The
Family
I Lost

BOOKS BY ALI MERCER

Lost Daughter
His Secret Family
My Mother's Choice
The Marriage Lie

Ali Mercer

The
Family
I Lost

bookouture

Published by Bookouture in 2022

An imprint of Storyfire Ltd.
Carmelite House
50 Victoria Embankment
London EC4Y 0DZ

www.bookouture.com

ISBN: 978-1-80314-400-9
eBook ISBN: 978-1-80314-401-6

For Lyn and Ray

FOREWORD
JULIE

1978

Their daughter stands out in the drab visitors' room like anything that catches the light when it is gloomy. Her hair is in wispy bunches and she's wearing a pale green velvet-and-net fairy dress with bedraggled wings at the back. She is sitting up very straight at a bolted-down table opposite her dad.

Julie has warned her that although her dad could give her a quick hug when he first saw her, after that he'd have to stay seated and would not be free to get up and move around. Lisa had accepted this without question, just as she had accepted without question the news that he had done something bad and was in prison, which, now she was nearly five, she was fully old enough to know was where bad people went. She loved him, and it was obvious she didn't really believe that he was bad.

The distinction between 'bad man' and 'man who did a bad thing' had seemed important to Julie at the time, something for both her and Lisa to hang onto. A small, redemptive possibility after all the tragedy and disaster. But now they are all here in this room that smells of disinfectant and sweat and old cigarette smoke, and she can't kid herself that it really matters.

After all, he's still here. And the dead are still dead. And her family will never forgive her.

Her mum, her dad, her sister – they have all decided that Lisa counts for nothing. Out of everything that has been said and done since that summer afternoon at the farmhouse, that is perhaps what cuts most deeply. She doesn't really care any more about them deciding to cut her off. She understands it. But Lisa? How could they do it? How could they reject an innocent child out of hand like that?

She clears her throat and says in a low voice to her ex-husband, 'How are you getting on?'

It's a stupid question, because she knows just by looking at him. He looks terrible – puffy-faced, tired and bleak. But she has to say something. They have less than an hour, and a clock mounted on the wall on the far side of the room is ticking the time away. Prison officers are stationed here and there, watching, and all around them other families are keeping their voices low and their eyes down, leaning across the bolted-down tables, not touching. There seems to be an unspoken mutual agreement that the prisoners and their visitors will allow each other as much privacy as possible.

Mike shrugs. 'It is what it is.'

She remembers her dad saying, *I hope they lock him up and throw away the key*. She had been horrified by that, but if she is honest with herself she isn't sure how she feels about Mike coming out one day either. It's not that she wants him to suffer – how could he suffer any more than he has already, and will continue to do? Whether he's inside or not will make no difference to that. They are both serving a different kind of sentence, one that will never end. A sentence of grief and guilt and regret. What she's not sure about is him back on the outside, free to be a dad to Lisa again.

In the past he'd been no great shakes as a dad – sometimes there, sometimes not, unreliable, usually broke. But after everything that's happened... Would he want to redeem himself? Would he try?

How would Lisa, who is so sweet and docile now, feel about him when she is a little older and more independent and has a mind of her own, and finds out what he has done? Come to that, how would Lisa feel about Julie herself?

Anyway, all that is a long way off, and for now, what Lisa doesn't know can't hurt her...

Lisa is sitting bolt upright next to Julie, her legs crossed neatly at the ankles and her hands clasped on the table, wide-eyed, on her very best behaviour. She'd got up early without protest to come here – a three-and-a-half-hour journey by train and bus, the same again ahead of them when the visiting hour is up. Lisa had been scared of the sniffer dogs but hadn't made a fuss, which was just as well because the very last thing Julie had needed at that point was for her to kick off.

She's a good kid. Always has been. She deserves all the love in the world. Not to be rejected by most of her family for something that was not her fault.

Julie says to her, 'Why don't you go and have a look at the toys?'

There is a small play area – really just an empty corner – next to them, with a few of the kind of toys you might find in a doctor's surgery or a hospital waiting room: one of those metal frames with wooden beads threaded on curvy wires, some stacking cups and a tub of plastic bricks. Nothing that would hold any immediate appeal for Lisa.

Lisa looks doubtful and casts an appealing glance in her dad's direction, as if asking Julie to reconsider. Obviously, she remembers that Mike isn't allowed to get down and play with her. But Mike doesn't say anything and Lisa obediently climbs down from her seat, goes over to the play area and starts pushing the beads along the wires on the frame. Julie has the impression that she's trying to play as quietly as possible, as if to avoid drawing attention to herself and annoying her parents or anybody else.

Mike says, 'It's so good to see you. Both of you.'

She keeps watching Lisa. She can't bring herself to meet his eyes. 'She's a bright little thing,' she says. 'She's getting ever so good at reading now. Her writing's coming on, too.'

'I can believe it,' Mike says, and hearing the pride in his voice makes it possible for her to face him. It's so strange to see his wrecked face wreathed in smiles, but there it is – he looks almost happy.

'Maybe she'll write to you, one day,' she says.

His expression abruptly changes. His smile disappears, and he is sombre again. 'Maybe,' he says. 'I wouldn't expect her to. How's your sister?'

She shrugs. She shouldn't, but she does. Because what has her sister got to do with her now? Nothing. Next to nothing.

'All right, from what I know,' she says.

'What about your parents?'

Another, slightly bigger shrug. 'I asked them to let me have our stuff from when we were staying there, and they wouldn't.'

'What do you mean? What stuff?'

She hesitates. It would have been better not to say anything. She doesn't want to push him over the edge, and this is no place for an outburst. Especially not with Lisa watching.

'Julie... what stuff?'

'Clothes. Books. Unopened birthday presents,' she says. 'I didn't pack half of it. I was on complete autopilot. I mean, I don't actually remember leaving the place at all.'

He glances across at Lisa. 'How's she doing with it all? Does she ever talk about it?'

'No. I don't think she remembers.'

And this would be a blessing, surely, if it was true. Wouldn't it be better if Lisa could forget? If they could move on just as the two of them, mother and child, as if there had never been anyone else...

But then the memory comes back to Julie very vividly and painfully – the night, not that long after it all happened, when she had found Lisa weeping in the dark, her pillow soaked with tears.

She had asked what was wrong but Lisa had just carried on crying and it had been obvious she couldn't find the words to say it. So Julie had stroked Lisa's damp hair back from her forehead and she had said, *Everything you lose comes back to you eventually. I promise you, one day, when you need it the most, the person you're missing now will be right there to help you through it.* And even though this was a promise she could in no way guarantee, Lisa had seemed to believe her, and to be soothed, and had calmed down enough to go back to sleep.

'I hate knowing that your family won't see you any more,' Mike says. 'Or Lisa either.'

'You know what, in a way I think it makes things easier. It's just her and me now. That's all I have to worry about.'

'Yeah, right. Single mum and single daughter. I guess that's manageable, isn't it?'

She feels the blood rush to her face, a sure sign of guilt. He sounds so bitter, and what he's said is so close to what she has just been thinking herself. His words hit home like an accusation: *You want to forget, don't you? You want to deny all of it, and all of us. You can't bear the truth and you're more than ready to live a lie. You want to pretend it never happened.*

But he's in here, inside, doing his time. It's down to her now to decide how to handle things. What right does he have to make her feel bad about it?

'Mike, this is not the time to go picking a fight,' she says. 'I'm here, aren't I? I came, and I brought Lisa with me. Isn't that enough?'

She breaks off, suppresses a sob and leans forward to rest her head on her arms on the table.

'Don't make a scene,' Mike says in a low voice. 'You'd better sit up. There's a prison officer looking over this way. If they think you're getting upset they might ask you to leave.'

'I'm not *getting* upset. I *am* upset,' she says, and then she does sit up because they have even less time left now, and she owes it to Lisa to see this through, if only for the rest of the visiting hour.

Lisa hesitantly returns to the table, and Julie gives her one of the snacks she has been allowed to bring in with her – everything else is sitting in a locker outside the visiting room. It's a chocolate bar, and after Lisa has finished it her hands are sticky and Julie wipes them with a tissue. She is conscious of Mike taking all of this in, as if trying to imprint it on his memory – the normality of it, the ordinary, everyday to and fro of caring for a child.

Mike asks Lisa how she's been getting on at nursery school, and she says her class has been talking about what they want to be when they grow up. After a brief, wounded pause he asks her what she has in mind. It costs him an effort to ask, Julie can see that. Probably because the last thing Mike would ever want is for their little girl to end up being anything like him.

After all, what is he now? A prisoner. A criminal, convicted of one of the most serious of all crimes. No – the longer Lisa can go on not knowing what he has done, the better...

Julie expects Lisa to say she wants to be a fairy, or an artist, or a gardener – all answers she has given to the same question in the past. But instead, Lisa sucks in her cheeks as if thinking hard and then says, 'I want to be a coping lady.'

'Yeah? A coping lady? What's that, exactly?' Mike's face has brightened again. It's almost unbearable to see how tenderly he is looking at their daughter – it's like a light that has come on somewhere inside.

'A coping lady helps people cope,' Lisa says, as if this is something everybody should know about and have access to. 'You phone up, and she comes and helps you.'

'They must be very busy, these coping ladies,' Julie says. 'Given all the problems everybody has. Their phones would be ringing all the time. Some people probably wouldn't even be able to get through.'

Lisa looks briefly troubled by this. Then her face clears. 'I think they sometimes just know, without you having to ring,' she says.

'I should think they'd be very expensive, though,' Julie says. 'I mean, some problems are pretty hard work.'

'Maybe they sometimes work for free,' Lisa says thoughtfully. 'Or you just leave them a fifty-pence piece, like the tooth fairy. Or a carrot and some sherry, like for Santa.'

'Well, that'll see you right, if you're paid in carrots and sherry and fifty-pence pieces,' Mike says, and he laughs. He actually laughs.

With that the tension between them seems to lift, and for the rest of the hour they manage to talk and there are no poisoned silences, no recriminations and no distress. It's like magic. As if, for the time they have left, they have agreed to set everything else aside, and just be here with their daughter.

But then, just before they are due to leave, Mike leans forwards and says to Julie, 'You make sure you take good care of her,' and there's something even more final than goodbye about it. As if he's not expecting there to be another visit.

Her throat suddenly feels too tight to speak, and all she can do is nod.

He knows. He knows she's not going to want to come here again. He knows, and he's not going to make a scene. He's not going to make it hard for her. It's as if he has already forgiven her. Even though it means that on top of everything else he has lost, he is going to lose Lisa too.

As she walks out holding Lisa's hand she can feel his eyes on her back, following them both. She senses something stirring in her wake as if it has just been released and cast forward into the future, as quiet and potentially powerful as a promise whispered to a sleepy child.

But she doesn't look back. Lisa does, or tries to, just for a moment, and Julie tightens her grip on her hand and hurries her along. Then they are on the other side of the door, and she knows with dreadful and inexplicable certainty that they will never see him again.

PART ONE
LISA AND AMY

Winter 2008 to Spring 2009

ONE

LISA

December 2008

Lisa comes across the little red address book in one of the drawers in the kitchen, along with an old electricity bill reminder, a flier from the local Chinese takeaway and an assortment of junk: paper clips bent out of shape, biros with chewed ends and a lidless, dried-up tube of glue. It's the first thing she's come across in an hour or two of searching and sorting that might actually be worth keeping, and as she opens it a frisson runs down her spine.

There it is, under her fingers on the yellowed, gold-edged pages. Mum's handwriting, never quite on the line, a spiky, sloping scribble that looked as if it had been dashed off at speed.

It had always been hard to read, as if Mum didn't actually want anyone to be able to make out what she was writing down. Her shopping lists had been a nightmare. But then, by the time Lisa was fourteen, she'd graduated from running errands to planning their meals, budgeting for them and doing the shopping and cooking herself.

In spite of how long Mum had kept that same address book,

most of the pages are almost empty. That's not much of a surprise. Mum had been what you might call a very private person. *A loner*, was how Lisa described her to other people. *A bit of a recluse*. She didn't volunteer any other information about her family if she could help it.

She has also always avoided the subject of her mum's close and intimate relationship with the gin bottle. But that particular bit of denial has become harder to maintain lately, given how drunk they'd said her mum had been when she died, and given the number of empties Lisa has found stashed here and there around the place.

Clearly, Mum had felt ashamed enough of her drinking to want to hide the evidence from the neighbours. Or maybe it just hadn't been possible to fit it all in her recycling bin.

Lisa's chest tightens as if about to form a sob and she forces herself to breathe deep. The heating has been off and the house is very cold, but it still smells the same as ever: of bread, cigarette smoke and alcohol. Mum's handwriting blurs in front of her and she blinks to clear away the tears.

Today is for completing practical tasks, not for grief. She can't start weeping and wailing, not now, not here. She needs to save her tears for later, for a time when there is nothing else she is meant to be doing.

There's a load of clean crockery in a box outside in the hall, waiting to be loaded into the boot of her car and dropped off at the charity shop. If she doesn't get a move on, the shop will shut and she'll be too late...

But she carries on standing there in the kitchen, which she has almost, but not completely, emptied out, turning the pages of the address book, touching her mum's handwriting. Even though it seems like trespassing, she can't stop herself. The weird thing is that even though, earlier on, what had bothered her most about the house was how empty it felt, right now she half expects Mum to walk in and snatch the address book out of her hands.

And yet there's nothing to see. The longest entry in the address book is Lisa's own, which spills over one page and onto the next, eventually ending up with her current flat in Brickley, an hour's drive from here – she'd never really felt comfortable being any further away from Mum than that. They'd lived in Brickley when she was very little, so despite all her moving around, it seemed she'd just ended up right back where she'd started.

Is she imagining things, or is Mum's writing on those pages even crabbier and more illegible than elsewhere? It's a terse little record of the tension between them spiralling down the years, with each successive address scored through with a surprisingly firm black line.

The page before the list of her addresses, the opening of the P section, is missing. It has been ripped out. All that is left is a rim of tufted paper.

No prizes for guessing why *that* is. It would once have listed addresses for Mum's family. The Powers. People who Mum had never wanted to talk about, apart from to say, *We're better off without them*. Lisa had formed an impression of them as cruel, indifferent and rich, which meant she'd been inclined to agree with Mum on this without question.

She had no idea what her preconception of the Powers was based on – things she had overheard Mum saying after too much gin and tonic, probably. But who's to say she's got it wrong? They probably are stuck-up and nasty. They've certainly never been interested in having anything to do with her or Mum...

Although there was the business of her dad having been in prison, which could explain why they felt the way they did. A bit of an extreme reaction, perhaps. Ruthless. But understandable.

People didn't always stick by relatives who have been disgraced, and depending on the circumstances, you couldn't really blame them for turning their backs. Any kid has a cloud over them if one of their parents has done something wrong, and no wife is ever really free of the taint of a bad husband. Or of a husband who has committed a serious crime. Even if she was divorced from him. No matter how the law sees innocence, it's a different matter in the eyes of the world. Just being close to wrongdoing is a kind of guilt.

Is she really so different herself? Just knowing about the prison sentence had been enough. She had never pressed for more information about her dad. She had no memories of him, and for as long as she could remember she'd been aware that Mum really didn't want to talk about him. Once or twice she had been bold enough, or tactless enough, to bring the subject up, and Mum had refused to tell her what he'd done. *You're better off not knowing,* she had said. And Lisa had believed her, and had never tried to find out what had become of him after his release.

Too late to ask now...

She knows his name – Mike Brierley – but only from her birth certificate. *We didn't keep anything of his,* Mum had told her. *Not his surname, not anything else. I went back to my maiden name the minute I was divorced, and I made sure you did, too. Not that being a Power means a whole lot more to me. But you've got to be called something.*

As she sorted through her mum's paperwork and belongings, she'd wondered if she might come across something that would give her a few more clues about him. She doesn't even know for certain whether he's still alive. But she has found nothing, so far. Not even a marriage certificate or a wedding photo. Mum seemed to have done an uncharacteristically efficient job of erasing all traces of him from her life.

Anyway, it's not as if she *needs* to know. She is who she is.

She doesn't need to go digging into the past to find herself. She tries to live in the present and keeps her sights set on the future; she isn't interested in ancient family history. Some people in her situation might feel differently, might even have gone digging before now, but that's not her. Besides, she never would have wanted to upset Mum, and now that Mum has gone she is more glad than ever that she had never sought to rock the boat, and risk wrecking the one close relationship she had. Heaven knows, it had been fraught enough already.

It's just that she never would have imagined quite how alone in the world she would feel once she no longer had her mother to worry about...

She is about to close the address book and put it away when she spots an unexpected name at the bottom of the first page of her own old addresses.

Amy Power. And then there's a landline phone number and an Oxfordshire address. *5a Mary Close, Kettlebridge.*

Hadn't Mum once told her that she'd grown up in Oxfordshire, in the countryside?

Amy. She must be a relative. But where did she fit in?

Mum had a sister – though Lisa can't remember now how she knows that, or what exactly Mum had said about her, apart from the name. Diane. Mostly, Lisa's family history is a blank, and a blank that she had always felt she couldn't – and shouldn't – ask her mum to help her fill in. The small nuggets of information that she has picked up along the way are like souvenirs kept tucked out of sight, rarely thought about, not part of everyday life, but secretly important nevertheless. That's how she feels about Diane, her mysterious aunt. But she has never heard of any Amy before.

Whatever Amy's place in the family, presumably she was an apple who hadn't fallen far from the tree. Unlike Lisa and her mum, who had fallen so far that they were clean out of sight. And presumably out of mind as well.

Anyway, as far as Lisa knows, she and this Amy have never met. Mum had been ostracised and rejected by all the Powers, and that had always made Lisa feel even more protective of her, because Mum literally had no one else. It had just been the two of them against the world, and that had been hard and exhausting at times but at least Lisa had always felt needed. She had even taken a lonely kind of pride in taking care of Mum as best she could.

She had never asked anyone for help, and nobody had ever offered it, and she probably wouldn't have trusted them if they had. She had been defensive and secretive about Mum's drinking, just as Mum herself had been, though she had never felt responsible for it. Somehow she had always known that Mum's sadness and irritability and drinking were separate from her, and not her fault.

Did she really want to have anything to do with people who could be as harsh and unforgiving as Mum's family had been?

But that didn't mean she had to behave the same way. Should she at least try to get in touch with Amy Power, the only family member, beside herself, left in Mum's address book – who was probably only there because of an oversight, because she'd been on a different page to the rest?

It couldn't hurt to make contact, could it? Not to invite Amy to the funeral, since that wasn't what Mum had wanted – her will had been emphatically clear. She wanted a natural burial somewhere in the countryside, and she didn't care who came as long as the only family member present was Lisa herself. But Lisa could at least let that side of the family know that Mum had passed away.

Perhaps she should wait until after the funeral. But if she puts it off, will she ever get round to it?

She puts the address book in the cardboard box of paperwork she is going to take back to her flat. There isn't much in it. A fat concertina folder that she hasn't yet finished going

through, which so far has turned out to contain a random assortment of receipts and bank statements and cheque book stubs,
along with postcards and birthday and Christmas cards from
Lisa herself. A passport that went out of date in the early 1980s.
A stack of old bills, mostly addressed to Ms Julie Power, though
some had been sent to Miss or Mrs, which would probably have
annoyed her. 'I haven't been a spinster for quite some time, or
married, either. If they can't get it right, I'd rather they didn't
put down anything at all,' Lisa remembers her saying.

It saddens her to realise how little her mum had, and how
little even of that she is planning to keep. There are a few
mementoes in a separate cardboard box – a big pile of old drawings Lisa must have done as a kid, and various framed photos
that her mum had out on display, all of Lisa at various life
stages: on the swing in the park, in school uniform as a teenager
with a bad haircut, dangling the keys to her first car. It breaks
Lisa's heart all over again to realise that however testy Mum had
sometimes been with her, she'd lived out her life surrounded by
those pictures. She'd been so proud of her. Even if she could
never bring herself to say so outright...

There was only one photo of the two of them together, out
on one of the daytrips that she occasionally nagged Mum into
going on with her, because Mum hadn't been particularly keen
on looking at photos of herself. And there were no pictures at all
of Lisa with anybody else. There was half of that picture of her
with her last boyfriend, standing in sunshine in a square in
Montmartre. Mum had liked the photo, and when Lisa broke
up with the boyfriend she'd simply cut him out of it.

Anyway, she's done as much as she can for one day. She
carries out the cardboard boxes and puts them in the boot of her
car, locks up carefully behind her and sets off for the nearest
charity shop, making it just in time to drop off her mum's
crockery.

The traffic is awful on the way to Brickley, and the hour-long drive takes two. By the time she's back in her flat and has brought in the cardboard boxes of Mum's stuff and fixed herself something to eat, she's exhausted. She settles on her bed to watch TV – she doesn't have a separate living room, or space for a sofa – and soon dozes off.

And finds herself somewhere she doesn't recognise, in a garden. With her mum.

Mum is talking to her, telling her something urgent and important, but there's a storm rising and the sound of the wind in the trees is too loud for her to make out the words. She tries to step towards her, but the wind is too strong, it's buffeting her and won't allow her to move any closer...

The dream is so vivid that on waking she is immediately disappointed to find that it wasn't real. It's the first time she has dreamed about Mum since losing her a few weeks before.

She rummages in her chest of drawers for notepaper and a pen, and composes a letter to Amy Power straight off the top of her head, without allowing herself to hesitate. When she drops it into a post box on the way to work the next day she has a strange sense of having committed to something, or started something, even though logically she knows it's quite possible that she will never hear back.

TWO

AMY

January 2009

The family room is the second warmest room at Hillview House, after the kitchen, which is next door. Or alternatively, you could say the family room is the second least cold room. Even then it isn't exactly cosy, even though Amy is coming up for six months pregnant and better insulated than usual against the Oxfordshire cold.

Calling it the family room makes it sound much more modern and comfortable than it actually is. Still, at this time of year it's infinitely preferable to the main living room, which is freezing unless you get the fire going, and then scalding if you're close to the fire and icy everywhere else.

She runs her hands over her baby bump and admires the contrast between the orangey-pink of her freshly varnished nails and the blue of her engagement sapphire – the best Joe had been able to afford. *Blue like your eyes*, he had said when he first presented her with it. He'd been looking at her so adoringly that she'd managed to resist the temptation to correct him, but really, depending on the light and how closely you examined them, her eyes were barely blue at all. They were nearer to grey, or green if it was about to rain.

Anyway, at least he'd got the size right. The ring had been a perfect fit. But now it was probably time to take it off. When she was pregnant before, her fingers had swollen up so much by the last trimester that she'd had to wear it on a chain round her neck, along with her wedding band, till after she'd given birth.

The cold air is whistling round the gaps in the frame of the window next to her, hitting the back of her neck. Maybe, if the field trip Joe is going on this summer goes well, and he ends up moving up the ranks at work, there will be more money, and she might finally be able to replace the absurdly draughty old windows. It would be good to do it before next winter.

But also, that could be tricky.

She wouldn't want to get a quote from the company she used to work for, and it might occur to Joe to ask why not. He'd probably assume that she'd get a favourable rate if she did. And there was no way she could even begin to explain.

But he might not ask. There were sometimes advantages to having a husband who wasn't very practical, and who tended to leave household matters to you to sort out. Not that she was exactly keen on all that stuff herself.

Still, Joe probably wouldn't get a pay rise anyway.

'No, you *can't* have that.'

It's so close to what she's been thinking that it makes her start. But it's only Tilly, talking under her breath, making one of her dolls argue with one of her other dolls. She has been playing quite nicely on the rug for the last half hour or so, or at least, she hasn't been making any demands, and using the maternal super-power of selective attention, Amy has pretty much been able to forget that she's there. But not any more.

How on earth is she going to manage Tilly and a newborn baby without losing it completely? Especially with Joe disappearing over the summer. And before that, there's the labour and birth to get through.

Joe wants to be there for the delivery, same as with Tilly. And he's so excited – has been ever since the shock of finding out she was pregnant again wore off. It wasn't exactly planned, and it wasn't exactly as if they'd been having lots of sex. But still, he'd got his head round it remarkably quickly. *A little brother or sister for Tilly! She'll be thrilled.* And Amy had been obliged to suppress the instinct to protest: *Yes, I'm sure it's thrilling for Tilly – but what about me?*

It would have been embarrassingly childish to complain about him thinking about things from their daughter's point of view. And if he'd registered that Amy's feelings were more complicated and mixed than his, he would probably have been worried and upset, and any attempt she might have made to explain would almost certainly have only made things worse.

Joe always sees the best in things, and in people. Even if it isn't there. But sometimes she can't help but feel frustrated with his tendency to look on the bright side, especially when he's not the one who's going to have to deal with the worst of the trials ahead.

He cooks when he's around at home, he had changed Tilly's nappy occasionally when she was little and he plays with her sometimes, but he has no idea what it's like to be the default parent. Plus it's almost as if he's completely forgotten what the whole birth thing is like. How awful it is. Which she hasn't, of course.

The midwives calling you Mum because they couldn't be bothered to remember your name, because your name didn't matter anyway. The stitches, the broken nights, the screaming, the vomiting, the mastitis, the dirty nappies, the constant laundry, the baby fat to lose, the nagging from the health visitor about this, that and the other. The endless repetition. The constant hope and expectation from pretty much everyone –

including her husband, and Grandma Elsie – that you should be blissfully happy and fulfilled because, after all, you're a wife and mother. What more could any woman want?

Much, much more, to be honest. But there is no point at all in thinking about that. Not unless she wants to drive herself out of her mind.

And what had Joe said to her when she'd tried telling him how difficult it all was? *You could always go back to work, if you wanted. I know childcare is expensive, but you'd probably earn enough to cover it. Maybe there's something going at your old place. They might even offer you something part-time. You could always get in touch with them, just to check it out...*

As if *that* was an option.

Anyway, she can't change anything. Can't undo any of it. Too late now. She just has to be sensible, keep her head down, keep it together, keep going. Stay sane.

All alone over the summer, with Tilly and her new baby, while Joe is off looking at plant samples on the other side of the world.

Still, it's not as if she will be totally on her own. Mrs Paley will be coming in to clean, thank goodness – Joe had tried to suggest that they could cut back on that, but she'd put her foot down. And Tyler will be around every now and then, mowing the lawn or whatever. You couldn't really get rid of Mrs Paley and keep Tyler on – you couldn't sack someone's mum and expect her son to carry on being willing to work for you. Or so she'd said to Joe when he floated the idea, which had been a while back now, soon after she'd inherited the place and they'd moved in.

She had pointed out that their names would be mud in the village if they let either, or both, of the Paleys go. Whereas, as it was, they could rely on the Paleys to be discreet. You couldn't put a price on trust, could you? Not when it came to the people you let into your home.

Mrs Paley had worked for the family for ages – longer even than Amy had known Joe, since the days when Amy's mum was still alive, but was too sick with the cancer that had eventually killed her to keep up with household chores. And Tyler had been looking after the garden for years now too, ever since Amy's grandad had got too frail to manage it. The two of them as good as came with the house, and they were needed still. Or so she had told Joe when he had questioned whether they should stay. Too late now to wonder if that had been a mistake.

Is it a good thing or a bad thing to have Tyler around over the summer stretching ahead of her, while Joe is away?

She doesn't really want to think about it. Nothing much she can do about it, not without stirring up trouble, and maybe prompting people to ask questions that don't need asking. Anyway, he'll probably keep his distance. She can't imagine that nursing mothers and screeching babies are his thing.

She looks out at the garden – mostly an uninspiring view at the moment. Wet lawn and bare branches, a palette of dank green and brown, all looking the worse for wear after taking a battering in last night's heavy rainfall. Even the snowdrops aren't out yet.

Then a sudden movement somewhere beyond Tilly's playhouse catches her eye.

Tyler must be down there now, tree trimming. She can't watch him properly because the playhouse is in the way, but she can see the long, leafless fronds of the weeping willow threshing about as he gets to work.

And she can't help herself; the picture just pops into her mind without her making any effort to conjure it up. Tyler's strong back and shoulders in the grey vest he is wearing today, the muscles sliding under his smooth skin, the rings of sweat under his arms.

As long as she's known him, right back from the days when they were both teenagers hanging out in Kettlebridge, he's always been one of those men who doesn't seem to feel the cold. Joe, being a townie from the south, doesn't venture out at this time of year without being bundled up in a warm woollen coat. Tyler, though... Tyler isn't one for sensible layers.

She imagines the small grunt of satisfied exertion he'll let out when he's got through the branch he's pruning now, the shivering sound it will make as it falls to the ground...

'Mummy, can I see your nails?'

Reluctantly, she tears herself away from what she can see of Tyler's labours and looks down at her daughter.

Tilly has abandoned the game she has been playing on the rug and is gazing up at Amy with big, admiring, pleading eyes. It's perfectly clear what she is really saying: *Play with me. Pay attention to me. Stop looking out of that window and thinking whatever you're thinking, think about me instead.*

Amy suppresses a sigh and stretches out her right hand so Tilly can inspect it.

'Better not touch,' she says, 'though they should be just about dry.'

Passion crush, it's called. It's the colour of the inside of a ripe peach, and it would be perfect with a tan and a white T-shirt and denim shorts and sandals. Or it will be, in summer, if she can get back in shape by then.

Still, even now, it's a little protest against the January gloom. A pick-me-up. Heaven knows she needs it.

If Joe sees that she's done her nails, he'll probably start worrying about whether the chemicals in the polish could be harmful for the baby.

But he might not even notice. And she can't really object to his obliviousness, because there have been so many times when it's been a blessing.

'They're so pretty,' Tilly says admiringly. 'Will you paint my nails?'

Amy withdraws her hand. 'I don't think so. Remember you're going back to school tomorrow.'

Tilly looks crestfallen, and Amy immediately feels bad even though she's been perfectly reasonable.

'Maybe it's time you had a snack,' she says brightly. 'How about some fruit?'

'I had a banana already. I'm not really hungry,' Tilly says listlessly.

'OK, well, would you fetch me a peach? One of the nice new ones we got yesterday. Make sure you give it a rinse, and pat it dry on some kitchen paper. I'll need a plate, too. Oh, and you could check if the post has come while you're at it.'

Not that she's expecting anything nice. That maternity wear catalogue might have come – the expensive stuff – but Joe would probably balk at the prices. And even if she does get away with ordering one or two new things, she'll still look the size of a house.

Tilly brightens at being entrusted with a task to do and scurries off. Amy hauls herself out of the armchair and steps around Tilly's collection of toy animals spread out on the rug – each one an overpriced little treat bought by Joe on Saturday morning trips to Kettlebridge, which is how easy it is to be beloved if you're a father. She switches on the TV, which hesitates and blinks and then comes to life and rattles out the theme tune of one of the more boring children's shows.

Hopefully it will keep Tilly entertained till lunchtime. Pretty good going, to have kept it switched off all morning... She's well past feeling guilty about how much TV Tilly watches, and has learned to bite her tongue when other mums talk about rationing viewing time. They're all so virtuous. And crazy. What's not to like about a quiet child who is totally absorbed in watching a screen? Absolutely nothing, that's what.

The room darkens. It's raining again. She turns on the reading light, settles down in the armchair and picks up a magazine, but leaves it in her lap unopened. There's something off-putting about the smugly pretty, slender young woman on the cover. A not-pregnant woman. The baby squirms inside her. Sometimes he's violently mobile – more so than Tilly had been – but he's been mostly quiet today, almost as if he's as tired as she is, and also wants to rest.

Tilly comes back in with her head bowed and the peach on a plate which she is carrying with both hands, as carefully as if it is a crown at a coronation. She has a letter tucked under her chin. She passes Amy the peach on the plate and says, 'I chose the best for you, Mummy.'

'Thank you,' Amy says graciously, and rests the plate on top of the magazine on her lap. 'What have you got there?'

Tilly hands over the letter.

'I think the person who sent it made a mistake. It says it's for Amy Power,' she says.

Amy studies the envelope. Her heartbeat accelerates. It's been redirected from their old address, the little semi in Kettle-bridge they'd lived in when Tilly was a baby. She recognises the round, conscientious handwriting of the woman who'd taken over the lease when they left. But the original handwriting is unfamiliar.

Who could it be? It must be someone who knows where she used to live, but not that she got married to Joe after having Tilly and took his name, and that her grandad died and left her his house.

She opens it, takes out the letter and quickly reads it, then folds it and puts it back into the envelope and tucks it under her magazine.

There's no way she can deal with this now. A cousin is the absolute last thing she needs. She should just chuck it out, forget about it...

But she can't quite bring herself to do that. It seems so final. Maybe one of these days she might feel differently. After all,

Grandma Elsie wouldn't be around forever. Things could change. And you never knew what might be round the corner.

She should just tuck the letter away somewhere. File it for future reference. After all, it's worth knowing where this Lisa Power is, even if she doesn't want to get in touch with her right now. But she'll have to put the letter somewhere Joe won't find it. If he sees it, he'll try and talk her into doing something about it, because he's like that – always inclined to give people the benefit of the doubt, and sentimental about family.

Which is another mixed blessing. It can be annoying that he feels that way – he's so earnest about that kind of thing – but it does mean that he's willing to tolerate the slightly peculiar set-up here. And to put up with Grandma Elsie. Who, until today, was the only surviving relative either of them had to worry about, as far as they knew.

Tilly says, 'Mummy, who's your letter from?'

'Never you mind,' Amy says. 'Nobody important.'

Because really, what can she be expected to do about it? An aunt she has never met is dead. Julie, her mum's disgraced sister. Someone who could never be forgiven, and was best forgotten. And now a cousin she has also never met is giving her an address in Brickley, less than thirty miles away, and an email and a phone number, and is suggesting that maybe they could meet up for a coffee in Oxford sometime, or Brickley if Amy's ever out that way.

She could mention the news about her aunt Julie to Grandma Elsie, who would probably be pleased, if anything. No love lost there, for very understandable reasons. But then she'd probably forget it almost as soon as she'd been told. What marbles she has left seem to be rapidly disappearing. And her reactions can be very unpredictable and sometimes rather aggressive, so perhaps it isn't worth it.

As for this Lisa Power – perhaps it would be best not to encourage her. Who knows what her motives really are? What if she was thinking of challenging Grandad's will? Could she, given that a couple of years have already gone by since he passed away? Oh well, if she tried it on, they'd just have to dredge up some money from somewhere for a solicitor, and get it handled by lawyers.

But this woman has just lost her mum. Amy knows full well how devastating that is. Maybe she should send a sympathy card. She's probably got one lurking in a drawer somewhere. That couldn't hurt, could it? She didn't have to commit to meeting up if she wasn't sure about it. It was hard to think about planning anything with a new baby on the way, let alone potentially difficult get-togethers with long-lost relatives.

'But Mummy,' Tilly tries again, 'who is it from?'

'You know how sometimes we get junk mail? It's a bit like that,' Amy says. 'Not every letter is important. Now will you watch your programme?'

Tilly pouts. 'Aren't you going to try your peach?'

'I suppose,' Amy concedes.

She takes the peach in her hand, feels the soft, dense weight of it, and holds it to her nose to smell it, as if it's a flower. It's sweet to the point of cloying. She can almost taste it already.

Her mouth waters. 'You chose a good one.'

Tilly beams. *Don't*, Amy finds herself wanting to say. *Don't love me like that. It won't do you any good, and anyway, it's too much. I really don't deserve it.*

She bites into the peach. It's perfectly ripe. Tilly looks on proudly as juice spurts down Amy's chin. It tastes good. So good. Who cares if it makes a mess?

There's an abrupt knock at the door and without waiting for her to reply, Tyler comes in.

He's taken his shoes off, the way he always does if he's stepping into the house. He's still in the sleeveless T-shirt and jeans he'd had on when he arrived that morning – he must have a jacket somewhere, maybe in his car. He has worked up a light sweat, and his hair is damp and his T-shirt is spattered with rain.

Her fingertips tighten on the velvety skin of the peach.

'It's just started tipping it down out there again, so I'm going to head off now,' Tyler says, and runs a hand through his hair. 'I'll be back next week.'

She swallows and wipes her chin with the back of her hand. She can't figure out whether she's giddy or hungry or hot. Or all three, all at once. But anyway, it's not *her* fault. She isn't doing anything, not right now. It's Tyler who is making it happen.

Tyler's gaze flickers down to the magazine resting in her lap, then up to the peach in her hand and her sticky face. One eyebrow goes up, and his lip curls.

'Anyway, I'd better leave you to it,' he says. 'I can see you're busy.'

And with that he turns and leaves.

She bites into the peach again. Her cheeks feel very hot. Probably she's gone bright red. Just as well Tilly, who can be frighteningly observant, is now too absorbed by the TV to notice.

THREE

LISA

The funeral wishes included in Mum's will had come as a surprise – not the part about having no family members present aside from Lisa, which was pretty much a given, but the bit about wanting to be buried in the countryside. Mum had never really seemed like a country lover. Her garden was a backyard for smoking in and she regarded wildlife as a nuisance that occasionally strayed indoors. But then, it also surprised Lisa that she'd been organised enough to leave a will. It seemed like a gesture of love – not a sentimental one, but a practical one. An attempt to make things easier for Lisa to sort out her affairs.

Well, if her mum wanted a countryside burial, that was what she was going to have, and it was going to be as beautiful and meaningful as Lisa could make it – though beauty and meaning might be too much to hope for from a field in the back of beyond in the gloom of January.

There wouldn't be many mourners, but how many do you need? How many is a fitting tribute to a life? Some terrible people have been seen off by crowds lining the streets. Lisa would be there, and Holly, who lived in the flat next to hers, Donna, who'd cut Mum's hair, Paul, the owner of the bakery where Mum had worked, and Marie, the nosy neighbour who'd raised the alarm when she hadn't seen or heard Mum for a day or two. Marie's intervention had prompted Lisa to go round and find Mum sprawled unconscious on the living room floor, having fallen in a drunken stupor and hurt herself. Lisa had called an ambulance only for Mum to die of a hospital-acquired infection a couple of weeks later. They had tried to save her. But it seemed to Lisa that her mum had given up on herself long before.

Five mourners, plus the undertaker Lisa had chosen because he sounded calm and patient on the phone – a tall, unhurried, gentle man whose broad forehead was almost unnaturally smooth, as if his line of work had made him immune to everyday worries, and who looked immaculate in his black suit even in a windswept field with no sign of civilisation in sight. There was also the celebrant who the undertaker had recommended to lead the ceremony, a practical woman with a can-do spirit who didn't seem at all fazed by either the location or the small size of the gathering.

It doesn't quite feel like a celebration of Mum's life, but it does feel like an acknowledgement. It's an acknowledgment of something too big for words – the impossibility of saying goodbye to somebody you love.

The day itself is bright and clear. Everybody finds their way, even though the burial ground is on the edge of a farm at the end of an obscure country lane where sat-nav doesn't seem to work. They park in one field and make their way to another. The view is of low bare hills, green and brown under a grey sky and raked by a cold breeze. In the field where Mum is to be laid to rest, there are saplings planted along a walkway. A tall, sculpted stone stands at the far end, overlooking the dip of the valley and the hills, to serve as a collective monument.

Almost as high as the stone is the pile of earth nearby, next to the hole that has been dug for Mum's grave. That's another surprise, how deep it had been necessary to dig. There are wooden planks across the grave to rest the coffin on and long strips of cloth that they will use, once the planks are eased from under her, to lower her into the ground.

Her coffin is made of cardboard. *It's what you wanted, Mum*, Lisa finds herself saying in her head as she stands beside the grave. *It's what you asked for. I would never have guessed that you'd want it this way. But perhaps there was a lot I didn't know about you.*

But there's no reply. Just the soft sound of the breeze in the grass and somebody suppressing a cough.

Lisa can't take in any of the words, although it had seemed important beforehand to figure out what would be said, and she had spent time mulling it over, deliberating, trying to work out what would be respectful and personal at the same time. She reads a poem. A short one. Her voice doesn't sound like hers. But that doesn't matter. What does it matter if she does not feel herself? What right does she have to carry on as normal when Mum has stopped?

They lower the coffin into the grave and Lisa drops some flowers down onto it. Pink roses. She had bought Mum flowers from time to time, and Mum had always seemed pleased with them, but in a distracted way, as if she felt Lisa giving them to her was a mistake. As if being presented with something nice meant some kind of disappointment must be lurking round the corner, to redress the balance.

And then Lisa reaches for one of the spades that has been left leaning against the pile of earth by the graveside. She scoops up the dark, heavy earth, and sends it down to scatter on top of the flowers. It feels like an act of vandalism. But a necessary one.

The others join her. It takes a while to fill a grave that deep, and it's warm work. The sun comes out and she takes her coat off and lays it on the grass. By and by the earth is level and she lays some more roses on top of it.

It looks like what it is, a freshly dug patch of earth that will soon, come spring and summer, be indistinguishable from the meadow around it, although the burial ground administrator will keep a record of the precise coordinates. There won't be a permanent marker. Maybe that would matter to some people, but it hadn't mattered to Mum and it doesn't bother Lisa that when she goes there again, it won't be obvious precisely where Mum is. It helps, in a way. Mum will just be part of that place and that view. And that seems like a fitting way to remember her.

She's part of the landscape now. The wishes of the dead carry weight, and Lisa hopes she has done enough to fulfil her mum's. She wouldn't want to have let her down. And she hopes her mum is at peace, and that she found that peace in time to be conscious of it. Maybe even after she had fallen, when she was hopeless and alone and in pain, in spite of everything.

Afterwards, the mourners say goodbye by their cars and go their separate ways. The others have work to get back to, or commitments they need to keep. They tell her they are sorry for her loss and she thanks them for coming, and these ritual exchanges feel both formal and a little awkward, but in the end, it's the awkwardness that is consoling. She can see in their eyes that they would like to be able to say or do more to comfort her, and their sympathy is like a soft, invisible shield around her, protecting her from the sadness of the day.

As she gets into her car and prepares to drive home she feels a wave of regret that her attempt to reach out to Amy Power had come to nothing. Somehow, even though there is not much that is more final than a funeral, and it is surely now definitively too late for anything to make any difference, Mum's relationship with her estranged family still feels like unfinished business.

FOUR

AMY

At least she had been only ten minutes late for school pick-up. She somehow seems to be incapable of making it on time, more so this term than ever before. It has got to the stage where the other waiting parents and Tilly's class teacher look at her with a kind of impatient sympathy when she waddles into the playground, as if to say, *We know it's hard, but everybody else copes – why can't you?*

Occasionally, some of the newcomers at the school gate try to be friendly towards her, but she never responds and they soon give up. People who have been around for longer know better than to try. She knows they think she's stand-offish and she doesn't care. She doesn't need their sympathy any more than she wants their judgement. The last thing she would ever do is confide in any of them. The less they know about her, the better.

Older people aren't quite so sensitive to being brushed off as people her own age, however, and there are one or two who make a point of stopping for a chat if they spot her on her way through the village, which she is no way in the mood for today.

She picks up the pace, hurrying Tilly along. Tilly protests, but Amy ignores her. They have nearly made it to the lane that leads up the hill – the turning is in sight, just the other side of the main road – when she sees someone she knows walking towards them.

It's Russell Bright, managing director of Millingford Double Glazing, her old boss. And he looks very much as if he wants to talk to her.

No. No, not now. She really is in no fit state for this. With her hair barely brushed and no make-up on, in a moth-eaten wrap coat that doesn't quite reach around her bump and saggy jogging bottoms and trainers – this is no time to see *him*. Especially not with Tilly dragging her feet beside her. And anyway, what on earth is he doing here?

There's no hope now of making it to the lane before Russell reaches her, and she can hardly pretend not to have seen him. Better just tough it out, however difficult that might be with Tilly at her side, watching and waiting, her sharp little ears poised to take in whatever is said and digest it and probably innocently report it back to Joe later.

She faces Russell with something as close to a smile as she can manage. He certainly doesn't look like a threat. He's a pretty ordinary, nondescript middle-aged man, with curlyish hair and a square face and broad shoulders, who isn't actually that tall but has learned to project himself so he seems bigger than he is.

He looks as if he's bulked up a bit, maybe. Been hitting the gym. He's wearing a navy-blue overcoat over a navy-blue wool jumper and jeans, which is odd for a working day – he always used to wear a suit. But it's odd him being here at all. Maybe he's taking some time off.

'Hello, Amy. I've been wondering when I was going to bump into you,' Russell says.

He leans forward and pecks her on the cheek, and she does her best not to flinch and veer away from him. The best way to play this is very, very low-key. If Tilly is too bored by their conversation to take any notice of it, so much the better.

'I see congratulations are in order,' Russell goes on. 'You're blooming, as they say.'

'Hardly,' she says, with a short, sharp laugh that is meant to be a kind of warning. 'What are you doing here?'

'I live here,' he says. Then, on seeing her reaction, 'Yes, we're virtually neighbours now. I'm the newest regular at your local pub. They told me a bit about you, though I didn't make the connection straight away. They said there was a couple with a kid who'd inherited the old farmhouse on top of the hill, and then I remembered you said you had family here and put two and two together. I've been looking out for you, actually. I knew we'd meet sooner or later. It's a small place, isn't it? Small but charming. I've just moved into a cottage on the high street. The one with the blue door.'

He nods in the direction he's just come from, towards a sweet-looking little stone-built house nestling between a new build screened by a high brick wall and a row of half-timbered cottages.

'Oh,' she says stupidly. 'I thought you lived in Millingford. Near the business.'

'Well, I did, but not any more. As you can see.'

'What made you decide to move here?'

'It wasn't the chance of proximity to you, believe it or not,' he says, smiling the way people do when they make a small joke at your expense. 'Springhill is a good location. Quiet, pretty, but there's a good fast road not too far away. The right place just came up at the right time.'

'You fancied being a bit more out in the countryside, then.'

'Something like that.'

He comes closer and stoops to peer at Tilly, and says, 'So what's your name?'

Tilly looks at him blankly. Amy suppresses the impulse to

tell him to get lost – in a village as in marriage, diplomacy is always the better part of valour. She says, 'This is Tilly.'

'Tilly,' Russell repeats. 'Short for Matilda?'

'Yes. Matilda Alice Longcross.' Amy pronounces the surname with just a hint of emphasis, a reminder that she, too, is married now.

He gives her a quick, sideways look, more amused than appraising, and she can't help but feel vaguely humiliated, even though the last thing she wants, or needs, is for him to still be attracted to her.

'I see,' he says. 'How very Victorian.' And then, speaking unnecessarily loudly, as if Tilly is either stupid or slightly deaf: 'And how old are you, Matilda Alice Longcross?'

Tilly glances at Amy as if to check for permission to speak. 'Nearly seven,' she says hesitantly.

Russell straightens up. 'Nearly seven,' he repeats. 'I see. Spring is the nicest time of year for a birthday, I always think. My birthday is in the spring too.' He turns to Amy. 'It's good to see you looking so well,' he says. 'I must say I was a bit surprised when you started your family. You didn't strike me as being ready to settle down. But anyway, I take my hat off to you, you and, er, what's your husband's name? Keith? John? I'm sorry, I'm sure you did tell me back before you finished work, but it's slipped my mind.'

'Joe,' she says. 'His name is Joe.'

'Yes. Joe,' he says thoughtfully. 'Well, congratulations to both of you. You're obviously flourishing.' But he isn't even looking at her. He is studying Tilly, who looks painfully uncomfortable, as if she suspects she has done something wrong and is about to be told off. 'Anyway, I hope it won't bother you, seeing me about the place.'

'Oh, I'm sure I'll cope,' Amy says, as coolly as she can manage. 'After all, quite a lot of water has flowed under the bridge. I think, on the whole, it's best to let bygones be bygones, don't you? Especially now we're as good as neighbours, as you say.'

He looks her up and down. She can feel her cheeks growing hot. She never normally blushes so easily; it's a weird side-effect of being pregnant. She seems to be prone to all kinds of uncontrollable feelings, including embarrassment.

'Hm,' he says, then glances up the hill at her house. 'Well, if you ever want a competitive quote for replacement windows, I'm sure I could make you a very reasonable offer.'

'Thanks, Russell. I'll bear that in mind.' He's probably joking, though it's hard to tell. Humour never had been Russell's strong suit. Anyway, there's no way she's going to admit that they can't afford it. Or tell him he's the last person on earth she would ever choose to let into her house.

'You do that,' Russell says. He is smiling, though his eyes are cold.

'Well, we'd better get going. Good luck in your new home.'

She doesn't actually wish him luck at all. And she's going to have to keep on doing this, being nice to him whenever their paths cross... It's going to drive her crazy. She really wants to slap him round the face and storm off, but that is completely impossible. Especially with Tilly watching.

'Thanks. I'm very pleased with it.'

'What about your wife? Didn't she get a say?'

The question is out of her mouth before she gets the chance to stop herself. It's a rebuke as much as anything else, a reminder to Russell to tread carefully, because he, too, has something to lose.

The wife had been a big deal, once upon a time. Or at least a *presence*. A blonde, nervy, well-groomed, guilt-inducing presence. Is Amy going to have to get used to bumping into her too, now?

Russell raises his eyebrows and looks at her as if she's made a regrettable faux pas. His smile tightens. 'Oh, she isn't coming.'

'I'm sorry – she what?'

He bares his teeth in an expression that is closer to a grimace than a grin. 'She isn't coming,' he says. 'We're divorced. Look, I really do hope things aren't going to be awkward between us. There's absolutely no reason why they should be. Is there?'

'Absolutely none,' Amy says firmly.

She can't bring herself to say she's sorry about his wife. Sorry *for* her, maybe, though she hadn't felt that way at the time. Looking back, she can't help but wonder what that marriage had been like on the inside.

'I'm sure I'll see you around,' she adds. 'Come on, Tilly.'

She grabs Tilly's hand and is about to cross the road when a speeding car nips round the corner and shoots past in front of them, close enough to make her heart lurch.

'You want to take care,' Russell says, 'especially in your condition. Bye-bye, Tilly. It was nice to meet you.'

'Bye-bye,' Tilly says, and offers him a gappy smile before Amy drags her away from him across the road.

Once they reach the lane she lets go of Tilly's hand. She's really too old to need hand-holding, but sometimes it's the best way to get her to wherever you need her to go.

Tilly says, 'Mummy? Who was that man?'

Russell almost certainly won't be able to hear, even if he's lingering. She refuses to look back and check if he's still watching her. Doesn't want to give him the satisfaction.

Of all the times and all the places for him to move – why does it have to be here, and why now? When she has so much else to worry about. If he sticks around she's bound to have to introduce him to Joe sooner or later. And then even Joe, oblivious as he often is, will probably guess that something is up. And she won't be able to tell him.

'He's nobody important,' she tells Tilly. 'He just moved into the village. Years ago, before I had you, I used to work for him.'

'Why don't you like him?'

'Who says I don't like him? I like him fine.'

'You didn't seem like you liked him,' Tilly persists. 'He seems scary.'

'He's definitely not scary. Pathetic perhaps.'

'What does pathetic mean?'

'Someone you feel a bit sorry for.'

Tilly digests this. 'But you don't feel sorry for him.'

'Really, Tilly, stop going on about it. Let's just get home,' she snaps, and speeds up so that Tilly will be trying too hard to keep up to ask any more questions.

Should she tell Joe about Russell? She could just play it down, try to turn it into a funny anecdote...

No, the less said the better. If Russell turns into a problem, she'll fix it. But there's no real reason to assume that he will. He's here, but that doesn't mean he's taking any particular interest in her. Sure, it's an inconvenience. From her point of view, it's a piece of bad luck. But she can shrug it off. She'll have to.

She should just focus on being the best, most loving, most supportive, self-denying wife she can be. Russell belongs to a different life, so different she might as well have been somebody else entirely.

Back in the house, in the couple of hours before Joe comes back from work, she tidies up, does a load of washing, bakes a cake and cooks a meal from scratch, and after he's come home and they've had dinner and cleared up, she makes time to play with Tilly. When she and Joe have both said goodnight, they go down to the family room and she settles on the sofa while he finds their place in the DVD from their latest box set, the happily married couple's substitute for sex.

'You look exhausted,' Joe says as he sits down next to her.

'Thanks. Good to know.'

'Beautiful and exhausted, obviously,' he says, and presses play on the remote control.

Then he offers her a back rub. She doesn't really want him to touch her in that way, to let him be good to her. It's too close, too intimate, too tender. But she thanks him and submits to the touch of his hands on her skin, and even manages to persuade herself that he's making her feel better.

The trick to all of it, to lying, pulling the wool over people's eyes, hiding the evidence and not getting caught, is just not to feel guilty. Once you've realised that, you can cope with anything.

FIVE

LISA

Lisa is out of practice at parties. She hasn't been going out that much lately, and it's been a while since she went to a social occasion where she doesn't already know most of the other people, let alone to a proper public event. But less than two months after her mum's funeral, she finds herself in a large bright room in a swanky London venue, hiding behind a pillar with a glass of wine and wondering who, if anybody, she should attempt to talk to.

It's an unseasonably warm February day and everyone is shiny-faced and smiling. It is, after all, a celebration, and all in a good cause – most of the people milling around the room have taken part in a national swimathon to raise money for charity, and the charity has organised this event to say thank you.

The room is buzzing with conversation. Lisa decides she doesn't care about spotting someone she recognises from her swimming club to talk to. She's just happy to be here, soaking in the nervous excitement in the air as the initial awkwardness is eased by the treat of the free wine, and people begin to mingle.

She might have stayed there like that until the speeches started, concealed by the pillar and watching the others, if it wasn't for the man who's had his back to her for at least the last ten minutes. He's so oblivious to her presence that when he moves back to make way for someone who is passing through, he inadvertently stands fair and square on her foot. She gasps in surprise and he turns round and is all apologies.

'Don't worry, don't worry, I'm fine,' she says automatically.

He is taller than her, dark-haired, his face in shadow, peering down at her chest. No. Not her chest. Her name label. He looks up and says, 'Lisa Power. It's an unusual name.'

'It means "poor",' she says. 'At least, that's one of the possible meanings.'

'I suppose that makes sense,' he says.

'I hope you don't mean I look poor.'

What is wrong with her? She's so rusty at this. He'll probably think she's trying to flirt with him. Which she isn't, definitely not, and now she's embarrassed and he's probably going to move away as soon as decently possible.

But he just half smiles, as if not sure whether he has offended her.

'I just meant that the words sound similar,' he says. 'Poor and power. You can see how one might turn into the other.'

The two women he had been talking to before turn round, look her up and down and carry on chatting to each other. One of them is wearing blue velvet and looks rather warm, and the other is in coffee-coloured chiffon. They're both more dressed up than Lisa, who's in a long red dress picked up on impulse in the January sales, which makes her feel a little self-conscious because it's both brighter and a little more low-cut than anything she'd usually wear. The other women don't seem unfriendly, just curious, and perhaps a bit disappointed to have lost the handsome doctor they'd been talking to.

Because he is a doctor, according to the name label pinned to the lapel of his jacket: *Dr Joe Longcross*. It sounds like a kind doctor from a Dickens novel. Someone who might try to help abandoned orphans and desperate mothers in the slums. Today he's dressed semi-formally in an open-necked shirt with a dark suit. His hair is a little unruly and his shirt is slightly creased, and she wonders who does his ironing. It could be the woman in blue velvet, or the one in coffee-coloured chiffon. His wife, wherever she is. Or someone he pays?

Maybe he does it for himself...

He says, 'I noticed your name because I'm married to another Power. Or at least, it was her maiden name. She thought about keeping it, and I think some of the family would have liked her to, but in the end she didn't.'

'Well, there's a coincidence.'

'It certainly is.'

Her mouth is dry all of a sudden, and she swallows down some more wine. It's just a weird coincidence. It has to be.

She says, 'Is your wife here?'

Her tone is more interrogative than she'd meant it to be, as if she is accusing him of something. He looks faintly surprised.

'No, she's at home with our little girl,' he says, and his face lights up at the opportunity to mention his daughter. Clearly, she is in the company of a devoted dad, something she always finds all the more touching because she doesn't remember her own dad. It's touching in a slightly painful way, though. It's the kind of pain that goes with knowing that other people have something precious that you missed out on, and being glad for them and reminded of its absence from your own life at the same time.

'How old's your daughter?'

'Just turned seven.'

He takes a phone out of his pocket, glances at a message and dismisses it. It's a touchscreen phone and looks like a fairly recent model, not like the old thing she's carrying around because she's trying to put off spending the money on getting something better.

'She's not in bed yet,' he says, putting the phone back into his pocket and pulling a face that suggests the message he just got from his wife had made him feel bad about her being stuck doing the childcare back home.

Had his wife *meant* to make him feel bad? Possibly. Perhaps that was all part of the normal give-and-take of marriage – go out if you want, but don't expect to feel good about it. Normally Lisa would be inclined to sympathise with the parent who was left behind in this situation rather than the one who was out for the evening, but this time she finds herself siding with Dr Joe Longcross. After all, he doesn't exactly seem like the partying type.

'It's still pretty early,' she says, checking her watch. It's just gone eight o'clock.

He grimaces as if the situation back home is more delicate than he can easily explain. Anyway, he probably wouldn't even attempt to explain it to her, a stranger at a party. That was something she'd noticed about the fidelity of married couples. A big part of it was not telling other people what was going on.

'Thing is, we're expecting another baby, and she's pretty knackered,' he says.

'Oh, I see. Well, congratulations.'

'Thank you. I wasn't too sure about coming tonight, to be honest. But she encouraged me.' He says this ruefully, but he looks proud of her willingness to let him go. It's plain that he both adores his wife and worries about her, and that, too, both touches Lisa and leaves her feeling a little melancholy, because there is no one in her life right now who would talk about her that way.

'When's the baby due?'

'Beginning of April. Not long now. We're thrilled, obviously. But it's going to be a bit of a challenge.'

'Of course. Stands to reason. How does your little girl feel about it?'

'Oh... she's very excited.'

He doesn't ask if Lisa has children. Maybe he doesn't think it's a tactful thing to ask, or assumes that she would mention it if she did.

Out of the corner of her eye she glimpses movement by the platform at one end of the room. Somebody is edging their way through the people clustered there, and the crowd is politely parting and then reforming as they pass through. It must be nearly time for the speeches. Any minute now someone from the charity they've been fundraising for will take to the stage.

It's a missing persons helpline. She can almost hear what her mum would have had to say about that: *That's you down to a T, isn't it? Always trying to do good deeds and rescue other people. Maybe, once in a while, you ought to concentrate on helping yourself.*

'Lisa?'

The doctor's gaze is fixed on her face. He looks sombre, as if he's about to come out with a diagnosis she might not wish to hear.

'Yes?'

He clears his throat. 'My wife is called Amy,' he says. 'When we met she was Amy Power. Does that ring any bells?'

It doesn't mean anything. Anything at all. No name belongs just to one person. There are probably hundreds, no, thousands of Amy Powers out there, all living their separate lives, nothing to do with her and nothing to do with him.

And nothing to do with the unanswered letter she'd written, or her mysterious aunt Diane, or any of the other relatives Mum hadn't wanted at the funeral...

Just as clearly as if it's right in front of her, she can see her mum's handwriting in the address book. The note added under the list of her own addresses, after the torn-out page. Left there as if by accident. The sense of trespassing and danger that she'd felt as she'd stood there and read it.

She becomes aware of holding her breath and lets it out.

'The thing is, you do have a little bit of a look of her,' Joe says.

He reaches into his pocket and takes out his phone again, taps the screen and holds it out to her. 'See what I mean?'

It isn't really a choice. She can't not see. The faces on the screen are close enough to touch.

Amy. And Amy's daughter.

Without thinking to ask for permission, she takes hold of the phone to steady it and slant it so the reflected light shining on it slides away and she can get a better view.

'I don't think she does look much like me,' she says.

And this is true, but it is not the whole truth.

Lisa thinks of herself as someone who people don't tend to notice unless they're looking for someone to trust – to ask for directions, perhaps, or for an honest opinion about which colour top to choose in a shop. She has a round, almost childish face, big brown eyes, straight dark hair, and a smile that is shy unless she forgets herself. By way of contrast, Amy is strikingly pretty. She has a bold, rather imperious gaze, thick, slightly brassy-looking fair hair that contrasts with her dark, strongly defined eyebrows, broad, high cheekbones and a snub nose. Her expression is almost sulky. She's smiling for the camera, but it's not far off a pout.

There is definitely something about her that is familiar. The tilt of Amy's head and the way she is looking at the camera reminds Lisa of Mum.

It's the same slightly aggrieved, hawkish gaze, like a challenge from someone who is not resigned to losing, and the same desultory, sultry edginess. She looks moody, and as if she'd be a handful – but still, she has a kind of resentful glamour, just as Mum had once had.

But it's not Amy who Lisa is really drawn to. It's the little girl next to her, widening her eyes for the camera, her wispy hair pulled back into slightly untidy bunches that look as if she might have done them herself.

'Cute kid,' she says, and passes the phone back to Joe as the hum of conversation around them comes to an abrupt stop.

Nobody is looking their way. People are turning in the other direction, towards the stage. The speeches are about to start.

Joe looks puzzled, and not far off being embarrassed. 'I'm sorry,' he says. 'I don't know, I just... thought I might be onto something. I guess you don't see the resemblance.'

She stares up at him. Should she admit that he's right? Or deny it all and say a polite but firm goodbye?

Suddenly, she is overwhelmed by a surge of longing that seems to come from nowhere. What she yearns for is kin. People who she belongs to and is tied to by blood, the tie that continues to exist even if you chose to ignore it. It seems such a comforting thing, to have someone in the world who looks like you and for it not to be a coincidence.

'I don't think I look like your wife,' she says. 'But your little girl looks a bit like I did when I was a kid. What's her name?'

'Tilly. Short for Matilda.'

'Matilda. That's nice. She looks very sweet.'

'She is. Most of the time.'

'I have a cousin called Amy Power. But we've never met. Her mum and mine were sisters. I grew up with my mum, and we didn't have anything to do with her side of the family. Or my dad's, come to that. I don't know what happened to my dad, and my mum passed away a bit before Christmas.'

He immediately looks touchingly concerned. He reaches out as if he's about to clasp her hand or embrace her and then withdraws, as if he's thought better of it.

'I'm so sorry to hear that.' he says.

'Thank you. I think Mum was ready to go, in a way. She wasn't a very happy woman, for one reason or another. She'd had a hard life. But I did try writing to Amy, to let her know. I found an address. Somewhere in a place called Kettlebridge, in Oxfordshire. I don't know if it was right. I never heard back from her.'

'We used to live in Kettlebridge,' Joe says. 'The address would have been Mary Close.'

Lisa clears her throat. 'I see,' she says. 'Well then, it seems you're right. Your Amy Power and mine would appear to be one and the same.'

Her breath catches in her chest. She can't help but remember Mum's funeral, the cold and the views and the quiet field and the small huddle of mourners around the deep grave, not all that far away from these other surviving relatives who hadn't known and hadn't come.

'I'm so sorry, I'm not feeling well. I'm going to have to get some air,' she says, and turns and pushes her way through to find a space where she will be able to be alone again.

* * *

It turns out that she's gone the wrong way. Instead of finding herself back at the stairs that lead down to the exit, she finds herself facing a row of arched French windows that give onto a large first-floor terrace. One of the windows has been left slightly open, and she heads out past wicker sofas and tables littered with abandoned glasses of wine to stand by the balustrade and look out at the public garden below.

The sound of the speeches fades and is replaced by the background noise of London – traffic, the beep of a pedestrian crossing, the honk of a boat's horn on the river just beyond the tall trees obscuring the view in front of her. The cool air helps her to compose herself, and she finds a tissue in her bag and blows her nose just as Joe joins her.

He says, 'Are you OK?'

'Yeah,' she says. 'I'm sorry, I don't think I can really talk about it. Not right now.'

He glances at her. 'OK,' he says.

They stand there in silence for a little while. A burst of applause reaches them from the room at their backs.

'Look,' Joe says, and points. 'You can just about see the Thames.'

She looks, and there it is, a broad grey ribbon of water just visible through the screen of foliage.

He says, 'Well, I'm glad we ran into each other. I haven't met many of Amy's relatives.'

'What are her parents' names? If I'm remembering rightly, my mum told me she had a sister called Diane.'

'Yes, that's right. Elliott and Diane. But they're both dead now. Her dad passed away before she was born and she lost her mum to breast cancer a while back, soon after we started going out. Her Grandma Elsie is still with us, but apart from that, as far as I'm aware, you're the only surviving relative she has. Outside of our immediate family, of course. We're a pretty tight little unit.'

Lisa digests this. There was just so much her mum hadn't talked about. She'd never mentioned Elliott. And as for Diane... Had Mum known about what had happened to Diane? She'd never said anything about it. If she *had* known, wasn't that rather heartless? Had she had a chance to see Diane before she died, and turned it down? Was it possible that her mum had been harsh and unforgiving, too? Or had it been Diane's choice for them to remain estranged right up till the bitter end?

No way of knowing, now. Unless Amy can tell her. Or Amy's Grandma Elsie, maybe. Because surely this old lady is Lisa's grandmother too.

'You mentioned Grandma Elsie,' she says. 'Am I right in thinking that's Amy's grandmother on her mum's side?'

He regards her cautiously, as if not completely convinced

that it is a good idea to go into this. 'Yes, that's right. Diane's mum.'

'Which would make her my Grandma Elsie too.'

He nods. She turns away and tries to focus on the glimpse of distant river and calm herself. To think, rather than just to feel. Because she barely knows how to feel. Perhaps she should feel happy. But instead she is gripped by a vague sense of panic, as if she has gone from being alone to being under threat. Which is not the right reaction, not at all.

She makes an effort to pull herself together. What's wrong with her? Surely she should respond to what he's told her with a bit of compassion. Because Amy is parentless as well. Another adult orphan. And she looks as if she's maybe a couple of years younger than Lisa. She can barely be out of her twenties. Both of them have lost both their parents while still relatively young. Under very different circumstances, though, because Lisa's dad could still be out there somewhere, still alive, for all she knows.

'I'm sorry to hear about Amy's parents. It must have been very sad for her to lose her mum,' she says.

'Yeah, it had a big impact on her, as you'd expect. We had Tilly not that long after Diane died, and I guess Amy really felt the loss of her mum then, you know, and that her mum had missed out on getting to be a grandmother.'

'I bet,' Lisa says, and then, with a sudden rush, as if she's confessing to something she herself has done wrong, 'You should probably be aware that Amy might not be particularly pleased that you met me. My dad went to prison years ago, back when I was little. We'd already lost contact with his side of the family, and after that Mum's people didn't want anything to do with us either.'

'I have heard something about that,' he says gently.

'I've no idea what happened to him afterwards, or where he is now. Maybe Mum didn't know either. But anyway, it's too late to ask her.' She looks at him fiercely. 'I don't even know exactly what he did.'

Joe hesitates. 'I'm not sure it's my place to tell you.'

'Please, Joe. To be honest with you, I've always been a bit scared of finding out. But meeting you like this... I don't know, I feel like it's now or never.'

He sighs. 'Amy would know more. I think it was manslaughter. A drunken brawl.'

And she begins to cry. 'I'm sorry,' she says through tears.

'Don't be.'

'I mean... for getting so worked up. Crying on you like this. I'm sure it's the last thing you wanted from your evening out in town before the new baby arrives.' She sniffs. 'It's just... I thought it was probably something like that. But because Mum wouldn't say... You imagine all kinds of things, don't you, when you don't know... It seemed like it might be easier not to know.'

'It's not your fault,' he says gently. 'You didn't do anything, and you suffered too. It's called being a secondary victim, isn't it? When you are one of the other people who are affected by something like that.'

And then she is sobbing too hard to speak. Joe reaches out, quite naturally, and takes her in his arms and holds her, and she lets him. They stand there, swaying slightly, for all the world like the perfect couple, and only move apart when another round of applause rings out from the gathering of fundraisers they had all but forgotten about.

SIX

AMY

Tyler is pulling up ground elder near the laurel when she approaches him. She clears her throat and he straightens up and turns to face her and she says, 'I just wanted to remind you we've got someone coming for lunch.'

'Yeah, you said. Do you want me to go?'

'No, not necessarily. I mean, it's up to you. I just wanted to warn you.'

'Warn me? Why, what have you got planned?'

'Just lunch, that's all. Not a big deal. So it's fine if you want to carry on, you know, if you're happy with that. We're not going to eat outside or anything. We might come out here for a look round, but I don't suppose it'll take long.'

'Well, if it's all the same to you, I wouldn't mind cracking on a bit. It's been hard to get much done lately, with the weather being the way it has been, and I've got a load of other stuff on in the week.'

'Yeah, sure, whatever.'

'I mean, I won't start strimming hedges or anything. I'll be pretty quiet. What's the big deal, anyway? Who have you got coming?'

She hadn't been planning to say – she has been trying to keep it hush-hush, at least until she has a better sense of how it's going to pan out. But when it comes to it, she can't resist.

'My long-lost cousin, actually,' she says with a shrug, as if such things happen all the time. 'Joe met her at some event or other in London, and now she's coming here.'

'No way. Really? You mean the one whose dad...'

She lifts her chin and looks down her nose at him, not an easy feat given that he's a good foot taller than she is. She says, 'Yes. That one.'

'What are you doing that for? I'm guessing that was Joe's idea, was it?'

She shrugs again. 'Kind of. It was my idea, too. It's kind of an exploratory, get-to-know-you kind of thing. She doesn't actually seem to know anything about what happened.'

'You're kidding. You mean you asked her here and she doesn't even know why she probably shouldn't come? What are you going to do, drop it on her over lunch? Well, that'll make her choke on her peas.'

'She knows her dad killed someone,' Amy says coolly. 'I think that's enough to be getting on with. Anyway, look, don't say anything to anyone, OK? It's probably just a one-off. I know it's not likely to get back to Grandma Elsie, and she probably wouldn't understand even if it did, but some of her carers might know people in the village, and you never know what someone might come out with.'

'I won't mention it. But... are *you* OK with it?'

'Yeah. I mean, she's just a person, isn't she? It happened just before I was born, so she must have been a little tiny kid. It's not as if it's her fault.'

It is only as she is saying this that she realises it is true. She has only ever heard that side of the family mentioned with disdain, if at all. But Lisa really had been entirely blameless. As innocent as the baby Amy is carrying now, or as Tilly, who exists so much in her own world, and understands so little of what is going on between the adults around her.

'That's generous of you,' Tyler says slowly. 'Other people might not be quite so forgiving.' He reaches out as if to take hold of her, lightly touches the top of one of her arms and then lets his hand fall back to his side. 'You should put yourself first,' he tells her.

'Oh, don't worry, I will,' she snaps, suddenly irritated with him. After all, what right does he have to advise her about anything? 'Anyway, what do you care?'

'Amy, please,' he says. 'Don't you think we should have a talk sometime? An honest talk?'

'Don't do this, Tyler. Not now, not when we've got a visitor about to arrive,' she says, and turns away, because even though she's anxious about meeting her cousin, even that is preferable to a heart-to-heart with Tyler.

Something in the grass snags on her skirt and she tugs it loose and strides on without looking back, round Tilly's playhouse and across the lawn and back to the waiting house.

SEVEN

LISA

Even when she's on her way, she still half expects something to stop her getting there. A signal failure, perhaps, or flash flooding. But the train just keeps going. It's a slow weekend service that stops at several little towns and villages as it rattles away from the suburbs of Brickley and into the rolling landscape of Oxfordshire hills and fields, heading north-west and climbing.

She still can't quite believe she's made it this far. First of all, Amy had actually rung her up and invited her to lunch, and had been unexpectedly friendly, if a little overdramatic: *Long-lost cousin Lisa! What a turn-up for the books! I nearly fell off my chair when Joe told me. You must come and see us here at Hillview House. How are you fixed next weekend? OK, the one after? Saturday it is, then!*

The phone call had come through one evening when she was sitting on her bed watching TV, vaguely conscious of the splash of water against the wall next to her where her neighbour Holly was using the shower in her flat. As soon as Lisa realised it was Amy on the phone, everything else had faded into the background. She'd been automatically polite and enthusiastic – *great to hear from you, yes, I'd love to come* – and then, after

Amy finished the call (*so sorry, I have to dash*) she'd found herself sitting on the bed, still staring at the phone in her hand, gradually becoming aware of the sound of water again.

It had been almost unreal, after all this time, to have had contact. Then the nerves had set in. She'd told herself not to worry – the visit would surely be a happy occasion, though it wouldn't do to expect too much. But she still felt wary. It didn't help that she suspected Amy had only got in touch with her because of Joe's intervention, however enthusiastic she'd sounded.

Then an obstacle had intervened at the eleventh hour – her car had died, and she'd been told it was not worth repairing, which was OK in the short term because her current job was in easy walking distance of her flat, but was also a pain, because she can't really afford to replace it. Then Amy had said her not having a car was no problem – she didn't drive herself and had never learned, but Joe would be happy to come and pick her up from the nearest station.

Lisa is the only person who gets off at the stop Amy had told her to look out for. The ticket hall is locked, so she goes out through the gate at the side and there is Joe, waiting for her in a dusty old family estate car. As she picks up the pace to walk over to him her heart skips a beat, and she just has time to wonder if there's more to her response than nerves before he gets out to greet her.

Joe and Amy's house is up on a hill, as its name suggests, surrounded by open countryside and overlooking the village below. The view is idyllic, especially on a clear day like today: Springhill with its thatched cottages and the surrounding curves of green fields dotted with woodland, stretching for miles before fading into a bluish haze at the horizon.

The house, though... The house isn't quite so picturesque.

There's something mournful about it. Mournful and neglected, which surprises her. The white paint on the roughcast façade looks as if it could do with touching up, and the two rows of windows are set in crooked red wooden frames that probably need replacing. It looks like a tired face peering through sore eyes. Still, it's striking, a memorable landmark. That could be why she feels that there's something familiar about it, almost as if she's seen it somewhere before – maybe in a photograph, or an illustration from a book.

Joe pulls up in a gravelled area to one side, next to a pick-up truck with a neat row of bags of garden waste in the back.

'We've got someone doing some work in the garden at the moment,' Joe says. 'I expect he'll be gone soon. Hope you don't mind.'

'Of course not. It all looks so beautiful, it must be a lot to maintain. I've never actually had a garden myself. I just about manage to look after a couple of houseplants, and that's it.'

They go round to the front of the house, past a vivid display of daffodils. 'I've been trying to get Tilly interested in growing things,' Joe says. 'We've set aside a corner for her to grow whatever she wants. She's planted it with love-in-a-mist, because that's what she likes best.'

'That's nice. I guess you must find doing stuff in the garden is a good way to unwind after the stress of work.'

'I suppose it is, though you could argue it's a bit of a busman's holiday.'

'What do you mean? I thought you were a doctor.'

'I am. But not a medical doctor. I'm not out and about in a white coat saving lives. I'm an academic. I have a PhD in botany, and I work in plant science.'

'Oh, I just assumed...'

'Some of my friends at the swimming club call me Doc,' he says. 'It's a silly in-joke. One of them put it down on the paperwork for the swimathon, and it ended up on my name label. I wouldn't want you to think I make a big deal of using it as some kind of honorary title.'

'If I had an honorary title I'd want to use it all the time. Why shouldn't you? You don't have to be so self-effacing about it.' She holds up the cellophane-wrapped bouquet she has brought with her. 'You probably won't be too impressed by these.'

'On the contrary,' he says gravely. 'Gypsophila is beautiful. You know they call it baby's breath? I guess because it looks so delicate and innocent.'

They've reached the front door. He gets out his key and lets them in, and she follows him into a white-painted hallway with bright rugs on the red-tiled floor and an old oak staircase to one side. It's dim in spite of the bright sunshine outside, and the sound of birdsong from the garden is instantly silenced by the thick walls.

There's definitely a connection – a sense of familiarity. But maybe she just feels that way because she wants to – because part of her wants and needs a place and people to belong to, if only for a little while.

'Mind your head,' Joe says as they pass the staircase, and she ducks just in time. 'The ceiling's a bit low here. This part of the house, near the kitchen, is the oldest bit of the building, along with the master bedroom overhead. It's seventeenth-century, I think. Dates back to the English civil war, and people weren't so tall in those days.'

She turns back and sees that the space under the staircase, instead of being fitted with a door as most understairs cupboards are, is covered with a red velvet curtain, as if it might lead to a miniature stage. Then they pass through a low, heavy door into a long kitchen with a high vaulted roof edged with dark-painted beams.

Does she really recognise it, or is it just a trick her mind is playing on her, a kind of déjà vu? She must be more over-wrought than she'd realised.

There is a wood-burner to one side, opposite a row of the kind of standard pine units you might see in any suburban house. At the end of the room is a large paned window, and in front of it a small girl is sitting at a square wooden table, drawing.

She is wearing a shiny pink dress that looks slightly too small for her and her hair is pulled back into two straggly plaits. She's a slight, delicately built child, fine-boned as a little bird. Her head is bowed over the picture she is working on, and she is concentrating so hard that she doesn't immediately look up when they come in.

'This is Tilly,' Joe says. 'Tilly, this is Lisa, the lady I told you about.'

Tilly looks up and gives them both a gap-toothed smile. 'Look, Daddy, I'm drawing instead of watching TV,' she says.

'That's good, because if you sit in front of the TV for too long you might end up with square eyes.' Joe pulls his eyes open wide with his fingers and rolls them, and Tilly cackles explosively and then covers her hand with her mouth. Joe says, 'Where's Mummy?'

'She went out into the garden,' Tilly says, 'and then she came back in and went upstairs. I think maybe she wasn't feeling very well.'

'OK, I'll go and track her down,' Joe says. 'Sorry, Lisa – back in a minute.'

He withdraws and heads back into the hallway, leaving the two of them alone together. Lisa runs an inch of water into the sink and puts her flowers in it, then sits down next to Tilly at the table.

There's no sound of movement or conversation from upstairs. Maybe the old house is too solidly built for any noise to reach down here. Tilly doesn't seem concerned, and has gone straight back to her drawing. She has an illustrated book open on the table in front of her and is copying from it as she works on colouring in a row of blue flowers.

'Your dad told me you like love-in-a-mist,' Lisa says. 'Is that what you're drawing?'

'It is,' Tilly says. 'I like them because they're blue and blue is my favourite colour. But mainly, I like them because of their name. My daddy bought me this book.'

Lisa leans forward to look more closely at the open book. *Love-in-a-mist, also known as nigella or devil-in-the-bush. Symbolic of love, bonds between people and mystery.* The book doesn't seem to have been written with children in mind, but perhaps Joe had chosen it because of the pictures. Her heart twists inside her at the thought of Joe and Tilly seated at this very table in front of the same book, Joe reading it out loud and breaking off to explain the more difficult words, Tilly listening intently.

'I like blue flowers too,' she tells Tilly. 'I like bluebells and forget-me-nots.'

'Sometimes people call them weeds,' Tilly says. 'My daddy says a weed is just a plant in the wrong place.' She turns over a couple of pages in the illustrated book till she finds a bluebell, and starts to copy it. 'My mummy is having a baby soon.'

'Yes, I heard.'

'Do you have any children?'

'No, I don't.'

'Why not?'

Tilly's pencil is poised above the paper, perfectly still. She is watching Lisa intently, as if she really wants to know.

'You don't *have* to have babies, you know. Lots of people don't. There are plenty of other interesting things you can do.'

'Like going on an aeroplane,' Tilly says thoughtfully.

'Yes. Or doing an interesting job.'

'Do you do an interesting job?'

'At the moment I work in an office where I type up reports for people who want to buy houses. But I've done other things in the past.'

Tilly starts drawing again. She says, 'Did you ever work in a shop? I'd like to work in a sweet shop.'

'Yeah, years ago I worked in a supermarket.' She'd still been living with Mum at the time, trying to get through her A levels, desperate to leave home but conflicted about leaving Mum behind on her own. She'd carried on feeling like that all through her working life – worrying about Mum, wanting her independence – no matter what job she'd been doing, or where she'd moved to.

Tilly says, 'What did you do there? Were you one of the ladies on the tills?'

'No, I used to put all the food on the shelves ready for when the people came in with their trolleys in the morning.'

Tilly's eyes widen and her mouth forms a little circle as if she is about to whistle in admiration. 'You mean you worked in the night-time? When nobody else was there? I would love to be in a shop in the night-time. Especially if it was a bed shop, so you could go to sleep in one of the beds.'

'I don't know, I think it's nice to sleep at home,' Lisa says. 'But I do quite like working at night.'

An eddy of cold air stirs the hairs on the back of her neck. Someone has pushed open the door from the hallway. She turns and sees Amy approaching with Joe behind her, and gets to her feet to greet her.

Amy doesn't look quite as groomed as in the photo Lisa had seen on Joe's phone, but that's hardly surprising. Her resemblance to Lisa's mum is even more unmistakable in the flesh. She's wearing a faded green shirt that just about buttons up across her bump – maybe it's an old one of Joe's – and a long dark stretchy skirt, and she looks ready to give birth any day now, though her due date isn't for another couple of weeks. Her hair is slightly messed up and her face is flushed, as if she has just been sleeping, or perhaps crying.

'I'm so sorry,' she says, coming forward to give Lisa a hug. 'I came over a bit dizzy, so I thought I'd lie down for five minutes. I'm all right now. Just one of those things. It's lovely to meet you at last, after all these years... The whole of my life!'

Amy's smile is warm, but her embrace is brief and slightly stiff, as if she doesn't really want to get too close. She withdraws almost instantly and spots Lisa's flowers in the sink. 'Did you bring those? Thank you. That's very sweet.'

'You're welcome. Thank you for inviting me. This is a lovely house.'

'It's certainly got character. That's what people usually say. And views, of course.'

Amy turns away to retrieve a vase from a cupboard, and Lisa spots a broken stem of goosegrass sticking to the back of her skirt but hesitates to point it out. Joe stoops to pick it off and presents it to Amy with a jokey comment: 'What on earth have you been doing? It looks like you've been rolling round in the hay.' Amy shoots him a look composed of equal parts indignation and embarrassment, grabs the goosegrass and shoves it into one of the bins by the sink. Lisa is glad she hadn't said anything.

Amy trims the stalks of the flowers and arranges them, and Joe attempts to make small talk with Lisa about her journey. Then Amy says she'll take Lisa off on a tour of the house, and they leave Joe to sort out the lunch.

Lisa expects to see room after room filled with luxuriously comfortable furniture and valuable ornaments – a home equipped not with hand-me-downs and bargains, but with things that had been picked out and invested in. To her surprise, it isn't like that. It's much more sparse. It feels like somewhere that is rented rather than owned, as if Amy and Joe and Tilly could be given notice and asked to leave at any moment.

They start with a cavernous, rather gloomy living room,

with a couple of armchairs and a sofa covered in patchwork throws arranged around a long, ancient-looking fireplace. There are several framed photos of Amy, some with Joe next to her and one or two with Tilly too, but none of anybody else, as far as Lisa can see. Next there's a dining room with a long table covered with a dark blue oilcloth and a dusty bowl of pot-pourri on one windowsill, and finally a smaller living room overlooking the back garden.

Amy calls this room the family room, and it feels as if it's actually used, with a sofa and an armchair arranged round the TV and a couple of canvas storage boxes to one side stuffed with fluffy toys and nylon dressing-up outfits. By the rug, there's a scattering of jigsaw pieces next to a tiara with a missing plastic gem.

'Sorry for the mess. I did ask Tilly to tidy,' Amy says, nudging a soft toy out of the way with her foot, and Lisa makes the usual noises about how it isn't messy at all. Which it isn't, really.

They go back into the hallway and up the oaken stairs, which feel surprisingly solid, as if carved out of stone rather than wood.

First they peek into the master bedroom, which is dominated by the most imposing bed Lisa has ever seen outside of a stately home, a huge four-poster carved out of shining reddish-brown wood. It's an opulent room with lots of mirrors – on the dressing-table, on the wardrobe doors, hanging on the wall – reflecting carefully selected ornaments: a tall pale green alabaster vase, framed photos of Amy and Joe on their wedding day, and assorted candles in brass holders. The air smells faintly of expensive perfume.

'I picked the bed up at auction after we moved here, and got it fixed up,' Amy says. 'Bit over the top maybe, but I like it.'

They move on to Tilly's room, which has a little bed in one corner, with a raggedy, important-looking bear snuggled up in the pink bedlinen. There's a pink pop-up tent in the corner opposite.

'Typical, isn't it,' Amy comments, waving a hand in the direction of the tent. 'All this space, and all she wants is somewhere small to hide.' Lisa feels a pang of sympathy for Tilly; it's a generous-sized room, impeccably tidy, and the bed is surrounded by empty space and looks rather lonely. She can see why Tilly might want a little den to tuck herself away in.

'This is for our new arrival,' Amy says, opening the door to the next room, which has been freshly painted yellow and furnished with a white cot with a mobile attached to the frame. There's a small pile of bedding, still in its wrapping, lying on the brand-new mattress. Next to the cot is a square window looking out onto a large weeping willow at the end of the back garden.

'There's not much upstairs, just the converted attic that Joe uses as his study,' Amy says. 'Shall we go and see how he's getting on with the lunch?'

Lisa murmurs something about how that sounds like a good idea. But instead of retreating straight away, she steps hesitantly into the room, towards the window.

That tree... she's absolutely sure she recognises it. It's a beautiful tree, but the sight of it makes her feel sick at the pit of her stomach, as if she's only just realised that she's forgotten something crucial, or made some terrible, irrevocable mistake.

EIGHT

LISA

It isn't until they've settled down to eat that she begins to feel better. It's the best meal she's had in as long as she can remember. There is a big pasta salad with sweet, fat cherry tomatoes and mozzarella and basil, and another salad with roasted courgettes and aubergines and red peppers scattered with rosemary. Then there is a little bowl of grated carrot and a jug of home-made dressing with chopped mint and dill, and crusty bread and a dish of butter and cheeses on a board, some with skins and some without.

Lisa compliments the food, and Joe says, 'Well, it's a special occasion. It's not every day a long-lost cousin comes to visit,' and they drink a toast to her.

As their glasses clink – filled with elderflower cordial all round – Lisa is happy and at ease, and the nerves and uncertainty she'd felt earlier fade away. They talk about this and that: the baby, Joe's forthcoming research trip to New Zealand, the primary school in the village that Tilly goes to. Next to Lisa, Tilly carefully takes out bits of her salad she doesn't want to eat and nibbles at the rest.

When they've finished, Tilly is allowed to get down and Joe

sets about making coffee and clearing the table. Then the phone rings somewhere outside the kitchen and Amy goes off to answer it. Lisa suddenly finds herself alone with Joe, who finishes stacking the dishwasher and comes back to the table to join her.

'Amy was nervous about meeting you,' he says. 'This is actually a big deal for her. She's been quite on edge the last few weeks, but I think she's relaxed now that she can see for herself what you're like.'

And Lisa can't help herself. She's flattered. More than flattered. It's as if her heart is both light and expanding, like a balloon being pumped full of air.

'It's lovely to have the chance to meet her,' she says. 'And your daughter. And to see this place. Especially because not so long ago, it seemed like I had no family at all.' She stops herself. 'I'm sorry if that sounds over the top,' she adds. 'I'm just so pleased to be here.'

'I can imagine,' Joe says. 'I didn't have family around me when I was growing up. I know what it's like to be alone in the world. How ashamed it can make you feel. Even though it's nothing to be ashamed of.'

He is looking at her with a softness that makes her feel weak. It's just kindness. That's all. But it is also powerful and maybe dangerous. Something inside her is beginning to give way – the little wall of resistance that keeps her safe from other people.

Then Amy comes back in, and Joe's attention immediately shifts.

'I've really screwed up this time,' Amy says, and drops down onto a chair in a dramatic pose of despair.

'It can't be that bad,' Joe says reasonably. 'What's happened?'

Amy's face is the shade of red that goes with either humiliation or fever. 'Don't do that,' she snaps. 'Don't make out that I'm overreacting.'

'OK, well, why don't you tell me?'

'I'm trying to,' Amy says. 'That was Flora's mum, calling to see if Tilly's still coming to Flora's party. Which is happening now. Right now. I'd got it in my head that it was tomorrow. And then, what with one thing and another, I just didn't think about it at all.' She looks slightly accusingly at Lisa.

'Oh. Well, that's not the end of the world, is it? These things happen,' Joe says reasonably. 'Can't you just pop her round there?'

'They live near Oxford. It's miles away. You'd have to drive her,' Amy says.

'Maybe she could just give it a miss,' Joe suggests.

'That is not going to work. You know how miserable she is at school. She's always complaining that she has no friends and nobody ever talks to her. She was lucky to get an invite. When she figures out the party happened without her, we'll never hear the last of it.'

Maybe drawn by some sixth sense, or perhaps because she has picked up that her social life is under discussion, Tilly chooses that moment to reappear. 'Mummy? What are you talking about?'

Amy stares at her in blank despair. Joe looks helpless. And Lisa finds herself saying, 'Joe, why don't you just go on over and take her? You don't need to hang round here on my account.'

'If you go, Flora's mum will nag you to stay,' Amy says to Joe. 'The kids are supposed to be making their own teddy bears, and she needs a couple of parents to stick around. I think she's panicking. Most of them have already dumped their kids and run.'

'I don't mind helping out at the party, but if I do, how are we going to get you back to the station?' Joe says to Lisa. 'I could take you now, but it's a bit of a rush for you.' He turns to Amy.

'Or maybe Tyler could take her on his way home?' For Lisa's benefit, he adds, 'Tyler's our gardener. He was here this morning, but I don't know if he's still around.'

'Oh no, that wouldn't do,' Amy says. 'We shouldn't ask him to go out of his way. Anyway, I expect he's gone by now.'

'No worries, I can get a taxi,' Lisa chips in. 'That'll be no problem at all.'

'Great. OK, that's settled, then,' Joe says, looking both grateful and relieved. Amy exhales, and Tilly manages a tentative smile. Out of the blue, it seems that it's in Lisa's gift to make them all happy.

Tilly is eager to go straight away, and pudding is forgotten. Amy tells Joe to stop off at the newsagent's and let Tilly pick out a card and a magazine and some sweets to give as a present, and Joe and Tilly head off.

As they make their way to the kitchen door Tilly instinctively reaches for Joe's hand and he takes hers, just for a moment, and it's a sight for sore eyes – the tall man stooping slightly, the little girl who would clearly follow him anywhere. That trust. It's so touching to see it. Lisa is embarrassed to find herself near to tears, but Amy hasn't noticed. Instead, she stretches and suppresses a yawn and checks her watch. It's a slender, metallic bracelet, an elegant thing – a gift from Joe, probably.

And now it's just the two of them. Her and Amy. This is it. Her chance to open up the fraught subject of family history. But she can't think of how to start, and then Amy yawns again and says, 'I've the most splitting headache. I really think I'm going to need to have a lie down.'

Lisa hesitates, then gives Amy the response she seems to be angling for.

'Maybe I should head off now, then,' she says. 'You've been really kind to invite me here, but I can see you've got a lot going on at the moment and I really don't want to outstay my welcome.'

'Yeah, maybe that would be for the best,' Amy says, and stretches again. 'Sorry. My energy comes and goes. I guess it's just one of those pregnancy things.'

'I'm sure it must be exhausting,' Lisa says politely.

Amy gets to her feet and says, 'I'd probably better call for a taxi sooner rather than later. They can take a while to arrive, out here in the sticks.'

'Sure,' Lisa says. She feels, not insulted, but mildly surprised that Amy now seems so eager to get rid of her. She says, 'Amy...?'

An expression of blind panic crosses Amy's face, as if she's genuinely scared of what Lisa might ask her and where that conversation might lead them. Then she quickly composes herself and gives Lisa a patient but slightly weary smile.

'Yes?'

'Maybe this isn't a good time to ask... I know you're not feeling well. But there's so much I don't know about our family, and I've been wondering if you might be able to help me fill in some of the gaps.'

Amy grimaces as if Lisa has just demanded something that is beyond her right now. She moves forward a step or two and folds her arms.

'What like?'

'Well...'

Lisa doesn't know where to start. What does she really want, answers or comfort? It seems absurd, as if she's about to pose an abstract philosophical question to this tired, harassed, heavily pregnant woman who just wants her out of her house.

'I guess I wanted to see if you could tell me anything more about my dad,' she says. 'Pretty much all I know about him is his name. Mike Brierley. And I know he went to prison. Joe told me it was manslaughter, that he got into a fight and the other person died. But I've no idea where he is now, or even if he's still alive.'

Amy screws up her face as if this is as uncomfortable for her as it is for Lisa. 'I'm sorry, I don't think I can help you with that one. When I was growing up nobody talked about him. It was kind of like a taboo subject. I don't know what happened to him.'

Lisa gives a small, helpless shrug. 'OK,' she says. 'There are probably other ways I could try and track him down. I guess, I'm really honest, I never tried that hard to find out. It's just that, being here with you, I thought it was worth asking.'

Amy nods and smiles sympathetically, obviously considering that the subject is now closed. Lisa says, 'You know, this house does feel weirdly familiar. Almost as if I've been here before.'

'Perhaps you have,' Amy says, with a small smile. 'But doesn't it matter more that you've been here today?'

'I'm really glad to have had the chance to come. It was good of you to invite me,' Lisa says. 'It's been great to meet you, and Joe and Tilly too.'

'It's been a pleasure,' Amy says firmly. She glances at her watch again. 'I guess I'd better go and call this taxi for you.'

'Sure. Thank you,' Lisa says, and Amy goes off to use the landline phone in the hall.

Lisa stares at the flowers she had brought with her, now in the vase on the worktop Amy had put them in. Gypsophila, Joe had called it. Baby's breath, the symbol of innocence.

She is deadly tired, surely as tired as Amy is. It's as if she's been hypnotised, lulled not into a false sense of security but into complete inaction. When Amy comes back in she seems brisk and efficient, a hostess in the process of despatching her visitor, and Lisa's willingness to tackle difficult questions has deserted her.

'We're in luck,' Amy says. 'They said they can get someone

here in quarter of an hour or so. Normally it would be longer than that.' She checks her watch. 'Joe should almost be at the party by now.'

'He seems like a very devoted dad.'

'He is,' Amy says shortly. She is still standing, arms folded across her bump, as if hoping the taxi might come even sooner than expected. 'But the bar is pretty low, it seems to me. If a man does anything for his child, or anybody else, everybody thinks it's completely amazing. If a woman does it, it's just normal.'

'I didn't mean to sound one-sided,' Lisa says. 'You're obviously a brilliant mum too.'

Amy makes a small scoffing noise and makes a show of spreading out her right hand and inspecting her peachy nail polish. 'I don't think that's obvious at all. It's certainly not obvious to me.'

Lisa doesn't know what to say. It's certainly true that Joe seems closer to Tilly than Amy does. Then Amy looks up and their eyes meet and she sees that Amy knows exactly what she's thinking and, even worse, agrees with her.

There's something so intimate about this little moment of shared knowledge that it's almost claustrophobic. It's as if Amy is a victim in some secret way and finds this humiliating for anyone else to witness or acknowledge, however fleetingly.

'She's obviously having a really lovely childhood,' Lisa says. Then she gets to her feet and says, 'Tell you what, how about we have a quick look at the garden before the taxi comes?'

'Sure,' Amy says. She seems relieved. She goes over to the back door and holds it open for Lisa to go through, and Lisa steps out into suddenly strong sunlight and air that is sweet and heady with the scents of blossom and new growth.

The sense of familiarity that has ebbed and flowed since she first set foot in the house comes rushing back, stronger than ever. She hesitates, half tempted to beat a retreat, but it's too late to change her mind and go back because Amy is outside now, too, and walking ahead, and she finds herself following her.

They pass through a kitchen garden with rosemary and mint growing between uneven paving stones, along with a patch of tiny seedlings that are perhaps Tilly's love-in-a-mist. At the back of the house there is a patio overlooking the freshly mown lawn. It's very quiet, and there's no sign of Tyler or anyone else.

The lawn is circled by bushes and shrubs and trees, some of which are heavy with blossom – white on the ancient, gnarled apple trees, delicate pink on the plum tree. The tallest of all the trees is the weeping willow she'd noticed from the window of the baby's bedroom. Standing a little way in front of it is a playhouse made of chipboard painted white, with flowered curtains at the windows and a pitched roof made of faded black asphalt.

The playhouse looks new, but not brand new, as if it has weathered perhaps a couple of winters. It doesn't appear to be prefabricated, or shop-bought – it looks as if someone had built it, perhaps over a couple of weekends, taking their time to get it right. Joe must have put it up for Tilly. She can almost see him working here, tools and materials laid out on the lawn, measuring and fixing, making the playhouse robust enough to last.

Amy says something about checking to see if Tyler's working round at the front of the house and takes off. It doesn't bother Lisa to have her disappear. It makes it easier for her to explore. She strikes out across the grass and around the playhouse, gravitating instinctively towards the willow tree.

Stepping into the shelter of the branches is like entering a green cave. There is none of the dread she'd felt earlier when she saw the willow from the upstairs window. She looks up at the little pieces of sky visible through the canopy of the leaves, and presses her hand against the rough bark and imagines the roots deep below her in the earth, a secret network reaching out like creeping fingers and holding her up. The whisper of the breeze in the leaves is as soothing as the sound of flowing water.

Hadn't she climbed a weeping willow once, when she was young? She has a very faint memory of being perched high among the branches, like a bird, with the blue sky all around her and the long fronds of green leaves falling to the ground beneath her. Could it have been here? Or maybe it was something she had seen on TV. It hadn't happened anywhere she and Mum had ever lived together, that's for sure. They'd never had a garden big enough to have a tree like this one.

She moves on to the far side of the garden, where the lawn narrows between a border running along the side of the house and a flowering hawthorn hedge separating the garden from the neighbouring field.

The border next to the house is a tangle of budding purple lilac and yellow roses. It must be lovely when everything's in full bloom, but it's also a little neglected – it must be a while since Tyler, or anybody else, attended to it. Through the branches, partly obscured by stems and new leaves and weeds, she sees a small grate at ground level, set across a shallow well in front of a basement window.

She goes a little closer and stoops to look in. Something cracks – a twig underfoot. The rose has sent out a long spike of bloomless growth that snags her sleeve as she leans in closer. When she disentangles herself, the hook of one of the thorns pricks the back of her hand and draws blood.

All she can see through the window is the top of a bookcase with a row of books on it. It's too gloomy inside for it to be easy to tell, but it looks as if the books have been there long enough for the edges of their pages to begin to turn yellow.

'Lisa? Where are you?'

It's Amy. Lisa straightens up and hurries back across the lawn towards her.

'Where did you get to?' Amy says. 'Your taxi just arrived.'

She looks sullen but vindicated, as if something she has been dreading and putting off is now done with. She must have found the whole visit a strain, and be glad it's over.

'I'm sorry. I was just admiring the garden.' It's a lie. She was snooping, though she has no idea what she was looking for or what she expected to find.

'I guess I tend to take it for granted,' Amy says. 'Are you into gardening?'

'Me? Not really. I don't have any outdoor space. A few pots on the windowsill is about my limit.'

'I think it would be mine too. I mean, I have to confess, I don't actually have a lot to do with it.'

They pass a man in a vest and jeans putting tools back into a shed next to the gravelled parking area. Amy drops her voice and says, 'That's Tyler's department, mainly.' Then, more loudly, 'Joe does bits and pieces when he's around and has the time, of course.'

Tyler doesn't acknowledge either of them and carries on with the task at hand. If he's overheard them, he is choosing to ignore them. Perhaps he doesn't like to be talked about. Lisa doesn't try to say hello to him and neither does Amy, and they walk on to the gravelled parking area where the taxi is waiting.

'Thank you so much for coming,' Amy says, turning to Lisa with her warmest smile, and suddenly it's hard to picture her any other way.

'Thank you for inviting me. And for lunch, and showing me round. It's been great. Really great. All of it,' Lisa says, and finds she means it.

'It's been so good to meet you. Sorry it was cut a bit short. You must come again sometime. Maybe after I've had the baby,' Amy says, and rests her hands on either side of her bump. It seems not so much a protective gesture as a statement, a way of saying that the pregnancy is now in charge.

'I'd like that,' Lisa says, and then Amy leans forward to kiss her on the cheek. It's a light, decorous embrace that doesn't bring their bodies into contact, but still, it makes it seem possible that Amy might really mean it, and that maybe, over time, if Lisa visits again, they'll get to know each other better, and might even become close.

'Good luck with it. I mean, with the baby and everything,' Lisa says as Amy withdraws.

Was that all right to say? Amy doesn't seem to mind. 'Thanks,' she says. 'I'm trying not to think about it. Live in the present, that's what I say.'

'Good for you. That's probably what we should all do,' Lisa says.

Amy waves as she gets into the taxi, but has already headed back into the house by the time it pulls away.

NINE

AMY

April 2009

It had not been the first thing she thought when they put her
new baby in her arms – she'd been too busy admiring his perfect
little hands and fingers, his perfect eyelashes and eyelids, his
perfect round cheeks, his perfect everything. But it had
occurred to her soon afterwards, and she began to study his face
not just because it was his and she was smitten with it, but to
check for answers to the inevitable question: *Who does he look
like?*

Joe asked the same thing while they were still in hospital,
waiting to be discharged, and answered it himself without any
prompting from her. 'Your grandad,' he said. 'Look at his
eyebrows, the shape of his head and his neck. He's the spit
image of him.'

And it was true. Rowan really did have a look of her
grandad, and also of Amy herself.

She'd been crabby with Joe right through the late stages of
pregnancy, when she'd been suffering from heartburn and
insomnia and swollen ankles and also, generally, intense irrita-

tion, not helped by the fear of what she might end up saying to him when the brakes were off. But somehow, miraculously, she'd got through the gas and air, and labour and birth, without blurting out anything she shouldn't. She'd ended up screaming too much to be tempted to articulate a confession, even if she'd felt like it.

It is so good to be on the other side of the birth, and she is so elated to have delivered a gorgeous, healthy baby boy, that on the way home she promises herself she is going to be a really good wife and mother from here on in, and really believes it might be possible.

Rowan is so different to Tilly. She knows it's wrong to compare them, and that no loving mother should do it. But it's also irresistible. Surely it's OK to say to Joe, as she does from time to time, how lucky she is that Rowan is such a contented baby, and how much easier it all is second time round? Tilly had fussed so much, and been so colicky and demanding, and had such trouble feeding and teething – not that any of that had been Tilly's fault, of course, poor skinny little thing that she'd been.

Anyway, it won't matter if Tilly overhears, as long as she doesn't think that Rowan being an easy baby also makes him easier to love.

The days pass in a blur of feeding and sleeping and nappies and feeding again. She is determined to breastfeed Rowan for at least the first few months. She hadn't managed it for very long with Tilly. This time it's going to be different. And it is. As Rowan begins to put on weight his appetite grows, and she spend hours and hours in her favourite armchair with him in her arms, nursing him while watching TV.

She's glad that she'd followed through on the impulse to put Tyler straight that day when Lisa had come to visit. She'd been thinking about it all through lunch, wondering whether she should say something, and when and how. And then she had taken Lisa out to show her the garden and the impulse had become overwhelming. She'd done it right then and there – put Tyler back in his box. It hadn't taken long. After all, there had not been very much to say.

You said you wanted to have an honest talk. Well, I just wanted to tell you we have nothing to talk about. Yes, I am absolutely sure about that, so neither of us need even think about it ever again.

He had stared at her as if she'd shocked him. Which was fair enough, since she'd come out with it so suddenly. Also, he'd looked as if he didn't quite believe her. Which had terrified her and also, in a weird way, had been totally thrilling. Who knows what she might have done or said right then if he had called her bluff... But anyway, then Lisa's taxi had arrived, and after Lisa had gone Tyler had just got into his truck and driven off, too, without saying anything more. And he has kept his distance ever since, and said as little to her as possible.

He had accepted it. All he'd really wanted to hear was that there was nothing for him to worry about. Which was entirely disappointing and predictable, but also made things easier. It wasn't as if she had a choice, not really. What else was she going to do but carry on and make the best of things, just like she had before?

April gives way to May and May gives way to June, and then it is high summer and time for Joe to take off for the other side of the world. As he begins to pack, and Tilly becomes increasingly tearful and withdrawn and uncooperative, she realises belatedly just how much he has been doing to keep Tilly off her back, and how much more difficult life is going to be once he has gone.

Joe says not to come to the airport to say goodbye. But Tilly wants to go, and because he's going to be leaving on a Saturday they don't have the excuse of school. Tilly bursts into tears and pleads, and Amy has to be firm and practical and explain that she'd have to bring Rowan with them and she couldn't drive, so either they'd have all have to come back by public transport, which would take forever, or by taxi, which would cost a fortune. But Tilly stands her ground, and folds her arms and glares at Amy in defiance.

'He's only saying he doesn't mind if we don't go to the airport with him because he knows you don't want to,' she says, and this is so accurate that it makes Amy wince. They end up having a shouting match that concludes with Tilly screaming, not for the first time and probably not the last, that she hates her, then running up to her room and slamming the door as if she's suddenly turned into a teenager.

Then, of course, Joe is the one who coaxes Tilly out. He knocks on her door and asks her if she would like hot chocolate with marshmallows in it, and when she has said yes, and is sitting opposite him at the kitchen and sniffling self-pityingly in between picking out her marshmallows and eating them, he gives her a good talking-to – but does it so gently and kindly that she barely protests. Amy, who is rather resentfully washing up, can't help but admire how calm and reasonable he sounds.

'You will be on your very best behaviour for Mummy while I'm away, won't you? I want you to promise me that you'll do as much to help her as you possibly can. Because you know she's going to be feeding Rowan a lot, and she's going to get tired, and she's going to need your help.'

'But Daddy,' Tilly begins, and then hesitates. 'Mummy doesn't even *want* me to help.'

'She does,' Joe says. 'And so do I. And it's really easy for you to help. Every time you read a book, or play a game, or draw a picture, that's helping. The best way of all for you to help is to be happy.'

And Tilly pauses, and sniffs again and says forlornly that she will do her best but it is a big promise, and drinks some more of her hot chocolate.

'Don't forget, I'll be calling you up on the phone in the evenings sometimes, when you're about to go to bed. That will be morning for me. And we'll do Skype, and you'll be able to see me on the computer screen and I'll be able to see you,' Joe tells her.

'Will you call often, Daddy?'

'Of course I will. I'll call so often you'll be very bored talking to me, and you'll probably want to run off and play. Or just fall asleep.'

Tilly giggles, and then asks Joe where in New Zealand he is going first, and Amy stops listening because she's heard all this a hundred times before. Joe's itinerary is pinned up on one of the kitchen cupboards, and Tilly has located as many of the places as possible in her atlas and has asked Joe an endless series of questions about them, all of which he has responded to with the same patience. He never seemed to be afraid of saying he didn't know something, or that he would check and tell her later, and had taken to jotting down what she wanted to know in a little notebook and responding later on, when Amy would have assumed that she'd forgotten all about it.

Finally, the day arrives when he is due to leave. His taxi to the airport is booked for mid-morning, but he's typically well-organised and is ready hours before, so has time to sit at the kitchen table and draw pictures of flowers with Tilly. Amy leaves them to it, and takes Rowan with her to feed him in the family room in her usual chair.

When the doorbell rings the baby is sleeping peacefully in her arms, and her first reaction is annoyance that he's probably going to be disturbed. But then she remembers this is it – the big farewell. Rowan blearily opens his eyes but doesn't cry and she carries him out into the hallway and converges on Joe and Tilly coming in from the kitchen.

Joe holds out his finger for Rowan to clutch and bows down to plant a tiny kiss on his forehead. Rowan gurgles and gives him one of his brand-new gummy smiles. Tilly waits patiently to one side for her turn to say goodbye. She looks very pale, and has dark shadows under her eyes – she'd had trouble dozing off the night before, and had come back downstairs a couple of times after she was supposed to have gone to bed. Joe had been as patient as ever, soothing her, coaxing her to try again to go to sleep. Amy can only hope she isn't going to make a habit of it.

Then Joe hugs Tilly very tightly and she clings to him and starts crying.

'Don't, Tilly,' Amy says. 'Try to be brave, there's a good girl. You're not going to make your dad feel very happy on his journey carrying on like that, are you?'

But Joe says, 'It's OK. She doesn't have to be brave,' and Amy is quite sure she catches Tilly giving her a little sidelong look, as if she has somehow scored a point over her.

'Daddy, you will come back, won't you?' Tilly says. 'You won't die in a plane crash, or anything like that? Because if you did die, I think I would die too.'

'Don't be so morbid, Tilly. That's no way to talk,' Amy says.

Joe ignores her. 'Of course I'll come back,' he says to Tilly. 'Take care of the love-in-a-mist. If your mum helps you, you should be able to email me photos, and I'll be able to look at them from the other side of the world.'

Tilly is still clinging to him. 'Will you see me when you're asleep and dreaming, Daddy?'

'I will,' Joe says. 'And if I ever have a nap in the daytime, we'll actually be asleep at the same time. Maybe we'll meet in our dreams.'

Tilly seems comforted by this, though once again Amy feels excluded – neither of them ever talk about seeing *her* in their dreams. Or Rowan.

The doorbell rings again, and Amy moves a little closer to Joe and says, 'Well, I guess this is it.'

He gazes at her as if trying to fix her features on his

memory, and she stares back at him and suddenly it's as if she is seeing him clearly for the first time in months. How could she have forgotten how attractive he is? She has taken him so very much for granted...

Tilly is still clinging to his leg. He leans forward over Rowan to peck Amy on the cheek and just for a moment, it's like being in a huddle in a team game. The family of four. A tiny taste of the lives they might share together later, as a unit, the holidays and squabbles and school-morning turns in the bathroom. And it's a sweet, safe feeling, worth all the sacrifices and compromises, and all the things she has to try to push to the back of her mind.

Then the doorbell rings again and Joe says, 'I really must go now,' and Tilly releases him.

Amy takes Rowan outside to watch as Joe carries his case to the taxi and puts it in the boot. Tilly reluctantly joins them. Her face is wet with tears but at least she manages not to bawl, or sniff, though from time to time she lets out a strange gulping sound. They wave Joe off, and the minute the taxi is out of sight Tilly turns and rushes back into the house.

When Amy follows her in the house is silent. She stands at the foot of the stairs with Rowan in her arms and listens. Not so much as a sob or a sigh. But it's unusual to hear anything from upstairs if you're on the ground floor – the old oak beams in the ceiling are so thick, they seem to absorb any noise. Tilly's probably crying her eyes out in her room.

She should check up on her. Suggest a treat to cheer her up. Ice cream, maybe, or a chocolate biscuit and a fizzy drink – it's too warm a day for hot chocolate. How about a favourite film? *The Little Mermaid*? She could watch it with her... Perhaps it wouldn't be so bad, Joe being away. It might even be a chance for them to bond.

She goes upstairs and pauses to listen outside Tilly's door before knocking.

Tilly is talking to herself. Playing. Well, that's a good sign. A remarkable recovery, all things considered. Amy can't quite make out the words. She leans in closer and focuses all her attention on the one-sided conversation taking place on the other side of Tilly's bedroom door.

Then she distinctly hears Tilly say, 'No, Alice, I promise I would never do that. I know it's dangerous to climb the willow tree.'

All the hairs on the back of Amy's neck stand on end. She grabs hold of the door handle to steady herself and breathes deep. Tilly is just playing. A game of 'let's pretend'. After all, Alice is Tilly's middle name. And maybe she likes it. Yes, that must be it. That's all there is to it.

Tilly is alone in her room, for sure, and there can't possibly be anyone else in there with her. Because there's no such thing as ghosts. And there is no little girl called Alice at Hillview House. Not any more.

PART TWO

LISA

Spring and Summer 2009

TEN

All through April, Lisa wonders if Amy has had the baby yet; in May, she wonders whether they will ever get in touch to tell her. She hesitates to be the first to make contact. What if something's happened? And if she hasn't heard from them simply because they're a busy, happy family with a new baby, would it be presumptuous of her to intrude? Eventually, she texts Amy to say she hopes all is well and to say again how good it was to meet her. But she doesn't hear back.

Blossom scatters on the pavement outside her rented flat like pink snow, then quickly turns brown and is crushed to mush underfoot. She carries on sifting through her mum's papers and personal effects, though it's dispiriting, as if she's gradually erasing her mum's existence, or at least going through another kind of goodbye.

Finally, she clears out the last of her mum's furniture, and the house is empty and then, much more quickly than Lisa expected, it is sold. The proceeds just about cover the mortgage and various debts that Mum had kept quiet about during her lifetime, with a little bit left over. Then a cardboard box of bits and pieces in a corner of Lisa's bedroom is all that's left.

Mum comes back to her in her dreams, but is in shadows and doesn't speak. Lisa goes for long swims, long enough for her mind to empty out so she doesn't fret about either the future or the past. She test drives a couple of cars, but doesn't buy one; a big purchase like that seems like a commitment she is not in the right state of mind to make. The sense of drift and of impermanence is a strange kind of comfort. She knows that sooner or later something will snap her out of it, but she doesn't know what.

Her booking at her temp job is extended, and she stays on because the work is soothing in its way – the surveyors' reports to be typed up and edited and formatted, the lists of flaws and features and caveats, the ceiling roses and original fireplaces and party walls. She works from four till midnight, Tuesday to Saturday, which wouldn't exactly be compatible with an active social life, but for the time being she doesn't feel like going out much anyway.

Every evening when she settles at her desk at work, she takes in the traces left behind by the woman who sits there during the day: little crumbs of rice cake on the computer keyboard, a cardigan hung on the back of the chair for when the air-conditioning is a little too efficient, a lone camomile teabag abandoned by the desk tidy. There's a photo, too – a framed snapshot of a pretty blonde around Lisa's age, with a kind-looking husband and two sweet little kids.

From six o'clock onwards she's the only person in the office, apart from the security guard who pops his head round the door every now and then but doesn't want to chat any more than she does. And that suits her just fine. She has almost forgotten she is waiting for something when she finally gets a phone call out of the blue.

It's nearly ten o'clock, a bit late for anyone to contact her. The patch of summer sky visible above rooftops through the window next to her has finally darkened, and she has pulled down the blind. Not so very long ago, the only person who would have rung her at this time was Mum. Must be a wrong number...

Lisa pauses the recording she is working on and answers the call.

'Lisa? Is that you? It's me. Amy.'

Amy sounds panicky and upset. Lisa's heartbeat accelerates the way it used to do when she got distress calls from her mum, when she'd locked herself out or lost something or got another court summons over a bill she'd neglected to pay.

'Yeah, it's me,' Lisa says. 'Is everything OK?'

'I never got in touch to tell you I had the baby. Well, I did. I have a little boy. He's called Rowan.'

'Congratulations! That's wonderful news. So how are you all? How's it going?'

Then Amy begins to cry. Undignified, snotty, unrestrained sobbing. 'I'm sorry,' she says after a while. 'I suppose it's not going very well. Joe's gone away, and I'm struggling.'

And then she starts talking about the day Joe left, and how tomorrow is the first day of the holidays and the childminder she had found in the village has suddenly decided she can't take Tilly after all, and what is she supposed to do?

Lisa listens, and says little, and tries to sound as soothing as possible. She is surely not the most obvious person for Amy to turn to, but maybe it makes it easier that they barely know each other. Her guess is that Amy is weeping like this on the phone to her because right now, she has no one else to talk to.

Somewhere in the background a baby lets out an experimental wail.

'That's him,' Amy says. 'I think he's teething.' She sniffs. 'I honestly have absolutely no idea how I'm going to get through this. All I want to do is check into a hotel and drink whisky till I fall asleep.'

She starts to cry again, and the baby's distress picks up pace.

'Can you hear that?' Amy says between sobs. 'I'm feeding him all the time, which is fine, and I want to do it, but then Tilly is on at me constantly, being angry, asking for things, getting in my face. I know she wants my undivided attention, but how can I give that to her? I can't. It's not possible. So there it is, Lisa. I'm a terrible mother. A terrible person, full stop.'

'You're being much too hard on yourself. You've obviously had a bad day, but I promise you things will seem different in the morning, once you've had some sleep.'

'You weren't here. You didn't see. You don't know what I did.'

The way she says this gives Lisa the chills. Amy sounds both guilty and defiant, as if she knows that what she is about to say might be shocking, but is going to go ahead and say it anyway.

'Amy... what do you mean? What *did* you do?'

'I smacked Tilly. Just a little smack. But I did it out of anger, and the look she gave me afterwards just made me feel terrible. And then she said, "Why did you hit me?"'

'Well...' Lisa is at a loss for words. She *is* horrified, because... well, poor Tilly. And what if it is worse than Amy has just said?

There is no reason to think that. But still. *Why did you hit me?* To Tilly, that was what it had been. A blow, not just a smack.

Amy says, 'I know it's terrible. I know. But she keeps going on about this imaginary pretend friend of hers, and it's driving me nuts. And then she told me she hated me. Again. And then I said, "Guess what? I hate you too," and she grabbed a handful of my hair and pulled it. I knew she meant to hurt me, and I smacked her to make her stop. But I know it was wrong. Joe would never do anything like that. But now he's gone, and it's all down to me, and I don't think I'm up to it, Lisa. I really don't.'

Lisa says, 'When did this happen?'

'This evening. She's gone to bed now, thank goodness.'

'Have you talked to Joe about any of this?'

'No. What can he do about it? He's in New Zealand. It'll only worry him.'

'Is there anyone else who could help you? I don't know, like a friend in the village or something.'

Amy gives a short, bitter laugh. 'No. I'm not very popular at the school gate. And anyway, other mums always want a quid pro quo, and I'm in no position to help anyone else out in return. And it's not like I've got any family to turn to – my mum's dead, my grandmother's in a home...' Amy stops herself. 'I'm sorry. I didn't mean that the way it sounded. I mean, you *are* family. And here I am, ringing you up when you probably have much better things to be doing.'

Lisa hesitates. She could back off right now, tell Amy she's at work and has a target to meet, end the call.

But she can't. Because Amy's right. She *is* family, in spite of everything. And Amy has turned to her.

She remembers how her mum had been when she was growing up. Exhausted. Crying. Drinking. And occasionally, lashing out. For Mum, there had been nobody to lean on and no help from anywhere, apart from Lisa herself. If there had been just one person she could have called on – a friend, a neighbour, a relative, any other adult – wouldn't everything have been different?

'Look, Amy... this might not be something you'd want, but I'm not working tomorrow,' she says. 'I could come and see you, if you like. Maybe I could take Tilly to the park. Give you a break.'

The baby's crying accelerates. Amy pauses, then lets out a whistling breath. 'Would you? Would you really? That would be amazing,' she says. 'Thank you, thank you, thank you. Honestly, I can't thank you enough. You're a lifesaver. If I know you're coming tomorrow, I think I might actually be able to get through tonight.'

'I'll see you in the morning, then,' Lisa says. 'I'm sure you'll feel better if you can get some sleep, even if it's just a few hours. I'll text you when my train gets to the station, and then I'll jump in a taxi. I could pick up a few bits and pieces and bring them with me. Milk, bread, nappies, chocolate, whatever. Just let me know tomorrow if there's anything you need.'

Amy begins to cry again. 'I've been so rubbish,' she says. 'And you're being so lovely and kind.'

'It's my pleasure,' Lisa says. 'It's family, isn't it?'

When Lisa arrives at Hillview House the next day it takes Amy a while to answer the front door. She looks bleary and unfocused, as if she's slept a little but not nearly enough, and her hair is wet from the shower. She's wearing a grubby T-shirt and pyjama bottoms, and all her movements are slow and stiff. It's as if she's aged several decades since Lisa saw her last and is on the verge of grinding to a halt.

Inside, the house smells like the aftermath of disaster – closed in, unhappy, neglected. Amy takes her through to the kitchen, which isn't filthy – the floor and sink look as if somebody has had a go at them fairly recently. But it's untidy in a way that probably makes it harder to keep clean. There's an accumulation of debris on the worktops: a pizza box, take-away containers, a few dirty mugs.

'Excuse the mess,' Amy says. 'At least we've still got someone coming in to clean once a week. The place would look even worse if she didn't.'

Lisa sets down the bags of shopping she has brought and starts putting things away in the fridge. 'I brought the milk,' she says. 'I can make us tea in a sec, if you'd like some.'

'I should have offered, shouldn't I?' Amy says, and fills the kettle and puts it on. 'The catering's been a bit hit-and-miss since Joe went. Tilly's had tinned pasta and fish fingers for tea so often she's started turning her nose up at them. And I just can't really be bothered to eat, somehow. I guess the upside is the baby weight's just fallen off me. It's the crash diet of the rubbish cook.'

She opens the dishwasher, takes a mug out, inspects it with a look of disgust and puts it back again. 'I must have forgotten to run it. Sorry, I'm not being a very good hostess. At least Rowan's having a nap. That gives us a bit of a reprieve.' She suppresses a yawn.

'Where's Tilly?'

'In the garden. I think. She doesn't seem to like me very much at the moment. Doesn't want to be anywhere near me.'

'I'm sure that's not true.'

'There are times when the feeling's mutual, to be honest. I know that sounds bad. But sometimes when she kicks off...' Amy shrugs. 'I just can't be doing with it. I literally don't have the energy. I'm surprised I can actually find the words to talk to you, and carry on standing here.'

'Why don't you go to bed? Have a nap until Rowan wakes up. I can keep an eye on Tilly.' Lisa rummages in the shopping bags for the colouring pencils and sketchpads she'd bought, and puts them on the table. 'I remembered she likes drawing. I bought these for her, and there's a big gingerbread biscuit some-where. Is it OK if I give them to her?'

'That's so kind of you,' Amy says. 'Thank you. Yes, do give them to her. I'm sure she'll be thrilled.'

'I got these for Rowan,' Lisa says, and takes out a couple of plastic toys and a sleepsuit, also bought in a rush on the way. 'I hope they're OK.'

Amy takes the sleepsuit, holds it up and examines it. Her face softens and brightens. 'Oh, that is sweet.' She offers Lisa something close to a smile, but at the same time her eyes have begun to swim with tears. 'He's such a gorgeous baby,' she says. 'I honestly don't deserve him.'

'Honestly, Amy, you should go and sleep.'

'Yes. You're right. Thank you.' She turns as if to go, then hesitates. 'Don't be freaked out if Tilly goes on about her imaginary friend, by the way. She does it all the time. It's a new obsession of hers. I'm sure it doesn't mean anything, and it's just a phase. But I have to say, I am really looking forward to the day when it passes.'

'OK. I think I can handle that. What's the imaginary friend called?'

'Alice,' Amy says, with a tense little smile. 'It's Tilly's middle name.' She lifts up the sleepsuit again. 'Thanks for this. It looks the right size, and it's good to have a clean one. I keep running out.'

She heads out of the kitchen, taking the sleepsuit with her. Lisa throws out a rotten cucumber from the bottom of the fridge and turns on the dishwasher. She folds down the pizza box and puts it in the recycling, scrapes out the remains of a rancid-looking curry and rinses the takeaway containers. She half expects Tilly to walk in at any moment, but there is no sign of her.

Does Tilly even know she's coming? She had assumed Amy would have told her, but maybe not. Last thing she wants is to frighten the poor kid by showing up out of the blue, apparently uninvited, and taking over the kitchen.

When she's finished washing up she takes the gingerbread man outside with her. The air is sweet with the scents of midsummer: new fruit beginning to ripen, roses in their first flush. Tilly's love-in-a-mist is in full flower, the blue blooms surrounded by the delicate green lace of its leaves. Beyond the kitchen garden she can see the car Joe had used to pick her up from the station, standing on the stretch of gravel leading to the exit to the main road.

She makes her way across the lawn and crouches down to knock on the playhouse door.

'Go away,' is the muffled response. 'I hate you.'

'It's Lisa,' she says. 'Remember me? I'm your mum's cousin. I have something for you. A gingerbread biscuit with icing on. Would you like to see? It's OK if you decide you don't want it. It looks pretty tasty to me, though. I wouldn't mind eating it myself.'

There is a pause before the door of the playhouse swings open and Tilly peers out. Lisa holds out the biscuit and Tilly takes it, rips off the cellophane wrapping and bites off the gingerbread man's head, then swallows and says thank you as an afterthought.

She looks pale and exhausted, and a little thinner than before. Has she had any breakfast that morning? She is wearing a striped pink-and-blue cotton dress, a better fit than the too-small party dress Lisa had first seen her in, though it could do with a wash and has a big triangular rip in the skirt. Her legs are dirty, as if she's been kneeling to grub around in the earth in the garden, and her feet are bare. The aura of sadness around her is so strong it's almost visible, like a soft, shadowy halo.

Lisa says, 'Is it OK if I come in?'

Tilly hesitates, then nods and withdraws, and Lisa ducks her head and goes in.

Someone – Joe, presumably – has painstakingly lined the walls with red flock wallpaper, covered the inside of the pitched roof with white-painted chipboard and cut down a remnant of old brown carpet to fit on the floor. There is not much inside: a doll's cot and a few toys – the well-worn teddy bear Lisa had seen in Tilly's bedroom and a newer-looking bear in a pink dress, a couple of small, realistic-looking animals made of rubbery plastic and a Barbie in underwear with only one shoe.

Tilly sits down cross-legged. Lisa follows suit, settling down opposite her. She wants very badly to reach out and give Tilly a hug, but knows it would be premature, and Tilly would probably find it intrusive. She doesn't want Tilly to think she is acting out of pity, either. People want respect, not pity. Even seven year olds. Especially seven year olds.

Besides, Tilly is still eating.

'Thank you for the biscuit,' Tilly says, and bites off the gingerbread man's arm.

'I'm glad you like it,' Lisa says. 'You have a very nice playhouse.'

Tilly chews and nods. 'My dad made it for me.'

'I know you must be missing him.'

Tilly looks at her as if assessing whether or not she has the right to say something like that. 'I'm glad you came,' she says eventually.

'So am I. I brought something else for you, by the way. It's in the house. Would you like to come and see?'

'I don't like surprises,' Tilly says gloomily. Then, with a slight tremble of her lower lip and a hopeful glance: 'Unless it's a puppy?'

'Sorry. It's not quite that exciting. It's a drawing pad and some pencils. I hope you still like drawing. If not, you can always give them to someone else.'

Tilly gives a small shrug. 'I'll keep them. Alice likes drawing too.'

'Alice?'

'My friend,' Tilly says defiantly.

'Oh. Yes. Your friend. Your mum mentioned her.'

'Mum doesn't like her.'

'I'm sure that isn't true. She probably just hasn't got to know her yet.'

'She just doesn't like me having friends,' Tilly says. 'Most of the time she gets her way. Nobody at school likes me.'

'I'm sure that's not true either.'

'You don't know,' Tilly says reproachfully. 'You're not there.

There was one day when they let me hold the end of the skipping rope. But they don't really want me around. Why did you come here? It's not very much fun without Dad.'

Lisa takes her time to consider her reply. She wants to be as truthful as she can, and she suspects Tilly will be able to tell if she isn't. She also senses that her relationship with Tilly is in the balance. She needs to earn Tilly's trust. If she can't, what hope does she have of helping her?

'All kinds of reasons,' she says. 'I wanted to come back and see you again. I'm hoping to get to know you and your mum a bit better. You're my only family.' And then she smiles at Tilly and says, 'Also, I like you. Maybe if I'd have known you when I was your age, we would actually have been friends.'

Tilly also considers her reply for a moment. 'I quite like you too,' she says.

'Well, that's something, isn't it? That's a lot better than if you absolutely hated and despised me, for example.'

Tilly rewards her with a tiny ghost of a smile. 'I'd like to do some drawing, and so would Alice,' she says. 'Let's go in the house.'

As they make their way back across the lawn together Tilly's little hand snakes out and finds Lisa's. Lisa takes it and holds it. It feels like being forgiven and needed and trusted all in one, and Tilly will probably never understand quite how much it means to her.

ELEVEN

Somehow Lisa ends up staying till the evening, even though she had originally meant to leave that afternoon. Then Amy is busy feeding Rowan and Tilly says she's hungry, so she volunteers to cook.

It doesn't take long. She makes sausage and mash, using the potatoes she'd brought with her, and sings along quietly to the radio as she cooks. She has the kitchen to herself. Amy is in the family room, and Tilly has tidied her pens and paper away and gone up to play in her bedroom, claiming this was her friend Alice's idea. When the food is ready she calls them both in and Amy is the first to arrive, carrying Rowan.

Amy eases Rowan – who is fast asleep – into his bouncing cradle, a sort of baby armchair formed of a deckchair-like sling of fabric on a metal frame. She moves the cradle to rest on the floor by her place at the table, then sits down, turns her attention to her food and helps herself to gravy.

'Lump-free,' she says. 'You obviously have the knack.'

Lisa settles next to her. Should they wait for Tilly? Amy obviously doesn't think so – she is already tucking in. Then

Tilly comes in and marches up to the table and says to Lisa, 'You're sitting in Alice's chair.'

'Don't be so rude, Tilly,' Amy snaps at her. 'You're too old to keep going on about this nonsense. It has to stop.'

The corners of Tilly's mouth turn down. Lisa says, 'I can sit in the other chair, Tilly, if that would be better?'

'That's Daddy's chair,' Tilly says. She is scowling now, but it is clear she is not far from bursting into tears.

'Well, do you think it might be OK with Alice if I borrowed her chair, just while we eat dinner? Perhaps she could share yours.'

'It's OK. She doesn't mind,' Tilly says, brightening slightly. 'She says it's all right for you to sit there.'

'That's very kind of her,' Lisa says.

Amy rolls her eyes in exasperation but doesn't comment, and Tilly settles down to eat. Lisa shows her how to make volcanoes out of gravy and mashed potato, and a very dim, hazy memory comes back to her of her mum showing her the same thing.

Amy looks on forbearingly as Tilly smiles and eats and clears her plate. Then Rowan starts whimpering and Amy says, 'He probably needs his nappy changing. I'll go and do his bath,' and takes him out.

Lisa clears the table and says to Tilly, 'Do you think you might like to do some more drawing before your bathtime? Those pictures you did of fairies were really good.'

Tilly considers this and then, with the air of one granting a favour, agrees, and fetches her drawing things and gets to work.

Lisa finds that she's unexpectedly happy, happier than she can remember being for ages. It's so cosy and peaceful in the kitchen with the summer evening sunlight pitching in and the scratch of Tilly's pencil and the distant sound of Rowan's bath running upstairs.

Tilly is drawing a garden, with a green lawn and a row of

daffodils in front of a bush of big pink flowers that are easily identifiable as roses.

'Those are beautiful flowers,' Lisa says.

'It is a magic garden,' Tilly says. 'That's why there are flowers that don't come out at the same time. You can have anything you like in this garden. You can have snowdrops at the same time as love-in-a-mist, and the only weeds are pretty ones.' She starts drawing a big fat orange pumpkin. 'Are you going to read me my bedtime story today?'

Lisa grimaces. 'Oh, Tilly... I would like to, but I should really be heading off soon.'

Tilly pulls a face, as if this is an option she hadn't considered and is too polite to dismiss out of hand. 'Daddy isn't going to call tonight, so it won't be very late. Mum doesn't like reading to me and she's too busy with Rowan. Dad always used to do it. I would like you to, and Alice wants you to. I'm quite good but Alice is sometimes really naughty if she doesn't get her way.'

'OK, well, we'll see. If not today, maybe another time.'

Lisa tackles the washing up, and a little later Amy comes back down to the kitchen with a baby-shampoo-scented Rowan in her arms. She glances at Tilly's garden picture without much interest before asking her to tidy her drawing things away and go and have her bath.

'I'm going to see if I can get Rowan down in his cot,' she tells Lisa once Tilly has gone. 'And then I think I'm just about ready to turn in myself. I'm dead beat.'

'I should probably be heading off,' Lisa says, taking off her apron and hanging it back on the hook by the cupboards.

A look of blind panic crosses Amy's face. 'Oh no, don't go!' She reaches out and rests her hand lightly on Lisa's forearm. 'Honestly, you're a miracle worker. Tilly's like a different child. The way she scoffed down that meal! Usually, she just pushes her food round her plate and sulks. Having you here is like having Mary Poppins in the house. I know this is a lot to ask...

but do you think there's any chance you can stay the night? Just this once? Unless you've got things you have to get back for, of course... There's a spare bed in Joe's office in the attic. I think it's pretty comfy. He used to retreat up there when I was really heavily pregnant and couldn't sleep, and when I'd just had Rowan and was up a lot in the night...'

Lisa hesitates, but more because she feels as if she ought to than because she is genuinely unsure.

'I'd like to,' she says, and Amy beams at her in relief.

Tilly's bedtime story is a chapter of the first Harry Potter book. Tilly listens attentively and without comment, her new bear and old bear carefully arranged on the pillow next to her with a space left for Alice on her other side. There is a small silver torch in pride of place on her bedside table, and when Lisa comments on it Tilly tells her Joe gave it to her when Rowan was born.

'So we could go out at night and look for hedgehogs together,' she explains sadly. 'Maybe in the autumn, when he's back.'

After the first chapter Lisa gives in to Tilly's pleas and reads another, and then goes downstairs to see if Amy would like to say goodnight. Amy seems to have given up on the idea of an early night, and is sitting in front of the TV in the family room, nursing a glass of white wine. She trudges up to Tilly's room with Lisa following at a tactful distance.

'Night-night. Sleep well,' Amy says, and reaches for the switch on Tilly's bedside light.

'Mum? Could I please have a light on? Just a little one, so it isn't quite so dark.'

'Come on, Tilly. Only babies like Rowan and tiny little children have nightlights, not big girls like you.'

'But Alice would really like one. She gets frightened when she can't see.'

'Well, she'll just have to learn to be brave then, won't she,' Amy says, and reaches forward to switch off the bedside light. The room is instantly plunged into darkness.

'Just go to sleep now,' Amy says, and comes out and firmly shuts the door.

Out in the corridor Lisa's heart twists with pity, thinking of Tilly in the darkness. At least she has her torch within reach, although she might get a telling-off if Amy catches her using it.

There is a small, soft sound that might be a carefully muffled sob, followed by silence.

'She'll be fine,' Amy says. 'Come on down with me and have a glass of wine. I can't tell you how nice it is to have some adult company.'

She is already walking away, hurrying down the stairs, and Lisa follows her. She feels bad for having failed to intervene on Tilly's behalf. Surely there's a right way to do it, without seeming to criticise. Wouldn't Joe do that if he was here? She passes on the wine and they settle in the family room, Amy in her usual armchair, Lisa curled up in a corner of the sofa. She can't help but feel nervous, as if she is facing a job interview. Or something worse.

'I think you must be my guardian angel,' Amy says, and raises her glass to Lisa. 'It's amazing to have them both down so early.'

'Glad I could help.'

'You're good with kids, aren't you? I'm not sure anyone would say the same for me. I wasn't much good with them before I had my own, and I don't think I'm that much better now. But you seem to know what you're doing. Especially for someone who doesn't have any kids of her own, if you don't mind me saying so.'

Did she mind? Not especially. Amy had said she was good with Tilly. That was enough to be going on with. 'Thanks,' she says.

'What do you do, anyway? You're not a teacher, are you? You seem like a teacher.'

'I'm not, actually. Right now I'm temping in an admin job.'

'Oh. Is that because you're between jobs or something? You seem too sorted to be a temp. It's the kind of thing I used to do, before I got married and had the children.'

'I'm doing it because I got made redundant last year,' Lisa says. 'I was working in estate management, and I'd only just started, so when there was a downturn I was the first one they let go. Before that I was an assistant manager in a couple of hotels. I moved jobs a couple of times to be near to different men – does that ever work out? I never went to college or anything like that. I have thought sometimes that maybe I should change direction and study to do something else, but I've never been sure what.'

'I really don't want to go back to work,' Amy says, with a slight shudder. 'I know that probably sounds bad, and I ought to want to, but I just don't. I did all kinds of different things when I was younger. Some of it was OK, I suppose. I worked in bars and clubs, mainly. Sometimes in offices. But I seemed to get fired a lot. Then my mum died, and I got pregnant with Tilly, and Joe and I moved in together and it was all about family, so...' She shrugs. 'I never really had a plan. It was just the way things turned out.'

'I was sorry to hear about you losing your mum,' Lisa says. 'And your dad.'

'Oh. Yes. Thank you.' She frowns. 'Joe told you about that, didn't he? When he met you at that party. What did he say, exactly?'

'Just that your dad died before you were born, and your mum passed away quite early on in your relationship. He said she had cancer.' Amy is still frowning, and Lisa hopes she hasn't got Joe into any trouble. Is Amy annoyed because she thinks this information is too personal for Joe to have shared with somebody he'd only just met, cousin or not? Or is it because she thinks it's her story to tell? She decides not to ask what had happened to Elliott, Amy's dad. From the look on Amy's face, now is not the time to press for information on sensitive subjects.

Then Amy sets down her wine glass, stretches and lets out a long sigh. 'Well, I guess we're both orphans, aren't we? Or as good as. You wanted to know more about the family, didn't you? Do you know about the bakery our grandparents used to run in Kettlebridge? It's a sports shop now. Before she had me, my mum used to work there. They sold it soon after I was born.'

'My mum worked in a bakery too. I thought it was brilliant because she used to bring home the leftover pastries. She was still working there when she died.'

'Where did she live?'

'In Chalmington. That's where I grew up. Do you know it? It's a little town just over the Northamptonshire border. It's not that far from here.'

'Rings a bell,' Amy says. 'Joe might have driven through it on the way to somewhere else.'

'Do you have any old photos?' Lisa asks suddenly. 'We didn't have any pictures of the family at home.'

She would have expected it to be upsetting to have this conversation, and it is, but it's also intriguing to have a glimpse of her mum's background.

'There are lots of pictures me growing up. Beyond that, not much. I think Grandma Elsie must have had a pretty brutal purge at some stage. I'll see what I can dig out for you tomorrow, if you like.'

'That would be good,' Lisa says. 'If you have time, and if it's not too much of a pain. I'd be really interested to see them.'

'Sure. Least I can do.'

Amy sips her wine again. Lisa wills her to get up and fetch the photos now, but she doesn't make a move. Instead, she sets her glass down and looks at Lisa searchingly, as if she, rather than Lisa, is the one with unanswered questions about days gone by.

'I don't believe in letting the past wreck the future,' she says. 'That's one thing to be said for having children. They keep you focused on the present. What matters is the here and now, and right now, I'm really glad you're here.'

'I'm glad to be here, too,' Lisa says. They smile at each other, and Lisa feels herself beginning to relax. Is it really possible that her cousin could turn into a friend? Maybe it is. Maybe, as they get to know each other better and to trust each other more, it won't feel so much like tiptoeing on eggshells.

Amy raises her glass to her. 'I probably shouldn't be drinking this, but I figure one glass can't hurt, and I'm not going to be feeding the baby for another couple of hours. Thank you for not disapproving. Or for not telling me if you do. Anyway, here's to you.' She finishes her wine and sets her glass down. 'I'm so pleased you can stay a bit longer. It's nice to get the chance to spend a bit of time together. It seemed like Tilly was pretty happy to see you too.'

Lisa clears her throat. It's probably as good an opportunity as any. 'You know, it probably wouldn't do any harm to let Tilly have a nightlight, at least for a while,' she says. 'It's probably not unusual for a child to regress a bit at a time of change. It's just like you or me going back to something that's familiar and comforting if we feel stressed or anxious.'

She braces herself for Amy's reaction. Amy might well think this is none of her business. But Amy just pauses to think it over and then nods in agreement.

'Well, if you think it'll help. I think her old one is still in a drawer somewhere. I must fish it out sometime.' She sighs. 'Anything for a peaceful life.'

Right on cue, Rowan starts crying. 'So much for us having a chance to chat,' Amy says regretfully. 'Anyway, to be continued.

I'd better go and try to settle him.' She hurries off upstairs to see to him, leaving Lisa staring at the faint fingerprints on her empty glass.

When Amy comes back downstairs she looks drained and exhausted. She finds some bedding for Lisa, but Lisa tells her to go and get some sleep and she'll make up the bed in the attic herself. Amy gratefully withdraws.

Joe's office, which doubles up as a spare room, is a plain, white-walled room under the eaves, with a ceiling that slopes steeply to either side of the bed under the window, and a desk with a computer and a printer on it at the other end. The window is still open, and the air coming through it is surprisingly cold. As Lisa pulls it shut she sees that the view beyond the glass is inky black. When she looks more closely she can just make out the tops of the trees to the side of the house, a more textured, denser mass of darkness than the sky.

She draws the thin, chintzy curtains. She doesn't feel at all sleepy. She feels alert and vigilant, as if she could stay awake for hours, and perhaps ought to, watching and waiting. But for what?

It is very quiet. There are none of the night sounds that she is used to back at her place in Brickley: no traffic, no police helicopter, no neighbour moving around in the next flat, nobody arguing in the street.

She catches something like a faint whispering sound, and nearly jumps out of her skin. But no, she is just imagining things. It's the old house shrinking into itself and resettling as the evening temperature dips, like an old lady adjusting herself to a sudden chill.

As she lies down to go to sleep she is conscious of the dark pressing in on the house from all sides, the miles of fields and woods all around them, and the distance to the nearest cluster of houses in the village below. But the bed is soft and she is just the right amount of warm, and as she relaxes the night seems to settle over her like a blanket.

So much about this house is familiar. When she first came that was eerie and disconcerting but now, suddenly, it is not. She is almost certain that she has been here before, when she was very little, too small to remember. And perhaps she will never find out any more about the circumstances of that visit, but surely she must have been here with her mum, and the thought of that is reassuring in itself.

Anyway, the present is what matters, as Amy had said. Right now, this seems the best and safest place in the world to sink into a deep and comforting sleep.

TWELVE

The next morning, Amy suggests they walk down into the village. By the time they're all ready to leave the house it is almost lunchtime and rather warm and Amy is irritable, but says they might as well stick with the plan anyway. She leads the way, charging down the hill with the rattling pushchair, and Lisa and Tilly trudge along stoically in her wake.

They wander along the main road to an algae-covered pond overlooked by weeping willows. Amy seems to be on edge, as if she half expects to see somebody she doesn't want to. Or maybe she's just keen to get back to the house before Rowan starts crying again. She has told Amy she doesn't really like feeding in public, and finds it difficult to spend any length of time out and about.

There's an old church opposite the pond, overlooking the village from the vantage point of a small swell of ground. It's small, with a low tower, built of pale, weathered honey-coloured stone. The churchyard is dotted with gravestones, some of them tilted and weathered, others straight and new, and there is a bench in one corner, in the shadow cast by a cluster of tall yew trees. Lisa suggests that they could rest there for a minute or two, but Amy is keen to keep going. She chivvies her and Tilly on down the narrow lane next to the churchyard towards a play park where Tilly has a brief go on the swings before Amy decides it is time to head home.

On the way back Amy looks back over her shoulder at Tilly and snaps at her to keep up, then refocuses her attention on getting the pushchair up the hill.

'I don't know why she has to go so fast all the time,' Tilly mutters. 'Rowan isn't even crying yet. And Alice is out of puff.'

'I must be very silly, because I didn't realise Alice was with us,' Lisa says, trying to speak just loud enough for only Tilly to hear. 'Is she walking on the other side of you?'

'Oh, yes,' Tilly says serenely. 'Can you not see her?'

And Lisa catches sight of something out of the corner of her eye that shouldn't be there. Or, just for a moment, she thinks she does. It's a long shadow beside hers and Tilly's, reaching forward to merge into the shadows cast by Amy and the pushchair. As if there really is another person walking with them. But it can't be so, it must be an illusion. Perhaps it's the shadow of a tree they are just passing, a sapling growing by the wayside.

Then the sun dips behind a cloud, the light fades instantly and the shadows disappear. All there is at their feet is stones and dust.

'No, I can't see Alice, I'm afraid,' she says. 'But that doesn't mean she's not there. I can't see the sun right now, or the stars or the moon, but they're all still up there in the sky above us and I expect other people somewhere else in the world are looking up at them.'

'You shouldn't look at the sun,' Tilly admonishes her. 'It is bad for your eyes. The moon and stars are OK, though.'

Amy has reached the house and is unlocking the door. She doesn't seem to be listening, or even aware that they're having a conversation. Lisa says, 'Is Alice with you all the time?'

'No, not if it's boring. She doesn't stay if it's a telly programme she doesn't like.'

'I'm a bit worried that if I can't see her, I might walk right through her. Could that happen, do you think? And would she mind if I did? I wouldn't want her to think I was being rude.'

Tilly rewards her for this attempt to play along with another smile, though it's a bit more inscrutable this time. 'I don't think she'd mind,' she says thoughtfully. 'She'd understand that you can't help it. She thinks it's quite funny when people do that. It tickles. You might find it a little bit strange, though. Like walking through cobwebs.'

'Oh well, that doesn't sound too bad.'

'Do you like spiders? We get some very big ones in our house. Me and Alice are going to keep one as a pet.'

'I don't know if that would work, Tilly. Spiders are wild things. They like to be free. Also, you might find it tricky to catch the flies for it. Unless you know how to make a web?'

'Silly,' Tilly says indulgently. 'Me and Alice are only pretending. Nobody would really keep a spider as a pet.'

Amy has gone on into the house, leaving the door open. Tilly and Lisa slow down as they approach it. Tilly looks furtively ahead into the hallway to check whether Amy's still in earshot before saying in a low voice, 'Why does Mum get so angry about Alice?'

'Often when people get angry, it's because they're a little bit frightened about something. Maybe it's because she's worried about you.'

'No,' Tilly says firmly. 'That's not it.'

'Tilly, for what it's worth...'

Tilly looks trustingly up at her.

'Maybe don't talk to your mum so much about Alice,' Lisa says finally. 'Some people just don't like to talk about things they can't see.'

Tilly nods thoughtfully as she takes this in, and they go on into the house.

Lisa half thought Amy might have forgotten that she'd asked if she could see some family photos. She wasn't sure whether to remind her. But after lunch, once Rowan is settled in his bouncing cradle and sound asleep, Amy takes Lisa into the main living room, the one that feels as if it is scarcely used, and fishes a couple of albums out of a cabinet behind the sofa. Tilly comes to join them and perches on a corner of the sofa next to Amy, and Amy looks at her slightly askance, as if not sure whether she can be trusted to behave herself, but doesn't object.

She starts with some recent pictures: Rowan in Joe's arms in hospital, red-faced and apparently already exhausted by the effort involved in being alive, Joe proud and relieved. Christmas, Amy pregnant by the tree and leaning forward to put a star on the top, Tilly hanging back and smiling shyly for the camera. And then someone new appears: a long-limbed, bony woman sitting in one of the overstuffed living room armchairs with a purple paper hat askew on her bluntly cropped grey hair, seemingly both dazed by the festivities and disapproving of them.

'That's Grandma Elsie,' Amy says, tapping Grandma Elsie's brooding, deeply lined face with her forefinger. 'I think you can see that she isn't really that with it any more. She wasn't terribly happy about Grandad leaving the house to me, but there wasn't a lot she could do about it, and he'd sorted her out with a nice little retirement apartment in Kettlebridge, so that was all right. But then she started getting quite confused, and *I* couldn't look after her – I had too much on my plate already – so Joe and I found her a care home. It's a lovely place, not like you might think, and not too far away, so we go and see her when we can, and sometimes we bring her back here. She perked up no end when we showed her Rowan. I think she'd been hanging on to see if I'd have another baby, to be honest.'

Further back: Tilly's first day at school, first steps, first shoes, and first smile – 'At least, that's what we were trying for, though maybe it was just wind,' Amy says, glancing at Tilly almost affectionately. Tilly is studying the photos with polite interest, like a well-behaved pupil sitting through a history lesson that's a repeat of something she's already learned.

There's a whole album dedicated to Amy and Joe's wedding. Grandma Elsie is there in pastels and a robust hat, a stark contrast to her later self – proud, happy, vindicated, as if she personally has triumphed over the odds to preside over this family celebration. And next to her is Amy and Lisa's grandfather, a thin, upright, reserved-looking man with mournful eyes and a surprisingly sweet smile. He didn't look quite as you'd expect a former baker to look – he'd obviously never overindulged in the bread and pastries that must have been his stock-in- trade.

Next, it's a glimpse of Amy's life before she had Tilly. 'I don't look like that in a bikini any more,' Amy says rather sadly when they come to a snap of her on a beach holiday with Joe, both of them radiating the kind of happiness that goes with romance and sunshine and sand and the sea. Then there's a picture of Joe with his arms around her, looking at her with unalloyed adoration while she pouts at the camera, and Amy in skin-tight jeans and a skimpy top, actually smiling for once, standing on the front doorstep of a small suburban house, which Amy tells Lisa is the address she'd written to when she first tried to get in touch with her.

'That's pretty much it for the more recent ones,' Amy says, closing the album. 'Go any further back and you're into the annals of my adolescence and childhood, and there's rather a lot to look at, because my mum did an album for every year of my life until I turned eighteen and left home.'

She rolls her eyes and smiles as if she is proud her mum had gone to so much effort, but aware that it might seem over the top.

'I'd like to see them,' Lisa says.

'Tell you what, I'll start by showing you the last one and the first one. For contrast.' She disappears behind the sofa and emerges with two more albums. 'Let's start at the end,' she says, opening one of the albums at the back. 'You can laugh at my teen fashions.'

The kitchen at Hillview House. Walls a different, paler colour, wine on the table, Amy as a moody teen with black lipstick.

'That's my mum,' Amy says, pointing to the plump blonde woman sitting on the other side of the table, smiling nervously as if she didn't really want to be photographed at all. 'Your aunt Diane.'

They all peer at the photo together. Tilly studies it with interest, too, though she has presumably seen it before. Diane has large glasses, a round face and a blonde bob that seems to be styled so that she can hide behind it as much as possible, with a fringe that falls into her eyes. She looks almost like Amy's polar opposite – self-effacing, shy, keen to please.

Amy sighs. 'I don't think I was a very good daughter to her,' she says. 'I made her life hell, actually. I was pretty naughty – running round with boys, staying out late, getting in trouble at school, drinking too much and coming home and throwing up all over the bathroom floor. All that classic teenage stuff. I bet *you* weren't like that.'

'Well... no.' Lisa hesitates. 'Not because I was a goody two-shoes,' she says. 'I just felt I couldn't afford to be. Mum was pretty unhappy most of the time, and she drank quite a bit, and I guess I just didn't associate drinking with going out and having a good time. Plus, I felt like it was down to me to try and hold everything together. So I was the one clearing up after her.

Creeping round in the morning when she had a hangover, that kind of thing.'

'That sounds tough,' Amy says gently.

'Yeah, well... It was what it was. I couldn't wait to leave, to be honest with you. But I still felt responsible for her. I'd circle around, you know, going away and coming back. Sometimes I'd panic about her and drive back from wherever I was just so I could check up on her. She wasn't always very good at answering the phone.' She hesitates, then plunges on. 'Before she died, she had an accident in the house and fell and hurt herself. She'd been drinking, and it was her neighbour who raised the alarm, because she hadn't seen her. I sometimes think about that, about her lying there in pain and not being able to get the phone. It haunts me, to be honest.'

'I'm sure you were as good a daughter as it was possible for anyone to be, under the circumstances. She must have been very proud of you,' Amy says, and reaches out and squeezes her arm. The unlooked-for kindness nearly tips Lisa over the edge. For a moment she thinks she is about to cry.

'Your mum must have been proud of you too,' she says. 'And if she could see you now she'd be even more proud.'

But Amy suddenly stiffens and turns away, and closes the album.

'Yes, well, no point dwelling on might-have-beens,' she says. 'Tell you what, let's go back to the beginning. Are you ready for the baby pictures?'

Lisa says she is, and Amy looks through the first album with her. Amy as a baby appears in numerous outfits, smiling, screwing her face up in disgust, holding different toys, at the centre of every photo. Other people appear in the background, holding her or watching her, occasionally fretfully, but usually with delight. The story the album tells is that baby Amy had been at the heart of the family, and the star of the show wherever she went. Lisa can't help but think of herself and her mum in a house not all that far away, ignored and forgotten, struggling to get by.

Towards the back of the album, carefully arranged across a couple of pages, is a selection of pictures of Elliott, Amy's dad, who looks unassuming and mild-mannered and conscientious, like the kind of man you might expect to see stocking up for DIY projects in the hardware store, or carefully washing his car at the weekend. He has gingery hair with a slightly receding hairline, and the beginnings of a paunch – signs of the early onset of a middle age he had never reached. He looks as if he would have made solid husband material, although, as Amy points out, he had never actually married her mum.

'What happened to him?' Lisa asks.

'Heart attack,' Amy says. 'They were planning to tie the knot after they'd had me. I'm not really sure why they didn't before, because they'd been together for a while – no one ever wanted to talk about it. Mum did once let slip that my dad had been married before. I got the impression his first wife might have dug her heels in and been difficult about giving him a divorce – you know, made him wait. I think it was a really big deal for her, that she never got her day in white. And it mattered to my grandparents too – they were quite old-fashioned about that kind of thing. So everybody was absolutely delighted when I said yes to Joe. I think they cared more about it than I did.'

There are black-and-white pictures of Lisa and Amy's grandparents' 1950s wedding in an envelope tucked into the last page of the album – earnest, nervous groom, and wasp-waisted, triumphant bride – and of Diane as a chubby toddler in a sun bonnet, and as a girl with a pudding-basin haircut and a shy smile.

'Are there any more of the old pictures anywhere?' Lisa asks. She can't quite believe that there are no pictures of her mum anywhere in this house, as a baby or a girl or a young woman, even if she's just in the background of a photograph of someone else. After all, she'd been part of the family for more than a quarter of a century, however thoroughly she'd been estranged from them later.

'Sorry,' Amy says. 'Like I said, Grandma Elsie was pretty ruthless about chucking stuff out.'

Lisa feels vaguely cheated. She's made it this far, she's on the inside of the family that she'd been excluded from for so long, and she still hasn't found what she's looking for. She's seen pictures of her uncle and aunt and grandfather, all of whom are no longer around: she's seen her grandmother, and now she knows exactly where Amy's hawkish, autocratic, disappointed look – the one her mum had too – had come from. But she still hasn't really found out any more about her own parents.

Is Amy holding out on her? Maybe there was more to it. Had her mum perhaps been accused of being involved in some way with what her dad had done? Maybe she had been there, and had failed to intervene. Or she could have tried to give him an alibi, or cover up what had happened, in a way that could have dragged the rest of the family down with him?

Maybe Amy knows things she isn't sharing. But why would she hold back? Maybe because Lisa is an outsider and the offspring of the black sheep of the family, and she doesn't entirely trust her yet. Or maybe Amy is in the dark too.

Amy asks her to stay Sunday night, too, and she does. She finally leaves on Monday lunchtime, leaving herself just enough time to get back to her flat and change before work. When her taxi arrives, they all crowd round her in the hallway to say goodbye. Tilly presses a drawing on her. It turns out to be of the two of them in the garden, holding hands. Rowan gives her one of his best gummy smiles, and Amy embraces her and looks her in the eye and says, 'Thank you for putting up with me. I know

I've been all over the place lately. Please, come and see us again soon.'

On the way to the station the sun is shining and she is elated. But as her train travels south, back towards Brickley, it begins to rain, and her mood shifts. The view of the grey sky and green hills is blurred by the water streaming across the window next to her, as if it's dissolving, and she is bereft. It's as if she's left behind the only part of her life that means something, and the only place where it makes sense to be.

She gets Tilly's picture out of the carrier bag Amy had given her to take it away in, unfolds it and studies it. The taller, rounded, smiling figure that is somehow unmistakably her, and the smaller, smiling figure that is Tilly, surrounded by greenery and flowers. It makes her heart ache.

She shouldn't expect too much. Shouldn't get her hopes up. After all, great hopes can lead to great disappointment... and it just seems so dangerously needy.

Yes, they have had a good weekend, and she'd felt something slide into place, as if she was somewhere she was meant to be. But the bond between her and Amy is so new – it's not as if there's a shared history of family gatherings and holidays and visits to draw on, the kind of security that comes from knowing someone over nearly half a lifetime. Instead, there's a shared history of silence and shame and secrets.

It's not just what happens between two people, the conversations they have and the way they treat each other, that makes for closeness. It's everything around them. And what have she and Amy got? Almost nothing: a coincidence, an unsettling sense of familiarity. Two visits. An old house and a garden with a willow tree at the end of it. Photo albums that she and her mum have been edited out of. Rowan with his charming smile, and Tilly, battling her loneliness with the help of her imaginary friend.

But then, to Lisa's surprise and delight, Amy gets in touch with her that very evening, when she is still at work.

She knows as soon as she hears her phone ring who it's likely to be, and moves to answer it with such haste that she knocks over a not-quite-finished cup of tea. It doesn't even occur to her to worry about the mess she's made on what is also somebody else's desk.

'Amy! How are you? You all right?'

'Yeah, yeah, fine. Finally got both the kids down, so, you know... thought I'd give you a call. You got back OK, then?'

'Yeah, made it in on time.' Though she has already texted Amy to say this, and to thank her again.

'How's it going? You busy?'

Lisa looks round at her desk, the computer screen in front of her with a document open – *further inspection of the party wall may be required to ensure fire safety* – the puddle of spilt tea next to her mouse, the photo of her daytime colleague's children.

'Not really,' she says. 'It's pretty boring, actually.' Which is more honest than she would usually be.

'Oh, join the club. It's not exactly thrilling here either.'

There is a small pause. Then Amy goes on. 'Look, you're probably busy, but if you're free next weekend, we'd love to see you again. If you've time.'

She says it quickly, as if she's afraid of being rebuffed, but there is something in her voice that is stronger than fear of social embarrassment, and much sweeter to hear. She *wants* Lisa to come back. It's not just that she needs the company, or distraction, or a bit of help with the kids while Joe's away – or is going through the motions because she thinks she ought to. She *wants* her there.

It is music to Lisa's ears. Any reservations she might have had melt away, along with the niggling memory of her unanswered questions. If she wants to enjoy this, she's going to have to cast off the dead hand of the past.

'I'd love to come,' she says.

Amy exhales. 'Phew. Great. Brilliant. Tilly will be delighted. Me, too, of course. And I promise I'll get your bed made up ready for you this time.'

Then Lisa picks up the faint sound of Rowan crying in the background. Amy says she'll have to go and they say goodbye. As Lisa puts her phone back in her bag she is suddenly completely happy again, and floats through the rest of her hours at work as if she's just won the lottery.

She looks forward to the visit avidly all week. She dreams about it. And when she arrives on Friday morning and rings the doorbell, Tilly answers it and barrels right into her arms.

Amy puts the flowers Lisa's brought for her in a vase – pink roses this time, a replacement for the gypsophila which must have gone over by now, because it isn't on display any more. Then Amy makes coffee for them both and apologises for only having decaffeinated to offer. She seems nervous, as if she wants to be a good hostess but isn't sure her efforts will be up to scratch. Lisa wants to reassure her but doesn't know how to do it without being patronising.

Lisa has brought Tilly another gingerbread biscuit, a gingerbread lady this time, and Amy says she can have it in front of the TV in the family room and puts on a DVD for her – it's *Spirited Away*, a Japanese animated film Lisa hasn't seen. But Tilly obviously has, and settles down in front of it with the air of a child who is about to fall under a magic spell, and will neither create nor welcome any interruptions for as long as the spell lasts.

'Come on, then. Let's go have our coffee,' Amy says to Lisa, scooping Rowan up from his playmat. Lisa begins to suspect that Amy actually wants to talk to her about something, and is trying to make sure that Tilly won't eavesdrop.

They settle on opposite sides of the kitchen table – Lisa is in the place Tilly had said was for her pretend friend Alice, and hopes Tilly won't object this time if she comes back in and sees her there, though that seems unlikely to happen for at least the next hour or so. Lisa sips her coffee. Amy latches Rowan on and starts to feed him. Apart from the sound of suckling, the room is silent.

Amy clears her throat. 'So, I have something I wanted to ask you.'

Lisa's heartbeat accelerates. 'Sure. Try me.'

Amy leans across the table, moving carefully so as not to dislodge Rowan, and picks up a raisin swirl from the selection of Danish pastries Lisa has brought with her. She puts it on the plate in front of her and breaks off a piece, but doesn't eat it and looks up at Lisa instead.

'This is probably going to sound crazy,' she says. 'But I've been thinking about it, on and off, ever since you came last weekend, so... here goes. I'd love it if you could stay for longer.'

Lisa is so taken aback that all she can do is stare at her.

'Well, that sounds great and I'm sure I'd love it too, but how much longer do you mean? Because, you know, I have work and stuff.' Already her mind is racing ahead, coming up with all the reasons why she could and should say yes.

'I know. But it's a temp job, right? And it sounds like you're not really into it. But, you know, if you are, and I've got that wrong, just say, obviously, and I'll shut up about it.'

She pauses, and Lisa grimaces, and Amy grins and carries on. 'Yeah. Thought so. Well then... unless you have other plans... you would be very much more than welcome to come and stay here over the summer, while Joe's away. I've talked about it with him, and he thinks it's a great idea. I haven't run it past Tilly, but that's because if I do I know I'll never hear the last of it. She keeps asking about you. All week, she's been checking whether you were still going to come and when you were going to arrive. Alice wants you here, apparently.' She pulls a face as if to say that although she isn't usually keen on Tilly's imaginary friend, on this occasion she agrees with her, and so is inclined to be more tolerant. 'You and Tilly really seem to have hit it off – it's like there's a rapport there. She's not like that with everybody, you know. And it would make the world of difference to me to have you here.'

'But we don't really know each other,' Lisa says slowly.

'Well, this will fix that. Won't it?' Amy says, with perhaps the most irresistibly pleading smile Lisa has ever seen. 'No rush, I know I've sprung this on you out of the blue. I realise you're probably going to want to think about it. And obviously, we'd have to sort out something to do with money. I mean, I don't know if you've got a mortgage to cover...'

'No,' Lisa says, thinking of her tiny flat back in Brickley, and her kitchen under the eaves that, in sharp contrast to this one, can only accommodate two people standing if they choose precisely the right spot. 'I have a rental contract. But I wouldn't want you to give me money.'

'It wouldn't be like giving. It would just be making sure you don't end up out of pocket. Oh, please say you will. I know I'm not always the easiest person, and I can be flaky and selfish and annoying. But I'm trying to do better, I really am. I'm trying to *be* better.'

Lisa hesitates. There are plenty of reasons why she should say no. It's too much, too soon. And there's the matter of the bad blood between them, or at least, between their parents. But none of that seems to matter very much, because it is clear that Amy really does want her here, and it is equally clear to her that she wants to stay.

'OK,' she says. 'I mean, there will be a few things to figure out. I think I need to give a week's notice on my temp job – I wouldn't want to just walk out on them. And I'd need to talk to my landlord. But, if you're sure... I'd love to come and spend the summer with you.'

Amy exhales and beams at her. 'I'm so glad,' she says. 'It just seems like it was meant to be. You're the right person at the exact right time. To be honest, I can't quite believe my luck. It's almost like someone's looking out for me.'

'You know, it's actually the right time for me too,' Lisa says, thinking of the field where she had buried her mum, and returning to her flat by herself afterwards, and how even a space that only has room for one can feel lonely.

Rowan has stopped feeding and drifted off to sleep, leaving Amy free to reach out without disturbing him. She holds out her hand and they shake on it. Amy's touch is firm and warm and sure. For some reason Lisa thinks of contracts signed in blood, and the kind of pacts you aren't supposed to make.

Amy says, 'I think we have a deal.'

'I think we do,' Lisa agrees.

Rowan stirs and lets out a faint whinnying cry, then falls silent. There is a burst of swelling music from the film Tilly is watching in the family room, and then that fades too. Amy looks tenderly down at Rowan and then back at Lisa again, and the gratitude and relief on her face is more than enough to chase away any lingering doubts Lisa might have had.

She is suddenly as certain as it is possible to be that she is doing exactly the right thing, and, as Amy had said, is the right person in the right place at the right time, just as if it had been meant to be.

THIRTEEN

It's surprisingly easy for Lisa to put her life on hold. She gives up the temp job; her landlord agrees to let her hold onto her flat over the summer at a slightly reduced rent, which Amy and Joe insist on covering for her. All she has to do is pack a couple of bags, lock up behind her and go.

She immediately finds herself almost entirely responsible for keeping Tilly occupied and entertained. They draw up a wishlist of places to go and things to do, and Tilly writes *The Grand Plan* at the top of it and carefully illustrates it. They stick it up on one of the kitchen cupboards, next to Joe's itinerary for his trip to New Zealand, ready to tick each item off once they have done it.

Over the weeks that follow, they bake biscuits and scones and jam tarts, launder all Tilly's dolls' clothes and hang them up to dry, and paint and model with clay. They attempt to knit, not very successfully. They find wellies that fit and go stream dipping with a couple of old jam jars and a sieve, and catch nothing but murk and an old sweet wrapper, but are delighted to see dragonflies and damselflies and a painted lady butterfly, all of which Tilly draws when they get back home. And Lisa watches her, and feels rewarded by each smile, every sign of enthusiasm, and each moment when Tilly loses herself in what she is doing.

Amy promises to ask Joe to try to sort out the insurance so Lisa can drive the family car, but he seems to take a while to get round to it – probably too busy inspecting plant samples on the other side of the world. In the meantime, they're limited to activities they can get to on foot or public transport. Tilly has a bike but isn't particularly confident on it, so that isn't an option either, although Lisa takes Tilly out now and then to ride round the village green for practice. She takes her back to the play-ground near the church, too, and is pleased to see her bold and sure-footed on the big climbing-frame, but careful with smaller children in the queue for the high slide.

Lisa familiarises herself with the maps kept in the drawer of the hall table, which show various local footpaths and bridle-ways. They walk to the newsagent's in the village to buy sweets, then on to the nearest farm shop for fresh eggs and to pick their own strawberries. As time goes on they venture further from the house and go for long treks in the countryside, following the course of the stream that flows down from its source near the Flowing Spring pub, or making great loops around the surrounding hills and woods.

Once or twice a week, Lisa leaves the attic bedroom in the evening so that Amy and then Tilly can talk to Joe on Skype on the computer that stands on the desk opposite her bed. After these exchanges Tilly tends to be more than usually quiet and thoughtful, as if talking to her dad has reminded her all over again how much she misses him. Lisa helps her use the computer to look up the different places Joe is travelling through and find out more about them, and that seems to help.

Every now and then, they catch the bus which passes through the village about once an hour. In Kettlebridge they swim in an open-air pool that Tilly says Joe used to take her to, then eat ice cream by the river. Lisa finds the sports shop that used to be Power's Bakery, but it has none of the familiarity of Hillview House. If she has ever been there before, it made no impression on her – it's just another old building in a row of other old buildings facing the town square. But she holds Tilly's hand a little more tightly than usual as they cross the road and head into the sixties shopping precinct opposite, where they find a real, live, working bakery, and pick out some treats to take home for tea.

They take the bus in the opposite direction and end up in Oxford, where they look at dinosaur bones in a museum and orchids in a glasshouse in the botanical garden. Lisa knows, as Tilly studies them, that she is thinking of Joe, and that this is a place she has been to with him. Back home after that, Lisa tentatively suggests adding gardening to The Grand Plan, but Tilly shakes her head, and her eyes begin to brim with tears.

'It would make me think of Daddy too much,' she says. A few fat drops fall and splash down on to her cheeks. She wipes them away and looks anxiously up at Lisa, as if the tears are a disgrace that she is about to be told off for.

'Would you like me to help you look after your love-in-a-mist? We could dry some of the flowers and keep them to show your dad when he gets home.'

'Oh yes, that's a good idea. I think Alice would like that too,' Tilly says, instantly brightening.

So love-in-a-mist is added to The Grand Plan. They pick a selection of the flowers and hang them upside down to dry in the walk-in larder in the kitchen, and then put them in a jam jar on Tilly's bedside table. Sometimes Lisa sees Tilly looking at them fondly just before lights-out time after the night-time story. It seems the flowers are a comfort to her, and that is just another affirmation, if any were needed, that Lisa had been right to accept Amy's invitation to stay.

Alice, the pretend friend, sometimes has to be accommodated – allocated an empty seat on the bus, or allowed an invisible snack – but she is mentioned less frequently as the days go by. Tilly begins to look less tired and pale and a little less thin, and sometimes Lisa hears her singing when she thinks no one is listening.

Occasionally, there are setbacks. One day Tilly suddenly loses her appetite, and complains of slightly vague symptoms – wormy tummy, fuzzy head – that seem to vanish as soon as Lisa mentions them to Amy. Lisa wonders if the symptoms are related to anxiety and suggests that a doctor's appointment might be worth pursuing, but Amy just says, 'I'm not taking her to the doctor if there's nothing physically wrong with her. They won't thank me for wasting their time. She's fine, anyway. It's that overactive imagination of hers again, I expect.'

When Lisa tries to persist, Amy responds with a flash of temper. '*I'm* her mum. Taking her to the doctor is *my* responsibility, and I honestly don't think she needs to go.' And Lisa decides to drop the subject, though she keeps a note of what happened and when, just in case it recurs. To her relief, it doesn't. There are no nightmares, and there are many more good days than bad.

There are not many social encounters. Lisa has bought a swingball set to put up in the garden, and although Tilly is soon a dab hand at that, she refuses point blank to go to a free tennis tryout at the leisure centre in Kettlebridge. There is one play-date with a schoolfriend who lives on the outskirts of the village, and a return visit that Lisa anxiously supervises, but when Lisa asks if there are other friends Tilly would like to see, Tilly says airily that they are all on holiday.

'And anyway, I have Alice,' she adds, as if this should be self-evident. 'She doesn't always like coming to strange houses. She doesn't feel welcome.'

When Lisa tries to sound Amy out on the subject, Amy just shrugs and says it's true that a lot of people are away, and she's sure Tilly's social life will pick up when the new school term begins.

'There's really not a lot going on right now,' she says. 'All the mum and baby groups have stopped for the summer – otherwise I suppose I might try to take Rowan out to a couple of things. Though it's not really my scene. Anyway, all that will kick off soon enough, in the autumn.'

Amy is less snappy with Tilly than when Lisa first arrived, but still doesn't make much effort to spend time with her: she seems more than happy for Lisa to pick up the slack. She spends hours feeding Rowan and reading or watching TV, sitting with him on a rug in the garden and taking him out for occasional walks. She never meets up with any mum friends. Apart from Lisa and the phone and Skype calls with Joe, the only other adults she has any contact with are Mrs Paley, who comes in once a week to clean, and Mrs Paley's son Tyler, the gardener – and neither of them are exactly talkative.

Lisa worries that she's too isolated and that it's not good for her, but Amy brushes aside her suggestion that she could babysit Rowan if Amy ever wanted to go out: 'How can you? You can't breastfeed him, can you?' Then Amy finally succeeds in persuading Rowan to accept a bottle of formula milk, and is delighted with this development – 'It means I can actually give him to someone else!' But when Lisa repeats the offer of babysitting she says she thinks Rowan is still too young for her to leave him. 'Maybe one day. But it would be taking on a lot for you to look after the two of them. It'll keep. There's no rush.'

In mid-August, the weather abruptly turns bad. For several days they are all marooned in the house by steady rain, apart from brief trips to the village in head-to-toe waterproofs. Inside, Tilly makes hopeful attempts to play with Rowan, who treats her to gummy smiles and allows her to pass him his favourite rattle, and to hold him on her lap. Lisa listens to Tilly's bright chatter about all the things Rowan might enjoy playing with when he is a little bit older, and all the toys she is prepared to share with him, and marvels at the little girl's lack of resentment and jealousy. She can't help but wonder, if she'd had a sibling, whether she would have been anything like as kind-hearted.

Amy encourages these scenes of sibling bonding and takes pictures of them to show to Joe. Lisa initially tries to stay out of the way but then Amy tells her to move in closer, and snaps a few photos of the three of them. Later on, Amy brings the camera up to the attic while Rowan is napping in his cot, and after a bit of fiddling round with leads and on-screen prompts they manage to print out a selection of the photos. 'For you to keep,' Amy says. 'A little memento.' And Lisa has a lump in her throat as she thanks her, because all of this is so much more than she had hoped for.

After Amy has gone back downstairs Lisa sticks her favourite of the photos up on the wardrobe door next to the picture Tilly had drawn for her at the end of her first visit, of the two of them together in the garden. One day, these things will just be souvenirs of a time gone by. But while she is here she is determined to make the most of it. As she stands there looking at herself with her cousin's children in her arms, and listens to the rain pattering on the farmhouse roof, she is profoundly grateful to have been given the chance to be close to them.

FOURTEEN

The bad weather takes its toll, and finally the day comes when Tilly doesn't want to settle to anything. It isn't pouring outside, but it is drizzling and windy, and while Lisa is hopeful that it might clear up later, for now, they need to find something to do inside – except they already seem to have exhausted just about every possible option.

Amy has taken Rowan to the vaccination clinic in Kettlebridge on the bus, so they have the family room to themselves, but Tilly doesn't want to watch any more TV. She won't draw, won't play a board game, won't read, can't be bothered to cook, doesn't want to make jewellery out of wires and beads, isn't interested in any of her toys. And she makes it clear that Alice doesn't want to do any of these things, either.

Eventually, Lisa asks, 'So what *would* you like to do?' and Tilly's face brightens.

'I know,' she says. 'Alice has a good idea. Let's play hide and seek.'

Something tells Lisa this might not be a good idea at all. But also, she can see that Tilly would love to have her thumping around the place, nearly coming across her hiding place and missing it. Tilly wants a chance to outwit her.

'OK,' she says. 'And after we've played for a bit we'll do something I choose. Deal?'

'Deal,' Tilly agrees.

Tilly hides first, and Lisa spots her early on but spins out looking for as long as possible. It's the quivering of the dining room tablecloth that gives her away. Eventually the sound of Tilly's giggling becomes too loud to ignore, and Lisa duly tracks her down, slowly circling the table and talking loudly to herself about how confusing it is to be able to hear Tilly and not to see her before finally lifting the edge of the tablecloth and being rewarded by Tilly's squeal of delight.

Next, it's Lisa's turn to hide. She retreats into the kitchen larder, leaving the door very slightly ajar and expecting Tilly to find her almost straight away. But Tilly blunders through the kitchen and misses her.

She is just beginning to wonder if she should give herself away – by coughing, perhaps, or knocking something over that she knows won't break – when Tilly flings open the larder door with a grin of triumph.

'There you are,' Tilly says. 'Alice thought you might be here.'

'Clever Alice,' Lisa says, and emerges sheepishly, because there's really no other way to emerge from a cupboard, whatever your reasons for being there. 'It's my turn now, isn't it? I mean, it's my turn to choose what we play.'

But Tilly is having none of it. She folds her arms and pouts. 'You forgot Alice. It's her turn to hide now. We will look for her together. I'll tell you when we've found her, because you can't see her.'

Lisa gives in. They both cover their eyes and count to ten, then begin to search the house. They work their way through the kitchen, the living room, the hall, the family room, the bathroom, Tilly's room and Rowan's room, and Lisa begins to wonder if Tilly is planning to draw this out indefinitely.

'I hope Alice isn't in your mum's room,' she says. 'Because I don't think that would really be allowed.'

Tilly shakes her head. 'No, she wouldn't go in there. We'll have to try upstairs.'

Lisa follows Tilly up to the attic. Her bedroom and bathroom are exactly as she had left them earlier, sparsely furnished and mostly bare, Joe's computer and printer on the desk, the white paintwork lit up by patches of sunlight spattered with raindrop shadows.

'If she's not up here, I think we've run out of places to look,' she says to Tilly as they return to the attic landing.

Tilly screws up her face in concentration. 'There is one more place we can try,' she says, and takes off at a rapid pace down the stairs.

She doesn't stop on the first-floor landing, and Lisa briefly loses sight of her, then glimpses her again scurrying down the last few steps to the hall and turning in the direction of the kitchen.

But when Lisa reaches the bottom of the stairs the hallway is empty. All the doors are firmly closed, and she hasn't heard any of them open and shut. Tilly has vanished into thin air.

Her heart stops and then restarts in a big, lolloping beat. Where on earth could Tilly have vanished to?

Then she finds Tilly standing at the back of the staircase, holding back the red velvet curtain that usually hangs there. She looks wickedly daring. The bright sunlight falling onto the curtain is reflected onto her skin and gives it a faint reddish tinge. She reaches past the curtain to hit a light switch and slips into the suddenly bright space beyond it.

'Tilly! We're not meant to go down here.'

Too late. Lisa follows her. The soft dead weight of the red velvet clings and resists as she pushes past it and down a steep little row of steps to find herself in a low-ceilinged, windowless, cobwebby passageway, painted a yellowing shade of white. There is thin brown carpet underfoot, and the light fitting – a dome fixed to the sloping underside of the stairs – gives off a flickering glow. At the other end of the short passageway, just beyond Tilly, is a door.

'She must be through there,' Tilly says, pointing at the door. 'There's some keys in the drawer in the little table in the hall. There's probably one there that would work.'

'Tilly, I really don't think that's a good idea. Let's go back up.'

But Tilly's only response is to freeze and put a finger to her lips.

The next moment, Lisa hears it too – the sound of a key turning in a lock. She's disoriented enough for her first thought to be that it's coming from the other side of the door she is looking at. Then she realises that it's coming from upstairs, from outside.

It's not Mrs Paley's day to clean. It can only be Amy with Rowan, back earlier than expected.

She and Tilly exchange glances for just long enough to establish a conspiracy. *Let's keep quiet about this.* Then Tilly pushes past her and races up the steps. Lisa hurries up to the hallway behind her, pulls the curtain across, and remembers almost a fraction too late to reach back in and turn the light off.

'Hello? Anyone in?'

Amy has left Rowan in the pushchair by the front door, and is looking at her reflection in the hall mirror and fluffing out her hair.

'Hello, Mummy,' Tilly says. She approaches her, then comes to a halt at a safe distance. Amy glances at her and says, 'I was wondering where you'd got to,' then turns back to the mirror.

'We were just playing hide and seek,' Tilly says.

Lisa comes forward to stand just behind Tilly and says, 'Was Rowan good about having his injections?'

'Didn't have any. I'd got the wrong day, can you believe it? I think you might be right, and I've been in the house too much. Going stir crazy without realising it. You can't hide away your whole life, can you? It's just not good for you.'

'No, definitely not,' Lisa agrees.

Amy leaves the mirror and homes in on Tilly to brush a bit of cobweb off her shoulder. Tilly flinches, then stiffens and stoically submits to her mother's attention.

'Honestly, what have you been up to? You look like a little urchin,' Amy says. 'Anybody would think I'd been neglecting you.'

She lifts Rowan out of his pushchair and swings him up high, making him gurgle with pleasure.

'There's my boy,' she says. 'What a good boy. Everybody likes to see you, don't they? Of course they do. And why wouldn't they?'

She brings him down to rest so that he's curled up on her front, his face squashed against her shoulder. 'Would you mind fixing me a cup of tea, Lisa?' she says. 'I'm absolutely parched. I'm going to change Rowan and then feed him – I've probably made him wait for about as long as I can get away with.'

'Sure,' Lisa says as Amy heads upstairs to the bathroom without waiting for a reply. She has a slight but unmistakable bounce in her step as she goes upstairs, as if something unexpectedly good has just come along and helped to lift her out of the mire in which she's been stuck.

· · ·

When Lisa brings in the tea, Amy is standing by the window looking out at the garden with Rowan in her arms. Tilly is listlessly lining up a couple of dolls on the rug at her feet. Rowan is making a soft mewling noise, like an unhappy kitten, and Tilly begins talking in a sing-song voice under her breath about how it's time to go back to school.

'Come and sit down, Lisa,' Amy says. 'I want to have a word with you about something.'

Lisa puts Amy's tea down on the occasional table and sits on the sofa, trying to shrug off the feeling of being a housemaid who has been summoned for a telling-off. Amy settles into her usual armchair and unbuttons a couple of buttons on her shirt to latch Rowan onto her breast. The baby's plaintive complaining is almost immediately replaced by the soft, wet sound of contented suckling.

'Like magic,' Amy says, closing her eyes as if to better appreciate the relative calm and quiet. Then she opens them wide and fixes her gaze on Tilly, with the look that means she expects what she wants to be done and will brook no argument. 'Tilly, would you go up and tidy your room? Mrs Paley is coming tomorrow, and she'll want to vacuum it.'

'But it's already tidy,' Tilly protests.

Amy raises her eyebrows at her as if she can't quite believe Tilly would deliberately defy her and Tilly gives in, reluctantly gets to her feet and slouches off.

'Close the door behind you,' Amy calls after her. Tilly bangs it shut, conjuring up, not for the first time, the spectre of the sulky teen she might become one day.

'Right,' Amy says, and exhales. 'Lisa, I have to talk to you about something, and it's a bit awkward so I've been putting it off. But there's no time like the present, is there?' She pauses as if expecting some kind of affirmation.

'Guess not,' Lisa says.

Her heart is thudding. That can't be right, surely – that her cousin, who she has been living with so closely – as closely as a sister – can so easily set her nerves on edge? Has she done something wrong somehow? She can't think she has – not that Amy knows about, anyway, and even if Amy knows that Tilly has just been exploring the steps down to the basement, surely that wouldn't be that big a deal?

Amy composes her features into the kind of expression that people put on when they know what they are about to say might be hurtful or confusing, but are determined to go ahead and say it anyway.

'I've already spoken to you about our grandmother,' she says. 'Grandma Elsie.' She sighs. 'A difficult character, to be honest, and she really hasn't improved with age. Now she's difficult *and* confused. Anyway, she always visits in the summer, and I feel I really ought to keep it going this year. She's due to come next weekend. And what always used to happen, when Joe was here, was that he would keep Tilly out of her way, and go down to the village, or to the playground or whatever. I was wondering if you might be willing to do that.'

'But won't she want to see Tilly?'

'Yes, I suppose,' Amy concedes, easing Rowan off her breast and stroking his cheek with her forefinger. 'Look, it wouldn't be for that long. Just a couple of hours between lunch and teatime, and then the visit will be over.'

Lisa pauses, considering. It feels horrible, as if she's just swallowed down something that is going to make herself sick. Amy is telling her to get out and stay out because her own grandmother won't want to meet her. At the same time, on the face of it, she can see that what Amy is suggesting makes sense. It's just that it seems so unfair.

'You'd be doing me the most enormous favour,' Amy says, and gives her that winning smile that tends to have the magical effect of making Lisa's objections melt away, whatever they might be. 'Me *and* Tilly. And Rowan, too, because as soon as things start falling apart round here my milk supply seems to dry up, and then...' She pulls a face suggestive of extreme discomfort. 'Well, then things can get very difficult.'

'OK,' Lisa says slowly. 'If that's what you think would be best. I'm sure I can find something to do with Tilly, whatever the weather. How are you going to get her here? Grandma Elsie, I mean.' It feels weird calling her by the name Amy uses for her. Lisa doesn't feel inclined to acknowledge this person as a relative at all.

'Oh, don't worry about that,' Amy says. 'I'm going to ask Tyler to give me a lift.'

'Tyler Paley? The gardener? What, he's going to give your grandma a lift in his truck?'

'*Our* grandma,' Amy says reproachfully, as if Grandma Elsie is a burden that Lisa is lucky to have been able to avoid. 'And he has another car, silly. Which is his pride and joy, actually, and absolutely spotless. I'm not suggesting Grandma Elsie hitch a ride in the cab with a load of tree trimmings bouncing round in the back.'

'OK, well, whatever you think's best,' Lisa says. 'I'll be interested to meet her, if only in passing. I suppose if she's a bit confused, as you say, it might not be a good idea to ask her about the past? Or is it the kind of thing where she can remember events that took place years ago, and is hazy about what happened more recently?'

She says this with a sick sense of inevitability. If anybody could fill in the gaps for her, it should be Grandma Elsie – but going by what Amy is saying, she will probably be unwilling or unable to do so, and Amy seems to be keen to keep them apart.

'Oh no, no, you mustn't ask her anything,' Amy says. 'She'll get very upset. The thing is, most of the time she's pretty harmless, but if she gets worked up – well, the same as any of us – she can get very aggressive. I mean, I know it sounds ridiculous, but she can actually be quite frightening. She may be old, but she's still strong.'

'Right.'

Amy looks her directly in the eyes. A slow blush creeps along her cheeks.

'I don't want her to know who you are,' she says. 'We'll have to say you're a friend who's staying to help out, or a nanny or something. Is that OK?'

'You want me to pretend to be your nanny,' Lisa says slowly.

The blush on Amy's cheeks darkens. 'I'm sorry, that was crass of me,' she says. 'I'm a bit stressed about it, to be honest, and not really thinking straight. We'll just say you're a friend who's here to help out. That's the truth, isn't it?'

And there's that smile, again. But Lisa doesn't feel like being won over, not this time. Or at least, not yet.

'It doesn't seem very practical,' she objects. 'Won't my surname be a bit of a giveaway?'

'We won't tell her your surname,' Amy says. 'I'm not saying you have to lie. If she wants to know, fair enough, we'll just deal with the consequences. But I don't think she will.' She pauses. 'I know it's not ideal. But I honestly think it's the best we can do.'

'You *are* asking me to lie,' Lisa says slowly. 'I am going to meet my own grandmother for the first time that I can remember. And maybe it will be the only time. And you don't want me to tell her who I am.'

'Yes, but only because if she finds out she'll probably lose the plot completely. I'm actually looking out for you, Lisa, believe it or not. Believe me, this does not have the potential to be some kind of sweet, meaningful encounter. She isn't like that. I'm not cheating you of anything, OK? Let's just play it safe.'

'That's easy for you to say. You grew up with her.'

'Do you think I want her to come here?' Amy is almost shouting now. It's quite clear to Lisa that she doesn't really want to go through with the visit at all. 'Look, I have to invite her. I'm obliged to do it. And I don't want to have to go on about this, because I know how bad it sounds, especially given everything you've done for me and my children over the last few weeks, but you would seriously be persona non grata. I can't stress enough how viscerally she used to react to anything that even reminded her of your mother. Now, I don't want to upset you. As far as I'm concerned, all that is done and dusted and in the past. You know that. I told you that already. But you have to remember that it's actually a pretty big deal you being here at all.'

Suddenly, Lisa is really angry – the kind of angry that is not far off bursting into tears, and the indignity of it makes her even more furious.

'Oh, I see. I need to know my place. I'm meant to be grateful and shut up, and carry on looking after your daughter till your husband gets back. And after that, who knows?'

Rowan's eyes flicker open – their raised voices must have disturbed him – and his little mouth turns down in a grimace of despair. He roots for the breast again and Amy latches him on. When she next speaks her voice is clear and steady.

'As far as I'm concerned, Grandma Elsie coming is a minor inconvenience. Or it can be, if we handle it right,' she says. 'I love having you here. I want you to stay. But I have to do this. It's difficult for me too. Please, Lisa, I'm begging you. Don't make it any harder than it already is.'

The door opens and Tilly comes in. Both Amy and Lisa fall silent and watch her as she makes her way across the carpet to where Lisa is sitting.

'I heard you both shouting,' Tilly says. 'What are you arguing about?'

'Grandma Elsie is going to visit,' Amy says. 'I don't think we should tell her Lisa is my cousin, because she is funny about family things. What do you think?'

Tilly turns very pale. 'I don't think you should tell her either,' she says, shaking her head. 'She is not a good person to tell things to.'

'Quite,' Amy agrees. 'And no mentioning imaginary friends, all right, Tilly?'

Tilly shakes her head. 'No. I won't say anything to her at all.' She reaches out and takes Lisa's hand. Hers is ice-cold. 'Will you come and see how tidy I made my room?'

Lisa allows herself to be pulled up. 'OK.'

On the way up the stairs with Tilly she experiences a sudden little thrum of hatred for her cousin. And then, as she looks round Tilly's room – the little tent in the corner, the jam jar of dried love-in-a-mist, the torch, the teddy bears – her anger begins to fade. This is part of what family life is, after all, isn't it? Obligations, some of them painful. Swallowing your pride. Giving up on what you want because of what other people need, and yielding when they can't.

She is used to this feeling – the bitterness of the perhaps unjustified compromise. She had lived through years of it with her mum, biting her tongue, tolerating Mum's moods, not confronting her. And that is exactly how she feels now: in the wrong and in the right at the same time.

Usually, at Hillview House, Lisa sleeps deeply and dreamlessly. But that night she tosses and turns, and when she finally drops off she dreams about going down a long flight of steps into the dark, then along a tunnel and down more steps, a spiral staircase this time, and finally along another tunnel with a very faint glowing red light at the end.

There is no sign of Tilly. She has no idea what she is looking for. She only knows that she is afraid of what will happen if she doesn't find it.

Just as the red glow is beginning to intensify, and the tunnel seems to be coming to an end, she wakes with a start to find herself alone in the attic in the dark, gripped by a terrible and inexplicable sense of dread and regret.

FIFTEEN

On the day Grandma Elsie is due to visit there's an almost audible hum of tension in the air. Amy is up early, mopping and vacuuming, and Tilly puts on a frilly dress Lisa has never seen before and keeps fiddling with the collar. Tyler shows up on the dot of eleven to take Amy to pick the old lady up, wearing an ironed shirt and chinos, his hair oddly slick with gel. The car Amy had described as his pride and joy turns out to be an old Ford that shines as if it has just been polished up by hand.

Lisa wonders if Amy is paying Tyler for his time. Then she notices the way he watches Amy as she carries Rowan in his car seat out of the house and leans across to fix it into place. It's quite something to see Amy in action – the way she straightens up and shakes out her hair and smiles, the mixture of self-consciousness and confidence that makes her come across as both vulnerable and proud. Perhaps Lisa is not the only one who is open to Amy's powers of persuasion.

At least she knows when Amy is going to work on her. If Tyler is aware of being used, would he still look at her that way? And what about Joe? Maybe Joe can see what Amy is like and loves her anyway. Or perhaps he is wilfully blind to the aspects of her character that can make her hard to deal with – the self-absorption, the impulsiveness, the changing moods...

Amy has decided that Tilly should stay behind with Lisa. Tilly doesn't seem to have any objections to this arrangement but is very quiet. She concentrates on drawing at the kitchen table while Lisa lays the rarely used dining room table, tops and tails a batch of green runner beans freshly picked from the garden, and wraps salmon in foil ready to bake.

When Lisa has prepared as much as she can, she settles down next to Tilly and flicks through one of Amy's magazines. Then she remembers to check that Tilly hasn't forgotten how Amy wants this visit to be played.

'I just wanted to make sure you remember not to mention me being your mum's cousin,' she says. 'It might make your Grandma Elsie upset.'

'She's not my Grandma Elsie. She's Mum's Grandma Elsie,' Tilly says. 'She's my *Great*-Grandma Elsie. And yes, I remember. We're lying.'

'Not lying,' Lisa says. 'Just... not telling.'

Tilly shoots her a dubious look. 'Isn't that the same thing?'

The sound of tyres on gravel floats in through the open window. Lisa says, 'I think they're back.'

Tilly doesn't answer and carries on colouring, but her shoulders stiffen. Amy comes in first, through the back door, carrying Rowan in his car seat and looking harassed.

'Hi, Lisa, Tilly, how's it all going back here?' she says. Without waiting for a reply, she puts Rowan down by the kitchen table and goes back to offer Grandma Elsie an arm to help her over the ledge of the door.

'I can manage,' Grandma Elsie says stiffly, but she does briefly grip Amy's arm as she steps in, then releases it. Outside, the gravel crunches as Tyler turns, then revs the engine and drives away.

Grandma Elsie shuffles forward so she can lean on the

kitchen table, but remains standing. She looks around the
kitchen as if taking stock. Her expression is that of someone
who doesn't look for the best in people, or places, and would be
surprised to find it. She glances at Tilly but doesn't soften, then
turns to Lisa and says, 'Who are you?'

'That's Lisa, who's been helping out with the children,'
Amy says with a stiff little smile. It's clear that she's not that
comfortable with the lie, either. 'Don't you remember? I did tell
you.'

'Hmm,' Grandma Elsie says, and sniffs the air as if smelling
a rat. 'Yes. You did tell me. The nanny. But who needs a nanny
when you have a husband like Joe?'

'Joe's not here, Grandma Elsie,' Amy says with the kind of
exaggerated patience that isn't really patience at all. 'He's in
New Zealand. And Lisa isn't really a nanny.'

Grandma Elsie studies Lisa as if considering what she
might possibly be, if not a nanny. 'Well, are you paying her?'

'Let's not talk about money,' Amy says. 'Tilly, why don't you
come and give Grandma Elsie a hug?'

Tilly dutifully gets to her feet and comes over to offer
Grandma Elsie a tentative embrace, and Grandma Elsie drapes
one arm lightly around Tilly's shoulders. Then Tilly sits down
again and Grandma Elsie eases herself into the chair next to
her, opposite Lisa.

'Actually, Grandma, if you don't mind, I think it would be
better if we went through to the sitting room,' Amy says. 'You'll
be much more comfortable there, and we can leave Lisa in
peace. It won't take long to get the lunch going, will it, Lisa?
About half an hour?'

'Sure,' Lisa says, and turns the oven on.

'All in good time, all in good time. I've only just sat down,'
Grandma Elsie says. 'I spent hours of my life in this kitchen. I
can at least have five minutes more, can't I?' She looks around

the kitchen again. 'It seems very yellow in here. Have you had it painted?'

'We had it done last year. You've seen it before,' Amy says. 'We thought it would make it brighter.'

Grandma Elsie closes her eyes tightly and screws up her face in concentration, then relaxes it and opens her eyes again. '*Brighter*,' she says gloomily. 'Like a disco.'

Amy reaches forward to pick up the rattle Rowan has just dropped on the floor. When she gives it back to him he rewards her with a huge, adoring grin before sticking it back in his mouth.

'Is that hygienic?' Grandma Elsie says. She looks down at the floor and scuffs it with her toe. 'It doesn't look especially clean.'

'Doesn't it? It should do,' Amy says. In spite of all her last-minute attempts to clean the house, she doesn't appear insulted, more mildly surprised, as if the state of the kitchen floor is nothing to do with her, and is unworthy of anyone's attention anyway. She stoops down in front of Rowan and says to Grandma Elsie, 'Would you like to hold him?'

'I suppose so,' Grandma Elsie says, and Amy takes Rowan out of the car seat and puts him on her lap. He looks slightly startled and not completely convinced about the suitability of his new resting place, but goes along with it for now and carries on chewing his rattle.

Grandma Elsie says to Amy, 'May I see the cake?'

'Of course,' Amy says. She goes over to the supermarket sponge cake standing in a box on the side and brings it back to the table, holding it out for Grandma Elsie to inspect.

'Hm,' Grandma Elsie says. 'You've got candles?'

'Yes, we've got candles.'

Candles? Lisa's first impression of Grandma Elsie had been that she was not quite as confused as Amy had suggested, but now she is beginning to wonder. Amy's policy seems to be to humour her as far as possible. Maybe, after all, it's the right thing to do. Lisa decides not to comment, or to point out that it isn't anybody's birthday.

'It'll do,' Grandma Elsie says, and Amy puts the cake back.

Grandma Elsie leans forward and sniffs the top of Rowan's head, breathing in his baby smell, and he wraps his tiny chubby hand round her wrinkled forefinger. Then Grandma Elsie attempts to jiggle him up and down, and Rowan breaks off from biting his rattle to emit a small whimper of protest.

'Maybe you should take him back,' Grandma Elsie says to Amy. 'Can we go through to the living room now? This chair's rather hard. Old bones need padding, you know.'

'Yes, good idea,' Amy says with the sort of exasperated brightness that people use to reproach others for not going along with what they'd said in the first place, though her irritation seems to go straight over Grandma Elsie's head.

She takes Rowan from Grandma Elsie and helps her out, offering her an elbow to hang on to while holding Rowan in place with her other arm. Tilly glances at Lisa with something approaching sympathy, as if Lisa has been unfairly excluded, and then scuttles after them, clutching her drawing book and a selection of pencils, and closes the kitchen door behind her.

Their voices fade into silence. There could almost be nobody else in the house. Lisa stands in front of the sink and looks out at the garden, at Tilly's playhouse and the big old willow tree. There's a breeze today, and the whispering sound of the leaves drifts through the open window, but the air seems thick and hard to breathe. She feels as if she has become unmoored somehow, or been cut adrift. As if she'd never really had a place here, or been welcome.

She could just go upstairs and pack her things and walk out. Catch a bus, then a train. Go home. Back to her real home, which is locked up and waiting for her return. The little rented flat on the top floor of a converted Victorian house in Brickley, where, if you open the kitchen window and lean out, you can hear the roar of traffic from the nearby dual carriageway, but you can also see the cherry tree that grows in front of the house next door.

Then she thinks of Tilly, who hasn't been out all day, and who will probably be relieved to get away from the house. And Joe, who is due to ring that evening. And Amy, who never usually cleans anything. And Rowan, because surely that's Rowan she can hear, letting out a thin, keening wail as if stricken by sudden grief.

The crying stops. Lisa pulls herself together and reminds herself that she is needed here. And besides, this is just one day. One awkward, uncomfortable day, but no reason to leave. She turns away to put the salmon in the oven.

She eats half a sandwich alone in the kitchen while the others have their salmon and potatoes and beans, garnished with rosemary from the garden. Her sandwich is weirdly tasteless, and she gives up on it and throws the rest of it away.

The meal she's prepared for the others seems to go down all right. There's not much left on the plates when Amy brings them back through – even Tilly seems to have managed a decent lunch. Amy fixes Rowan a bottle, which seems to keep him happy, because Lisa doesn't hear him cry again. Amy takes out strawberries and cream for pudding, and Lisa is halfway through filling the dishwasher when Amy carries in the rest of the dirty crockery.

'Thank you so much,' Amy says heartily, setting down the tray. 'You're an absolute star. I don't know what I'd do without you.' She drops her voice. 'It's always difficult. I think it's a little bit harder each time I see her. Don't worry about the clearing up, I'll sort it all out later. Are you still OK to go down to the village? We're all done, for now anyway, and I think Tilly's itching to get down from the table.'

Lisa says yes, of course, she can head off whenever Tilly's ready. She tries to sound cheerful and willing but feels fake, as if she is just playing a part and Amy is too. Amy says she'll send Tilly out to her, and Lisa goes out to the hall to get the spare house keys from their place in the bowl on the table by the door.

She remembers what Tilly had said when they were playing hide and seek, about there being other keys in the drawer, and pulls it out to have a look. Sure enough, there they are, a couple of keys in their own little compartment. It's surprisingly tidy – Joe's influence, perhaps. She suspects that if it was left to Amy, it would soon silt up with random junk, just like the drawers in her mum's house.

Grandma Elsie is saying something, but she can't make out the words. Then the dining room door opens and she slams the drawer shut, scoops up the spare house keys from the bowl and shoves them in her pocket. Her reflection in the hall mirror looks furtive and frightened, like a bad thief.

Tilly comes out looking crushed, as if she's just had to sit an unpleasant test and is sure she's got most of the answers wrong. But she perks up when she sees Lisa, and Lisa's spirits lift, too, as they leave the house together and step out into the sunshine.

They don't rush. Lisa is conscious of spinning everything out for as long as possible, and encourages Tilly to dawdle. After all, Amy had made it pretty clear that she wants them out of the way for as much of the afternoon as possible.

She buys them both ice cream from the village shop, and they wander along the main road from one end to the other, and stand in the shadow of the willow trees to look down at the algae-covered pond. Then Tilly asks to go to the park. As they move on, out of the corner of her eye, Lisa sees the shadow of someone walking close by.

A man. A tall, thickset, solitary man. No dog. No children. She tenses slightly and then tells herself she's being ridiculous. This is Springhill at two thirty on an August afternoon. Nothing is going to happen to her here, and lone men are as entitled to stroll round scenic English villages as anybody else.

They go down the narrow lane by the churchyard with him behind them, and when they turn off into the park he is still following them. She decides he looks harmless enough: a bit older than her with sandy-coloured curly hair and nondescript clothes – a short-sleeved check shirt, chinos, trainers.

Tilly runs off to climb on the monkey bars, forgetting to be careful of her best dress, and Lisa sits down on the bench where she can see her. The stranger settles on the bench at her side, but not too close, more up the other end. Well, that's OK. She can hardly complain about that. There's at least a foot or two of air between them. And he's not doing anything objectionable. He's just sitting there, looking at the grass and the trees, enjoying a gorgeous summer afternoon.

He says, 'Beautiful day, isn't it?'

She reminds herself that this is a village, and village people are friendly, friendlier than people in towns. They think nothing of making small talk to people they don't know.

'Yes, lovely.'

He has to squint into the sunlight to look at her. He smiles, and she automatically smiles back. The smile gives him a dimple that might have made him look cute once, when he was a boy. He has a long, slightly doughy face under a bullish forehead, and his cheeks are beginning to sag, as if a combination of gravity and gloom has dragged them down.

He says, 'You're a friend of Amy's, aren't you? I've seen you around with Tilly.' He looks away from her towards Tilly, who has abandoned the monkey bars and is climbing up the tall slide.

'I'm Amy's cousin,' Lisa says. 'I've been staying over the summer.'

He sucks in his breath in a way that reminds her of the mechanic who'd told her that her car wasn't worth fixing, just before he delivered the bad news.

'Her cousin. Right. I see. Sorry, I'm just a bit surprised. I didn't think she was that close with her family. Not on her mum's side, I'm guessing?'

'Yeah, on her mum's side. Why, what do you know about it?'

He moves his hands in a quick, dismissive little gesture, as if he'd wipe out what he's just said if he could. 'I didn't mean any offence. Don't take this the wrong way, but with Amy you never really know what to believe anyway.'

She hesitates. She knows she should spring to Amy's defence. At the same time, what he's said seems to her to have some truth in it. Amy certainly has the persuasive skills to be a good liar, and she's just done a pretty convincing job of deceiving Grandma Elsie.

Maybe this man had been romantically involved with Amy at some point, or had wanted to be. Why else would he speak about her like that, with that mix of intimacy and disdain? Probably Amy left a trail of broken hearts behind her before she settled down with Joe. What would it be like to be like that? To be used to commanding people's attention in that way, and leaving them still thinking about you?

But also, this man shouldn't talk about Amy like that here, with Tilly more or less within earshot.

She says, 'So how do you know her?'

'She used to work for me,' he says. He is not watching Tilly any more, but is gazing at the trees that mark the edge of the park and the line of houses just beyond it. 'I'm in double glazing, and she was my PA for a bit. Quite a long time ago now. But she's not the kind of person you forget.'

'I'm sure she isn't,' Lisa says soothingly, though she has no idea why she should feel the need to soothe him.

He holds out his hand for her to shake and introduces himself: 'I'm Russell Bright.' His clasp is tight and meaty. She tells him her name and he says, 'Say hello to Amy from me.' She promises she will, though she can't imagine that Amy will be particularly pleased to hear from him.

'You see that house over there? The red-brick Victorian place with the gables? I did their windows, years ago now,' he says. 'They had a conservatory put on too. Business was better then. These days, people always think they can get something cheaper off the internet.'

'I can imagine that must be difficult.'

He shrugs. 'It's a dog-eat-dog world. If you don't survive, you don't deserve to be in business anyway.' He looks at her more closely. 'What do you do, anyway? When you're not doing Amy's mothering for her?'

'That's not what I'm doing,' she says. 'I don't think you should talk about her like that.'

He cracks a grin. It makes him look cheeky, like someone who'd be fun down the pub.

'OK, fair enough,' he says.

After a minute's silence he reaches into his pocket and brings out a small packet of mints. He offers her one. She refuses. He shrugs and takes one for himself and starts sucking it, then puts the packet away.

He pushes his mint into his cheek with his tongue and says, 'So how did she talk you into coming here, then?'

'It was really a lucky coincidence.' She is beginning to feel repulsed by him, and it's an effort to remain polite. 'She just happened to need someone at a time when I was free to help. Plus she has a nice big attic she could put me up in.'

'Yeah, right,' he says, and swallows. 'Amy's good at that. Making other people think what she wants is what they want. Guess she made a sucker out of you, didn't she? Well, don't feel bad about it. You're not the first.'

While she is still digesting this he gets to his feet. 'Anyway, it was nice meeting you,' he says. 'I expect I'll see you around.'

And with that he ambles off towards the treeline. He has an uptight, slightly awkward walk, as if he's used to striding briskly from one place to another and doesn't quite know how to move when he has no reason to rush.

Tilly gets off the swing and comes over to her. She says, 'Who was that man?'

'Just someone your mum used to work for, a long time ago.'

'I've met him before,' Tilly says, pulling a face as if it is not a pleasant memory. 'He wanted to talk to Mum once when she was collecting me from school. Can we go back home now?'

Lisa consults her watch. It's half past three. It seems ridiculous to say they haven't been out for long enough yet. To have to keep Tilly away from the house just because her great-grandmother's there, however difficult or confused she may be.

'Yes, I think we could make a start on getting back up that hill,' she says. 'But don't go too fast, because remember, I'm older than you and my legs are feeling a bit tired.'

She is rewarded by a smile and the unthinking trust with which Tilly reaches out to hold her hand as they set off.

SIXTEEN

Back in the house, a little of the tension seems to have gone out of the air. It's like walking into the aftermath of something – not necessarily an argument, but some other kind of confrontation that has been defused, or a threat that has been seen off.

Grandma Elsie and Amy are in the main living room still. Grandma Elsie is talking about something in the kind of firm, wearily angry voice that people use for opinions they have expressed before and expect to express again. If she's been banging on like that since they left, Amy probably won't mind too much if they interrupt.

Lisa knocks on the door to let Amy know they're back and, yes, Amy definitely sounds relieved as she calls them in. The two women are sitting at a polite distance from each other, Grandma Elsie very upright on an armchair, Amy with her feet tucked up under her on the sofa. Grandma Elsie is flushed and watery-eyed, as if she has recently been crying, and Amy has the stiff, long-suffering air of someone who's been stuck in a doctor's waiting room while time drags on and is desperate to get out. Rowan, meanwhile, is obliviously cheerful, lying on his playmat on the floor and looking up with interest at the different soft and shiny shapes suspended from a cushioned arch that reaches over his head.

Amy says to Tilly, 'Did you have a nice walk?'

Tilly nods, keeping a wary eye on Grandma Elsie.

'We met somebody who knows you,' Lisa says to Amy. 'Some guy you used to work for. He said his name is Russell Bright.'

'Oh, him,' Amy says. 'He seems to be spending a lot of time hanging round the village.'

'He said his business isn't doing too well.'

'Well, maybe he should try and do a bit more work,' Amy says. 'Tilly, would you like some cake?' Tilly nods, though she looks a little doubtful. 'Why don't you go into the kitchen with Lisa and she can give you some? We made a start on it, but there's still plenty left. Then you can come back in here and keep me and Grandma Elsie company until it's time for her to go.'

Lisa takes this as her cue to leave and retreats towards the door, and Tilly follows suit.

'Help yourself to a bit of cake, too, Lisa, if you want,' Amy says. 'Just leave some for Grandma Elsie to take back to the home with her.'

'Sure, thanks,' Lisa says.

Amy uncurls herself, stretches and stands up. 'I've got lots of new photos to show you,' she says to Grandma Elsie. 'There are some gorgeous ones of Rowan.'

'I'm sure there are,' Grandma Elsie says, though she sounds a little gloomy. 'The Power women always make pretty babies.'

Amy moves round to the cabinet behind the sofa where the photo albums are kept, and Lisa and Tilly make their escape.

The kitchen smells very faintly of sugar and burning, and the icing on top of the cake is pocked with little circular marks where candle holders have been stuck in and then pulled out. Maybe the old lady had got her dates muddled up, and genuinely thought there was a special occasion to celebrate, and Amy has humoured her. Or maybe she just really likes birthday cake.

Lisa and Tilly both have a slice at the kitchen table, and then Lisa puts the cake back in the box and says, 'You should probably go join the others. Your drawing things are all still in there.'

'I want you to come too,' Tilly says.

'I don't think that'd be a good idea,' Lisa says. 'I've got some other stuff to do, anyway.'

'Like what?'

Lisa shrugs. 'I always have stuff to do, Tilly.'

'So do I,' Tilly says. 'But *I* still have to go back in there.' She lets out a very small, infinitely weary sigh, and trudges off in the direction of the living room.

Lisa tidies away the tea-things and retreats up to the attic. She pictures Grandma Elsie with her head bowed, poring over the baby pictures that Lisa herself had admired not so long ago. And then she imagines Grandma Elsie standing over a bonfire in the garden, the photos she no longer wants curling into ash at her feet, her face fierce and triumphant in the reflected light of the flames.

There are always pictures that don't make it into the albums. But in their case, it's half the family that's missing.

She had told Tilly that she has plenty to do, and she does – there's always a bank statement to check, a friend to email. Not to mention the future to think about. The not-so-distant future, because Joe will be back soon and it has always been understood that she will move out then. She ought to get back in touch with her temp agency and her landlord, think about applying for jobs...

Or maybe she should look for somewhere to live closer to

here, in the countryside. It would be cheaper, and it would be easier to stay in touch.

She turns on the computer and starts composing a message to Holly, her neighbour back in Brickley, but finds she keeps starting sentences and then deleting them. She doesn't know what to say.

I've got close enough to my cousin to think of her as a friend, but I don't trust her the way I would like to and I feel sorry for her daughter. My grandmother hates my mother so much, my cousin suggested pretending that I'm the nanny. I met a weird stranger today who knew Amy, and he gave me the creeps, but he said she's a liar and I half wanted to believe him. I feel a connection to this place but sometimes it scares me. I think maybe it wasn't smart to let my guard down as far as I have. And right now, I really don't know what I'm doing here.

No, she can't say any of that. It makes her sound like someone who's got herself into a situation she ought to leave. And maybe she has, but she still doesn't feel ready to go.

There's still a very faint smell of burning candles, but perhaps she is imagining things because how could that reach up here from the kitchen? She is jumpy and out of sorts, and has been all day. Nothing adds up. She can't make sense of it to anyone else because she doesn't understand it herself.

She knows she is missing something. She feels disorientated. Lost. Part of it is the grief she has been learning to live with ever since she lost her mum. But it is also because she has allowed herself to forget how much she doesn't know.

A spider crawls across her desk and she catches it with a cup and a postcard and gets up onto the bed to put it out of the window, the way her mum had shown her to do. Mum had always been so careful to avoid killing anything, if killing could possibly be avoided. *You have to respect life*, she had told Lisa once. Even though she had often seemed to hate her own.

That beautiful view, the blue sky, the green curves of the weeping willow... all that space. Her whole flat would fit in this one attic room. How come it suddenly feels so much like a trap?

It strikes her that if someone was outside the house and looked up and saw her face in the window, she would look like a little ghost.

She is still there, kneeling on the bed and looking down at the garden, when the door behind her is flung open and Grandma Elsie comes in.

SEVENTEEN

At first the old lady doesn't say anything. She is standing on the rug by the desk, between Lisa and the door. Lisa realises she's been cornered. She drops the cup and postcard and quickly gets down off the bed. Then she pulls herself up to her fullest height and says, 'Can I help you? Are you looking for something?'

Grandma Elsie comes closer, almost close enough to reach across and touch her. She raises her hand and points at Lisa accusingly.

'I know who you are,' she says. 'You're Lisa Power. Julie's girl. I always did wonder if you'd come out of the woodwork one of these fine days. Anyway, you can't pull the wool over my eyes that easily. I don't know what you think you're doing here, but I am on to you. If you do anything to hurt Amy or her children, I swear I will make you pay for it. I will hurt you back. You may take me for a fool, but I am stronger than I look and I promise you there's life in me yet.'

'I don't want to hurt anybody,' Lisa protests. 'That's the last thing I want to do. I'm here because I want to help.'

'You want to help,' Grandma Elsie says disbelievingly. 'If

that's true, the best thing you can do is stay as far away as possible.' She shakes her head. 'What was she thinking? What was Joe thinking? Does he know you're here?' Another possibility strikes her, and she screws her face up in disgust. 'Did your mother put you up to it? Julie can stoop pretty low, but I never would have thought she'd play a trick like this.'

'My mother is dead,' Lisa says.

Grandma Elsie steps back. She looks shocked to the core. She folds her arms across her chest and seems to shrink into a smaller version of herself.

Lisa feels obliged to say something more, to offer some kind of explanation, because how can she leave it there? This is this woman's child she is talking about. How such a bitter estrangement could have come about and then lasted so long is a mystery to her. But Grandma Elsie must have loved Mum once. There has to have been a time when she cared, even if it was only when Mum was young.

'She died just before Christmas,' Lisa says. 'She fell and hurt herself, and then she contracted an infection in hospital and she died.'

Grandma Elsie says, 'Why didn't anybody tell me?'

She is eyeing Lisa suspiciously, as if Lisa has been personally responsible for keeping this information from her. Then her expression tightens into a ferocious scowl and she points at Lisa again and jabs her finger at her. 'The problem with your mother is she didn't know what side she was on.'

Amy comes hurrying in with Rowan clasped to her front.

'Grandma Elsie! How on earth did you get up here? I thought you were just going to use the bathroom. Are you all right? Is everything OK?'

Grandma Elsie's lower lip trembles. 'Nothing is OK,' she says. 'Nothing has been OK since Alice's birthday.'

The room seems to freeze. Rowan stirs and lets out a weak

little cry. Amy hushes him and pats his back and sways a little from side to side to soothe him.

'You should have told me,' Grandma Elsie says to Amy, and points at Lisa. 'About *her*. Today of all days.'

'Grandma Elsie, please, don't upset yourself,' Amy says. 'Look, it really did just come about by chance. It was actually Joe who met Lisa, and then one thing led to another...'

'One thing always leads to another,' Grandma Elsie says stiffly, 'unless you make a determined effort to stop it.'

'We just didn't want to upset you,' Amy says soothingly.

Grandma Elsie lets out a short, scornful laugh. 'Me? After everything I have been through? You think *she* can upset me?'

'No,' Amy says. 'Not really. I just didn't want to add anything more to the things you're already sad about. Especially not today. But I'm sorry. It was wrong of me. It was very special today, wasn't it? It was beautiful. I've put a piece of the cake in a Tupperware box for you to take back to the home with you.'

Amy continues to gently rock Rowan to and fro. Grandma Elsie watches them and her expression shifts again. Now she looks tortured. It's as if an intense inner struggle is playing itself out so quickly that one mood blurs into the next, like cards being shuffled: distress gives way to horror and confusion and shame, and finally, she looks bland and soft, as if she's completely lost sight of what she was so devastated about the moment before. She simpers a little and offers Amy an ingratiating smile.

'I'm so sorry, Amy. I don't know why I ended up here,' she says. 'I think I was looking for something. I didn't mean for you to worry. Been all over today, haven't I? Up, down and in my lady's chamber.'

'Don't worry at all, it's no problem,' Amy says. 'You must be very tired. Would you like to come downstairs now? Tyler's here, and he wants to take us for a little drive.'

Lisa notices that Amy doesn't explicitly say that Tyler's going to take Grandma Elsie back to her care home, presumably to avoid the old lady getting upset at the prospect of leaving behind a place that she still clearly feels attached to.

'Tyler? Who's that?' Grandma Elsie stares at her in alarm.

'You know Tyler. He helps us in the garden.'

'Oh yes. Such a worry to his mother. Poor Grace. Or he used to be. But these days, I think he's turning into quite a nice young man.' Grandma Elsie appears willing to allow herself to be mollified. Amy moves round so she's between her and Lisa, and gently ushers her towards the door.

'Take it slowly, mind. The steps can be slippy,' she says.

Grandma Elsie heads on out through the door. Once she has gone Amy looks back at Lisa and hisses, 'What did you say to her?'

'I told her my mum is dead. But I don't think she took it in.'

Amy's face clears. 'OK. That's not too bad, then. No harm done. She might not even remember anything about it. You never really know, with her.'

'Amy,' Lisa says. 'Who is Alice?'

Amy shakes her head. 'Not now. We'll talk later, I promise, but now is really not the time. Tyler's here and he's waiting. I have to go. We won't be long. Remember, Tilly's staying here with you.'

She moves off towards the stairs without waiting for Lisa's reply.

Lisa thinks of Tilly somewhere downstairs, waiting for the visit to be over. Amy's so preoccupied, and in such a rush to get Grandma Elsie out of there, she's quite capable of walking out with Rowan and slamming the door, leaving Tilly alone in the hall without reassuring her that Lisa is still here. And Lisa can't bear the thought of Tilly starting to go through the house, room by room, to look for her. The hide and seek game all over again, but with Tilly fearing that this time it is for real, that Lisa really has vanished.

She hurries off down the stairs behind Amy, who has gone down at quite a pace, obviously not wanting to leave Grandma Elsie to her own devices again.

EIGHTEEN

Lisa hangs back out of sight in the hall while Tilly says goodbye to Grandma Elsie, and tells herself that she will challenge Amy later, when she gets back. She will be direct and clear and ask Amy to tell her what she knows. Who Alice is, and why the family is so divided.

It's not just for her sake, it's for Tilly's too. No child should have to grow up in a family where so little makes sense, and it seems not only safer but also more bearable to keep it that way...

More *manageable*. The truth in this family has been managed like a bad office, where what matters is not what people do or how they treat each other but that they turn up when required.

Amy steers Grandma Elsie out to the car, then returns for Rowan, who is already strapped into his car seat. She doesn't acknowledge Lisa at all. Nor does Tilly, until Amy has gone. Then she turns to Lisa, half hopeful and half anxious – as if Lisa might rebuff her, or tell her off for something she doesn't know she's done – and says, 'What can I do until dinnertime?'

Lisa makes her suggestion, and Tilly looks pleased and agrees. They go through to the family room, where Lisa puts on the DVD of *The Little Mermaid* and they curl up on the sofa together. The familiar film, which is one of Tilly's favourites, works its magic. Tilly relaxes as soon as the opening scene unfolds, and seems to forget all the strangeness and strain of the day.

It's so comforting to feel Tilly's warm weight leaning against her side that the scene in the attic earlier seems completely unreal. Had Grandma Elsie really said, *Nothing has been OK since Alice's birthday?* And then, on being told that Lisa's mum, her own daughter, had passed away, *The problem with your mother is she didn't know what side she was on?* And to Lisa herself, *If you do anything to hurt Amy or her children, I swear I will make you pay for it?*

Lisa can't take it in. She doesn't take the film in either. It plays on, and Tilly laughs and presses her knuckles to her mouth during the scenes of storms and magical fighting, enraptured. Lisa's mind keeps circling round what Grandma Elsie had just said and the things that Amy had said to her earlier. *You must be my guardian angel. I don't believe in letting the past wreck the future. What matters is the here and now.*

And there was what Joe had said. *I'm not sure it's my place to tell you. Manslaughter. A drunken brawl. It's not your fault. It's called being a secondary victim.*

Whatever it is that Amy has yet to tell her, and has decided for reasons of her own – cowardice, convenience, maybe shame, maybe even kindness – to keep from her, it feels like something enormous and dark, something powerful enough to squeeze years of love and closeness out of both their lives and leave them with something false and partial, the broken outline of a family that has been in pieces for all these years.

And yet there's life in the family still. She's sure of it. And goodness too.

She cannot believe that her mum was a bad person or had done anything to deserve Grandma Elsie's harshness. Troubled, yes, but not bad. Anything else doesn't tally with her own memory. It doesn't add up: it isn't possible. Because Mum had loved her, and she had loved Mum.

Mum had been difficult and secretive but she had always been there. She had always been proud of Lisa, and happy to see her, even if the happiness had been so closely mixed up with sadness and bitterness that it was hard to tell it for what it was. And there had always been day-old bread, the kind that's good for toasting, right up until the day Mum died, and the smell of it mixed with the smell of cigarette smoke and alcohol, and that was the smell of home.

Here Lisa is with Tilly, and it feels like the easiest and most natural connection in the world. So why would her own grandmother have wanted to deny them this?

Eventually, the film finishes and Tilly comes into the kitchen with her and sits drawing pictures of mermaids and sea creatures while she makes their evening meal. Boiling water, pasta, pesto, tuna, grated cheese, cherry tomatoes. It's all so normal it should be reassuring and yet she does not feel reassured.

Nothing has been OK since Alice's birthday. Nothing. None of the meals, the bathtimes and bedtimes, the games, the mornings before school and the hometimes, the Christmases, the birthdays... Life has carried on here, just as it carried on in the house she grew up in. But at what cost? What had been forgotten or denied so that everybody can get on with the ruthless business of surviving, for all the years of Tilly's young life and maybe for most of her own?

Tilly has a pretend friend called Alice because that is her middle name; she is Matilda Alice Longcross. And yet there is another Alice, and Grandma Elsie had said that it began with her. *Nothing has been OK since Alice's birthday*. Does it follow that everything was OK before? So what could have happened to tear the family apart?

Lisa makes enough pasta for three and eats with Tilly, leaving Amy's share in the pot. If Amy doesn't want it, there's other stuff in the freezer and Lisa will have the leftovers tomorrow. Shouldn't be long now till Amy's back. Maybe they got caught up in traffic, or maybe Amy decided to spend a little time with Grandma Elsie at her care home, settling her. Tyler probably wouldn't mind waiting. Tyler didn't seem to mind anything where Amy was concerned.

Tilly watches a little bit of TV while she tidies up. The light coming into the kitchen begins to slope and fade but the evening is still bright. Such a beautiful summer day. A family should be happy on such a day.

Six thirty. Amy has been gone for two and a half hours on a one-hour round trip. Lisa can't remember now when she had said she'd be home, and she feels like the stereotype of a nagging wife: *Where are you? Dinner's going cold.* But she decides to text Amy anyway. She deliberates over how to phrase the message, then settles on:

What time do you think you'll be back? All well here. Hope all OK with you.

There is no reply.

She lets Tilly watch the last half hour of children's TV before it finishes for the day, half expecting Amy to walk through the door with Rowan at any minute. Because surely, even if they've got lost or had a flat tyre and Amy hadn't thought to call her or text her, it wouldn't be that much longer before she arrived back home? And then Amy would make sense of it all, and apologise, and the air would clear. Tilly would go to bed and Amy would put Rowan down in his cot and maybe then, finally, it would be possible for Lisa to say, *What was Grandma Elsie talking about?*

But where the hell is she?

What if there's been an accident? A car crash. Or something could have happened to Rowan.

But wouldn't someone let her know?

Maybe Amy's phone ran out of charge or something. Though Tyler must have a phone.

Would Amy be angry if she rang Grandma Elsie's care home? It might seem like crossing a line. But what else can she do? She helps Tilly build a tall, complex marble maze that uses all the best bits of the kit in the box, and leaves her playing with it as she goes to look for the number.

She doesn't know where Amy keeps her address book, or even if she has one, and she can't remember whether Amy had ever said what the care home is called. But there's a number saved in the phone under *Grandma* and she decides to give it a try. If Grandma Elsie herself answers the phone – though that seems unlikely – she'll just have to go ahead and ask where Amy is and hope for the best.

The line seems to ring forever. Eventually someone picks up and says, in a flat, dejected voice, 'Leafield Care Home, can I help you?'

Lisa begins to gabble. 'My name's Lisa Power, and my cousin Amy just brought my grandmother, Elsie Power, back to you after a visit. I was wondering whether Amy was still with you; I mean, still with my grandmother, because she hasn't arrived back yet.'

'Elsie Power?' The woman on the other end of the line sounds unconvinced, as if she's not sure she's ever heard of Elsie Power before.

'Yes, that's right, that's my grandmother. My cousin Amy, the one who brought her back to you, she would have had a baby with her. A little baby boy called Rowan.'

'OK, wait a minute,' the woman says brusquely. There's a creak and a thud as she puts the phone down and goes off somewhere, presumably to ask whether anybody knows about Elsie and Amy Power, and Amy's baby, but Lisa can't hear anything, and after a while the line goes dead.

She dials again, and this time somebody else answers. Lisa asks her question again and the new woman answers straight away. 'Yeah, the granddaughter was here with the baby. She left a while ago. Like maybe a couple of hours ago. Sorry, can't tell you any more than that. Is that OK?'

'Yes, thank you, everything's fine,' Lisa says automatically, because the instinct to make out that everything is OK, even if it isn't, is one of the strongest there is.

She hangs up, hesitates, checks her mobile. Still nothing from Amy. Nothing at all.

At what point does something unexplained and worrying become a full-blown, undeniable crisis? How long before she should call the police? Ring round hospitals? Call other people Amy knows?

Amy had been with Tyler. Surely she couldn't have been carjacked, or had an accident and been dragged off by a malevolent passer-by while she was waiting for help. Tyler would protect her, wouldn't he?

Or had Tyler done something to her or to Rowan?

No, no, that was impossible. He was surly and uncommunicative, but that didn't make him bad or dangerous. Just hard work. At least where Lisa was concerned.

There's a mobile number for Tyler saved in the phone. She tries that and it goes straight through to voicemail. Then she scrolls through the phone's address book and finds the entry for Tyler's mum, another mobile number saved respectfully under Mrs Paley.

Does Tyler live with her? He might do. They tend to come and go at different times, in different vehicles, but that doesn't mean anything. They could still share an address. She might still do his washing and reproach him for putting his feet up on the furniture.

She has the impression there isn't a Mr Paley around at home, but she couldn't say why exactly. Something she had overheard, or that Amy had said once? It strikes her how little she knows about the other adults who are part of the life of the house. Tyler and his mother are like her, in a way; they are there because they have a job to do. And Amy had suggested that they describe her to Grandma Elsie as a nanny. That still stings, even though Amy had quickly taken it back. The whole business of being asked to stay away during Grandma Elsie's visit has made Lisa feel precisely as if that's what she is: the hired help. Useful and valued, sure, but not part of the family.

Maybe Amy is not the only person at Hillview House who could answer Lisa's questions. Surely Mrs Paley must know a little about the family history as well. How long has she worked here? Lisa doesn't even know that.

Mrs Paley seems like an efficient, practical sort of woman who just wants to keep her head down and get through her work as quickly as possible and get out. Not someone who would welcome the chance to gossip about her employer. But if Lisa could find the right way to approach her, she might open up.

She presses the button to dial Mrs Paley's number. There. It's done now. The phone rings just long enough for her to begin to formulate a message to leave: *Sorry to disturb you like this out of the blue – it's Lisa Power here, and my cousin and her baby seem to have disappeared with your son...* And then Mrs Paley answers.

'Hello?' A TV blares in the background, then goes quiet. Lisa suspects she has interrupted Mrs Paley's viewing of a programme she likes. She sounds very slightly resentful.

Lisa explains who she is, and why she is calling. She feels suddenly foolish. She doesn't know if she is underreacting or overreacting, because nothing she has experienced before now has prepared her for how to react to her until-recently-estranged cousin leaving her in charge of a seven year old and disappearing with her baby and the gardener.

Has Amy ever done this before, to Joe? Disappeared without warning? She has no idea if this is exceptional, and if not, how worried she should be. Even after this summer, she barely knows Amy at all.

But then Mrs Paley says, 'Honestly, I'm sure there's nothing to worry about. Is Tilly all right?'

'Yes, she's fine. She's had her tea. She should go and have her bath in a sec.'

'Well, why don't you just deal with that for the time being? Maybe Amy was hungry and wanted to get a bite to eat, and to feed the baby. Most likely they've just stopped off somewhere. It's a beautiful summer evening, and it must have been a hard day for her. Who could blame her if she wants to have a breather?'

Her little girl waiting for her back home is the answer that comes to mind. Instead Lisa says, 'Then why wouldn't she call me? Neither of them are answering their phones.'

'You called Tyler too? Isn't that a little over the top? They must be in a spot with bad reception or something. You're out in the country now, you know. Phones don't always work, not everywhere. Why should you always be able to get hold of people immediately, anyway?'

'Well, it's useful to be able to get hold of them if you're expecting them back home. I'm just concerned, that's all.'

'Look, I'll see if I can make some enquiries,' Mrs Paley says. 'But I guarantee you this is a storm in a teacup and she'll walk through that front door safe and sound any minute now.'

'I was wondering if maybe I should call the police. Or how long I should leave it.'

'I think you definitely shouldn't do that,' Mrs Paley says firmly. 'All you'll do is cause embarrassment, to yourself and to your cousin. You need to cut her some slack here – and also, you need to give my boy some credit. Amy is in safe hands. Now, I'm going out this evening, but I'll have my mobile on me and I'll call you if I hear anything, and you can do the same for me. I see no need at all for this to go any further than ourselves. There are worse things people can do than take a little bit of time out when they need it. At least we know that old Mrs Power made it back to her care home safely. That's what really matters.'

With that she hangs up. Lisa tries calling Amy again and leaves another, slightly more anxious message. Then Tilly comes to her and says it is time for her bath and Lisa has to switch focus to taking care of her, just as Mrs Paley had told her to do.

Tilly makes her bath last for as long as possible, adding more hot water, bubble bath, *Little Mermaid* bath toys. As she is letting the water out the phone rings in the hall and Lisa rushes downstairs to answer it.

The phone line crackles. An unfamiliar, very distant-sounding male voice says, 'Hello? Is that Lisa?'

'Yes, it is. Who's this?'

'Lisa, it's Joe. How are you?'

'Joe! I'm OK, I'm fine. How are you?'

'Oh, it's not too bad over here on the other side of the world where it's winter and even the stars are different. But I'm really looking forward to coming home. Not too long now, just another couple of weeks. Is Amy there?'

'No... Grandma Elsie came to visit, and she's gone to take her back.'

Should she say more? She can't. It'll only worry him, and she doesn't know for sure whether there is any point in him worrying, and what can he do from where he is?

'Ah. OK. I see.'

'I'll ask her to call you the minute she gets back...'

'No. Don't worry. It'll keep till tomorrow. She'll be tired. She must have had a difficult day. I mean, it always is.'

'What do you mean?'

'What?'

'Why is it a difficult day? I can see that it's not easy having Grandma Elsie here. But is there some other reason? Because – I don't know – the whole thing has been weird. I took Tilly out for a bit and while we were gone they had a birthday cake, with candles and everything. But it isn't even anybody's birthday. And then Grandma Elsie came up to the attic when I was there and was pretty hostile, and Amy had to defuse the situation and coax her back downstairs, but before she took her away Grandma Elsie said something about Alice. She said, *Nothing's been OK since Alice's birthday*. I don't want to probe if it's none of my business, and I know Grandma Elsie is a bit confused and erratic and Amy's just trying to humour her, but still... do you know what she was talking about?'

At that moment Tilly rushes down the stairs in her pyjamas, smelling of strawberry bubble bath, her hair still slightly wet. Her face is glowing with excitement.

'Is it Daddy? Can I talk to him?'

Lisa hands over the receiver and Tilly takes it. She says, 'Daddy, is that really you?'

And Lisa backs off and retreats to the kitchen. She half expects Tilly to call her back to the phone so Joe can finish talking to her, but instead Tilly comes to find her about five minutes later and says Daddy had to go and he is going to call back tomorrow and talk to Mummy, and could she please have her bedtime story now?

Lisa is slightly disappointed not to have any answers to her questions, but part of her isn't surprised. If there is something of a conspiracy of silence going on, Joe is bound to be part of it, and would probably defer to Amy on keeping it that way.

Anyway, she's relieved that Tilly's going to go to bed happy, having spoken to her dad, and still hasn't so much as asked where Amy and Rowan are.

She follows Tilly into the hall. Tilly is telling her about what Joe had said, about how careful they are in New Zealand not to let any new plants or animals come in because they could mess up the delicate balance of everything that is already in the country, and destroy it. But Lisa doesn't really follow what she is saying, because as she moves towards the staircase she sees something that makes it impossible to concentrate on anything else.

The curtain that covers the space behind the stairs is hanging loose at one end where a curtain hook has come out of the ring. It looks as if someone has pulled it back harder than they needed to.

It wasn't like that before. She would have noticed. Which means that not so long ago, someone has been down to the basement where nobody ever goes. Which is maybe no big deal. But still – why?

She does her best not to seem distracted as she follows Tilly upstairs and waits for her to brush her teeth and reads her another chapter of Harry Potter. She tells Tilly she'll see her mum and Rowan in the morning, and Tilly accepts this as if it is an unnecessary statement of the obvious. Then Lisa turns the nightlight on and says goodnight.

She doesn't even wait ten minutes for Tilly to go off really deeply to sleep, and she gives no further thought to phoning the police. Instead she goes straight down the stairs to the hall table, takes the spare keys out of the bowl on top of it and the loose keys out of the drawer below, carefully pulls back the red curtain with its dangling end and goes down to the basement.

NINETEEN

Standing at the end of the dim, yellowing passageway, in front of the door, she holds up the bunch of spare house keys and examines them. She knows what most of them are for, but not all. She tries one at random, then a couple of others. No joy. She sticks them back in her pocket and tries one of the loose keys. It turns, and her heart gives a flutter of apprehension and anticipation. Then it sticks.

It takes what feels like a long time, too long, to get it out. She tries the next one much more cautiously.

It wouldn't do to get the wrong key stuck in the lock – it would be pretty obvious what she'd been up to. Thankfully it turns and the door gives way, and she stumbles into a cool, dim, open space.

She finds herself in a bedroom.

A child's bedroom. Sparsely furnished, dim, orderly and neat. There is a single light bulb overhead with a pink shade, but she doesn't turn it on. What light there is comes from the small window she had seen beyond the lilac in the border, the first time she went into the garden. The worn bricks of the window well are visible on the other side of the square pane of glass, reaching up to the flat black metal grid laid across the well at ground level.

The light has a faint greenish tinge from filtering through the leaves overhead, as if she's under stagnant water and everything is coloured by algae. It's like being in a prison. A prison from an old fairy story, designed for a child under a spell.

There's a faint ringing in her head, or maybe the ringing is real and it's the telephone upstairs, but she decides to ignore it. She's come too far now to stop and go back.

In front of the window is the small bookcase she had glimpsed from outside on the day of her first visit. There's also a small single bed she hadn't been able to see. The bed has been made up with a duvet cover printed with a big pink and black-and-white picture of Pierrot, and there's a pillow in a matching case. The bedlinen is not new. It's slightly faded but clean, and there are fresh crease marks in it where it has been folded and ironed. There's a pair of pink pyjamas lying neatly folded on the pillow and they, too, look freshly laundered but not new.

Next to the bed is a bedside table with a mushroom-coloured reading light and a large Micky Mouse alarm clock on it. A home-made woven dreamcatcher hangs from one corner of the bookcase, the kind of thing a child might make at school, and there are two shelves' worth of old books, some in good condition, others with broken spines and faded covers, bought second-hand, perhaps, at jumble sales or in charity shops. Or kept with someone in mind.

There's a selection of Enid Blyton stories: Famous Five, Secret Seven, Malory Towers, St Clare's. There's also a large illustrated edition of *Black Beauty*, and another of *Heidi*. Books for a girl. A girl of around Tilly's age...

To her left there is a small chest of drawers and a wardrobe, and on top of the chest of drawers is a small soft hairbrush, a purple glittery plastic comb and a pink-and-white box with a picture of Barbie as a ballerina.

She picks up the hairbrush and inspects it and sees a single blonde hair curled up in it. Short, as if from a fringe. The music box looks brand new. She opens it and a tiny ballerina with a net tutu springs up and rotates as a tinny version of the overture to *Swan Lake* begins to play. The music carries on as she opens the top drawer and sees that that there's a neatly folded pile of underwear inside. A girl's underwear. The drawer is lined with scented paper, and releases a faint smell of old lavender.

Opposite the wardrobe, pushed up against the wall to her right, is a folding Formica table with a couple of chairs on either side of it. It's clean – no dust – but there are a couple of crumbs on it. Without stopping to think, she picks one up on the tip of her finger and holds it to her tongue.

It's sweet. Very sweet. And then she allows herself to register perhaps the most peculiar thing of all, which is that the still air smells very faintly of candles and of icing sugar.

She turns to the wardrobe. It's small and white with curly gold plastic handles. The kind of wardrobe that a princessy little girl might like. She opens it and sees that there are clothes hanging there. Tilly-sized summer clothes. A yellow cardigan, a flowered sundress with a ruched bodice, a blue T-shirt, brown trousers. Plastic moth deterrent capsules hang at either end of the rail, giving off a strong smell of chemical lavender. They appear to be new.

There is a shelf at the top of the wardrobe, and on top of the shelf there is a thin blue cardboard document wallet. She reaches up to take it down, and as she moves it she hears something rustle. A piece of paper, lying underneath the folder. She takes that out, too, and sees her own handwriting.

Her letter. Her initial letter to Amy, sent to the wrong address, dated December last year.

Dear Amy, I'm sorry to get in touch with you out of the blue like this…

Amy had said she had never received the letter.

If she could lie about that, what else has she lied about?

Lisa takes both the letter and the folder over to the Formica table and pulls out a chair. The chair wobbles underneath her when she sits. Everything around her seems flimsy, as if it couldn't stand up to everyday use. Like a stage set.

She opens the folder and pulls out a sheaf of photographs.

Not that many. Perhaps four or five glossy prints in colours that suggest the past. Old summers, happier times. A smiling baby in a pushchair. A fair-haired toddler in wellies and a red coat in a country lane. The same child, by the look of it, growing into a little livewire of a kid with bright eyes and a challenging grin.

And then again, the same girl, but older now, more Tilly's age, barefoot on grass in a sundress with a smaller child crouching at her feet, the two of them deep in a game and oblivious to the camera. It looks as if the older child is telling the younger something important, and the younger child, who is around nursery-school age, is looking down at the grass, maybe watching ants crawl about.

She holds up the photo and examines it more closely. There's something very familiar about both the girls. She is sure – as far as it is possible for her to be sure about anything – that she has seen both of them before.

The older girl is wearing a sundress patterned with blue and yellow flowers and a ruched bodice. A sundress with a home-made look. It's the exact same sundress she has just seen hanging in the wardrobe.

But the younger girl... She's wearing a yellow sunhat with a pastel T-shirt and shorts. And Lisa has definitely seen that sunhat before. Hasn't she worn it? Wasn't it hers? And isn't the tree behind the girls the same old willow tree that is at the end of the lawn at Hillview House?

It's her. It has to be. Her at around age three or four, in the garden just beyond the basement window. She knew she'd been here before. And here's proof. But who is she with? And why have these photographs been hidden away, and why didn't Amy tell her about them? She must know they're here. But would Amy know who the girl was? At the time the photo in the garden was taken, Amy would have been a newborn or on the way. Or maybe not even expected yet.

And this room, this strange little room with its sparse arrangement of childish possessions. A place where Tilly had been told not to look. And Lisa herself had been asked to avoid it, too. Whatever is going on here, Amy had not wanted to tell her about it.

She closes her eyes and breathes in the cool, candle-scented air. Perhaps the strangest thing of all is that she doesn't feel frightened. Her heart is still fluttering with anxiety about Amy and her sudden disappearance and all the evidence that Amy has been keeping things from her. Secrets from the past, and perhaps also secrets from the present. But the room itself is still and quiet and calm, and she is not scared of it.

It has a little of the atmosphere of an old, beautiful church-yard, or of an ancient landmark – somewhere where the past and the present meet. And it feels like somewhere she was always meant to find, that has been waiting for her all this time. Which it has been, in a way. All summer, while she was playing with Tilly and cooking and talking to Amy and going upstairs to the attic to sleep, this was just under her feet.

The light flashes and changes and the air moves. The door squeaks open. She looks up to see Amy with Rowan in her arms, staring down at her with her most hawkish, disaffected gaze.

Amy says, 'What do you think you're doing? I told you not to come here.'

Lisa holds out the photograph of the two girls together in the garden so Amy can see it. 'I remember that yellow sunhat,' she says. 'It was mine. Why have you got a photo of me hidden in your basement? Who's the girl I'm with? And who is Alice?'

Amy takes the photo from her, holds it up and studies it. Then she reaches forward, carefully holding Rowan in place on her front with his chin resting on her shoulder, and drops the photo on the table between them.

'The older girl in the picture is Alice,' she says, 'and today is Alice's birthday. What happened to her wrecked our family. These are things that nobody has ever wanted to talk about.'

And then she offers a brief and rather grudging explanation. Lisa can barely take it in. She hears the words but they don't seem real. It's as if Amy is reading from a script, and trying to convince herself as well as Lisa. But Lisa can't believe it. She can barely believe that Amy does. Most of all, she can't believe how much her mum had failed to tell her.

PART THREE

JULIE

August 1977 to Spring 1978

TWENTY

Alice's birthday, August 1977

Julie sets her alarm for seven on the big day and forces herself up and out of bed straight away, rather than lying in the dim morning light and enjoying the chance to have a few uninterrupted waking minutes to herself. The attic curtains at Hillview House are unlined and don't keep out the sun, but on a promising summer day that's no hardship.

When she potters down to the first floor she sees that the only bedroom door that is open is her parents', revealing their modest, neatly made queen-sized bed. They always go to bed at the same time, and get up at the same time. They have that kind of marriage. Is that what it takes for a marriage to last? The idea still frightens her, which perhaps explains why, to her parents' lasting shame, she is now divorced.

Her mum is sitting at the kitchen table with yesterday's paper, doing the crossword. Dad must have gone to work already; even though he's supposed to be easing off, he finds it difficult to let go.

'There's tea in the pot. Help yourself,' Mum says. 'You sleep all right?'

'Yes,' Julie lies.

She'd actually had a really restless night, broken up by bad dreams that she couldn't remember on waking. Probably because she's anxious about Mike making good on his threat to turn up uninvited. Anyway, it won't help to tell Mum any of that. She pours out a cup of tea and sees that it's very strong and stewed. Mum must have been up for a while.

'Kitchen looks pretty,' Mum says. 'You did a good job.'

Julie had stayed up the night before, blowing up balloons, finding things in the kitchen to tie them to. She had felt a little sad to be doing this on her own. In many ways Mike had not been a great husband, but he had been very good at blowing up and tying balloons.

'Did my best,' she says, and cuts herself a couple of slices of bread for toasting. It's perfect for it – a day-old loaf, no doubt left over from yesterday. And there it is, the smell she most associates with her childhood and her parents, and that, in spite of everything, still makes her feel she's home.

Mum looks up at the kitchen clock. 'We'd best make tracks pretty soon if we're to make it to the bakery for eight,' she says.

Back in the days when Julie was still getting on with Mike, they'd laid bets each time they saw her parents about how long it would take for the bakery to come up. It's like another member of the family, perhaps a stern, hard-to-please parent or an equally demanding child. It stands for home and comfort and security but also for duty and responsibility, and for as long as she can remember, all she has wanted is to escape from it.

But today she is going back, even though it is a special day, because her sister is heavily pregnant and they are short-staffed. They had asked her, and she had agreed. She's a grown woman now, financially independent, and a mother, and she still finds it almost impossible to say no to her parents.

She spreads butter on her toast and adds some of her mum's home-made marmalade. 'I'll just eat this and pop up to say happy birthday to Alice, and then we can go,' she says, sitting down at the kitchen table.

'We do appreciate you coming in today, you know,' Mum tells her. 'We should only need you for the first couple of hours, until the morning rush dies down.'

'It's fine. Alice doesn't mind, and I'm glad to be able to help.' Another necessary lie.

Diane shuffles in, blinking behind her glasses, still in her outsize pink fluffy dressing-grown. She subsides heavily into the chair next to Julie. Mum is instantly solicitous and fetches her a cup of tea, which Diane accepts with the grace and fortitude of a particularly saintly invalid.

'The girls are awake,' Diane says to Julie. 'I could hear them chatting to each other. It was very sweet.' She runs a hand over her bump. 'I think this little one could hear them too. I get the feeling he can't wait to join the fun.'

'Or she,' Julie says. 'It could be a girl, you know.'

'Or she,' Diane concedes.

'You should both come and stay again next summer,' Mum says. 'Give your children a chance to get to know each other. It'll be lovely for them all to play together as they're growing up, and we might as well make the most of it now we've got the space.'

'That sounds perfect,' Diane says.

Julie gets up and puts her plate and cup by the sink. Diane says, 'Why don't you leave those, Julie? I can sort out the washing-up later. You and Mum had better be on your way.'

'OK, thanks. I won't be a minute,' Julie says, and heads upstairs.

The girls are sharing the smaller of the spare rooms on the first floor, with Diane in the other – there'd been no question of Diane being put up in the attic, and having to go up and down an extra flight of stairs. Julie could see the sense of this, but it meant her being in the attic, away from the girls, and it had felt like yet another reminder that she was at the bottom of the pecking order. Diane's fiancé Elliott had spent the night in the flat above the bakery in Kettlebridge, where he and Diane were living in not-quite-sin together; he would have been hard at work for a couple of hours already this morning, having got up at five to fire up the ovens.

As she reaches the landing she can hear the girls' voices, but she can't quite make out what they are saying. She can't resist the temptation to eavesdrop – it's a chance to spy on a world that she is not part of. The relationship between Alice and Lisa exists in part because of her, but it's separate from her, and she hopes with all her heart that it will outlive her. She pauses outside the door to listen.

Alice is explaining something to Lisa, patiently and painstakingly, like an adult talking to a young child. It's very touching to hear. It's as if Alice is already rehearsing the way she'll be if she has children of her own one day.

'When it is my birthday,' Alice is saying, 'I will always be four years older than you. I am seven and you are three. When you are seven, I will be eleven. When you are twenty, I will be twenty-four. When you are a hundred, I will be a hundred and four...'

Her girls. Her beautiful girls.

Sisters don't always get along, as she knows all too well. And they squabble sometimes, inevitably. But on the whole, Alice and Lisa make a pretty good duo, and she can't help but be proud of them and how well they get along.

Their personalities have turned out to be quite different, which probably helps. Two Alices in one family would be too much for anyone to cope with. Lisa is shy, placid and gentle, a watcher rather than a doer, and Alice is, in the best possible way, a handful. Lisa always wants to stick as close to her older sister as possible, so as not to miss out on any of the fun that is part of what you get with Alice, along with occasional chaos. And Alice takes great pleasure in showing Lisa things and telling her how they work, and congratulates her fulsomely whenever Lisa proves capable of doing something for herself.

They are both endearingly excited about the baby Diane is going to have, their little cousin... Unlike Diane herself, Alice is convinced it is going to be another little girl.

Maybe Mum's right. Maybe this could be an annual thing, getting together in the summer holidays, celebrating Alice's birthday together. Maybe it really is possible for the family to be closer. Especially with Mike out of the way, and Diane and Elliott making a success of taking on the bakery, and Mum and Dad beginning to step back.

After all, that's why she's here, isn't it? Her girls are like a bridge, and they have made it possible for her to return to the fold. She might have fallen out with her parents, but she never wanted to sever ties with them completely, and once she'd become a mum it had been clear to her that a permanent estrangement would be impossible. Children need to know where they come from. It's up to them to decide whether to keep on going back.

And she's pleased, finally, that she had agreed to help out at the bakery that morning. Mum was right, she'd been a bit neurotic about leaving Diane to babysit. OK, so Diane doesn't have much experience with kids – yet – but she's got plenty of common sense, and they're good girls, at the end of the day. They'll all be fine, and it's not for long. Julie will be back before she knows it.

She knocks on the girls' bedroom door and pushes it open. Alice must have drawn the curtains – the room is pink and white and light. The girls are both still in their pyjamas, sitting cross-legged and facing each other on the carpet like a teacher and a student at a yoga class.

Alice leaps up and cries out, 'Mummy!' as Julie comes in, and hurls herself at her and wraps her arms round her and holds her tight. Lisa gets up, too, and totters over to join in the hug.

'Happy birthday, Alice,' Julie says. 'Seven years old! You're getting to be such a big girl now.'

'I know I am, Mummy,' Alice says importantly. 'I've just been explaining to Lisa all about it. I am always going to be a little bit bigger than her, and that means I will always help you look after her.'

'Good girl, Alice. I hope you will,' Julie says. 'Sisters are very important. You need to take care of each other.'

As she embraces them and breathes in their smell – sleep-warm, familiar skin, bedlinen and strawberry shampoo – she is suddenly filled with an abundance of hope for the future. After all, it's going to be a beautiful day.

The morning at the bakery is trouble-free to begin with. To her surprise, she enjoys being back. She'd been press ganged into working there at the weekends as a teenager, and she'd done it reluctantly then, but now she finds herself taking pleasure in it: the smell of cakes and buns and bread, the greetings from customers who remember her, the satisfaction of the coins ringing in the till. She even begins to daydream about finding herself a similar job – she does admin for a builder's merchant at the moment, which is OK, but she could do with a change. Or maybe she could even move back round here and finally join the family business, just like her parents always used to hope she would do.

Then her dad bursts out of the kitchen and she knows at once that something has gone terribly wrong. That's the moment when everything begins to change and fall away, and when she looks back later, knowing what was to follow, she will often wish that she was the one who had not survived it.

TWENTY-ONE

'You'd better come to the office. Something's happened,' Dad
says. He turns to Mum, who is standing next to her, almost as an
afterthought. 'You too.'

Mum starts to stay something, but he ignores her and she
falters and falls silent. It is suddenly very quiet. The small
queue of waiting customers have frozen as if they, too, are
waiting to hear what is going on.

'I'm sorry, we're closed,' Dad says. 'Family emergency.'

They turn and hurry out. He goes out into the shop front
and bolts the door behind them, and turns round the *Open* sign.
Then he comes back through to the area behind the counter and
says to Julie, 'I think you need to hear this for yourself.'

She doesn't object. She has lost the ability to speak. He
ushers her through to the little office at the back, to the side of
the kitchen, with Mum following close behind them. She is
conscious of him watching her and Mum standing anxiously by,
close to either anger or tears or both, as she picks up the
receiver.

Her hand is trembling. Her whole body seems to be trembling, as if she has come down with a sudden fever.

'Julie, is that you? It's me. Diane.' Diane sounds weird, as if she's very far away. 'There's been an accident. I think you'd better come as soon as you can.'

'What do you mean, an accident? Who's had an accident?'

'It's Alice. She was in the willow tree. She was climbing, and then she fell.'

'But that's impossible. She wouldn't go climbing a huge great tree like that. She's never climbed a tree in her life.' As Julie says this, she realises that Alice has never before had access to a garden with a tree big enough to climb.

'I think you'd better come,' Diane says tonelessly.

'But she can't have fallen,' Julie repeats.

Very gently, her dad takes the phone from her. 'I'll drive,' he says, and puts the receiver back in its cradle.

As they follow him out she can't take in the questions that Mum is asking. She is able to move, but her brain feels as if it has been paralysed. All she can hear is what Diane had said: *She was climbing and then she fell.*

And then she begins to hear what Diane had *not* said. *She's fine, don't worry, but you need to get over here ASAP. They think she might have broken something, but she's going to be OK.*

Alice belongs in the present. But Diane had spoken of her in the past.

She was climbing and then she fell.

They don't talk on the way. Something strange has happened to time, making it slow and fast at the same time. And perhaps this is a kind of mercy. Because if what has happened to Alice is truly terrible, if it is the worst news she can imagine, then she never wants to find out. Much better never to arrive at the house, for time to be suspended and to stop right here, with them on their way, because what would be the point of time without Alice, what sense could she possibly make of anything without her child—

The sun is still shining. The countryside is still lovely.

Unnecessarily lovely, if what they are not telling her is true, and Alice is no longer here to see it.

It is only now that she realises how much her oldest child was at the heart of everything. Her reason for carrying on after the mess of her marriage and her divorce. Her hope for the future. Her prize.

And then her dad pulls up on the gravel beside the house, next to the ambulance and the police car, and she gets out and runs.

She crosses the lawn. Her breathing is hard and tight. It's like being in a dream, as if she herself is flying or falling towards disaster. Under the willow tree she can see a paramedic leaning over a small, prone, lifeless body in a yellow summer dress.

Alice.

She is seeing for herself what she had begun to fear the minute she heard Diane's voice on the phone in the bakery. Alice has gone. That spirited, wilful, independent presence. The oldest child. The firstborn. The big sister. That child is lying on the green grass in her yellow dress and the sky overhead on her birthday is still blue. But somehow she has gone.

A policeman approaches her and says, 'Are you Alice's mum?'

'Yes, I am. I'm Julie Power.'

'I'm sorry, I have to ask you to keep back for now. We have to let the paramedics do their work. They're trying to resuscitate her. If I could perhaps ask you to come with me?'

'How long have they been trying?'

'I think maybe half an hour or so.'

'Half an hour?'

They look at each other. Maybe this man, who has a long, soft, doleful face and a slightly drooping moustache to match, is a parent too. Maybe he's thinking of his own children. Of when he'd last held them close, or whether he'd parted from them on a cross word that morning. Isn't that what someone else's bad news always makes you think? Of your own dear ones, and whether you would have loved them well enough if it was your turn to say goodbye?

'Half an hour,' Julie repeats wonderingly.

What are the odds? Would it be a miracle if Alice were to revive now, and suddenly sit up and come back to consciousness and start talking?

But it is impossible for her to be dead. She will live. She has to live. She's the most vividly alive person Julie has ever known, a force of nature wrapped up in the body of a seven-year-old girl. And she was sitting cross-legged in her pink pyjamas just that morning, telling Lisa she'd always be four years older than her.

Julie allows the policeman to steer her round to the side of the house, to the scrubby patch of grass by the back door that Mum has been planning to turn into a herb garden. She is docile, in shock perhaps. She doesn't shriek and howl and tear her clothes and look for someone to attack. It's as if the maternal part of her that has grown used to protecting her children – from lack of money, or evil strangers, or Mike's drunken mood swings – is shielding Alice still, trying to avoid scaring her with the violence of her fear. Because being frightened is contagious. She knows that. Anything you feel rubs off on your children. Even if they don't always understand, they pick it up.

But Alice has been hurt. That means she has failed. Even if she was not here in the house at the time. Even if it was an accident. Alice is her child. Her responsibility. If anything happens to her, Julie is the one to blame.

All the other people around Alice, in the garden or the house or elsewhere, are like figures in a chorus. Julie is aware of them, but they don't hold her attention, not now, not while Alice is lying on the lawn, hurt, unconscious, being tended to. Not dying, though. Not that. Because that can't have happened.

That is just what she is beginning to think because it is what she is most afraid of.

The paramedics... the police... Lisa and Diane, who are presumably in the house. Her parents, who might be in the garden somewhere, or who have maybe gone inside. Mike, who will have to be told. Other people, with their needs and probable wants. Right now, none of them really matter. What is happening to Alice is huge and terrible enough to drown everything and everyone else out.

And yet she is glad that Alice is out of sight, even though she is Alice's mum, and had been the very first person to study her face, to look into her eyes, to hold her and be held by her – the grip of that tiny hand on her forefinger! Alice is a person as well as a child, and at extreme moments any person deserves privacy. And this is extreme. She understands that from the way she was ushered over here, where she can't see what is happening. And she has no right, and no desire, to watch the struggle going on over Alice's body.

All she wants is to see Alice walking on her own two feet again, whole and safe as she had been when Julie said goodbye that morning. To wrap her arms around her and feel her warm and breathing. She wouldn't scold her about climbing the tree, wouldn't make a big deal of it. Wouldn't need to. After all, Alice would have had a good scare and she'd have learned her lesson. She'd most likely never climb a tree again....

Inside, hidden away, is the pile of presents Julie had made her wait to open till that afternoon, when they would all be back in the house. Alice hadn't even seen her cake yet. The most beautiful cake the bakery had to offer, covered with smooth pale-blue icing and decorated with little icing-sugar flowers. A cake fit for a princess, tucked away in one of the kitchen cupboards. It was going to be such a wonderful surprise.

One of the paramedics comes away from the scene under the willow tree and approaches her. She's a brisk, purposeful, strong-looking woman with a ponytail, a bit younger than Julie. She looks like she knows what she's doing. She looks like this part of it is the absolute last thing she wants to do.

And Julie knows straight away, before the other woman has even started speaking, that the news she is bringing is the worst news in the world. And is the end of the world, as Julie has known it, and of the world she had helped to make and hoped to live the rest of her life in. The world that had Alice in it.

She listens to what the paramedic has to say, because what else can she do? She has to hear it. She doesn't fall down in a dead faint, or collapse into hysterics, or turn and run away. She is aware of clasping her hands as if to pray, even though she isn't religious and doesn't believe in prayer. *Please. Please, bring my child back to me.* She is conscious of the sound of leaves stirring in the breeze, of the grass underfoot, everything growing and alive. And Alice, not. Alice is the sudden still point in the middle of all of this, and in her own heart, which has surely stopped too, even though it seems to still be beating.

The paramedic looks Julie in the eyes as she talks to her, and Julie wants to look away and can't. It's as if she has fallen over a cliff-edge, and this woman is extending a hand to her and urging her to hold on. And she does hold on. She knows she has to, even if all she wants right now is to let go. Because it's not just her life that is at stake. She still has Lisa. She still has a child who needs her.

She hears the words. *Basal fracture of the skull. Her heart stopped.* And then she allows herself to be led across the lawn to see Alice and be with her again.

Alice who has already gone. A little girl on her seventh birthday, who will never get the chance to be anything more. Who will always be as perfect as she was that morning, so eager and excited for the day ahead, but willing to wait till tea-time for the presents she would never get to open.

It is like a painting. The broken child on the ground in her stained yellow dress, which has been cut open at the front so the paramedics could reach her chest. Her heart. They have been trying to shock Alice's heart, to restart it. But what hope could there have been? She must have been past saving from the moment she hit the ground.

They had tried. That was something. People who didn't even know Alice, and had never seen her before. They had tried and tried to change this bad new world they were all now in, so that Alice could return and put it back to rights.

Perhaps Julie is not the only one who feels the force of this as if she, too, has fallen, and all the air has rushed out of her lungs. She can hear the slightly harsh, ragged breathing of the woman standing just behind her, the paramedic who had seemed so strong, and it is the sound of someone fighting back tears. The moment of goodbye matters, even if you are not the one who is going to say it.

And then there is a white nest next to Alice's body, made of towels from the house. Soft, fluffy bathroom towels, not the old ones, ragged and worn, that the children use to play on in the garden. She registers the kindness of it even though she is beyond caring about her own comfort.

She lies down in the white nest and gently, very gently, takes Alice's hand.

There is blood, but she is barely conscious of it. The blood is neither here nor there, any more than it had been when it was her own blood caked in the tiny wisps of Alice's downy hair when she first held her, just after the birth.

That time comes back to her very vividly as she lies next to Alice now. The pulse under the skin under the hair with its clots of blood. The visible pulse of the newborn brain, the bones of the skull not yet fused into place across it to protect it. It had been just the two of them then, and it is like that now, except Alice has slipped away, leaving her body behind like the husk of something she never really needed.

'Wake up, Alice,' she says, very gently, because she knows in her heart of hearts that even if Alice could hear her, it's beyond her to obey. Alice has gone somewhere she can't follow. Somewhere it is not given to her to know about. But it is not nowhere, she is sure of that.

As she lies there and holds Alice's small and still-warm hand and listens to the sound of her own breathing and Alice's silence and the breeze riffling the willow leaves, it dawns on her that Alice has not vanished, and is instead somehow more present than she has ever been.

It's as if Alice has left behind more than her body, and more than traces – as if there is a shimmer lingering in the air that she has disappeared into, too faint or perhaps too bright to see. And the shimmer that was once Alice is there for Julie too, even though she is not yet ready to give herself up to it.

TWENTY-TWO

The time she spends lying there with Alice goes by as swiftly as seconds and as slowly as centuries. But eventually she has to let go of her hand and get up. Mum helps her to her feet and she goes back into Hillview House because she cannot bear to watch while they take Alice away. It begins to sink in that the disaster of Alice's fall means that she has forfeited a mother's ordinary right to care for and tend her child. Now strangers are going to do it. And this is not just the strangers' right, but their duty. Alice had looked so helpless lying there as Julie walked away, and now Julie is helpless too.

She sits down at the kitchen table while Mum fusses around with cups and the kettle, the way people do when something bad happens. Alice's birthday balloons are still bobbing all around them. The accident seems far-fetched and unreal, like an alien invasion or news of a plague on the way.

Perhaps someone will come in and tell them they've made a mistake, and Alice is sitting up and taking notice and is going to make a full recovery. She might just have a broken arm or leg, perhaps. Or cracked ribs, or a fractured collarbone. Concussion. Injuries that would require a short stay in hospital under observation, maybe even an operation followed by exercises to help her recover. These are the kind of things that actually happen – the kind of things that were difficult, but that you could get through and survive.

Then Diane comes into the kitchen.

Soft, pretty, conscientious Diane. The one of whom their mum had always said, *She'll make such a good mother*. Diane, who is just weeks away from having her own baby, and has approached impending motherhood with the sort of dewy-eyed hope and optimism that only a first-timer could ever be capable of. And who, in her own gentle, unassuming way, is wildly competitive and always had been. Who has been a better daughter than Julie, and probably a better sister, and who no doubt intends to be a better wife, which she would be able to do just by staying married, as Julie had failed to do...

Has Diane wanted to be a better mother too?

But all that has changed, because Diane had been the one in charge when Alice died. Her own niece. And yet Diane had always been good to Alice. And Alice had liked her. That in itself makes it impossible for Julie to hate her, although she might feel better if she could.

Diane comes closer and looks down at Julie, and Julie looks up at her.

Julie feels as if perhaps she should stand, reach out to Diane, embrace her. As if it is down to her to make the first move, and show that Diane has been forgiven, or at least exonerated.

But she stays sitting exactly as she is. Perhaps she does blame Diane. Why shouldn't she? Why should she care how terrible Diane must feel?

Mum stops fussing with the teapot, keeps quiet and maintains her distance. Sunshine streams into the ancient kitchen, illuminating the motes of dust suspended in the air so that they glitter like tiny particles of gold. The kitchen clock ticks quietly and relentlessly on overhead.

'You mustn't blame yourself,' Julie says to Diane. The words sound stiff and insincere, as if she means the opposite.

And then she finds herself saying, 'I never should have left you here with them both. If you're in no fit state to cope with a morning on your feet in a bakery, you're in no fit state to spend the morning looking after my children. I was worried that it would be too much for you. I should have talked to you about it. But I didn't even ask, and I let Mum convince me that it would be all right.'

'You can't blame me for this,' Mum says. She sounds shrill and frightened. 'How was I to know that Alice would go and do something like that the minute Diane's back was turned? How were any of us to know?'

'You didn't need to know. You just needed to watch,' Julie says to Diane.

Diane puts her hand to her face as if Julie has just hit her. She is suddenly ashen pale. Mum swoops forward just in time to catch her as she sinks gently down to the floor, as if guided by a choreographer. And then Diane sits up a little, in exactly the way Alice had failed to do, and she looks dazed but more like herself.

'You fainted,' Mum says to her. 'You stay there. I'll get you some water.'

Julie decides to leave them to it. She slips away and trudges upstairs to the room that Alice had shared with Lisa, and lies down on Alice's put-you-up bed.

The duvet cover is the one that Mum always reserves for Alice, pink with a Pierrot design. Julie closes her eyes and breathes in the smell of her: a sweet ghost of a smell, like the scent of soap on your hands after you've forgotten you washed them, or like flowers at a distance on a hot day. She remembers

standing in this same room with the girls just that morning, and
how tightly Alice had embraced her.

What it must have been like for Alice in those final
moments? The panic as she lost her grip or her foothold, the
impact, the pain. The darkness. Had she had time to realise
what was happening to her? Had she known that people were
trying to save her? Had she thought of her mum, her dad, her
sister? And had any of them, or anything, been any comfort
to her?

Then the bedroom door opens and someone comes in.

Not Mum or Dad, or Elliott or Diane. Someone small with
a light step. A child. With her eyes closed, in a state somewhere
between shock and hallucination and dreaming, she could
almost believe it is Alice.

She opens her eyes and sees that it's Lisa.

Lisa, who is just three years old. No one would expect her
to understand what has just happened. And yet it seems that in
some simple, fundamental way, she does. Almost as if she is
much older than she really is.

She comes quietly towards Julie, as if she thinks she might
be asleep and doesn't want to wake her. Then she comes closer
still and reaches out and puts her warm little hand in Julie's, for
all the world like an old-fashioned doctor on a home visit who is
trying to give reassurance. Her touch instantly reawakens the
very fresh and recent memory of lying with Alice out in the
quiet underneath the willow tree.

Lisa says, 'Mummy, are you all right?'

'I am all right, thank you, Lisa,' Julie says. 'I'm just sad.
Very, very sad.'

Lisa doesn't reply. Instead, she settles on her knees at Julie's
bedside and leans forward against the mattress, resting her head
on her free arm. The other is still stretched out towards Julie
and she carries on holding Julie's hand. The two of them are

perfectly still and there is no sound in the sunny room apart
from their breathing.

Julie closes her eyes again and is grateful that even in the
throes of horror and disaster it is still possible for her to find
some comfort. There is, after all, still a reason for her to carry on
living. But she remembers she has to get on the phone to Mike
and tell him what has happened, and then she can feel nothing
but dread.

TWENTY-THREE

It takes a while to get hold of Mike. When she does, at first he can't believe it. Then he is furious. She holds the phone at a slight distance from her ear and wonders why she had felt she ought to be the one to tell him. But who else could she have asked? Mum? Dad? Not Diane. Or Elliott. No, he is her ex-husband and the father of her children. She had to be the one to make the call.

She doesn't know how to tell him about the shimmer she had seen and not seen. She can't comfort him with that glimpse of knowledge that Alice is both gone and not gone, because she is barely sure of it herself: it's like something seen out of the corner of the eye that vanishes if you make a conscious effort to focus on it.

He makes her repeat what had happened. Once, then twice. And she tries her best to answer, but her replies don't seem to satisfy him. They seem inadequate to her too. None of it makes sense. How can it? Is she beginning to lose her mind? She feels as someone might who has been interrogated for a long time, who barely knows what the truth is any more. There's only one fact that really matters, which is that Alice is gone. And nothing is going to change that.

'So you weren't there? And she was climbing the tree? How long she was climbing it for? And where was Lisa when this was happening? And where was Diane, who was supposed to be looking after them both? Where was your sister when our little girl was about to fall to her death?'

'It wasn't Diane's fault,' Julie says mechanically. 'It happened so quickly. All she did was go back into the kitchen for a minute. It was an accident.'

What Mike wants is someone to blame and she won't give him that. She won't say it's Diane's fault. It's not that she isn't tempted to. She is. But she won't because she knows it wouldn't be true. And if she loses sight of the truth, she really will be completely lost.

Then Mike begins to cry. And he never cries. It's such a strange, shocking sound that at first Julie doesn't recognise it for what it is. He weeps at the thought of Alice in the mortuary, labelled and stored in a fridge, then being laid out on a slab, poked and prodded and examined. Alone or surrounded by strangers.

'We'll be able to see her,' Julie says, 'after the post-mortem. They'll release the body to the undertakers.'

'Well, how long will that be?'

'I don't know,' she whispers.

'You,' he says savagely, 'don't know anything.'

'Is there someone you can be with, Mike? Someone who can keep you company tonight?'

'Don't be like that. All caring and concerned. I thought I was supposed to be the bad parent. And you were meant to be a good mum. But look how that turned out. This happened on your watch, Julie. I'm never going to forgive you for this,' he says, and then he begins to cry convulsively again and she hangs up.

Without Mike's voice in her ear the living room seems very quiet. Too quiet. Without Alice around, the silence in this place is unbearable. Maybe she should just get in the car and take Lisa home. It's less than an hour to Brickley. They could be there by dinnertime. Why would she want to stay here any longer? How could she be expected to, when every time she looks out of the windows that face the garden and sees the willow tree, she remembers lying underneath it and holding Alice's hand for the last time? Diane has gone – Elliott had taken her to hospital to get her checked out, and then they had gone back to the flat above the bakery. She should go too.

But Mum makes it clear that she wants her to stay.

'Let me look after you,' she says. 'And Lisa. Till after the post-mortem, at least.'

And Julie gives in. It's like being trapped in the middle of a storm. Being here is unsafe, but to leave seems impossible.

The following morning Lisa does something naughty and quite out of character – she raids the biscuit jar and leaves chocolatey fingerprints on the upholstery of the living room sofa. Attention-seeking, perhaps. Or maybe it's the instinct to eat for comfort, a way of reminding herself that she is still alive.

The first Julie knows of this transgression is when Lisa comes to the kitchen table for lunch and it's clear she has been crying. Julie immediately assumes it must be because of Alice, and feels terrible – the poor little thing is grieving too, she has neglected her, she must try to find a way to make it better, and yet how can she? But then Mum explains what had happened, and Lisa sits at the table sniffing and eyeing the sandwich Mum has made for her as if it's a challenge from an enemy.

'Do stop fussing, Lisa, and eat up like a good girl,' Mum says. 'I hope you haven't spoiled your appetite.'

Lisa scowls. 'Don't want it.'

'Well, you're not getting anything else,' Mum says, and fixes her with a glare.

And that triggers a childhood memory Julie had long since buried and forgotten: sitting alone at the dining room table in the flat above the bakery with a plate of cold food in front of her. A chop under congealed gravy. Waxy new potatoes. Diane had finished and had been allowed to get down, and was watching TV with Dad. Mum had already cleared the table. And she had to sit there until she'd cleared her plate. But she couldn't begin to imagine how she was ever going to force it down.

'You don't have to eat it if you don't want it, Lisa,' Julie says quickly.

Lisa picks up one of the quarters of her sandwich and nibbles at it, then eats it and manages another quarter before looking up at Julie and saying plaintively, 'No more.'

'OK. Is there anything else you would like?'

Lisa shakes her head.

'OK, you can go and play, then.'

Lisa scampers off. Mum says, 'Obviously it's not my place to tell you what to do, but I think you'll find you need to stick to a few ground rules. Even little children can be quite manipulative, you know. They can be very good at working out what they can and can't get away with.'

'She's three years old, Mum. She's not exactly some kind of criminal mastermind.'

'Look, I wasn't going to tell you this,' Mum says. 'But after she stole the biscuits, she lied about it.'

'So what? She may only be three years old, but she's still smart enough to figure out when she's about to get into trouble.'

'Yes, but this was different, Julie. *She used Alice as an excuse.*' Mum lowers her voice to a whisper to mention Alice's name, as if someone – maybe even Alice herself – might overhear and start to raise hell. 'She said Alice told her to do it.'

Julie is at a loss for words. Mum says, 'I'm sorry, dear. I didn't want to upset you.'

'Oh, you haven't upset me.' Julie pushes back her chair and gets to her feet. She finds herself jabbing a finger at her mother's startled face. Suddenly, she is consumed by rage, as red-hot and destructive as a raging fire. 'You've made me furious.'

'I don't understand,' Mum says. She looks shattered, and as lost as a child accused of something they haven't done, which just makes Julie feel even more angry because Mum isn't the child here, Lisa is, and surely right now the last person whose feelings she should have to worry about is her mother.

'What does it matter if Lisa took a couple of biscuits? She can eat the whole packet for all I care. Her sister is dead!'

'I know, and you don't need to shout at me—'

'My daughter is dead, and all you can do is fuss about a few biscuit crumbs—'

Julie falls silent. Some sixth sense tells her that she is being watched, and she turns and sees Lisa standing in the doorway. Lisa looks absolutely crestfallen and wretched, as if she has just done the worst thing it would ever be possible to do. Then she turns tail and runs.

'It's obvious what happened,' Julie tells her mother. 'Obviously Alice must have said something about taking the biscuits when she was still alive. Lisa is only three years old. I think that under the circumstances, allowances can be made for her being a little bit confused about the sequence of time.'

Mum folds her arms and shakes her head. 'Julie, I know you are going through something terrible. We all are. Our hearts are broken. But even when everything is falling apart, children still need to know the difference between truth and lies and they need to know that the difference matters, and that the adults around them care about it.'

'They need to know that they're loved,' Julie tells her. 'That's all they need. And you don't love Lisa. You never have.'

'That is not true.'

'It is. You're not even interested in her. You were disappointed in her because she was another girl and you were hoping for a grandson. Just like you've always been disappointed in me. I guess it wasn't the kind of thing you wanted to have to tell your regulars about in the bakery. Your disgraced daughter. The first divorce in the family. Not that anybody who knew us would have been surprised.' She pauses to draw breath. 'You were fond of Alice. I'll give you that,' she says. 'Alice was the only thing I ever did that you were proud of. But now she's gone there's nothing left, is there?'

Her mother gets to her feet too. 'Maybe you've been thinking some of these things for a long time and maybe you haven't,' she says. 'But I can tell you this, no matter what's happened, I won't be spoken to like that in my own house.'

'Then we'll leave,' Julie says. 'And then that won't be a problem, will it?'

Mum's face crumples. 'Don't go,' she says. 'Not like this. I'm sorry, Julie. I didn't mean it.'

But Julie won't hear a word of it. As far as she's concerned, it's too late. She can't bear to stay a minute longer, and now it is finally clear to her what she needs to do, she can't imagine what good she had thought might come of trying to be closer to her family in the first place.

She packs in a rush. Mum comes upstairs once and pleads briefly with her to stay, then goes away again. Then her dad comes up. He's wearing the old shirt that he puts on to prune the roses – Mum must have called him in from the garden to talk to her. She tells him not to bother. Her mind is made up, and he won't be able to talk her out of leaving. He looks frightened and helpless, and she picks up their suitcase and pushes past him.

. . .

It is not until she is about halfway through the drive home that she realises she has left some of Alice's things behind.

The presents... What happened to them? And what about Alice's books, and her pyjamas? Maybe Mum had taken them when she spirited away Alice's bedding and moved Lisa's put-you-up bed into the attic with Julie. That had been prompted by Lisa asking when Alice was going to come to bed, as if she really did expect Alice to materialise out of nowhere and go to sleep next to her.

Maybe it would have been better to leave everything as it was, and let Lisa keep on asking questions and keep on answering them...

There are bound to be other things of Alice's left behind at the house. A few bits and pieces of washing in the laundry bag. Some toys, maybe. And what about her hairbrush? She can't remember packing it.

She is half tempted to turn around and go straight back, but she doesn't.

It's not far. She can pop back any time, or ask Mum to post things to her. It's not as if they've said goodbye for ever. It's just goodbye for now. And Mum will forgive her. She'll have to, won't she? How are they ever going to manage to carry on at all unless they can learn to forgive each other?

'It'll be good to get back home,' she says out loud.

But Lisa doesn't respond. Julie glances over her shoulder and sees that she has fallen asleep in the backseat. She looks pale and exhausted and very, very small. Poor little mite. Of course she is suffering too. It must be absolutely baffling for her. How could she be expected to understand it? How could anyone understand it?

Yes, it's high time they were back home.

Julie turns back to focus on the road ahead. She mustn't leave it too long before sorting through Alice's things. It wouldn't be fair to Lisa to have all of that around her. It would just confuse her.

Maybe one day Lisa won't even remember that there had been a time when she and her older sister had shared a room.

TWENTY-FOUR

A week later Julie takes Lisa on the bus to Kettlebridge, and on the way she tries to prepare herself to meet Mike for the first time since the accident. It's easier to think about Mike than Alice. She is so tired she doesn't really trust herself to drive, and she knows it's going to be a hard day.

Mike has been all over the place, and keeps ringing her up, which frankly she could do without. She understands it. He has lost Alice too. He'd been less close to her, in a day-to-day way, as the absent parent. But he adored her, always had. There'd even been a time when he'd threatened to go for custody – had suggested that he could have Alice, and she could have Lisa. Something she would never tell Lisa about, especially not now. Anyway, he'd given up soon enough.

They get off the bus in the centre of Kettlebridge and walk to the car park round the corner from the undertaker's. It's a hot day, maybe one of the last warm days of the summer. Her dad is waiting for them in his car with the windows wound down at the front to keep it cool. No sign of Mike yet. She suppresses a flash of irritation. There's still half an hour before they're due to meet. Plenty of time. Mike wouldn't be late for this. For something so important.

Oh, who is she trying to kid? Mike's always late. Barely in time for his own wedding. It would be entirely in character for him to keep her hanging round now.

Her dad gets out of the car and takes the overnight bag she'd packed for her and Lisa from her, and puts it in the boot. He says, 'Why don't you wait in the car? I'm sure he'll be here soon.'

'He'd better be,' she says.

Dad opens the rear passenger door for Lisa to climb in. Julie gets in at the front and Dad settles back into the driver's seat next to her.

'I've got something for a certain someone,' he says to Julie, with a wink cast back over his shoulder in Lisa's direction. 'Just a gingerbread biscuit from the bakery. Is it OK if I give it to her?'

'Sure, go ahead,' Julie says. 'As long as you're not worried about crumbs in the car.'

'I never worry about crumbs. Crumbs are a good sign,' Dad says. He turns back to Lisa and says, 'See that brown paper bag on the seat next to you? Open it up and you'll find something for you inside.'

Lisa's eyes open very wide and she murmurs a thank you and takes the gingerbread man out of the paper bag with slightly fearful gratitude, as if it's tempting fate to accept a gift. Her reservations seem to disappear as she starts eating.

Dad studies her briefly, as if to satisfy himself that she's preoccupied, and then turns back to Julie and says in a low voice, 'How's Mike going? I mean, how's he taking it?'

Julie shrugs. 'Badly. As you'd expect.'

Dad looks as if he's about to respond to this, but thinks better of it. 'Your mum's looking forward to seeing you,' he says instead.

'That's nice,' Julie says, and then feels mean. But she can't say she's looking forward to it too, because she isn't. She isn't looking forward to anything right now, and why should she?

She has agreed to go to Hillview House later, to have dinner with them all and then take Lisa back home the next day. She supposes she has to get used to it – to seeing Diane. Maybe it will make it easier when Diane has her baby. She doesn't want to have bitter feelings about that baby – and maybe when the baby's actually here, the bitterness will disappear – but she is afraid that she might.

Her parents want the best for her, she knows that. They always have. It's just that their ideas of what the best might mean has always been different to hers. And now she realises that she had the best when she had Alice, and she has lost it and she will never have it again.

But she has to at least stay alive. For Lisa's sake, if not for her own. Because no one wants to see Lisa an orphan as well as... what is the word for a sister who has lost a sister? Why is there no word for it?

Who would have thought that Alice – the noisy, naughty one, who had always seemed so emphatically alive – could have been so swiftly and completely obliterated?

And then Mike appears next to her, and stoops to speak to her through the open car window. 'Sorry I'm a bit late,' he says. 'Shall we go and do this, then?'

He looks like death. They all look like death. As if it's catching. Dad looks about a million years older since it happened. She gets out of the car, and Dad gets out and stands waiting to speak to Mike as he bends down to wave at Lisa. Then Dad holds out his hand for Mike to shake, and Mike takes it but looks at him with hearty distaste and drops it as soon as possible.

Dad says, 'Mike, how are you? It's terrible what's happened. We're all thinking of you.'

'Yeah, well, just make sure you take better care of Lisa than you did of Alice,' Mike says shortly.

Mike had objected to this part of the arrangement when they were discussing it beforehand – how could he be sure that Lisa would be safe, going back into the house where Julie's family had let Alice die? But Julie had said that Lisa would be better off with her parents babysitting than anyone else, and did he want to go to the undertaker's with her or not? Because they could hardly take Lisa with them. And in the end Mike had let it go.

'Thanks for doing this, Dad,' Julie says, going round to join them. 'I'll give you a ring when we're through, if you're still all right to pick us up.'

'No need,' Mike says stiffly. 'I can run you to Hillview House. It's not far.'

Dad hesitates, waiting for Julie to respond, and she says, 'Sure. That'd be good, thanks.' She doesn't relish the idea of getting a lift with her ex-husband, but she can see that he wants to be useful.

'Fine, then,' Dad says, looking deeply uncomfortable. 'I hope it goes all right. Or as well as it can do. Call me if you need anything, Julie.'

'I will,' she says. He gets back into his car and she and Mike wave goodbye to Lisa in unison as he drives off.

Then Mike turns to her with the fierce look that means he is truly, deeply frightened and says, 'I nearly didn't come.'

'But you did,' she says.

She is almost tempted to take his hand. But she doesn't, and after a second or two they set off towards the undertaker's together, both scrupulously observing the proper distance between a man and a woman who are no longer husband and wife.

She has dreamed about this moment: Alice on a metal trolley in cold blue light, with the still, shrouded shapes of the other dead lying in rows around them. In her dreams, Alice was sometimes lying there just as if sleeping, so that it was impossible to believe she was really dead, and Julie called out for help, crying out that there had been a terrible mistake, but nobody came. Other times, Alice was missing and there was nobody there, and that prompted a wild, irrational hope that Alice had somehow survived it all, and had got up and walked away, so that Julie had wept when she woke up and remembered her loss. Once there was a dead child laid out for her to see but it was not her own. It was someone she didn't recognise. And once she saw herself lying there, herself as a child, and on waking she cried because that dream was doubly true. She has lost Alice, and also, she has lost herself.

But now it is really happening, and it is nothing like her dreams.

In the dreams she was always alone in the place where she had come to see Alice. Now she has Mike with her, standing opposite her on the other side of Alice's body in a small, quiet, windowless room. The undertaker has discreetly withdrawn to give them privacy. There is nobody else here but Alice.

Julie had rung the undertaker in advance to ask, *Will it be OK for us to see her?* What she had meant was, *Will we be so distressed by seeing her now that we won't be able to remember her the way she was?*

And he had understood. Presumably this was the kind of thing that other people had had to find ways to ask. Gently and tactfully, he had let her know that for some bereaved people, it was important to see the body of the loved one they had lost, and if she did want to do this, he and his team would do their best to get Alice ready. But everybody was different, it was her choice – her ex-husband would need to make his own choice – and given a little time to think, she would probably find that she had the answer to her question inside herself.

She had been terrified of letting Alice down – of being

shocked, or even repulsed. Of not recognising her. Of Alice no longer looking like Alice. When she held Alice's hand under the willow tree Alice had only just gone, and it had been life and death that mattered then, not the details of Alice's injuries. Afterwards, she had been afraid of seeing Alice again – of what she would notice, and not be able to forget.

It is as if she and Alice are two lost explorers who have been forced to travel deeper and further in opposite directions. While Julie had been living in a violent blur of shock and grief and anger, of phone calls and explanations and despair, Alice had been handled by others, labelled and stored, transported, and then dressed and prepared to be seen. Julie had been afraid that being in the same room with Alice's remains would only remind her of the now infinite and unbridgeable gulf between them; the separation between the living and the dead.

But she had given herself time to think, as the undertaker had suggested, and it had come to her that she wanted to see Alice for one last time, in spite of all her fears. And to go with Mike. Mike had been afraid, too, and she had said to him, *You might regret it, but you might also regret it if you stay away. There's no way of knowing. You have to choose. You have to take that step in the dark.* And now here they are.

Alice is lying with her head resting on a pillow and her eyes closed, her body covered by a dark red blanket. Her arms have been arranged so that they are outside the covers. She is wearing the polka-dot nightdress that Julie had brought over to the undertaker's – they'd discussed what Alice should be wearing and what her hair should look like, strange conversations and yet tender and important. She had recognised that the undertaker was trying to give Alice back to them, in a way. To get it right, so that when she and Mike saw her it wasn't as if she had been tampered with by a stranger.

Alice's hair is loose, brushed, tidier than it would have been in life. But at least it has been parted on the right side. The light is muted, but it is still too bright for comfort – it is the kind of light Julie associates with offices after dark in winter, and hospitals and schools. Institutional light. Candlelight would have been easier, the gloom of a bedroom with the curtains drawn. It hurts to look. But that is really nothing to do with the light, it's because it hurts to see.

Her daughter is right there, close enough to touch, and yet Julie does not reach out to her. It's hard to conjure up her spirit, or to feel her presence. What Julie feels is her absence. Glancing at Mike's stricken face, she knows they are united in this at least.

Mike sniffs and rubs his eyes. He says, 'They put make-up on her.'

Julie had known that they would do this, and she had noticed it and at the same time had not wanted to notice it. She had wanted to see the effect they had been trying to create, not the tricks they had used to do it. She says, 'They've done their best.'

'It doesn't really look like her,' Mike says. Then, 'Your sister has a lot to answer for.'

'We've been through this. You know as well as I do that it was an accident.'

They are both keeping their voices down. It's impossible not to behave as if Alice is sleeping, and will be disturbed and upset if she hears them arguing. And at the same time, here more than anywhere it is impossible to escape the fact that they have lost her.

It strikes Julie that if she and Mike were not already divorced, what happened to Alice would have finished them off. Even so, and even though he is on the verge of being hostile, she feels unexpectedly close to him. There should be a word for it, for the tie between them – the tie between any two people who have a child or children together. Not a blood tie. It's a life tie. And it's still there even though Alice is no longer living.

She can bear to stand here with Mike, and be patient with him, because he is the only other adult in the world who understands just how much is missing in a world without Alice in it.

Mike says, 'Did you ask Lisa what your sister was doing while Alice was climbing that tree?'

'Lisa's a three year old who's just lost her sister. I'm not about to interrogate her as if she's in a court of law. Let's not talk about this now, Mike. Not here,' she says.

'I'm not the one at fault here,' Mike tells her. 'This is on your family. They turned you against me and helped wreck our marriage, and if that wasn't enough, their stupid attitudes and their carelessness and their obsession with their business have cost Alice her life. This is on them, and it's on you for letting them bully you and tell you how to bring up your kids.'

'They loved Alice. They're as devastated as we are.'

'They are not. You know they're not. Diane's going to have her baby soon and then she'll get married to Elliott and she'll have another one, or two, or even three. She won't suffer what we'll suffer. She hasn't lost what we've lost. The only thing that would teach her that would be if she lost a child of her own.'

Julie shifts from one foot to the other. She is suddenly aware of feeling very cold, so cold she is shivering.

'Don't talk like that,' she says. 'You shouldn't say such things. Not ever. And especially not here.' She looks down at Alice again. 'We're here to say goodbye, not to fight over her.'

'You know it would never have happened if we were still together. You would have been there. I wouldn't have let you help out at their bakery on our daughter's birthday, just because Diane's pregnant and your parents think she ought to be sitting round on her backside like a queen. And I wouldn't have let you leave our kids with your sister for her to neglect them.'

She doesn't reply. Instead she reaches out to touch him, but he brushes her hand away and looks at her with real fury, and she knows that he is seeing not just her, but everything that has gone wrong for him and pushed his life further and further away from what he had once hoped it might be. Her hand falls back to her side, and then, without even thinking about it, she reaches out and takes Alice's hand.

It is not Alice as she remembers her, who, right from the moment of her arrival, had been so quick to respond and grasp her in return. Alice is cold and lifeless. But holding her still feels like love, and she takes comfort from it.

Afterwards, once they are settled in Mike's car and he is about to drive her back to Springhill, he turns to her and says, 'I'm sorry for the way I behaved back in there.'

'It's OK,' she says, and is surprised to find she means it.

'You were right. I shouldn't have said those things.' He shakes his head. 'It was just... I was beside myself.'

'It was hard.'

He shakes his head again. 'But *you* could do it. How come you could handle that and I can't?'

'I don't feel like I can handle anything.'

'But you can. I don't know what it is about you, but somehow you just keep going. You know what, Lisa's lucky to have you. And don't try telling me otherwise, because you know it's true.' His face contorts. 'Alice was lucky to have you too.'

'We're lucky to have *you*,' she says, though she has not always thought so. But now is not the time to be ungenerous.

'You're just saying that to be kind. I'm a waste of space, always have been. The only good thing I ever did was have my kids. And now...'

He freezes with his shoulders hunched and his hands fixed on the steering wheel, then reaches forward to turn the key in the ignition.

'Anyway, let's get out of here,' he says in a different, harder tone of voice, and she recognises that he's now gone past the point at which it is worth trying to talk to him.

He drives badly on the way back to her parents' house, not so much so that she is genuinely scared for her safety – it's hard to imagine ever really being scared for herself again – but enough to put her on edge. She doesn't think he's about to crash, and it's not as if it's all that far to go, but it isn't a stretch to imagine him getting into a confrontation with some other driver who he thinks has done something stupid, or deliberately obstructed him. It is almost a relief to spot the white façade of Hillview House, however reluctant she is to go back into it.

Mike pulls up without signalling opposite the church on the village high street, next to the turn-off for the lane that leads up to the house. He says, 'You can get out here, can't you? It's not far for you to walk. Don't take this the wrong way, but I really can't face your family at the moment. It's going to be bad enough seeing them at the funeral.'

'Here is fine,' she says. 'Thank you.' She hesitates, then goes on, 'You know, it's not going to help Lisa for you to have a grievance against her aunt and her grandparents.'

Mike turns away from her, lowers his head and tightens his fists. She's conscious of holding her breath. He doesn't seem to be breathing either.

'Just go, Julie,' he says.

And she does. Her legs feel shaky and weak as she makes her way up the hill, but she sets her sights on the old white farmhouse and doesn't look back, even though she hasn't heard the sound of the car moving on and she can't be sure he has gone.

Back in the house, there's an unfamiliar pot of something – it looks like a shepherd's pie – standing on the kitchen counter. 'Someone from the village brought it round. As if we're suddenly incapable of feeding ourselves,' Mum says when she sees Julie looking at it. She seems to have lost weight in the days since the accident, and looks harder and prouder than ever. 'I'll probably end up throwing it out.'

'Oh, don't do that,' Julie says. 'Maybe I could take it home with me. I could bring the pot back another time.' She leans over and sniffs it. 'On second thoughts,' she says, 'maybe not.'

In the big living room she holds a glass of beer she doesn't really want and watches a game show on TV with Dad and Elliott, who has just finished at the bakery and come over, while Diane helps Mum with dinner. Is Diane still shy of Julie, and trying to stay out of her way? Lisa plays listlessly with a row of dolls she is busy lining up and murmuring over. The game is probably senseless, but no more so than what Julie herself is doing, or any of the rest of them.

Then Julie finds herself at dinner, picking at her food, and then she is supervising bathtime and tucking Lisa up in her put-you-up bed in the attic, where Julie will sleep later. She and Mum had agreed, without even needing to discuss it, that it wouldn't do to put Lisa in the room she had shared with Alice.

Earlier in the day the sight of the garden had bothered Julie, and she is glad that all the curtains are drawn now and the blinds are down. The attic feels almost cosy. She is just about to turn out the light when Lisa looks at her with wide, unblinking eyes, and says, 'I made a wish, Mummy, and it didn't come true.'

Julie doesn't need to ask to know exactly what Lisa would have wished for. Wishes don't come true if you tell them. But what Lisa wants – for Alice to come back – could never happen anyway. And if wanting could change that, then the force of Julie's longing and desperation would have revived Alice right there under the willow tree where she was lost to them.

'Wishes don't always come true straight away, and they don't always happen in the way you expect,' she says, but unsurprisingly Lisa is not satisfied by this answer.

'I'm never going to wish for anything ever again,' Lisa says desolately.

Then she asks if Julie will leave her a light, and her voice trembles a little and it is clear to Julie that she is afraid. Perhaps she is scared of vanishing herself. Julie turns the landing light on and leaves the door propped open – Lisa seems to be happy with that. She takes the overnight bag and her towel out with her so she won't disturb Lisa by rummaging round for things later, and puts them on the landing by the bathroom. Then she goes down and joins the others in front of the TV.

It is not yet nine o'clock. The evening stretches ahead. How soon can she decently go to bed? But will she sleep? Diane and Elliott don't seem to be in any rush to leave, even though Diane looks tired out and Elliott has work in the morning. They are on the sofa next to her, and Elliott has his arm round Diane and is chafing her shoulder with his thumb. Once Julie has noticed this small gesture it begins to irritate her and quickly becomes unbearable. She gets up and says she is going to have a quick shower, if that's all right, which is the best excuse she can think of for leaving the room.

Mum looks up at her in alarm, as if she is behaving wildly. Or perhaps just being rude. But Dad says, 'Good idea. You go ahead. Saves a queue in the morning,' and she is grateful to him for backing her up.

Diane stirs and stretches and stifles a yawn. Her pregnancy is enormous and imposing. Already her baby has the presence of a fully-fledged person, a newcomer to the family, and somehow it's Alice who is the invisible one, the elephant in the room.

Diane says, 'Perhaps we should make tracks.'

Elliott checks his watch. 'How about at the end of this

programme?' He glances at Julie. 'When you've had your shower, we'll say goodbye before we go.'

Don't stay on my account, she feels like saying, but she doesn't. And actually, just spending time with them had not been the worst way she could have spent an evening. People underestimated the therapeutic value of TV, the way it let you be in company in a room without actually talking.

She peeks in on Lisa in the attic. Sound asleep. Well, at least that's something. She takes her stuff into the bathroom and gets into the shower, and lets it run and run, not worrying, for once, about using up all the hot water. And it's while she is standing there, trying and failing to think of nothing, that it happens.

TWENTY-FIVE

The sound of the shower is almost loud enough to drown it out, but she can hear enough to make out the raised voices downstairs and outside. She does her best to ignore them. All she wants to do is wash, get into her pyjamas and dressing-gown, say goodbye to Elliott and Diane and go to bed, and attempt to lose consciousness. Surely no one can expect anything more of her today. But then she finds herself listening anyway.

She can't make out the words, but there is one voice in particular that has no business being here. It's Mike, and he is at his worst, drunk, abusive and yelling.

So he hadn't gone back to his flat. He'd probably found somewhere to park, gone straight to the pub in the village and stayed there, right from when he'd dropped her off to now. No wonder he's steaming drunk.

She turns off the shower, steps out, grabs her towel and begins to dry herself. She had better go down and try to calm him. Defuse the situation. If she can't placate him, nobody can.

'Just let me talk to Julie,' she hears Mike say. 'She's the mother of my children. She was my wife. All I want is five minutes of her time.'

'I think you need to sleep it off.' It's Elliott. 'It's been a long day. Come back when you're sober and if Julie wants to talk to you then, she will.'

She doesn't want to talk to him. Not in the least. But it will be better if she does. Better than those two having a shouting match on the doorstep, anyway. She'll remind Mike of Lisa sleeping upstairs, who might wake up and be frightened. Perhaps she could offer to go out for a walk with him. The cool night air will clear his head. Or maybe she could persuade Mum and Dad to let him into the house. They could go into the small sitting room at the back that isn't used very much. She could give him a coffee, something to sober him up. And then it will just be a question of time, of waiting for the anger to leave him, and then waiting for him to cry and to sleep. In the morning he'll be hungover and ashamed and sorry, and both of them will go their separate ways.

He certainly can't be allowed to get back into his car in the state he's in. He'll end up killing himself. Or someone else. She'll have to try and get his keys off him.

And then something happens that puts an abrupt stop to all of her thoughts and plans.

She hears a scream. It's Diane. And she knows what it means. It's like the scream she heard come out of her own mouth when she first saw Alice underneath the willow tree. It's the sound you make when you're confronted with one of your worst nightmares.

She pulls on her dressing-gown and ties it round herself as she flies barefoot down the stairs.

Too slow. Too late.

The front door is wide open and outside, Diane is kneeling next to Elliott who is on his back on the ground, and she is still screaming. There is something dark and sticky-looking on Elliott's face. Blood. And Mike is standing there at a slight distance, further out in the dark but still illuminated by the light from the house, looking down at Elliott as if he doesn't believe what he is seeing.

Mum pushes past Julie almost as if she isn't there. She kneels down next to Elliott and says something sharp to Diane, who falls silent, and calls out to Julie, 'We need an ambulance. Your dad is calling the police. Tell them we need an ambulance too.'

Mike pivots towards Julie and for a split second their eyes meet. He subsides onto the gravel and sits there cross-legged, and she realises he is already waiting for someone to arrest him and take him away. Then she turns and runs to the living room to interrupt her dad on the phone.

TWENTY-SIX

Right up until the day before, she still doesn't know whether Mike will be able to attend Alice's funeral. He's being kept in custody until his trial, and it seems that it will depend on whether there are enough staff available on the day for two prison officers to accompany him. She is so exhausted, and so out of it, that the question of whether he will be able to come or not just seems like something else she has no control over.

She gets the impression that Mike hasn't exactly settled into life inside. Unsurprisingly. Probably he's been rubbing someone up the wrong way. Always had a gift for that, even at the best of times. This is the worst of times, and that particular character flaw isn't going to make anything any easier. The more he resists the authority of the justice system, the more determined it will be to keep hold of him. He's like a very small fly caught in a very large and complicated web, which is invisible to most passers-by but is now revealed to both her and him in all its inescapable power.

Finally, with the funeral looming the very next day, in the brief lull between getting back from the childminder's with Lisa after work and making a start on dinner, she gets a very short phone call from Mike to let her know that he's going to be able to make it.

Straight after she gets off the phone to him, she rings Mum to tell her. Mum had been very insistent that she needed to know whether or not Mike was going to be there. It had already been agreed, without Julie specifically inviting her or Diane openly refusing to come, that Diane would stay away.

Julie hadn't actually seen Diane or even spoken to her since she'd had her baby, though she knew from Mum that the baby was a little girl, and Diane had decided to call her Amy. Julie had sent a card and flowers and a little gift to Hillview House, where Diane has been staying since she came back from hospital. But she has no idea whether any of this had reached Diane. Mum might have decided not to pass it on, and she can't bring herself to check.

'Mum?' Julie says. 'I just wanted to let you know I heard from Mike. They're going to let him come after all.'

There is a short silence at the other end of the line. Her conversations with Mum are punctuated with these short, dense silences now, heavy with all the things that both of them are trying to leave unsaid.

Then Mum sighs and comes out with it. 'I think your father and I had better stay away, then.'

'OK,' Julie says slowly.

She had thought that she was beyond being upset about anything her parents might do or say. But then, she would never have imagined that they would choose not to attend their granddaughter's funeral.

That was another assumption gone. Was this how it was, that when disaster struck the world changed, and everything you thought you knew about people and what they could do, and what could be done to them, turned out to be wrong? Or has the world always been like this, and it was just luck that kept her and her children safe from it until now, when all their luck has run out?

It's so wrong. And unjust. In spite of her numbness, she can feel both anger and sadness stirring inside her.

She has arranged for Alice's funeral to take place at the church in Springhill, at the end of the lane that leads up to Hillview House. Mum had suggested the church, and had spoken to the vicar on her behalf.

Now it feels like she is going to be leaving Alice on enemy territory.

She says, 'Do you mind telling me why? Because this isn't about Mike. It's about Alice. You wouldn't even need to talk to him. All you need to do is be in the same space.'

'I know you're grieving, Julie. But you have got your head in the sand and sooner or later you're going to have to face the facts. We think he's forfeited his right to come tomorrow. I don't know why you don't feel the same.'

'He's Alice's father, whatever he's done or not done. And what happened was an accident. Just like what happened to Alice was an accident. There's no way Mike meant for it to turn out the way it did. He came to the house to talk to me. It was just bad luck that Elliott answered the door.'

'Stop defending him,' Mum says. 'Why do you have to be like this? Why are you trying to take his side? You're not even married to him any more. It can't be because of Lisa. Let's face it, she's better off without him. He's not going to be much of a father to her where he's going.'

'You seriously think he's going to go to prison over this?'

'I think he should. I want him to. He killed Elliott.'

'Mum, he didn't. What killed Elliott was a heart attack.'

'Yes, which only happened because Mike attacked him the way he did. Mike has ruined our lives and everything we hoped for from the future. This has broken your father. Put years on him. Can't you see that? Or can you see it and you don't care? He's going to sell the bakery, did you know that? He can't cope with it any more, and Diane can't do it on her own, not with a little baby. Twenty-five years of work, all gone. And our chance of a happy retirement. That's gone too.'

'It was gone the minute Diane turned her back on my children and let Alice climb that tree. You have all expected me to forgive her. Why can't you forgive Mike?'

'Because what Mike did has nothing in common with what happened to Alice! It is completely different. Losing Alice like that was a tragedy and none of us will ever, ever recover from it. Our hearts were already broken and then Mike took Elliott from us too.'

'But Alice's fall and what Mike did are connected. He only behaved like that because he had been to see his child's dead body that day. That was the only reason he was anywhere near your house. Because he'd given me a lift there afterwards. And that was why he'd been drinking.'

There is another silence, even longer and deeper than before.

'I think it's done something to you, Julie,' Mum says eventually. 'The shock of losing Alice. It's changed you. Because quite frankly I can't see why you're standing by him. He never stood by you.'

'It's not a question of standing by him,' Julie says. 'I'm just trying not to be vindictive. When terrible things happen, there isn't always someone to blame.'

'He messed round with other women. Never gave you enough money. Kept you jealous and anxious and broke. Drove a wedge between you and your family. You chose not to keep his surname, so part of you must know what I'm saying is right. You don't owe that man a thing.'

'Maybe not, but you owe it to me and to Lisa and Alice to be fair to him.'

'And you owe it to your sister and her new baby to cut ties with the man who killed her fiancé.'

There is another silence, the longest and most impenetrable of them all. All Julie can hear is the official-but-friendly tone of the children's news presenter on the TV in the living room next to the hallway where she is standing. She can't make out the words, though. She hopes Lisa is too busy watching to attempt to eavesdrop.

'You are saying that Mike shouldn't be able to come to his own child's funeral, at a time when he has not been convicted of anything,' she says. 'Even the law is not as cruel as that.'

'If that's how you feel, then I would prefer you not to call me again,' her mother says. 'I suppose we will see each other in court, when Mike's case comes to trial. And I have to tell you, if we get the chance to help the prosecution then we will.' And then she hangs up.

Julie's vision of the scene in front of her – the brown carpet, the striped wallpaper, the *Yellow Pages* on the telephone table – trembles as if someone has just hit her world with a hammer. Then she hangs up too.

In the end Mike makes it to the church ten minutes before the service is due to start, dressed in the black suit Julie had been allowed to send him. It's not too bad a fit, though he has lost a bit of weight. He looks pasty and tired. He isn't cuffed, which she supposes they ought to be grateful for. He sits in the pew behind her with a prison officer either side, and she is conscious of him at the beginning, of what he must be feeling. Then all she can think of is Alice and she can't stop crying.

The service is a blur of music and words and tears. There are no children present – she has left Lisa with the mum of one of Alice's friends. She hadn't even told Lisa where she was going. But Lisa had drawn a picture of Alice, a stick person with a big smile and a yellow triangle for a dress, and that is taped to the top of the little white coffin, framed by pink carnations and frail baby's breath piled on top of it.

There are a few rows of mourners. A couple of friends. Alice's swimming teacher. A neighbour. No family. She is grateful to the people who have come and at the same time she can't help but think that her life might be easier if she never had to see anyone who knew Alice ever again. It's the pity with which they look at her. Pity and wariness. They know too much about her. It just makes her want to go to earth somewhere.

Maybe one day she will. It would be a relief to be anonymous. To be of no interest to anybody. Why stay in Brickley? She could just put Lisa in the car and drive, stop somewhere that seemed like it might do. North, south, west, east, she doesn't care.

The service ends with piano music, a tune she had chosen because it sounds like a lullaby. The undertaker and his assistant carry Alice out; she was so small that it only takes the two of them. Outside it is a grey day, threatening drizzle. She looks on as the vicar speaks and Alice is lowered into the ground, and then she steps forward to drop a single rose into the grave. The rose is pink and its petals are bruised and already beginning to curl. She has never felt so lost.

Then she hears something behind her – a light sound, like a child's scurrying footsteps. She turns, half convinced she is going to see Alice right behind her. But she must have imagined it. There is, of course, no Alice, and there are no other children present. Instead she finds herself looking straight into Mike's eyes, and knows the bleak comfort of not suffering alone.

The next time she sees her parents and Diane is six months later, on the other side of the courtroom. At first, it's a shock. Then, gradually, she gets used to it. They avoid looking at her, and she avoids looking at them. It's almost as if they're strangers. Almost – but not quite.

The courtroom is like a cross between a classroom and a theatre. It's imposing and airless, and at times the proceedings take on a kind of ritual tedium: the court rises for the judge and sits again, papers are shuffled, people cough and fidget and stare blankly into space as if they have almost forgotten where they are. But the tension never slackens. The whole thing is terrifying, a process of prolonged torment meted out over claustrophobic hours and days and endless words. It doesn't help knowing that in due course it will be her turn to take the witness stand and speak.

She can't begin to imagine what it must be like for Mike, who sits with his shoulders hunched and his head down throughout, as if already in despair about the outcome. He is wearing the same black suit she had sent him for Alice's funeral. It is even looser on him now.

Her parents and Diane are all witnesses for the prosecution, and her parents testify first. In turn, they describe their impressions of Mike and his relationship with them, the loss of Alice, and what they had heard and seen after Mike saw Alice's body and came up to the house: the knock on the door, the altercation with Elliott, the assault and the aftermath. There's no doubting their sincerity or their distress. From time to time, they glance at Mike in the dock, but he never looks up.

Diane looks frail and vulnerable and convincing on the witness stand. She's more than lost the baby weight, and her modest black-and-white dress swims on her. It's empire-line, black with a white collar, and looks like a cross between a nun's habit and a maternity smock. She has no jewellery on other than her solitaire diamond engagement ring, unaccompanied by a wedding band. Because, as she tells the court, she and Elliott had been planning to get married after she had their baby. But now that would never happen.

The next day Julie finds herself the focus of the court's attention. First, she runs through her account of events with the counsel for the defence, and then it is time for the cross-examination. As the prosecution counsel's questions begin and she responds to them she feels as if she is bartering, offering up something of herself in exchange for the chance of freedom for the man she used to love. It's a sacrifice, of sorts, one that the jury may or may not choose to accept.

People can be cruel, people can be kind; it's always a high-wire act, playing to the gallery. But she is walking the wire, not for Mike, but for Alice, and she is going to tell the truth and the truth will see her through to the end.

Almost inevitably, she cries. And then she pulls herself together, sips some water and composes herself, and they carry on. Finally, it is over, and when she gets down from the witness stand she thinks of Alice and Lisa together on the morning of Alice's birthday, and of how she had stood outside the door of their bedroom at Hillview House and listened to them talking. *I will always be four years older than you*, Alice had said. *When you are twenty, I will be twenty-four. When you are a hundred, I will be a hundred and four...*

But Alice had been wrong. Alice would always be seven.

Mike speaks in his own defence but seems surly and unsure of himself, mumbles, avoids eye contact, and stands there as if he would like nothing more than to disappear. She feels his anxiety almost as if it is her own. Her whole body tingles with nervous tension, and her heartbeat is light and fast, like something small that is trapped and trying to escape.

The judge gives his summing-up and the court rises. It is time for the jury to do their work behind closed doors, and there is nothing she can do now but sit and wait.

. . .

In the end, the jury's deliberations take about three hours and are over by five o'clock, in decent time for them to get back home to their families for dinner. Mike is not guilty of murder, but pleads guilty to a charge of manslaughter on the grounds of diminished responsibility, with sentencing to follow.

When the verdict is read out he looks strangely relieved, and finally straightens up, as if something has been lifted from him. He meets Julie's eyes just for a moment. Then he is taken away, back into custody. On the other side of the courtroom, Diane bursts into tears and Mum comforts her. And Julie just carries on sitting there alone.

Afterwards, in the corridor outside the courtroom, she catches sight of her parents standing with Diane, who is holding her new baby. Little Amy. She wonders who's been looking after the child while Diane has been in court. Someone from the village, probably. There must be lots of well-wishers who have offered their support.

Baby Amy. Poor little thing. Poor little fatherless thing. She catches sight of Amy's pink face and button nose, her wide-open, toothless mouth. She nearly goes closer, but stops herself just in time. It's over. Her family as she knew it is finished. She only has Lisa now, and Lisa is with the childminder, and she needs to get back to pick her up.

She turns on her heel and walks out of the court. It doesn't occur to her till much later, when she is back home and Lisa is asleep and she has got through the best part of a bottle of wine, that she will probably never see her parents or her sister or her little baby niece again. Which would be for the best. There's nothing left for them. And if she has anything to do with it, Lisa will never see them again either.

PART FOUR

AMY

Summer 2001 to Summer 2009

TWENTY-SEVEN

Summer 2001

When Amy wakes up her bedroom is flooded with agonising white light. She must have forgotten to draw the curtains when she got in the night before. It's one of those mornings. Except this is not like any other hungover morning, because it is the day after her mum's funeral.

She has lost her mum. She had lost her dad before she was even born. And she had lost her sister too, just ten days before her dad's final, fatal heart attack. That was when everything had started to go wrong – when her sister died. Her legendary sister Alice, who had fallen out of the willow tree in their grandparents' garden and died on the day of her seventh birthday.

Alice's brief life was a secret, more or less, because Grandma Elsie had given her to understand that it was shaming to turn something so dreadful into a story, and offer it around like common gossip. This edict had been so powerful that even when Amy was off her head, as she'd been last night, it was a part of her history that she did not share.

She didn't often tell people about her dad either, unless

they asked. But talking about that loss had never been quite as much of a taboo. If anyone wanted to know if she had a sibling, she just said no. She always felt a little lurch of guilt at denying that Alice had ever existed, but that was preferable to the worse guilt she'd have felt if she'd actually started to explain. In any case, the truth would probably kill any conversation stone dead. It was the kind of thing people didn't know how to react to.

And now, in addition to all of that, she has lost her mum. Her life really was almost about as tragic as you could get.

Grief, loneliness, shame, self-pity and self-hatred wash over her, a combination that is no less painful for being familiar. With Mum gone, the only family she has left is her grandparents. And she has done her level best to be a disappointment to them.

Also, she has almost certainly messed things up with her boyfriend. Which wasn't such a big deal in the scheme of things. But still, she really liked Joe. She had even told him about Alice, not all that long after they'd first got together, on the condition that he should keep it to himself. 'Who would I tell? It's not the kind of thing I talk about,' he had said, and she'd felt all right about it because she knew that this was true. Joe was someone you could trust. He wasn't the sort who would make hay out of your tragic family backstory, and turn it into an anecdote.

Better face it, though. He's too good for her.

It had always been inevitable that she was going to do something to drive him away sooner or later. But why did it have to happen now, on top of everything else?

Joe had tried to persuade her to leave the pub after last orders last night, before the lock-in. Too late now to think that maybe he had a point. She'd been stupidly drunk and upset. Out of control. And then she'd slapped him. She can still see the distress and disgust on his face. She'd expected him to slap her back, because that was what usually happened, wasn't it?

Then you cried, and later you made up. How was she to know that Joe played by different rules?

But she should have known. He'd been so kind to her. A shoulder to cry on, even though they'd barely been an official couple when her mum started to get really sick, back in the spring when it became obvious that the end was getting close. He hadn't minded when she wasn't in the mood for sex. And he'd offered to come to her mum's funeral, even though they'd only been dating for four months. He hadn't resented her for telling him to back off and stay away, he'd come to meet her at the pub afterwards...

She's still dressed in yesterday's black skirt and white shirt, though the shirt smells of spilled beer. She doesn't seem to have remembered to remove her make-up, wash her face and brush her teeth, either.

Somehow she manages to get up and change and leave the house not more than the standard ten minutes late. Then she has a wait for the bus and when she's finally on board she narrowly avoids being sick as it follows the twists and turns of the road that leads south from Kettlebridge to Millingford, through fields and villages and woods, to the little industrial estate by the river.

Russell's Jaguar is already parked outside their unit, next to Micky the apprentice's little Honda. She's been beaten to it not only by the boss but also by the office junior. Anyway, it doesn't matter. Today of all days she has an excuse. Joe had tried to persuade her to take the day off, but she doesn't see the point in using up her tiny annual leave allowance on being away from work on a day when nobody's going to expect very much from her anyway. She'd rather be at work. It's not much of a distraction, but at least it's something else to think about.

She taps in the security code and goes in. It's already stuffy in the display area on the ground floor, and will be unpleasantly hot in the little office upstairs if the temperature starts to climb later – there are a couple of fans, but no air conditioning. Luckily, it's a grey morning, not much like summer at all. The air tastes of metal and glass and plastic, and as if it's been shut in all night, which it has.

With any luck Russell is down in the loading bay supervising the goods going onto the vans for the day's installations, and won't realise how late she is. Half an hour now. Still, it is the day after her mother's funeral. And at least she's made it in.

She goes up to the office and turns on her computer, which takes forever to wake up. Micky the apprentice, who sits opposite her, clears his throat and looks at her mournfully.

'How was it yesterday?'

'Fine, thanks,' she says briskly.

'That's good, because, you know, I'd be well cut up if it was me.'

'Well, it isn't you, is it?' she snaps, and after that he leaves her alone.

The phone rings a lot that morning, which is bad because it hurts her head but good in that it makes the time pass quicker. Russell appears and heads into his office without speaking to her. When she goes in to take him some tea and his post he is on the phone, and doesn't look up.

At lunchtime she walks a little way out of the industrial estate down the lane towards the river and along the towpath. The river is low and the grass is dry and rustles underfoot. There aren't many people around – a couple of dog-walkers, women with small children in tow. From time to time a boat goes past on the river, steered by a holidaymaker or someone old enough to have retired. It's the daytime life that you don't usually see if you're working in an office from nine till five, and suddenly she wants very much to step out of the world she has been part of – of work and going out and then working again – and to live to a different kind of rhythm, and be part of the quietness.

Her mum had worked part-time down at the council offices, but she'd had plenty of time at home at Hillview House. It had been clear that was where she really wanted to be. The job was just a means to an end – a way to earn the money to cover their groceries and to pay for clothes and the occasional treat, and to give Grandma Elsie and Grandad John something towards the utility bills. But all the time she was younger, Amy had been absolutely determined that she wouldn't lead a life like her mother's. It seemed so boring: the little job, the chores at home, the cooking, the TV in the evenings. Where was the fun? How long could you go on being sad about the past? And what was the point of trying to live carefully so that nothing else bad could happen, if that meant you ended up not really living at all?

But as she watches the water go by, it seems to her that maybe her mum had the right idea all along.

When Amy left home, she'd wanted to make a space for herself that was separate from her family – it didn't matter if it was small or dirty or noisy, a shared room in a house with people she didn't know and probably didn't like, it just had to be hers, a space where she could do what she wanted. She had called this freedom.

But even though she had tried to be a completely different person to her mother, she had loved her. Too late to show her that now, though. And that hurts her more than anything else she has ever felt.

And now what is she expected to do with herself – who is she supposed to be? There will never be anyone who she will matter to as much as she had mattered to Mum. As for her grandparents, she has surely burned her bridges with both of them... they had never openly said so but it had been obvious that they hated the way she'd run her mother ragged. Every Christmas they'd looked at her as if she was a returning prodigal who'd neglected to repent.

She gets to her feet and makes her way back to the office. Perhaps that would be a good place to start: her job. She should look for something else. She should have quit a while ago, but she hadn't had the energy, what with Mum being sick. She'd just wanted a job where she could turn up and get through the day without really thinking about it.

Joe still doesn't know that she'd been sleeping with Russell before they got together. He probably wouldn't mind if he did, or at least, he shouldn't do. It wasn't as if she'd two-timed him. Not really, not for very long, even if there had been a tiny bit of overlap. But she still doesn't want him to find out that she'd had a secret affair with her boss. He'd probably think it was sordid and disgusting, even if he tried not to show it. Which is what Amy thinks too, objectively.

After all, Russell is ostentatiously married, with a blonde, shiny, brittle wife who sometimes rings the office or drops by. Russell's wife had big, glassy, light blue eyes, and when she'd met Amy she'd looked right through her as if she didn't exist. Amy might have felt guilty if she hadn't been sure that she wasn't a threat. She'd never been in love with Russell, nor him with her, and she had never wanted to take him away from his wife. She was just someone who'd let Russell use her and had used him right back.

The question of when and where she and Russell might do it next had added a sort of dirty glitter to the business of showing up at work and sitting at a desk and getting a monthly pay packet. She'd put a stop to it pretty sharpish when she started seeing Joe, though. And Russell had been disappointed, but hadn't tried very hard to persuade her to carry on. All he had said was, 'Well, you know where I am if you change your mind.'

She has only been settled in front of her computer for about five minutes when Russell calls her into his office. As she goes in and sits down opposite his desk she feels both apprehensive and disdainful, because it seems inevitable that he's going to ask her how she is and how it went yesterday. Trying to be caring just doesn't seem like Russell's forte. He likes closing deals and driving nice cars and dining out and cheating on his wife – it's not that he's insensitive, he's got pretty acute antennae, but he usually takes the line that other people's misery is not his problem.

Then Russell clears his throat and says, 'I've had a phone call from an unhappy customer. Arthur Wright. Does it ring any bells?'

She shrugs, instantly feeling foolish for having thought he might be concerned about her. 'Not off the top of my head.'

Russell steeples his fingers and explains why Arthur Wright matters. He's a local councillor, a person of some importance in the community, and he lives in a nice big redbrick Victorian house in Springhill village, which, as she knows from having grown up there, is full of the kind of older properties that need the sort of sensitive approach to renovation he specialises in providing. Arthur Wright had been very happy with his new windows, but he hadn't yet received his guarantee paperwork, which he shouldn't have had to chase for. So could Amy please sort it?

Amy says yes, of course, then mutters something sullenly about how she's had a lot on her mind lately. It's not even as it's that big an oversight. How could he tell her off like this, after yesterday?

Russell leans back, folds his arms and studies her. And yes, there it is – the old, reliable look of lust, a kind of hot, wounded animal longing. You wouldn't exactly call him charismatic. But he behaves as if he's used to getting exactly what he wants, and sometimes that is appealing in itself. He's a showman, a salesman, a force to be reckoned with, with a strutting step and a nice line in expensive suits. He is not kind or tender, not to her, anyway, and she should have known better than to expect him to be.

'Can I give you a word of advice, Amy?'

She shrugs. 'If you want.'

'Don't make excuses. Ever. It's a weakness.'

She stares at him. Suddenly, like a told-off child, she feels the urge to cry. He is right, of course. She has been making excuses all these years, blaming everything on all the death and loss that had surrounded her from the very start.

'I'll sort out the paperwork today,' she says.

'Good girl,' he says approvingly. 'OK, Amy, that'll be all, though I could do with a coffee when you have a minute. Black, with one sugar. The usual.'

He still hasn't asked her about the funeral. As she gets up and goes out she can't quite believe how detached he has just been. It's almost as if they'd never been close.

She sorts out Arthur Wright's guarantee, as requested, and then a delivery arrives – the new brochure – and she and Micky have to lug a couple of boxes each up to the stationery store-room. Russell pops his head round his office door and asks her to post it out to the main client list by the end of the day, but the mail merge doesn't work, and she struggles with it and fiddles with it and only just has it all done and franked by five thirty, when the postman comes round.

Micky says goodbye and heads off. Russell puts his head round his office door again to check if the brochures went out and to ask if she has his itinerary and sales materials ready for the next day's meetings. She doesn't. She looks sadly at the clock and resigns herself to working late. It does cross her mind that maybe he is keeping her there deliberately, but she no sooner thinks this than she dismisses it. He wouldn't do that. Not after yesterday.

It's just the two of them in the building now. Other people on the industrial estate are leaving: the mechanics have finished for the day, and so has the undertaker and the carpet fitters. The feeling of being surrounded by empty space isn't unfamiliar. Not to someone who grew up in a farmhouse on the top of a hill. And anyway, it isn't spooky. It isn't even dark.

He's peering at figures on his computer screen when she takes his itinerary and documents in. He thanks her, and then he takes off his glasses and says, 'Do you fancy going for a drink? I'm buying. We could go to the pub on the other side of the river.'

She barely hesitates. Yes, she would like a drink. Why shouldn't she? Joe wouldn't mind. Anyway, he can hardly object, because he doesn't know about Russell, and he hasn't called her all day, and it's already over with Russell and it's probably over with Joe too, so what does it matter?

It's beautiful out – mild, clear, an idyllic summer evening. They don't talk much on the walk down the lane from the industrial estate and across the bridge. You don't need to talk when you're somewhere that makes just walking enough in itself. Life had seemed so flat and desolate and pointless just a few hours before, and suddenly it's not any more. She feels like a person who's living in three dimensions, who still has a future, who matters. And she tells herself that there's no reason to despair. She's still allowed to enjoy herself. She can afford to let go.

Russell buys her a gin and tonic and has half a lager himself, and they sit in the beer garden of the pub by the river. He apologises for having been hard on her earlier and asks how she is, and he's being so sympathetic and attentive that she is able to say quite honestly that she felt terrible before but she is much better now. And then she finds herself telling him about what it was like growing up in the farmhouse that looks down on Springhill village, and about how badly behaved she'd been at school and the things she'd got up to as a teenager. Talking about it makes her miss it all, in a way, like it was a story and she was the heroine of it. He listens sympathetically, and she decides that she's done him an injustice. He *is* nice, after all. Maybe they can even be friends, now that she isn't sleeping with him any more...

And then she finds herself telling Russell about Alice.

She has always felt like her history is twisted and that she is twisted, too, because of all the bad things that happened before she was born and that are rarely spoken about, apart from that ritual once a year when her mum and grandparents lit the birthday candles for her dead sister and went down into the basement and sang to her. Is it callous to sometimes feel frustrated that Alice's birthday is still a big deal every year? Probably. But Alice is the ultimate big sister, the one who is impossible to beat. You can never do better than a sister who is perfect because she is already dead. Alice's shadow is so huge, and so powerful, there's never been any point in Amy attempting to shine.

It's no excuse for the way Amy has carried on, of course. She probably would have been just as terrible a person if her older sister had lived. But then they could have had the regular sibling rivalry that other sisters had, the kind that was out in the open, more or less – the squabbles, the bickering and the making up.

Maybe, if Alice had survived into adulthood, she wouldn't have been quite so perfect. Maybe she never *had* been so perfect, and it was just the strange protective reverence with which her memory was treated that made her seem that way.

It's as if the brakes have been lifted off Amy's tongue. She finds herself talking urgently, desperately even, and it all comes spilling out. She tells Russell she'd rebelled for the pair of them. Alice had never stayed out late, never lied, never skived off school or smoked joints in the bathroom in the morning. But Amy had, because she'd had the chance to live the life Alice never got to lead.

'Like sleeping with the boss,' Russell says, smiling.

She feels his knee between her legs under the table and automatically finds herself giving him her best pert glance and saying, 'Yes, that too.'

Another drink. Well, why not. She doesn't mind if she does. That's probably his way of signalling that it's time to change the subject. He must feel he's heard quite enough about Alice. Which is fair enough. It's not exactly a cheerful topic. She should probably make an effort to be better company. It's still a beautiful evening and what else is she going to do, go back home to her houseshare all by herself and go sensibly to sleep? Why would she do that when that is absolutely not the kind of thing she does? No, she'll save that kind of thing for when she's old and tired, and until then she'll carry on being the last to leave a party and she'll drink for as long as someone else is buying.

After that he says it's probably time to get her something to eat, and he gets up and she trots along obediently behind him. She stumbles once or twice because she's wearing high-heeled wedges and her ankle hurts a bit, but she doesn't really feel it. The river looks pretty, wide and slow and gentle, but then they're back in the car, swinging away from the quiet of the darkening lane and she's content to lie back in the passenger seat and watch the lights floating past on the main road and the other traffic moving all around them, all so purposeful.

She feels as if she's suspended over emptiness, like a tightrope walker in a circus, performing for an audience she can't see. How do you live life to the fullest? She has no idea any more. It's all so slippery and exhausting, sometimes it's easiest just to let other people worry about where you're going.

Russell turns off the main road after a while and drives her through wooded countryside. The light is beginning to fade; night is on its way. They stop at an obscure pub for dinner and she drinks some wine and eats the food he orders for her and laughs some more. He is looking at her quite seriously and a small, cold, hard voice tells her that she is drunk and if she doesn't do something about it now, she'll end up back in his car with him. And then it is quite possible, likely even, that something else will happen.

'Maybe I should ask to call a taxi,' she says.

'Well, you could, but why would you when I can give you a lift wherever you want to go? Have dessert. Have a coffee.'

He is spending so much money on her – she hasn't exactly tried to choose the cheapest things on the menu. And it would be rude to rush off after he's made such an effort to cheer her up. She owes it to him to see it through. Doesn't she?

The coffee he orders her has whisky in it, but she drinks it anyway. When they finally leave it is dark outside and she realises she has run out of cigarettes. He says that as far as he's concerned that's no bad thing, and puts his hand on her knee in the car and kisses her. It's as familiar as the first coffee of the morning, the hair of the dog, the taste of smoke; pushy, heavy Russell, who wants what he wants when he wants it.

'What about your wife?' she says when they both pause for air and she pulls away from him.

'What about her?'

'I mean, this really doesn't bother you?'

'Well, it doesn't usually seem to bother you.'

'I guess she doesn't understand you.'

He starts the car. 'She has nothing to do with this. I understand *you*, which is what matters, isn't it?'

She doesn't disagree. She doesn't object or protest. She thinks about Joe and then puts him out of her mind. Joe is someone she doesn't deserve. What she does deserve is this. She carries on sitting next to Russell even though she feels ever so slightly sick about what is going to happen next. But it seems too late to stop it now.

He drives her to a hotel by a big roundabout and books them in, and inside he proceeds to show her how well he understands her and she lets him, and she gives it her all because this is a performance and that's what performers do.

But the minute it's over she hates herself. She hates herself even more than she had that morning when she woke up hungover. She cries while he is showering, and then she looks at the red marks on her arms and legs and wonders how long it will take the bruises to fade, because she is not going to be able to let Joe near her for all that time. If he ever wants to go anywhere near her ever again, which seems in doubt. And then she puts her clothes back on and gets back into Russell's car with him.

He says he'll drop her back at her place, and she thanks him. They sit in silence together as he drives. It is profoundly awkward, as if they've been forced together when they barely even know each other. She wishes she hadn't told him all that stuff about her family – hadn't spilled her guts about her dead sister, and all of that. It wasn't as if he cared. He probably wouldn't even remember. She feels almost more ashamed of having confided in him than of anything else.

When they get to Kettlebridge she asks him to let her out by the garage near her house so she can buy some more cigarettes. He pulls in, and she finally finds the courage to say, 'We shouldn't do this again.'

'Don't do that,' he says, shaking his head. 'Don't feel guilty. So you've got a boyfriend. So what? It's pretty obvious it isn't going to last.'

'You've never met him. You don't know anything about him.'

'I know enough to know he's just another of your experiments. If he was enough for you, you wouldn't have come back to me.'

'I haven't come back.'

He touches his finger to her lips. 'Never say never, Amy.'

And then she gets out of the car and goes into the garage, and he zooms off into the darkness.

He hadn't asked her whether she was still on the pill – he must have just assumed that she was. But she'd stopped taking it a couple of months earlier, because there was nothing about seeing Mum in the hospice that tallied with wanting to snuggle up with Joe in anything other than a brother-and-sister way. Joe had said he understood, he didn't mind, he'd wait for her for as long as it took.

The next day she makes it into work late, as usual, and is distracted and slightly inefficient, which isn't unusual either. Russell ignores her. But when she gets home Joe comes round with flowers. All her housemates are out and they cuddle up on the sofa in front of the TV and he expects nothing from her, nothing at all. Not even conversation. So, of course, she doesn't tell him about Russell.

A fortnight later it crosses her mind that there might be something up, but she starts taking the pill again anyway and Joe invites her round to his place and makes her dinner and takes her to his bed. It's very sweet and tender and awkward and he's so puppyish, so keen to please, that she feels as if she's been remade.

It isn't until four months later that she goes for the scan that confirms she's pregnant. She tells Joe and he takes his hands in hers and looks her in the eyes and says, 'I want this baby,' and she says, 'I do too.'

And then she persuades him that the absolute best thing for all of them – even if it doesn't make sense on the face of it – is for her to quit her job, move in with him and introduce him to her grandparents, and for her to throw herself on their mercy and ask them for whatever help they're going to need to make ends meet.

TWENTY-EIGHT

August 2009

She hadn't done anything really bad. Not this time. Or so she tries to tell herself as Tyler drives her and Rowan through the village and back up towards Hillview House, where Lisa is no doubt going out of her mind.

No, it wasn't bad. But it was stupid. How could she have been such an idiot? And yet it had seemed so harmless. She had deserved it, hadn't she? A little bit of time out. A breather, after the time she'd had with Grandma Elsie, and the scene the old lady had made when she went up to confront Lisa in the attic. And besides, it was always sad, marking Alice's birthday.

Luckily, Lisa doesn't strike her as the suspicious type. People like her – good people, who give other people the benefit of the doubt – don't expect anyone to behave the way Amy has treated Joe. To be so treacherous.

She glances at Rowan, who has gone back to sleep in his car seat. Well, that's something. Not for the first time, she is profoundly grateful that he's such a placid baby. Although if he fussed more, if he hadn't behaved so beautifully all afternoon, she never would have gone back to Tyler's place, and she wouldn't be in the fix she's in now. She'll be able to talk her way out of it, she's sure. But the thought of the way Lisa will look at her as she tries to explain just makes her want to curl up and die.

Tyler says, 'Everything all right?'

'Yes, of course. I just need to get back as soon as possible, that's all. This has all got out of hand.'

She doesn't turn towards him as she says it, but she catches sight of his lean, lightly muscled forearm as he reaches forward to change gear and slows down to let someone cross the road. His hand brushes her thigh and she flinches.

Problem is, when she gets too close to Tyler Paley something goes haywire, as if her body has a mind of its own and has decided to override hers. What is she meant to do about that? There's nothing she *can* do, apart from try harder to stay away from him.

Where did it all go so wrong? How had she ended up making such a terrible mess of things?

She hopes they don't see Russell now, as Tyler drives her back through the village. Though there's nothing incriminating about being in Tyler's car, not in itself. And she has Rowan with her, which makes it look innocent, doesn't it? But the way Russell would look at her if he spotted her, as if he knew exactly what a dreadful person she actually is – she really doesn't want to have to witness that.

The village is quiet, as you'd expect at this time on a weekday summer evening. It's well past rush hour but still light, though the sun is on its way towards the horizon. They pass Russell's little cottage on the high street with the blue front door and there's no sign of him, and she breathes a sigh of relief.

The problem is – aside from her being a dreadful person – as time goes on, her marriage feels more and more like work.

And not satisfying work, either. More the sort of work where you put in the hours because you can't figure out how to leave.

Sex with Joe – which has barely happened since she got pregnant with Rowan – is about trying to keep him happy, and trying to keep him happy makes her grumpy and resentful, and then that hurts him. She does make an effort, at least some of the time. She feels she owes it to him, which is another problem, because there's nothing sexy about having to pay someone their dues. However grateful or guilty you are. He makes an effort, too. But it has become increasingly rare for them to both be in the mood to make the effort at the same time.

And that was normal, when you were married with a young child, wasn't it? Not that it was really possible to know. She didn't know any other mums well enough to ask, and it wasn't the kind of thing people talked about, as far as she could tell. She didn't want to talk about it herself, not even with Joe. Especially not with Joe. When he'd tried, once or twice, she had rebuffed him, and accused him of not appreciating how demanding it was to be a mother. It was actually easier to have sex with him and get it over with than to discuss it. Though that was because she'd never wanted to face up to what he might have to say. And anyway, she couldn't risk an honest, open, warts-and-all exchange.

No doubt Joe's sad about the way things have been between them. There's still some of the old tenderness left, but even that is in short supply. And it *is* sad – it makes her wistful. It's sad to think of all the potential trapped inside her body, of everything she has to give that she just doesn't really want to give to her husband. Not any more. Though the very least she owes him is not to give it to anybody else.

If only Tyler had called her back the first time they met, maybe she would have got him out of her system then and everything would have turned out differently. Or maybe things would have worked out between them, and she would never have got involved with anyone else. Probably not, though, because she had only been seventeen at the time.

But who knew, because they'd met at Kettlebridge Fair and legend had it that if you kissed someone for the first time at the fair, sooner or later you'd end up married to them.

He'd approached her first. Even though Grandma Elsie thought she was much too much of a flirt, she was wary of being forward. The fair was a leftover of the old agricultural hiring fair that had taken place in the town every October since the Black Death, and it was going on all around them in the darkness, with rides and fast food stands the length of Gull Street, and tinny versions of pop tunes competing with the thrilled screams of drunk teenage girls.

She'd been there with a crowd and so was he, and she'd noticed him immediately: tall and thin with a shock of dark hair and an obviously bad attitude.

So, of course, she said yes when he suggested going on the dodgems together, and the waltzers, and then, for a change of pace and because she said she wanted to, the carousel, riding on neighbouring horses.

For the four minutes of the ride, gliding up and down next to him while the old-fashioned tinny fairground music played and the world turned into a whirl of bright paint and gilt-edged mirrors and coloured lights, she was as happy as she had ever been. Afterwards, they kissed and he tasted of candyfloss and cider and smoke, and then she was even happier.

And that was it. That had been all they had time for. Her friends found them and dragged her away. She had laughed and apologised and he just stood there watching her with the lights of the fair playing on him. He was wearing a T-shirt, despite the October chill in the air, and she still remembers the lurch of lust she'd felt at the sight of his bare arms, and how much she'd wanted to go straight back into them.

She managed to get his number off someone and rang him

about a week later, but he never called back. She hadn't been that surprised, because by then she'd heard that he had a girl-friend, and she'd been glad in a way, because what they'd already had was so perfect.

The church comes into view and she thinks of little Alice's grave in its quiet corner. It's a privilege, really, to still be alive. To have had the chance both to make mistakes and to keep on figuring out how to live with them.

Tyler turns onto the lane and says, 'Nearly there now.' She sees the white front of Hillview House up ahead in front of them and her heart sinks.

She is home a couple of hours late and she has been a bit thoughtless. That's it. She has to remember that. There's nothing more for her to confess to.

Tyler turns off the lane into the gravelled parking area and she sits and looks up at her home: the red-framed windows and the garden and the big willow tree at the back towering over everything. She supposes she ought to feel lucky but right now, she hates the place.

Tyler says, 'Are you sure you're OK?'

'Yeah. Fine.' She allows herself to look at him properly then. 'Thanks for the lift.'

He sighs. 'No problem. Well, I guess I'll see you around.'

'Sure,' she says.

She flips down the sun visor and peers at her reflection in the tiny rectangle of mirror. She doesn't have bed hair, which is just as well. All things considered, she doesn't look too bad.

'Thanks for the drink,' she says, flipping the sun visor up again. 'It was nice to see your place. But you really shouldn't have let me sleep like that.'

He shrugs. 'You seemed to need it.'

'Yes, well, what I need is irrelevant,' she snaps, and gets out of the car and slams the door shut with just a little more force than is required.

She really shouldn't have said that. He'll start thinking she means she needs *him*. And she doesn't. She just has a little weakness for him, that's all.

Rowan blinks at her sleepily from the back seat. She's woken him up. She should know better by now. You couldn't really afford to indulge in any display of emotion when you had kids.

She opens the door next to Rowan, unclips the seatbelt holding his car seat in place and lifts him out. She sets the car seat down on the gravel and leans into the car to grab the changing bag. Tyler watches her over his shoulder and says, 'I'm glad everything went OK with your grandma.'

'Barely. But at least it's over,' she says, and withdraws.

She closes the car door, more gently this time, shoulders her bag, picks up the car seat by the handle and trudges away from Tyler in the direction of the house.

Best not look back at Tyler and smile and wave. She shouldn't be too friendly with him. Even after what happened today. Especially after what happened today.

She decides to go in through the kitchen. Lisa almost certainly won't have locked up yet, and it'll save her rummaging for her front door key. As she goes on past the shed and into the herb garden, she can't help but remember the very first time she'd seen Tyler working at the house.

When Mum first hired a cleaning lady she hadn't mentioned her name, and Amy had not made the connection with the boy she'd kissed as a teenager at the fair. She was married to Joe and had Tilly by the time Grandma Elsie told her Grandad couldn't cope with the garden any more and Mrs Paley's son was helping out. Even then, the penny didn't drop until she came to visit with Tilly one day and actually saw him.

It had been autumn, and he'd been raking leaves out on the lawn. Even though there was a chill in the air he'd been wearing just a T-shirt and jeans, and his arms were bare. He was more careworn and less cocky than she remembered. But it was still him, and she'd definitely felt something – a sort of flutteriness inside, and a sudden sense of coming into focus. Just nostalgia, probably. But he had shown no sign of recognising her, and she had decided to carry on as if they'd never met before.

Behind her, she hears the crunch of Tyler turning the car on the gravel and pulling back out onto the lane. He's gone. She's on her own again. Apart from Rowan, wiggling his toes and gurgling in the car seat, and Tilly presumably asleep somewhere inside and Lisa waiting. Hopefully Lisa will have picked up the message Amy had left on the answerphone when they set out from Tyler's place, so she won't be worried. Just annoyed, probably, though being Lisa, she might try not to show it.

There is no noise coming from the house and the garden is very quiet, apart from the bright to and fro of birdsong. It's always beautiful here towards the end of a summer day. On impulse, or maybe just to put off making her excuses to Lisa, she carries the car seat round to the patio at the back and takes it in: the lawn, Tilly's playhouse, the overarching willow tree. Everything lush and peaceful and growing. You wouldn't think, seeing it like this, that anything like Alice's accident could ever have happened here. It doesn't seem like the scene of a tragedy.

Or the scene of a crime. Her dad had died because he had been attacked on the front doorstep, trying to protect the family from a drunken lunatic – her mum's sister's violent ex-husband, who had gone to jail for what he'd done. It's still astonishing to Amy that Lisa is so sweet-natured and caring and gentle, given what her parents seemed to have been like.

But you might imagine that a place like this could be the scene of a seduction...

Partly because she wants to, partly because it is irresistible, she allows herself to remember what had happened between her and Tyler here a little more than a year before.

Tilly had been at school, and she was lying on the sun lounger on the lawn in shorts and a bikini top with a magazine to look at. She couldn't see Tyler, but was distracted anyway by the thought of him sweating down the end of the garden, just out of sight. In the end she got up and went over to where he was working and offered him a drink. He said yes and she brought out a glass of water for him.

Standing near him, she had been acutely, painfully conscious of her body. Not what it looked like so much – though she couldn't help but think he was aware of that – but of how it felt as he noticed her. When he'd finished drinking she took his glass from him and put it back in the kitchen. And she could have left it there, and gone back to the sun lounger for the hour or so that was left before she was due to go and get Tilly from school. But instead she went right up to him and said, 'Do you mind if I ask you something?'

He was pulling up weeds from the border, and he took his gloves off and laid them on the grass next to his trowel before he straightened up and turned to talk to her.

'Fire ahead,' he said.

And she said, 'Do you remember meeting me when we were young?'

He said he didn't, so she told him exactly what had happened: the fair, their friends, the carousel, the kiss. Then he scratched his head and said, 'Well, I'm sure I would remember something like that.'

'Well, you should,' she said, and then she kissed him, and he froze for a moment and then kissed her back.

And that was that. They'd ended up in the shed by the side of the lawn on a couple of sun lounger cushions side by side on the dusty ground, next to the stacked-up flowerpots and the taped-up compost and the watering can, and she'd felt like someone else completely, not Amy Power or Longcross but someone who was totally free.

Afterwards he had said, 'I did remember, by the way. About the fair. I just didn't like to mention it.' And then, 'Don't you need to get Tilly?'

And she had checked her watch and panicked, standing up and pulling her clothes back on, running her hands through her hair. She'd said, 'This never happened,' and walked out of the shed and back into her life, arriving at school quarter of an hour late to politely expressed disapproval from the staff and sulky resentment from Tilly.

A week later Tyler had showed up to mow the lawn and both of them did a pretty decent job of ignoring each other. But a couple of weeks later her body had begun to turn soft and tender in a way that almost certainly meant just one thing. Her slip-up with Tyler – that was how she'd told herself to think of it, as an accident – had left her with something real and growing to remember it by.

She and Tyler had never talked about it. He'd tried that day when Lisa first came to see them, and she'd responded by storming over to him just before Lisa left, and telling him they had nothing to discuss. And he had just looked at her, a bit surprised and blank and maybe disappointed, but all he had said was, 'Uh-huh.' You couldn't get very far on 'uh-huh', could you? It wasn't exactly worth breaking up a marriage for.

Anyway, they had gone on like that, not really talking, until she'd bumped into him in Kettlebridge that day she'd taken Rowan in to have his vaccinations. Except she'd mixed up the dates, and Rowan didn't have an appointment after all. And she had told Tyler that, and she had said, *I'm so stupid, I mess everything up*. And he had looked at her and looked at Rowan and said, *You're not, and you don't*. She had said goodbye to him almost immediately, but even that had been enough to make her feel better than she had felt for months.

She picks up the car seat and retraces her steps to the herb garden, heading for the back door. Tilly's love-in-a-mist appeared to be flourishing. Would Tilly even have missed her at bedtime? Probably not. She was so attached to Lisa these days, it was almost enough to make Amy jealous.

There's no sign of Lisa in the kitchen. Amy lets herself in and flicks on the lights – it's late enough in the day to have become a little gloomy. What was it Grandma Elsie had said? That the kitchen looked like a disco? Actually, the yellow walls have always given Amy a headache. It was Joe who'd chosen the colour. He thought it was cheerful. And she has got used to it, but now she looks at it with fresh eyes, she can see what Grandma Elsie was getting at. It isn't exactly restful.

The washing-up has been done, the surfaces wiped down, and a loaf of bread is out on the worktop, defrosting for the next day. She's been so lucky to have had Lisa here all summer. And she's been so much happier than she expected to be. Maybe, in a way, it has been easier for her to be happy without Joe around. Apart from missing the children, has it perhaps been easier for him, too?

She puts down the car seat, dumps her bag and stoops to undo the belt holding Rowan in place. He gives her his best, most charming grin and she lifts him out, holds him in place on her front and straightens up. He's such a perfect armful. Such a warm, delicious little package. And beginning to fill out now too. He'd been so light as a newborn, he'd put her in mind of a sparrow or a mouse, or something else tiny and vulnerable. But now he's beginning to get more solid, it's his weight and not his lightness that she notices.

'Who's a good boy?' she murmurs. 'It's all going to be all right, isn't it, my boy? I've got you, and that's all that really matters.'

She gets a glass out of the cupboard and pours herself some water and sips it, still holding Rowan in place, then puts down the glass and sways from side to side in the way he likes and looks out of the kitchen window at the fading sunlight on the garden.

Maybe Lisa's watching TV in the family room, though Amy can't hear anything, not even faintly. Or Lisa could be reading, or doing something or other on the computer in the attic. She'd mentioned about getting in touch with her temp agency to find out if they had any jobs for her. Amy hadn't said anything because she didn't want to think about Lisa leaving. But at the same time, she can't really ask her to stay.

If only the summer didn't have to end. But it will, and Lisa will go and Joe will come back. The trick is to take it one day at a time, and not look too far ahead. If she can do that, she'll be able to manage all right.

At least the ritual of Alice's birthday is over for another year. It always makes her feel low, and this year more than ever it had felt like a creepy charade, especially because she hadn't been able to bring herself to explain it to Lisa. So when she came out of Grandma Elsie's care home with Rowan and got into the waiting car, and Tyler turned to her and said, 'You know what, you look like you could use a drink,' was it so surprising that she'd agreed?

He'd taken her to a pub by a bridge over the river Thames a little way north and west of Springhill, where the land was lower and flatter and the meadows were prone to flooding. The green grass of the lawns stretched as far as the riverbank and was fringed by weeping willows, and he'd left her there in the shade of the trees with Rowan while he went into the bar.

She had an old flannel cot sheet stuffed in her bag that she'd brought with her to put down on the carpet in Grandma Elsie's room at the care home, so Rowan could lie there and roll around and it wouldn't matter if he was sick. In the pub garden she'd laid it out on the grass and let Rowan lie on his back and look up at the interesting leaves and the sky, and mouth his rattle and laugh at nothing.

And then Tyler had come back from the bar with a small glass of white wine for her and a Diet Coke for himself. While she drank her wine they'd somehow got onto the subject of how Tyler had left Springhill for a while when he was younger, but had run up a mountain of gambling debt and had ended up having to move back in with his mum and start over. And then he'd mentioned that he'd just bought a place in Springhill at auction and was doing it up. She'd asked where it was and he had said, 'I'll show you, if you like. It's on Dark Lane.'

'Sure, I'd like to see it. We can swing by on the way back.'

After all, why not? What harm could it do?

On the drive back to Springhill her phone had rung and she fished it out of her bag in a panic, but it was just a reminder for a dentist's appointment later in the week, and she'd turned it off. She didn't particularly feel like being interrupted again. Anyway, she was just going to have the quickest possible look at Tyler's new place, and then she'd be heading back home.

His place turned out to look like a building site with an unfinished bungalow on it. When he'd asked her if she'd like to see inside, she felt it would be rude to say no. She'd picked her way across the dried-out, churned-up mud of the front garden, carrying Rowan, and Tyler had shown her into the entrance hall, which looked as if it had been recently replastered but needed decorating. Here and there she could see exposed wires, and the floor was concrete. Then they went through to what should probably have been a living room, except it had a king-size mattress on the floor in front of the French window and kitchen units in one corner.

'This is really as far as I've got,' he said.

The walls were painted white and the flooring was polished wood. The windows looked out onto the back garden, a stretch of dry earth and ragged grass and weeds surrounded by spirals of untamed brambles, with the green swell of someone else's fields beyond. There was a large wall-mounted

TV and a little kitchenette in one corner, which looked reasonably functional. Apart from the mattress, there was nowhere else to sit.

'It's looking good,' she said.

'I like that it's mine.'

She might have left then if Rowan hadn't started crying. She used the microwave to warm up the little carton of formula she'd brought with her and gave him his bottle. When he'd finished it he was quiet and she lay him down on a corner of Tyler's king-sized mattress and he slept.

And then, because it was warm in the room and she was really drowsy after the glass of wine and tired out by the strain of the day, she lay down, too, and put her head on one of his pillows, which was pleasingly bouncy and firm.

'I could actually go to sleep myself, right here,' she murmured.

If Tyler had said something then, she might have got up and insisted on going back. But he didn't say anything at all. He just stayed there, very close but not touching, and reached out just once to stroke her hair, and then withdrew. And it was all so soothing, and so comfortable, her eyes closed and she didn't stir until Rowan did.

Then she'd surfaced with a sharp intake of breath, checked her watch, realised she'd been asleep for more than an hour and panicked. She'd rung Lisa to say she'd be home soon, and she'd made Tyler drive her back up the hill straight away.

It's not the end of the world, is it? She'd gone for a drink with Tyler, she'd gone back to his place, she'd fed Rowan and she'd fallen asleep on Tyler's bed. It's not too bad, apart from the last bit, which Lisa definitely doesn't need to know about. It *is* bad that she hadn't called Lisa to explain where she was going and what she was doing. But Lisa thinks she's dizzy and unreliable anyway. She'll be able to say that one thing just led to another, and it will more or less be true. There's no reason for

Lisa to suspect that there's anything going on, or that there ever has been.

'None of them need know,' she murmurs to Rowan, who burbles cheerfully in response.

Anyway, she'd better get the apologising over with. She goes out into the hallway, and that's when she sees that the curtain at the back of the stairs has been pulled back, and realises that she isn't the only one who has spent that evening exploring somewhere she wasn't meant to go.

* * *

She has always hated coming down here. There's no grab rail, and it never feels safe. Another reason why she always told Tilly to stay away. With Rowan in her arms it feels even more precarious. She takes it slowly and carefully, even though the temptation is to race ahead, and sees that the door at the end of the passageway is ajar, as she had expected. She pushes it open and goes in.

Lisa is sitting at the table where she and Grandma Elsie had sung 'Happy Birthday' to Alice just that afternoon, before blowing out the candles on the cake. Lisa looks stunned and bewildered, which is not surprising given that she has just discovered what looks more or less like a child's bedroom hidden in the basement of the house, sparsely furnished with relics of the 1970s.

Amy snaps at her, 'What do you think you're doing? I told you not to come here.'

Lisa just stares at her, still dumbstruck. Then Amy sees that Lisa has found the folder of photographs she keeps in the wardrobe so Grandma Elsie can look at them while they're down here. Lisa holds up one of the pictures as if it's evidence of something terrible, as if to accuse Amy of something.

It's the photo of Alice in the garden with another child, a

toddler, and Lisa is saying that it's her, and she knows it is because she recognises the kid's yellow sunhat. Which strikes Amy as maddenly presumptuous, especially as Lisa is down in the basement, in the special place they keep for Alice, where Lisa has no right to be. But maybe it *is* Lisa in the photo – who knows? Does it matter? She doesn't get why Lisa's making such a big deal of it. Maybe it's a way of trying to defend herself from Amy's righteous indignation. Anyway, who remembers what sunhat they had when they were little?

It had never occurred to her that the toddler could be Lisa. She has always assumed that it was the child of some friend or other of her mum's. Had she assumed, or had she asked and been told that? She can't remember. Anyway, what does it matter? It's really Alice who matters.

No wonder Lisa is reacting so strangely. Amy has tried to keep quiet about Alice and all she has done is turn her into a mystery. And now she has no alternative but to clear it up. Lisa has forced her hand, and she's going to have to put her straight.

She takes the photo from Lisa and puts it back down on the table. Lisa is looking at her as if she could be some kind of monster. A kidnapper. Or, at the very least, a thief.

'The older girl in the photo is Alice,' she says. 'And today is Alice's birthday. What happened to her wrecked our family. These are things that nobody has ever wanted to talk about.'

She's just going to have to do it. Blurt it out. There's no other way. She takes a deep breath and says, 'Alice is my sister. *Was* my sister. My older sister. And this room is Alice's shrine.'

Lisa's mouth falls open but she doesn't say anything. She looks shocked and disorientated, which isn't quite the reaction Amy would have expected. Lisa is usually so compassionate and sympathetic. But here Amy is, opening up about the tragedy of her lost sister, and Lisa looks as if she doesn't know what to do with herself.

Amy ploughs on. 'Every year, Grandma Elsie and I come

down here with a cake for Alice and sing to her. She lost her life when she was seven years old, the same age Tilly is now, the summer that photo was taken. She climbed the willow tree in the back garden and fell, and died almost instantly.'

Lisa still doesn't say anything. It's almost as if she doesn't know whether to believe her. Amy hesitates, then decides that she might as well carry on and get it all out into the open. Be cruel to be kind. Or at least, be honest. Perhaps it's tactless of her, given Lisa's recent bereavement. But for now, she's had it with keeping things to herself.

'I'm sorry to be the one to tell you this, Lisa, but Grandma Elsie once told me your mum was supposed to be keeping an eye on both of you at the time, because my mum was heavily pregnant with me, and was meant to be resting. I think that was part of why there was such bad feeling about it between the two of them. Between your mum and my mum, I mean. Not that there was ever any suggestion it was anybody's fault.'

She might as well not have bothered trying to explain. Lisa doesn't seem to take any of this in. Instead she starts talking about the letter she had written to Amy last winter, and Amy remembers that she'd hidden it away down here so Joe wouldn't come across it. And then she finds herself forced onto the defensive, which is infuriating because surely Lisa is the one who's in the wrong here.

'I'm sorry,' she says. 'I just didn't feel up to answering it. Especially as I was pregnant, and finding everything a bit overwhelming. Surely you can understand that, now you know more about the history?'

But Lisa just looks at her balefully, as if nothing at all she's said can now be trusted.

Rowan is beginning to get restless, perhaps picking up on the weirdness of the atmosphere. And suddenly Amy just wants to get out. She can't bear it down here any more. She hasn't even broached the subject of what Lisa's dad had done yet. But given the way Lisa is glaring at her, now is not the time.

'I promise I will tell you everything,' she says. 'But first I have to see to Rowan. Put the photos back where you found them, and lock up behind you. And then we'll talk.'

Then she turns and hurries out, and this time she doesn't even remember to take it slowly on the steps.

PART FIVE
LISA, AMY AND JULIE

Summer 1977 to Summer 2009

TWENTY-NINE

LISA

Summer 2009

She stays in the basement for what seems like a long time, trying to absorb what Amy has just told her. No wonder Mum had turned to gin. A child had died while in her care. Her own niece. Alice. The little girl who had worn the flowered sundress hanging in the wardrobe in the basement, who must have made the dreamcatcher hanging off the bookcase and slept under that Pierrot duvet.

Amy has told her so, and Amy has no reason to lie. Not about this. Amy is sometimes unreliable, but this has to be true, even if Lisa's strongest instinct is to flatly refuse to believe it.

When she emerges the hallway is quiet, warm and dim. She puts the keys away in the hall table and checks the landline phone. There's a message on it from Amy, saying she's on her way. She must have called while Lisa was down in the basement – Lisa had even heard the phone, though she'd been too lost in what she was seeing to break off and answer it.

She rings Mrs Paley and leaves her a message to say Amy is back safely and it was all a false alarm, and is surprised to hear that her voice sounds calm and almost normal. She's glad, in a way, that she had spoken to Mrs Paley earlier. At least she'd told her not to bother the police.

Amy must be in the family room. Lisa can hear the muted patter of TV voices, broken up by laughter. She knocks on the door and waits, but Amy doesn't respond. Lisa has always been an outsider here. Now she feels like an intruder too.

She decides to go in anyway, and as she approaches Amy reaches for the remote control and turns the sound down on the TV. She must have already put Rowan in his cot and has curled up with a glass of wine in front of *Friends*.

'I'm really sorry,' Lisa says. 'I know it was unforgivable to go in there like that.'

'You broke in,' Amy says sharply, still not looking at her. 'It was locked and you knew you weren't meant to go down there. You broke in.'

'Yes,' Lisa says. 'I broke in.'

She has spent so long wanting answers about her parents, and now she has them, and it turns out that knowledge isn't liberating at all. It's suffocating and deadening. Her whole body feels weak and heavy with shame and sorrow, as if she is suffering the after-effects of a long, slow form of poison. She has to sit down on the sofa before her legs give way underneath her.

Amy seems to make an effort to compose herself before turning to face her.

'Those things of Alice's have been in the basement for more than thirty years,' she says, and her voice is surprisingly calm. 'Some of them are the birthday presents she never got round to opening. Some of them are the things she'd brought over from the flat above the bakery in Kettlebridge where my parents used to live. My grandad always used to say the best way to honour the past is to remember it. And we do. Alice died on her birthday and we don't let it go by as if it's a date that is best forgotten. It's a day of mourning in this house but we celebrate it too.'

'I had no idea,' Lisa tells her. 'Mum never even hinted that anything like this had happened. She just wouldn't talk about it, which I suppose makes sense now.' She has to force herself to say this. Maybe in time she'll be able to accept it, but it feels all wrong. 'I understand now how special that place is and how protective you must feel of it,' she goes on. 'It was absolutely crass and stupid of me to go barging in there.'

There is a small, heavy silence. Amy studies her thoughtfully, and her lips twitch as if there's something more to say but she can't quite bring herself to come out with it. Then she says, 'Well, now you know. Maybe it's for the best.'

'Maybe it is,' Lisa says. 'It's better for us not to have secrets between us. And I am so, so sorry to hear about what happened to your sister.'

Amy looks down at her hands, flexing them so that the sapphire on her ring finger glints kingfisher blue in the evening light. 'I hope we can just carry on as we were,' she says. 'You've made such a difference. You've kept me sane. You've given me space. Look, I know what it's like to lose your mum. When mine went it turned my world upside down. I thought the last thing you needed was to find out that your mum maybe wasn't quite the person you thought she was.'

'It's a shock,' Lisa says. 'I guess it explains why Grandma Elsie reacted to me the way she did. I know it shouldn't have come about this way, but I'm glad you told me.' She feels like choking as she says this, but somehow manages to come out with it. 'It must have been hard for you, growing up with something like this.'

Amy is quiet for what seems like a long time. Her eyes slowly fill with tears, which she wipes roughly away with the back of her hand.

'It's been part of my life since before I even understood

what it was,' she says, and looks up at Lisa again. 'I used to join in on Alice's birthday from when I was tiny, and they told me it was for my sister who had died and I just thought it was normal, to have half your family dead. Because Dad had gone as well. When I was a little bit older they told me I shouldn't talk about Alice to other kids. That spooked me a bit, but I guess it made me feel important. Like I had a secret. Something too big and important to just chat about. We didn't talk about her much in the family, either, and the same went for my dad. It wasn't a rule, as such, but I just knew not to go there. It was obvious it was too painful for everybody. Even little kids can tell when there's something they're not meant to bring up.

'Then, by the time I was eight or nine, it began to sink in. That this was actually a little kid who had never got as old as I was already, who was dead just because she'd climbed a tree in the garden and fell out of it.' She presses her hand to her mouth and takes a moment to compose herself. 'I'm going to tell Tilly about it eventually. I just want her to be old enough to understand. But given that I haven't even told my own daughter – and she's named after Alice – how could I have justified telling you?'

'The room... was that actually Alice's bedroom?'

'No, no. No one in their right mind would put a child to sleep there. It's much too gloomy. And it's cold down there, even in summer – did you notice? No, they just decided that would be a good place to store her things. When it was her birthday Mum always used to arrange everything as if it really was her room, and now I do the same.'

'I see now why Joe was so odd with me on the phone. He seemed like he knew something but didn't want to tell.'

The texture and tone of Amy's skin seems to change, and to turn bloodless. She picks up her glass of wine, sips it and sets it down again. 'When did Joe call?'

'Oh... when you were out. He said he'd try again tomorrow.

I think he had a busy day ahead of him. He spoke to Tilly. I think he just wanted to check you were OK.'

Amy seems reassured by this. Though why had she been so worried about missing Joe's call in the first place? It's not as if he was the type to get angry about something like that.

'He thought I should tell you about Alice,' Amy says. 'But he didn't push it. He's always been very accepting of it. Some people might find it rather macabre, having a shrine to a dead girl in the basement. That's the trouble with shrines. It's all very well when you start them, but what about the upkeep? What do you do with them as the years go by? Is there a point at which you say, enough is enough? Anyway, my grandad had a view on that. He wrote it into the letter of wishes he left along with his will, that he wanted me to keep on marking the day in the same way for as long as Grandma Elsie is alive, and can come and join me. So that's what I'm trying to abide by.'

'And what about Mrs Paley? And Tyler? I guess they know?'

'Yeah, they know. Neither of them is the sort to go round gossiping about what goes on here. They wouldn't get much work in the village if they were. Nobody really wants other people knowing what they get up to in their houses, or their gardens. And quite frankly, it's none of anybody else's business.'

Amy picks up her glass of wine again. She suddenly looks very small and vulnerable, like Tilly in her loneliest moods.

'Sometimes, when it comes down to it, it's a relief to get these things off your chest,' she says. 'I'm sorry you couldn't get hold of me earlier, and I'm sorry if you were worried. But it's a difficult day, as you'll appreciate. I just really needed some time away from the house.'

'Of course. I understand.'

'How was Tilly?'

'She was fine. She was very good, actually. Went to bed on time, no problems.'

'That's good. I didn't think she would miss me, somehow,' Amy says regretfully, and finishes her glass of wine.

'Amy... there is one other thing I wanted to ask you.'

Amy stiffens, as if apprehensive about whatever Lisa might be about to come out with. 'Yes?'

'I'm sorry to bring this up. I know it's been a long, hard day, and I can see you're worn out. But I have to ask. I know you didn't feel you could tell me about Alice, and I can see why. But do you know something more about my dad and what he did than you've been saying?'

'Oh, Lisa,' Amy says, and her eyes fill with tears again. 'The fight your dad got into... It was here, and it was after Alice had died. He'd been drinking in the pub in the village and he came to the house and attacked my dad on the doorstep and beat him up. My dad had a heart attack and died in hospital ten days later.'

Lisa stares down at her. So here it is, finally. The answer she's been looking for. It should be a moment of clarity, of relief even. And it does make sense. But it doesn't feel as if pieces of her childhood are falling into place. It's more like being trapped in a dark machine after a brutal shifting of gears.

'You're telling me that my dad was responsible for your dad's death,' she says. 'That he killed him.'

'He did,' Amy says.

Lisa takes in the words like a blow to the chest. It feels like an accusation, but it's worse than that. She can see that Amy is telling the truth. And some part of her is not surprised. Maybe she had suspected something like this all along, but just hadn't been able to bring herself to acknowledge it.

Amy wipes her tears away again. Her face contorts like a child on the edge of bawling. Then she makes a visible effort to pull herself together, and when she speaks again her voice is almost calm.

'But Lisa, all that was nothing to do with you. Or me. You

were tiny and I hadn't even been born yet. It's just the history we inherited. It doesn't have to affect us. We don't have to let it.'

'I see now why you didn't answer my letter,' Lisa says. 'Why would you have wanted to hear from me, or have anything to do with me? No wonder Grandma Elsie didn't want to have anything more to do with my parents. Or with me.'

'I didn't answer your letter because I'm a coward, and that's why I didn't tell you any of this,' Amy says. 'And now I don't know whether it would have been better if I had told you, or if you'd never found out at all.'

Lisa shakes her head. 'I needed to know. Even if it's hard.'

And it is. It's too big to take in. It's overwhelming. And it makes sense – in a horrible, twisted way, it adds up. But still, something in her recoils from it. If only she could have asked her mum about it. If only she could have heard it from her. But would that have made it any easier to stomach?

Amy gets to her feet. She reaches out and lightly squeezes Lisa's shoulder, then lets her hand fall back to her side.

'It must be a huge shock to you,' she says gently.

If Lisa could reach out, too, they could embrace and cry and comfort each other and be almost as close as sisters. But she just can't bring herself to do it. It feels all wrong. It's almost unbearable.

'You've been very generous,' she tells Amy. 'I don't know whether I would have done the same if I'd been in your shoes. And I'm sorry, for what it's worth. I know that doesn't change any of what happened, but I'm sorry it happened to you, and I'm glad you told me about it.'

She wants to be gracious, she wants to say and do the right thing, but it just feels like forcing out thanks for a gift she never wanted, and is going to have to carry around with her for the rest of her life.

'I think I need to go out,' she says. 'Go for a walk. Get some air and try and get my head round it.'

'OK,' Amy says, sitting down again. She looks as if she feels off-kilter and disorientated too. It's as if the revelation that should have brought them together has left them both feeling more lost and alone than before.

'Be careful, won't you?' Amy says. 'Though you should be safe. Nothing ever happens round here. Take a torch, maybe. There's a flashlight in the hall table. The lane isn't lit.'

'I'll be careful,' Lisa promises. 'I won't be long.'

As Lisa heads out Amy reaches for the remote control and turns the volume back up on the TV, and Lisa's goodbye is drowned out by a sudden blare of laughter.

* * *

In the hall Lisa catches sight of herself in the hall mirror and is startled by how wild she looks, not at all like her usual self. Maybe this is what it is, to be liberated – this mixture of unfocused energy and unease.

She finds the flashlight Amy had mentioned, sticks it in her jacket pocket and heads on out. The night air is surprisingly cool and the sky overhead is pitch black. When she looks up she can make out the stars, and as she keeps on looking more and more of them reveal themselves, some insistently bright and others almost invisibly faint, like pennies concealed under a depth of murky water.

Then she turns and looks back at the house, its white façade glowing faintly in the moonlight, its crooked windows all dark now at the front because the only illuminated window will be the one Amy is sitting by, at the back.

Mum must have suffered such agonies here... And Amy's mum too, and Grandma Elsie... Her dad, and Amy's dad. All of them. And what, if anything, had she witnessed herself, when she was here as a little child?

Nothing comes back to her at all. There's just the pale

house in front of her, calm and quiet as if all its troubles are over, and the night sky above, and the shadowy hills all around.

There's a faint, unsettling sound in the air, like a very distant shriek – some unfortunate hunted creature, perhaps. She turns her back on the house, flicks the flashlight on and makes her way down the hill.

* * *

When she comes to the main road through the village, the proportions of everything are so changed by darkness as to be almost unrecognisable. The old church looks huge and the willow trees are giants. There are no people around at all. It's like an exaggerated stage set for a scene in which she is the only character, a small, vulnerable figure making her way past all the entrances and exits a potential attacker could use.

She keeps walking, following the light of the flashlight, and round a bend in the road she sees an old building with lights in the windows and cars parked outside, and a painted sign showing a fountain of water jetting up from the ground.

It's the village pub, the Flowing Spring. Which surely must be the one her dad had been drinking in the night he had shattered Amy's family and destroyed what was left of his own. Maybe it's macabre, or misguided, but she carries on walking towards it, and then she finds herself pushing open the door and going in.

It's quiet enough for her to feel conspicuous as she heads towards the bar. It's a snug, bright little place, low-ceilinged with wood panelling and horse brasses and sconce lights on the walls. To either side, a few small huddles of people are clustered round tables in alcoves, deep in their separate conversations. They seem to notice her arrival, but carry on talking as if her appearance is not in itself enough to bother them.

The bartender has a pot belly and a long grey ponytail, and

is polishing glasses. She asks him for half a lager and sits at the bar to drink it. Was this where her dad had sat, drinking and brooding? What could possibly have been going through his mind in those last few hours before he'd made his fatal mistake?

It is a mystery to her why anybody, under any circumstances, would attack a man who had just lost a child. Some attempt might have been made to blame her mum for Alice's death, since she had been babysitting at the time. But even then...

It just didn't add up. And perhaps she would never know. Maybe that was how it was when a family was ripped apart, when blame and responsibility and grief got mixed up with catastrophic loss.

No, best accept it. This is the end of the line for her, as far as she can go or should go, and she should count herself lucky to know a little more than she did.

And then she thinks of her mum's lonely funeral, and how remote Amy had seemed as she was leaving, and she knows it's not enough. Maybe she's in denial. But what Amy has told her doesn't feel right. There has to be more to it. Something Amy's still holding back. Or maybe even something Amy herself doesn't know about.

A door opens somewhere behind her and a group of people come out, chatting and laughing. They are mostly, but not all, women, and judging by their pink faces and laughter, they have all just been having a good time. Some of them linger to say goodbye, and others head straight through the pub to the car park. She sees one familiar face – a man, tall and bullish with curly hair – and recognises him as Amy's old boss, Russell. He seems to be in a filthy temper, and leaves without a word to any of the people he was with. He doesn't acknowledge Lisa, either. She can't tell if that's because he hasn't seen her, or if he's just not in the mood for exchanging pleasantries with a near-stranger.

One of the women detaches herself from the group and comes over to the bar.

'Lisa? It is you, isn't it? I don't think I've ever seen you in here before.'

She's an attractive woman in her late forties or maybe early fifties, with bright eyes under heavy eyebrows, thick dark hair that is beginning to turn grey, and a well-made, lightly lined face. She's wearing a blue paisley pattern shirt and pale linen trousers with gold jewellery and sandals, and looks tanned and slightly weather-beaten. Lisa takes a minute or two to place her, because usually she sees her at Hillview House in an old T-shirt and jogging bottoms and trainers, pushing the vacuum cleaner or the mop around.

'Hi, Mrs Paley,' she says. 'I wasn't expecting to see anyone I knew. I mean, I don't think I actually know anybody else from the village apart from you and Tyler.'

'Please, call me Grace, and I don't live here, it's too expensive. Tyler's bought a doer-upper down the road at auction, but he's young and keen enough to do that kind of thing. I just come up here for pudding club once a month on a Thursday. There's a group of us –we're pudding club regulars. You should try it sometime. The food here is really good.'

'Thanks, but I probably won't be here this time next month,' Lisa says.

Grace perches on the barstool next to her and dumps her handbag on the bar. It's pink leather with gold buckles and snaffles and probably designer, though she seems quite casual about it.

'It's fake,' Grace says, following Lisa's line of sight. 'So Amy got back OK, in the end, right? That must have been a relief.'

'Yeah. I suppose.' Lisa picks up her glass, drains what's left of her beer and puts it down again. 'Can I get you a drink?'

'Not for me, thanks. I should be heading off in a minute,' Grace says, but makes no move to go.

Lisa remembers what Amy had said about both Grace Paley and Tyler knowing about the basement. It made sense that they *would* know, if they'd been working at the house for years. And she feels impelled to try to acknowledge what she's just discovered, in the same way that you might inspect a fresh scab or a new bruise, or feel for a missing tooth with your tongue.

'I found out a few things about the family today,' she says. 'I found out what they keep in the basement at Hillview House. Amy said you know about it too.'

Grace darts a look at the barman, who carries on polishing glasses as if oblivious. She drums her fingers on the bar counter. 'You find out things about people when you clean their houses,' she says. 'It happens. It's part of the job.'

'I'm struggling with it, to be honest,' Lisa says. 'I hope I'm not speaking out of turn to say that to you. But I grew up not knowing about any of that. It was Joe who told me what my dad had been put away for. And now I know who his victim was, and I can't begin to understand why he behaved the way he did.'

Grace sighs. 'I don't know what I can say to you, Lisa,' she says. 'You seem like a nice person, and I know Amy's been really happy to have you staying at the house, and you get on so well with Tilly. You know, in a funny way you remind me a little bit of Amy's mum. I started working for the family after she first got ill, and she never complained, even when she was really suffering. She was a nice lady, very sweet, very gentle. But she was tough too. After everything she'd been through, she dealt with the pain almost like she felt she deserved it.'

'Did she ever talk to you about my parents at all? I know so little about my dad. I don't know what happened to him after he was in prison, and Amy doesn't know either. Did you ever hear anyone say anything?'

Grace's face sinks. 'I'm sorry to be the one to tell you this, but he passed away. It must have been about five years ago, something like that? I remember old Mrs Power, Grandma Elsie, talking about it. She was still living at Hillview House then, and Mr Power was still alive, and Mrs and Mrs Longcross were living in Kettlebridge with Tilly, who was just a baby. Mrs Power said your dad had got into drugs after coming out of prison, and he'd overdosed and died. Your mum had been in touch with her to let her know.' She pulls a face. 'Mrs Power used to sometimes talk to me about things like that. Letting off steam, I suppose, whereas she kept her feelings under wraps with everyone else. She'd obviously never got anywhere near forgiving him. I think she felt he'd finally got his just deserts, and she probably didn't hold back from telling your mother so.'

The bottles hanging up behind the bar blur and spin as if Lisa has drunk much, much more than she really has. So that's it. Another dead end. Another loss. She realises that even though she has partly been expecting it, she is also unprepared for it. It's the possibility that has gone, the small daydream she has carried round with her and sometimes indulged in, the idea that one day she would be able to meet her dad, and he would be happy to see her, and she him.

She will never see him contented. She will never comfort him. And there can be no reconciliation.

'I'm so sorry,' Grace says, looking at her with concern. 'Your mum didn't tell you?'

Lisa shakes her head. 'No. Maybe she was ashamed. She always took the line that the less I knew about him, the better.'

'Perhaps I shouldn't have said anything,' Grace says doubtfully. 'It isn't really my business. But if I'd been in your mum's shoes, I would have wanted you to know whether your dad was alive or dead, whatever he might have done years before. I don't think it was right of her to keep it from you.'

'That's not all she kept from me. Not by a long chalk,' Lisa says. 'Maybe she always meant to break it to me one day, when the right moment came along. And then she ran out of time.

Anyway, I'm glad you told me.' Her voice sounds very small and very distant. 'I guess I should be going home.'

She stands up, and Grace stands up too.

'Are you sure you're OK? I could give you a lift up the hill if you wanted,' Grace says.

'Thank you, but I'm all right. I wouldn't want to impose, and anyway, the walk will do me good. I guess I'll see you at the house.'

'I guess so,' Grace says. 'You take care, now.'

Lisa is conscious of the older woman watching her as she makes her way to the exit, probably wondering how much longer she will stick it out at Hillview House in the light of what she's just learned. Maybe Grace wouldn't be surprised if she never saw Lisa again.

The next morning is grey and rainy and everyone is out of sorts. Amy complains of not having slept well, and Tilly seems tired too. They don't really talk. After lunch Amy successfully settles Rowan in his cot for a nap and says she is going down to the basement to sort out a few things. Lisa realises what she means – that she is going to pack away Alice's bits and pieces, the alarm clock, the dreamcatcher and so on, and store it away till next year.

She offers to help, but Amy rebuffs her. 'No, thanks, it'll be quicker if I do it myself. Much better if you keep an eye on Tilly.'

'Can I help?' Tilly pipes up, excited at the idea of being allowed somewhere she is not usually supposed to go. 'I could be very helpful. Or I could just watch and stay out of your way, Mummy.'

'No, you can't,' Amy snaps. 'I just need to get on with this on my own.'

Then Tilly runs up the stairs to her room and won't come

out, and Lisa is reduced to standing outside and pleading with her – very quietly, so as not to wake Rowan.

'Please, Tilly. I know you don't want to come down, but is there any chance you could let me in? Because, you know, I'm really getting fed up and lonely out here.'

Eventually the door swings open and Tilly grudgingly admits her, and they get out Tilly's plastic tea set and organise a pretend tea party for her teddy bears and Alice, with Tilly hosting from inside her pink pop-up tent. By the time she coaxes Tilly into coming back downstairs Amy seems to have finished sorting out the basement, and is back in the family room flicking through one of her magazines.

Tilly settles down to play with a selection of dolls and their outfits, and Lisa clears her throat, like a visitor who is no longer quite sure if she is wanted, to ask a question.

'Amy...'

Amy looks up from her magazine.

'Yes?'

'Can I have a word?'

Amy wearily gets up and follows Lisa out. Tilly carries on playing as if she hasn't heard anything, but Lisa knows she's listening. When she and Amy are out in the hall she pushes the door to and says, 'I just wanted to ask you something about what you told me yesterday. About Alice. I wondered if you could tell me where she's buried.'

'Oh, that's easy,' Amy says, looking relieved. Lisa fleetingly wonders if she'd been afraid of being asked about something else, though she can't for the life of her think what. 'She's in the churchyard in the village. Grandma Elsie never likes going there, for some reason.'

'Would you mind if I went down to have a look?'

'What, now?'

'If it's all the same to you.'

Amy shrugs. 'Sure. If you want. Be my guest. It's quite a

small stone, easy to miss. It's near the wall at the front, on the side by the cut-through that goes down to Tilly's school.' She hesitates. 'Look, are you all right?'

'Yes,' Lisa says firmly, though she's not sure that she is. 'You?'

Amy shrugs. 'So-so.'

'I'll feel better when I've done this,' Lisa says.

Amy studies her face doubtfully, as if she thinks Lisa is hoping for too much from this. She reaches out and very lightly brushes her hand against Lisa's arm, a gesture of sympathy that seems to say, *I know this is eating away at you, and I feel it too.*

'I hope it helps,' she says, and withdraws.

Amy is right that the stone would be easy to miss. Lisa knows what to look for and it still takes her several minutes of walking round the churchyard to find it. But eventually she comes to it: a small, rounded stone that must once have been white, but after more than three decades' worth of weathering is a mottled creamy-grey, softened by lichen.

The finely carved inscription is still clear enough to make out without difficulty.

ALICE POWER, 1970–1977: LOVE NEVER DIES.

There is a flash of blue in the long green grass in front of the stone, and when she crouches down to look more closely, she sees a patch of love-in-a-mist that must have seeded itself there.

THIRTY

AMY

As the time when Joe is due to call comes closer, Amy is increasingly nervous about talking to him. She can't help it, because even the truth sounds incriminating. To have gone to the pub with Tyler, and then to have gone back to his house and gone to sleep... If she explained that to Joe, would he even believe it? And if he did, wouldn't he question why Amy – who is a restless sleeper, and who has kicked him out of the marital bed for months at a time – should be so relaxed with Tyler as to doze off happily on his mattress?

And Tyler *had* touched her. He had stroked her hair. She *definitely* can't tell Joe that. Especially as remembering it makes her feel soft and fuzzy, like a teenager with a crush.

Meanwhile Lisa has been quiet and preoccupied all day, presumably still brooding on the discoveries about her parents and Alice, and doesn't seem to feel any better after coming back from her walk to the churchyard. Amy supposes she could try talking to her about it – and maybe she should – but she's wary of initiating a heart-to-heart about anything at the moment. Who knows where it might lead?

Joe has emailed her to suggest a Skype call just after dinner, but then the internet goes down, as it so often seems to do, and in the end they arrange for him to call the landline phone around half past nine, which at least gives her time for a calming glass of wine or two after Tilly has gone to bed and she's got Rowan settled in his cot.

Lisa has withdrawn too, saying something about being tired and wanting an early night, which Amy doesn't really believe – it just seems like she doesn't want to talk any more than Amy does. Well, dealing with Joe is enough – she'll worry about Lisa another day.

She takes Joe's call in the family room with the door firmly closed, even though both kids are sound asleep and Lisa has already gone to bed, and wouldn't be able to hear anything anyway. The line isn't bad; a little crackly, but it would be easy to believe Joe was just down the road rather than on the other side of the world. Which is not entirely a good thing. Even though she has tried to persuade herself that everything will be fine once he gets back – after all, it has to be – the idea of them being properly close again makes her nervous.

'So,' he says, 'how was it? How did Alice's birthday go?'

She hesitates. 'Well, it was all fine, apart from Lisa deciding to break into the basement while I was taking Grandma Elsie back to the care home afterwards. So then I obviously had to explain to her why it is as it is. I think it came as a bit of a shock, and she seems really down today. I just hope she isn't going to hold it against me.'

'Why would she do that?'

'I don't know. I guess it could be a case of shoot the messenger, maybe. We don't always like the people who tell us bad news. And now she knows about my sister. She seemed to really struggle with that. Maybe it was a mistake, but I told her that her mum was meant to be looking after Alice when she died. I thought it might help her make sense of it all. I mean, her mum must have felt terribly guilty. But it clearly wasn't easy to hear.

Plus she knows what her dad did to my dad. It must have been horrible to finally find out what her parents were responsible for.'

She feels quite magnanimous as she says this, and also put out, because it strikes her all over again that Lisa hadn't reacted quite as she should have done. Shouldn't she have been more sorry? Shouldn't she have appreciated all the more how generous Amy has been, inviting her here at all?

'I can see that it's a lot for her to get her head around,' Joe says. 'Maybe she's still digesting it. But it's probably for the best that she knows, isn't it? Surely it clears the air?'

Amy sighs. 'It doesn't seem to have done. Tilly's still going on about a pretend friend called Alice, and I would have thought that now she knows about actual Alice, Lisa might try to discourage her, but she hasn't. Not yet anyway.'

There is a pause at the other end of the line that is just long enough to make her wonder if there's a technical fault.

'I'm sorry that Tilly's upset you,' Joe says eventually. 'I'm sure if we sit her down and tell her about your sister she'll be much more careful. Do you think you would feel up to doing that with me when I get back?'

'You don't need to be there for me to explain it,' she snaps, and then, to try to justify herself for having been short with him, 'It's my family. I can handle it. It just hasn't been the right time yet, that's all.'

There is another, even longer pause. Then Joe says, 'It's my family too, Amy. That's what being married means.'

She has no answer to this, or at least, none that she can bring herself to give at the moment. Because it isn't really his family, is it? This is about *her* parents, *her* sister. But if she points this out, he'll just be hurt and go all quiet and sniffy and defensive. There's nothing worse than hurt Joe long-distance. Arguments from eleven thousand miles away are to be avoided at all costs.

'Look, you just need to hang on in there,' he goes on. 'I honestly think it would be better to explain things to Tilly when I'm there to help. Or if you really feel you can't wait, make sure Lisa's to hand somewhere.'

'Why should I do that? She's only just found out about it herself, and her parents were part of what happened. And like I said to you, she seems to be finding it hard to come to terms with.'

Another pause. Which is weird, because normally Joe would have backed down by now and would be trying to mollify her.

'I worry about the two of you,' he says finally. 'About you and Tilly, I mean. I've been thinking about it since I've been over here, and in a way, the distance has helped to make it clearer. Amy, I can hear the difference in your voice between the way you talk about Rowan and the way you talk about Tilly. I don't understand it, but I know it's there and I'm not imagining it. I don't want to have to spend the rest of our children's lives compensating for something Tilly's missing out on because you can't give it to her. I want to think you love our daughter as much I do. But sometimes I have to wonder.'

Her blood runs hot, then cold. He has never spoken to her like this before. Never told her off like this before, as if he's entitled to find her lacking, and to ask her to do better.

Then she goes on the attack. After all, it's the best form of defence.

'Joe, let me remind you of the obvious. You are not here. You left me here on my own with a seven year old and a tiny baby while you waltzed off to the other side of the world to concentrate on your career. For you to talk about compensating for what I'm not doing is just a joke. *I'm* the one compensating for you not being here.'

'No,' Joe says, 'Lisa is the one who is doing that. And when I get back, you and I need to have to have a proper talk about all of this.'

And then he ends the call. He doesn't even say he loves her first.

She puts the phone back in its cradle in the hall. Her heart is pounding. She is ashamed and angry, but she doesn't really have the right to be furious with Joe, not after the way she's behaved. What a disaster... If she had actually tried to tell him about falling asleep on Tyler's mattress, who knew how much worse it could have been?

But what if it wasn't actually Tyler who was the mistake? What if it was Joe who had been the wrong turning?

No sooner has she allowed herself to think this than she suppresses it. So what if Tyler seems to feel something for her? Whatever it is, it would never last. If he was going to attempt to lay claim to her, he would have done it by now. No – at the end of the day, he's a risk not worth taking, and she is going to have to cut him out.

She's just wound up and exhausted, that's the trouble. It feels as if every nerve in her body is on edge. She needs to relax, put her feet up, watch something on TV. Take it easy until it's time to give Rowan his last feed of the day at eleven, the one that will see him through the night. She might as well make the most of having a bit of time to herself.

So she'd just had a conversation with Joe that hadn't gone quite the way she would have wished – so what? It wasn't a total disaster. She still has her husband, her home, her children. Her life. Everything her grandparents and mum had wanted for her. Everything her dad would have wanted for her. She's come so far, now she just has to carry on keeping it together.

She heads into the kitchen to pour herself another glass from the bottle of wine she'd opened yesterday. The light is on, though she can't remember leaving it that way. If Joe was here he'd surely have turned it off. He was careful about things like that. Liable to gently remind you about the bills, or the planet. She didn't mind it when he explained that kind of thing to Tilly, but found it profoundly irritating if it was directed at her.

But that was marriage, wasn't it? The art of tolerating irritation.

As she stoops to retrieve the wine from the fridge someone steps forward behind her, from the corner by the back door, and says, 'Hello, Amy.'

The shock is so great that the bottle drops from her hand, falls as fast and hard as if she'd thrown it, and is instantly smashed to pieces on the stone floor. The fragments of glass and pooled wine at her feet look like a snapshot of a crime scene, and the sweet smell of the spilt alcohol is the only thing that persuades her it's real.

She knows him from his voice even before she straightens up and turns to face him. Russell. Of all the people... *Russell*, dressed in some kind of beige jacket and a check shirt and chinos and looking smug and sure of himself, as if any setbacks he might have experienced lately are behind him now. As if he has a perfectly good excuse for being here, and she's the one who is out of place.

He puts his finger to his lips. 'Don't be frightened,' he says, and takes a couple of paces towards her.

OK, so he wants her to keep quiet. That means he doesn't want to wake up the kids. Or Lisa. He does know Lisa is here, doesn't he? He knows Amy's not the only adult in the house. He must think he can accomplish whatever he's come here to do quickly, and without disturbing the rest of the household. That rules out murder, torture and burglary, surely. Maybe he just wants to talk.

'I'm not scared of you,' she says contemptuously, though her heart is in her mouth and tastes of metal, and her whole body is flooded with adrenaline. 'What do you think you're doing here? You can't just walk in here like this in the middle of the night.'

'Well, yes, obviously I can,' Russell says. 'And I have, haven't I? Your security is terrible. You can't have done anything to improve it since you moved in. You've got that gravelled area to the side, so you can hear if someone pulls up in a car, but then you have a path right up to the back door. I thought it would probably still be open, and it was. It amazes me you've never been burgled. For a family that's had more than its fair share of disaster, you do seem determined to push your luck.'

She folds her arms. What a fool she'd been to ever confide in a man like this, let alone to sleep with him. The callous reference to her family history is an outrage, but she can't afford to get worked up. She has to stay calm and think it through.

The phone is in the hall, so not exactly close, and she can't remember where her mobile is – in her handbag? Plugged in and charging in the family room? Her mind is a complete blank. Had she left it on the desk in the attic, next to the computer? No – if she had, surely Lisa would have found it and brought it down...

If only Lisa would wake up and come downstairs, surely then Russell would come to his senses and leave. He's behaving as if this – him being here – is completely normal. As if it's his right, and where he belongs every night. It's like he's in a weird kind of trance. Surely any reminder of the outside world – the phone ringing, Lisa appearing – would snap him out of it, and he'd apologise and stumble out.

She says, 'Get out now, or I'm going to call the police.'

That sounded pretty good. Pretty convincing. But it has no impact whatsoever. Russell settles heavily in a chair at the kitchen table, his legs spread disconcertingly wide. Taking up space. A man-sized space. In her kitchen! He doesn't appear to be in a hurry, or to respond to her threat with anything other than mild disappointment. Instead he gestures at the chair opposite her and says, 'Take a seat. I think you need to calm down.'

'I am not going to sit down with you, and I am not going to be calm! Who do you think you are? You need to leave.'

'You wouldn't be saying that if it was Tyler Paley sitting here rather than me,' he says, and watches her carefully to see what effect this has on her.

She feels the blood rush to her face. Why does this always happen where Tyler is concerned? 'I don't know what you're talking about,' she says.

'Oh yes, I think you do.'

'Have you completely lost your mind? You're making no sense at all.'

He taps the table in front of him. 'Sit down, Amy. You're not going to call anyone. And stop protesting your innocence. It really doesn't suit you.'

'How dare you speak to me like that!'

'I'm speaking to you like that because it's what you deserve,' he says. 'And in your heart of hearts you know it, and that's why you're still standing there.'

It must be the shock. She is rooted to the spot. She could try and get away and shout up the stairs for Lisa, or phone for help. But he's right. She isn't going to. Because she's too afraid of what he knows about her, and what he could tell her husband if he chooses to. The sex they'd had the day after her mum's funeral. The timing of it, almost nine months exactly before Tilly's arrival. And that wasn't all, either.

'I wouldn't have had to do it like this if you hadn't been so hostile,' he says. 'But it was just so easy. I can see when most of your lights go off from my bedroom. I don't even have to leave my house to keep an eye on your routine. I don't suppose you ever thought of that. Other people's points of view aren't your strong point, are they? Anyway, you seem to be on a schedule at nights these days. I guess that's probably Lisa's doing. She seems like a creature of habit.'

'That's disgusting,' she says. 'You've been spying on us. What a sad, sorry little man you are.'

'I just couldn't help but notice. And I was interested. You should be flattered. Anyway, we seem to have got off on the wrong foot. I'm sorry I startled you when I came in. I wouldn't have minded drinking some of that wine with you. Seems a waste. You know, those are some of my best memories of the time we spent together. You, me, a hotel room and a bottle of wine.'

'Honestly, looking at you right now, you make me want to vomit. I don't know why I ever let you touch me. I was too young to know any better.'

'There speaks the virtuous wife and loving mother. Come on, Amy, spare me the self-righteous horror. There's nothing worse than a hypocrite. I guess you must have convinced yourself that you wanted to be Mrs Longcross and all of that, but I don't think you have any idea what you really want or who you are. You're just making it up from one minute to the next.'

'I don't know what you think you've heard, but people round here have always gossiped about me. There's no basis to any of it, and nobody who matters would believe a word of it. You can't use that to bully me.'

'You're calling me a bully? Oh, come off it. You always have to be the victim, don't you? You treated me with absolute contempt when we met that time in the village. You could have at least pretended to be polite, for old times' sake. It would have been nice for me to feel I knew someone round here to talk to. I could have got a few things off my chest. I could have told you how I lost a load of money in my divorce, and now my business is going under and I'm probably going to have to go bankrupt. The cottage I'm in is rented, did you know that? You didn't, did you? You weren't even interested enough to look it up. Well, soon I won't even be able to afford that.' He slaps his hand against the table. 'Come on, sit down with me. It's just your pride that's stopping you. But it's really not in your interest to make a scene. Unless you want your cousin and your daughter and your husband and everybody else to know you've been sleeping with Tyler Paley.'

She makes no move towards him. 'You should be ashamed of yourself, coming here to say things like that about me.'

He lets out a short, dry little laugh of disbelief. 'I notice you don't deny it. You're the one who should be ashamed, and you know it. The only reason you aren't is because nobody knows what you've been up to.'

He reaches into his pocket and takes out a printed piece of paper, unfolds it and lays it down on the table. It's a photograph, blown up to A4 size, showing a parked car by an overgrown hedge, and two people going through a gap in the greenery towards an unfinished-looking house.

She steps closer and examines it with a sick feeling in the pit of her stomach. It's unmistakably her and Tyler on Dark Lane the day before. There she is, carrying Rowan in his car seat, and Tyler is holding her hand and she is looking up at him with clearly unfeigned delight.

Russell folds his arms and shakes his head. He seems to be enjoying himself.

'You've been a naughty girl, haven't you, Amy? There's a time stamp on that, of course, and I have others. I caught you arriving, and I caught you lying on his bed with him in front of that very big French window, and I caught you leaving. No point tearing that one up. I still have the originals. If your husband saw it, I think you'd have some explaining to do, wouldn't you? I mean, you might be able to talk your way out of it. You're obviously pretty good at manipulating him. But it's much easier to do that when someone trusts you. Loss of trust is very corrosive, Amy. Very damaging to a marriage. As I should know.'

'Put it away,' she says, and he obliges. 'What is this, black-mail? Is it money you want? Is that what all this is about?'

'Now, there's a nice way to talk to the father of your child,' he says drily.

All she can do is gape at him. She can't breathe. How can he stand here in her kitchen and say that, so matter-of-factly, as if he's entitled to come here at night and attack her like this? To throw out an accusation like that as if it's the kind of thing that ought to be out in the open for everybody to hear?

But it *is* in the open now, between the two of them at least. There it is, her dirty little secret, the thing that has always come between her and loving Tilly. Because right from when Tilly was a newborn, every now and then, something small but distinct about Tilly – the shape of her forehead and jaw, the way she frowned – had reminded her acutely of Russell. It was uncanny how her daughter's genetic heritage kept revealing itself, though only to Amy, who knew what to look for. It wasn't just the small resemblances, which were unnerving to spot in the features of a baby growing into a small girl, it was also expressions and habits. Even the way Tilly held her pencil when she drew reminded her of Russell signing letters back in the days when she used to work for him. And Russell having suddenly turned up in Springhill only made it worse.

It doesn't mean Tilly is *like* Russell. She has always been clear about that. But it has made it almost impossible for her to believe that there's any chance, however slim, that Joe could really be her father.

Russell says, 'Isn't it perfectly reasonable for me to want to check up on you after all this time? You could even say it's my right.'

Her arms and legs begin to shake and she can't stop them. She manages to say, 'I don't know what you're talking about.'

'Oh, come on, I think you do. All you need to do is look at her. It's supposed to be a little trick biology plays, isn't it?

Making a couple's first child look like the father, so the father feels reassured that he hasn't been cheated on. It's OK, Amy, calm down, I'm really not interested. I told you I didn't want children all those years ago, and I still don't. I haven't changed my mind, and your little secret is safe with me. *Both* your little secrets. I'm a pretty broad-minded guy, as you know. It really doesn't bother me that you're sleeping with your gardener.'

'Don't,' she says. 'That picture doesn't prove anything. It can't, because nothing happened.'

'I've been spending some time with Tyler's mum, did you know that? Your cleaner. She plays darts at the Flowing Spring, and she introduced me to the pudding club. Which is very good, actually, don't know if you've ever been? No? Well, it might be something to try sometime. Anyway, I took her out for lunch a little while ago, and she told me that she was worried about her son, and she thought he had feelings for a married woman but he wouldn't tell her who. And that was really as much of a clue as I needed, knowing you the way I do.' He grimaces. 'I'm very disappointed in Grace, actually. I would have thought she'd count herself lucky. It's not like she's fighting them off. But today she gave me the brush-off right in front of the rest of the pudding club crowd, when all I did was offer to settle her share of the bill. "Don't make assumptions," she told me. "You and I are friends. Nothing more." As if I'd want to be friends with someone like her! She's nearly fifty, for heaven's sake. And she's a cleaner. *She* was the one making assumptions. She humiliated me. But anyway, it doesn't matter, because she brought me to you.'

Amy has to suppress a wild urge to laugh at the thought of Mrs Paley putting Russell in his place.

'I'm sorry if your feelings were hurt,' she says. 'But that isn't my fault. And it's absolutely nothing to do with me.'

His face reddens. 'What do you know about feelings? You don't have any. You're shameless. The one thing that really did surprise me, though, the one thing that I wouldn't have expected even from you, was that you took your new baby along when you went to Tyler's place yesterday. I get that you have to take your opportunities where you can, but it's not exactly standard adultery, is it?'

'I was tired. I'd had a terrible day. The baby went to sleep, and so did I. That's all that happened,' she says. Her voice sounds hoarse, as if she's saying a line she's been rehearsing over and over, but that still doesn't sound convincing.

'Amy, sweetheart, you don't need to justify it to me. I'm not your husband,' he says, and then something shifts in his expression and he says, 'I suppose if what you say is true, it's quite touching, really. But I don't suppose Joe would see it that way.' He shakes his head. 'You didn't, did you, Amy? It's too good. Even for you. Tell me you didn't go and do it again.'

She stares at him in horror. 'I don't know what you mean.'

He begins to laugh. 'I have to say, it never would have crossed my mind. Rowan could be Tyler reborn and I wouldn't have seen it. All babies look alike to me. But this... You really have surpassed yourself this time, haven't you?' He looks up at her, beaming broadly, and lifts his hands in an expressive shrug. 'If Joe finds out about this, you're finished. Let's face it, Amy, a man might forgive his wife for accidentally conceiving one child with someone else and not telling him. Maybe, if he was very tolerant and forgiving. But there's not a man in the world who would forgive a woman who did that to him twice.'

'I don't understand,' she says slowly. 'After all this time, why would you do this to me? You let me go. We were over ages ago. Why would you want to wreck my life now?'

'Silly girl,' he says, almost affectionately. 'I don't want to wreck your life. Right now, all I want is to be part of it. I'm right, aren't I? I notice you don't deny it. Rowan is Tyler's baby. Well, have Tyler if you want, and I've certainly got no desire to break up your marriage. I only said all of that because it was the only way to make you listen to me. I just want us to be friends. After all, that's what friends are, isn't it? People who keep each other's secrets.' He gets up and approaches her, arms outstretched for an embrace. 'How about it?'

She reaches out and slaps him with all the force she can muster. He looks stunned and stumbles backwards, only just righting himself. A rough red mark shows up on his cheek, and she feels a huge rush of fear and fury and satisfaction.

'You're disgusting,' she says. 'And pathetic. What a creep! I'm ashamed I ever let you anywhere near me. Everything you've said is rubbish, and nobody in their right mind would believe you.' Her eyes flicker towards the knife block by the cooker. 'Now get out of my house before I stick you like the pig you are.'

They are interrupted by a thin wail from upstairs, hushed by the layer of oak beams and wooden floorboards, but still unmistakeably the sound of Rowan crying.

'Just go, Russell,' Amy says. 'Find someone else to have sick little fantasies about. Get out of here the way you came and we can both forget this ever happened.'

And he goes. He allows himself to be bundled out of the kitchen door and vanishes into the darkness. She locks up behind him and hurries upstairs to Rowan's room.

She's left him to cry for longer than she normally would; she can just about make out his face in the pale light of the night-light, screwed up tight in an expression of almost comical despair. He still looks dead tired, though – his face has the soft, baggy look of extreme sleepiness. She bends down over the cot and touches his velvety cheek with her forefinger, and he quietens.

The magic touch. Maybe he isn't really hungry yet. Maybe he'd picked up the sound of a strange man's voice in the kitchen, and just wanted reassurance. If she leaves him a little longer, maybe he will settle himself...

She sings to him very quietly, under her breath, because that always seems to soothe him. *Lavender's blue, dilly-dilly. Lavender's green.* It doesn't matter if you can't really remember the words. Rowan wriggles and grimaces and then is still. He lets out a final cry – more grumbling and resigned than panicky – and finally his breathing becomes calm and steady.

Thank goodness, she's done it. She's coaxed him back to sleep.

She lingers for a while, admiring him. What a beautiful baby he is! Russell's invasion of her house already seems far away and long ago. How could she ever have submitted to someone like that? Coming here with that picture and some outrageous guesswork, thinking he could pressure her into having some kind of relationship with him again... But she had just needed to face him down and be tough about it, and he'd given up and crawled back under his stone. He'd most likely have to move away, anyway, if he was going bankrupt. The village was pretty expensive these days, even to rent, and he probably wouldn't be able to afford it on whatever benefits he'd be allowed.

Then there is a tiny, barely audible click – a small mechanical sound, not ominous in itself – and Rowan's nightlight goes out.

Something must have tripped the fuse. It happens every once in a while – either the electrics in this house are temperamental or the fuse box is particularly sensitive, or both. Sometimes she hears the click first, and sometimes she only realises when she tries to turn on a light, or the kettle, and realises she can't. It only really matters if it's the circuit with the freezer that goes, and then the freezer starts defrosting and the food in it spoils.

She goes to the door, and sees that the landing is dark too. It must be all the upstairs lights that are affected. Now she has to get back downstairs without breaking her neck, and try to avoid stepping on any shards of broken glass from the wine bottle on her way to the fuse box in the kitchen. And she's going to have to clear all that up before morning. She can't exactly leave it for Lisa to come down to.

Out of force of habit, she closes Rowan's door quietly behind her. Then all the breath rushes out of her lungs as someone seizes her from behind and holds her close, his right arm reaching across her body to press something long and sharp against the left side of her face, along her cheekbone. She can see its edge with her left eye, dull silver and metallic, gleaming faintly in the darkness. The blade of a knife.

THIRTY-ONE

LISA

She dreams of tunnels and blue flowers, and then of a tall tree with a child climbing in it. The child is Alice, seven years old in a summer dress, daring and happy and sure-footed, holding on tightly as she ascends from one branch to next. When she reaches the very top she turns and smiles and waves and abruptly disappears. All that is left then is the blue sky and the bright light, and the thin green leaves of the weeping willow swaying and whispering like rippling water.

Then something jolts her awake, or maybe it's the dream itself that disturbs her. She comes to with tears on her face and remembers the love-in-a-mist Tilly had planted with Joe in the kitchen garden by the back door, and the same wildflowers growing on Alice's grave. And she thinks of meeting Joe all those months ago, how much she had been charmed by him, and how, if she was honest, her desire to see him again had played no small part in her getting in touch with Amy in the first place. Not because she had wanted Joe for herself. But because she'd liked him. He'd seemed so steady and gentle and kind. And she'd been lonelier than she cared to admit.

She is lying in a patch of moonlight, and the thin curtains

are stirring in the breeze from the open window above her bed. She closes the window, takes a fresh earplug from the little box on her bedside table to replace one that has fallen out at some point during the night, shuts her eyes and lets herself slip back into unconsciousness.

THIRTY-TWO

AMY

'I tried to talk to you,' he says in her ear. 'You wouldn't listen. All I want is for us to be friends the way we used to be. Remember?'

He could maim her, disfigure her. She could lose the sight of an eye. Russell could do that to her, and she could die here. That is suddenly possible. He could kill her and by and by Rowan would cry and she would not be able to feed him, and Lisa or Tilly would find her. And maybe they would catch him and maybe they wouldn't, but by then it would be much too late to save her.

She has to placate him. It's her only hope. It's the only chance she has to stave off whatever could be coming. To buy time. To bring this back from the edge. To save her skin.

And to keep the children safe, though he hasn't threatened them, he wouldn't...

She stands very still because she cannot think what else to do. She is here in her own house and yet she is right back where she was all those years ago when they were lovers, and the memory of shame and weakness floods back into her body until it barely feels like hers.

'I remember,' she says.

'Let's go to the bedroom. We can talk there,' he says, and releases her. She sees that the door to her bedroom is slightly open, and that there is a soft light coming from inside.

'Go on,' he says, and she does as he says.

He has lit the candles. Her candles, the expensive ones that she uses to cheer herself up on bad days, when Tilly plays up and it's raining outside and she wonders what on earth she's doing with her life in this place. Jasmine, fig, sandalwood. Christmas presents, birthday presents. Collectibles. She only ever uses one at a time, and he has lit all of them. On the dressing table, on the chest of drawers, on the bedside tables to either side of the four-poster bed.

'Sorry about the fuse box,' he says. 'You got me nervous with your talk of calling the police. I didn't think you actually would, but it seemed like it might be a distraction. And I put your mobile somewhere safe too. I find those things really don't help when it comes to having a proper conversation. But anyway, I'm sure you'll find it without too much trouble in the morning.' And then he gestures wildly with the knife. 'I mean, look at this! I never expected it to come to this. That got a rise out of you, didn't it? Of course, I never would have grabbed it if you hadn't said what you said before you threw me out. Didn't it occur to you that I'd just walk round to the first open window and climb back in?'

'Look, I'm sorry,' she says, though the words stick in her throat. 'I shouldn't have said the things I said. I appreciate you're having a bad time right now. Let's go downstairs and sit down together like you wanted, and we'll talk. We can talk all night if you want. We've got all the time in the world.'

'It's too late for that,' he says. 'Just be nice to me, Amy, that's all I want. It doesn't have to be difficult. You were nice to Tyler Paley, so why not me?'

Then she feels a sudden draught of air at her back, and Russell's focus switches from her to the door.

'Mummy? Is that you?'

A small, sweet, trusting voice. The voice of a child who is used to adults being kind to her, and who, for the first time, is not sure if it is safe to ask for help.

It's Tilly, holding her torch. The little torch Joe gave her. She is standing on the threshold, not daring to come in, because she knows she's not usually allowed. Amy is about to move towards her, but is held back by Russell's hand clamped on her upper arm.

'I'll deal with this,' he whispers in her ear. 'I guess this is the kind of thing parents have to get used to, isn't it? Unwelcome interruptions.' She feels the tip of the knife very gently nudging the small of her back, and freezes.

'My nightlight's not working,' Tilly says, choking a little as if she is about to cry. She rests the light of her torch on Lisa and then moves it up behind her towards Russell's face. 'Who are you?'

'I'm just a friend,' Russell says. 'Did nobody ever tell you not to bother the grown-ups when they're busy?'

Tilly's bottom lip trembles. 'I remember you,' she says. 'What are you doing here?'

'We're just playing a game,' Russell says smoothly. 'It's the best thing to do when the lights go out. It's hide and seek. You can play too. All you have to do is go and find somewhere to hide, and count to a hundred. Maybe two hundred, if you've found a really good place. And by and by Mummy will come and find you.'

Tilly frowns. 'What about you? Are you going to hide too?'

'In a while,' Russell says. 'But you can have a head start. Off you go now. And remember to close the door behind you.'

Tilly hesitates. It is quite clear that she is not sure this is at all right. Russell's hand trembles on Amy's arm. He is nervous. Perhaps this has already gone much further than he thought, or maybe he had already imagined all this unfolding exactly as it is now. He could have been thinking about it for years. Or it could be as much of a shock to him as it is to her. Because what is most shocking about it is that it is real, it is unfolding in the present moment, and that also makes it ordinary. It is now normal for her to stand in a dark bedroom with her ex-boyfriend holding a knife to her back. This is happening, and it is happening to her, and she does not know how to stop it, or if she can keep it from getting worse.

Then Tilly makes her move. The small plume of light from her torch circles as she whirls round and disappears as she slams the door shut. The candles flutter and the light waves. Amy catches sight of herself in the wardrobe mirror with Russell standing close behind her and clasping her almost as if supporting her, or to demonstrate his loyal affection.

'Look at us,' she says. 'The perfect couple.'

He looks, and smiles as if for a camera, and his grip on her loosens a little as he shifts his position so that they look more comfortable together. It's a moment of hesitation and it's as much of a chance as she's going to get. She wrenches herself away and grabs the chair that sits in front of the dressing table next to the wardrobe and swings it hard against his knees.

The knife flies out of his hand and falls out of sight somewhere on the carpet. He bellows in fury and stumbles backwards against the wardrobe and there's a crunching sound and a jingling of hangers from inside as it rocks and thuds back against the wall. The light shakes and flashes and she sees the mirrored panel on the front of the wardrobe has cracked and is sending the reflection of the candles in different directions.

She swings the chair at him again and jabs it at his face and he howls in rage and grabs it and pulls and she has to let go.

Then he is back on his feet and about to launch himself on her again, but suddenly Lisa is there, moving towards them, getting between her and him, shouting at her to get the children and run. Amy races towards the open door and is out of the room almost before she knows it.

THIRTY-THREE

LISA

Thank goodness Amy has the sense to run, to get the children out. Lisa catches sight of her flitting through the door and disappearing before the intruder hurls himself at her. She just has time to brace herself for the impact before he brings her down.

They crash down onto the floor with his full weight on her and he's too close to strike her but sinks his teeth deep into her shoulder like a dog worrying a bone. She screams and his teeth tighten as if she is nothing but meat, and she can believe that he would tear a chunk out of her if he could. She scrabbles with her free hand, reaching for his eyes, and his jaw slackens and she is able to move but then he rears up and punches her on the bridge of her nose and the hurt is outrageous, radiating out around the sockets of her eyes and her forehead and cheekbones. He takes hold of her face and bashes her skull against the floorboards as if it's a shell he's trying to crack open and she can't knee him in the groin, she can't free her hands, she can't get any purchase on anything, and she is screaming but she knows that won't make him stop. If anything it will make it worse, because he will want her to stop, too, and there is only one way for him to make that happen.

The light is reddening and darkening. Maybe she is bleeding behind her eyes or inside her brain and the blood fog is hazing what she can see. But then she smells smoke and hears the whisper and rustle of flames and knows the fire burning is not only in her head because she can see that he has noticed it too.

He is distracted just long enough for her to get a hand up to his face, to his eyes, and he recoils. She pulls away at the same time and reaches for the alabaster vase on the dressing table, the beautiful pale green one that she has always thought would feel good to hold. And she grasps it and swings it in a perfect arc towards him and it cracks against the side of his head.

He's down. No, he is trying to get up. He is unstoppable. He is going to keep coming for her and she is never going to be able to get away.

She makes it to the door and gets out and slams it shut behind her, and hurries towards the stairs through total darkness. Rowan's door is open and so is Tilly's. Both rooms are empty. Good. Amy has got them both out. They're safe and that's what counts, it doesn't matter so much what happens to her...

The door swings open behind her and the steps in front of her are suddenly illuminated. But then the light shifts and there is a rushing sound as if something has just exploded into flame, or as if she is falling from a great height, so fast that the air is pushing back against her like flowing water. She loses her balance and then she really is falling, and the darkness is rolling her into a ball and inside it there is nothingness, and that is where she lands.

When she comes to the house is burning.

Somewhere a smoke alarm is going off. She forces herself to straighten up and her dim view of the segment of ceiling above her head swims and corrects itself. She can't see him. Russell. Had it really been him? Is he still in the bedroom? Has he gone?

The curtains must have gone up in flames, or the drapes, or both. And next it will be the wooden frame of the four-poster bed, and then maybe the beams...

She can hear the fire roaring. Her vision darkens and blurs. But she has to move. She summons up every last vestige of willpower she has to haul herself up the next step, and then the next. The stairs in front of her flicker and give way to darkness and then she is conscious again and moving again, clawing at the banister posts, pulling and pushing, making use of anything that could propel her.

There is no sign of anyone on the first floor. The door to Amy's room is wide open and the four-poster bed is wreathed in crackling flames and obscured by clouds of smoke. She had never realised just how much of a house fire is smoke, that it is as much smoke as flame. The air is hot and dry and choking. She pulls the top of her T-shirt up over her nose and mouth and begins to make her way back down the stairs.

The air is darkening and that could be the smoke or it could be her eyes. She trips and grabs the banister to steady herself, and when she lets go she feels another hand takes hers.

A small, unmistakably real hand. A child's hand. She can't see who. The child's hand tugs at hers, firmly but not impatiently: *Let's go.*

And she moves. She lets herself be led all the way down to the foot of the stairs. It is still smoky down here and it is even darker, but it is easier to breathe. The front door is right there, and it is wide open. Fresh air. Safety. Just there waiting for her to walk out into it. But the persistent little hand in hers keeps pulling her along. She doesn't stop to rummage in the hall table for the flashlight. She keeps going all the way to the red curtain at the back of the staircase, and then she sees that it is only pulled halfway across.

The hand tugs hers again. *This way.* Down the little passageway. It's very dark. She feels for the handle of the basement door with her left hand and finds it is already unlocked and open. The shock of it is electric, an agonising rush of fear and hope that travels in an instant from the tips of her fingers through all of her nerves. She pulls the door open and sees the small light of Tilly's torch and hears crying.

And just like that, the little hand that has guided her all the way down here is gone.

She slams the door shut so the smoke won't follow them in. Tilly drops the torch and jumps up off the bed where she has been curled up and scuttles across the room to press herself against Lisa's body and wrap her arms around Lisa's legs. It is just the two of them and Lisa's heart feels as if it is burning and as if no flame could be more powerful.

The front door. That's the closest exit. She could get Tilly out that way. Or there's the back door, out into the garden from the kitchen. But the flames could be halfway down the banisters by now, and the smoke makes it so hard to see and to breathe. She's not sure she'll make it. She's not sure if Tilly will make it without her...

She says, 'There's a fire upstairs. We should be able to climb out of that window. Will you try for me?'

'But you're hurt,' Tilly says, and starts to cry again. There's a dark smudge of blood on her forehead. Lisa touches it in horror and realises it is her own, that it is covering her face and soaking her clothes.

'I'm OK,' she tells Tilly. 'But we have to get out of here.'

'What about the flowers we kept for my daddy? And my bears?' Tilly weeps. 'Will they be all burned up?'

'The fire engine will be here in a minute to save them,' Lisa says. 'But we have to save ourselves, and we have to do it right now. I need your help. Get your torch and shine the light at the window for me.'

Tilly breaks away and snatches the torch up from the floor and directs its beam onto the window. The handle has a lock set in the lever and the key is on the sill. Lisa reaches for the key, but then the lock doubles and triples in front of her. Three windows. Three possible exits. With a superhuman effort she refocuses her vision and gets the key into the lock. It turns. A sweet, tiny half circle, the difference between life and death.

She reaches for the handle but it's stuck. She bellows with exasperation and jiggles it and wrenches it because she can't have come this far only to be thwarted when the outside world is so close. Just the other side of a double-glazed pane of glass and a set of metal bars, the safety of the garden.

Then she hears something click – a mechanism shifting in the window frame – and the window swings towards her and the night air rushes in, sweet and fresh and scented with lilac.

She reaches up into the window well and grabs the bars of the grille, expecting another struggle, and then she pushes and the grille squeaks in protest and flips outward and away from the window like a hatch, then comes to rest and won't go any further, won't lie flat – there's resistance from the other side, it must be a branch of the lilac. But anyway, it is open enough.

She says to Tilly, 'You've done very well. I'm going to help you climb out, and then I'm going to follow you. OK?'

Tilly puts the torch down on the bed and scrambles through the window into the well, and then quite easily clambers out of it. Lisa withdraws to grab the torch off the bed. She switches it off and the room instantly darkens, lit only by the faint white glow of moonlight. She passes the torch up and Tilly takes it.

'Keep it off just for now,' Lisa says. 'There's a bad man out there somewhere and you don't want him to see you. Go round to the front of the house. Look for your mummy and Rowan, or for the fire engine. Don't put the torch on till you find people who are safe. There should be a group of them come to help. Or go down the lane to the village. Go as quick as you can. I'll come and find you. Go!'

Tilly turns away and disappears in a flurry of scratchy branches and rustling leaves.

The window is just big enough for Lisa to follow her. She rests the palms of her hands on the brick base of the window well and prepares to hoist herself through. She'll need to get a knee up onto the windowsill and push, and then she'll be out and she'll be safe and this will be over. She's so close, so close now...

But her arms and shoulders have lost all their strength and she can't pull or push herself any more. The room darkens completely, as if someone has just turned off a dimmer switch. From somewhere in the distance she hears the wail of a siren. She thinks of Tilly running through the garden in the moonlight and of Mum at rest in the quiet ground under the same moon. She remembers the hand that held hers and led her to where Tilly was. And then she is conscious of nothing at all.

THIRTY-FOUR

LISA

Summer 1977

Alice is still sleeping when Lisa wakes up, and it's funny to see her like that with her eyes shut and her mouth open. Then Alice wakes up, too, and Lisa remembers to say happy birthday. Alice is going to have a huge, huge pile of presents that will take ages to open, and Lisa has forever to wait until it's *her* birthday and she will be the one with a special cake and lots of new toys.

After Mummy has gone to help in the bakery Auntie Diane says to get dressed and have breakfast. She seems grumpy, and Lisa hopes that Alice won't do anything to make her worse. Lisa plays in the living room at the back of the house, the one that looks out onto the garden, for a bit – that's the thing about Grandma and Grandad's enormous house, there is always a space to go into, and it is easy to stay out of the grown-ups' way. But then Auntie Diane tells her to go out into the garden. Lisa takes her dolls out with her even though usually she is meant to play with them indoors, and Auntie Diane doesn't say anything, maybe because she doesn't know or isn't really looking.

Auntie Diane is sitting at the garden table in the shade at

the back of the house, knitting a tiny cardigan in pale blue wool for the baby that is growing in her tummy. Alice is there next to her, drawing in her book of pictures. She looks a little sad. After a while she says to Auntie Diane, 'Can we go to the park?' She is using the voice Mummy calls her whiny voice, which sometimes helps her get what she wants and sometimes doesn't.

'Maybe after lunch,' Auntie Diane says.

'Can I open one of my presents?'

'No, you cannot. You know you have to wait. Now don't look at me like that. What are you going to do if the wind changes?'

Alice tries to make her face less sulky, but it doesn't work. She says, 'That can't happen. Your face can't get stuck.'

Auntie Diane sighs and puts her knitting down on the table. 'Look, I have an important job for you. Keep an eye on your sister for me, will you? Make sure she doesn't eat the grass or anything like that.'

'She wouldn't eat grass. She isn't a cow.'

Auntie Diane stretches and sighs. 'Just do as I ask, there's a good girl.' She rubs her tummy. 'I need to go and find something to eat.'

'Can we have a snack too?' Alice asks.

'No you can't, or you won't eat your lunch and your mum will be annoyed with me.'

'But you're having a snack,' Alice points out.

'That's different. I am having a baby.'

'Yes, but it's my birthday.'

'And don't we all know it,' Auntie Diane mutters, and gets up and flounces into the house.

Alice pulls a face at Auntie Diane's back as she retreats, then comes over and kneels down next to Lisa. She looks at the dolls as if she would like to play with them herself.

'I have a good idea,' Alice says. 'Do you want to play dares?'

All Lisa can do is stare at her. She doesn't know what Alice means, but it sounds like trouble.

'You know what a dare is? It's really fun,' Alice persists. 'You think of something brave to do, and then you have to do it. If you don't, you're a cowardy custard and you lose the dare. We'll take turns thinking of things. Do you want to play?'

Lisa would rather play a nicer, safer game, but it seems like Alice is in the mood for this and nothing else, and she doesn't want to miss out on doing something together. She says, 'OK.'

'Good,' Alice says. 'I'll go first.' She takes Lisa by the hand and leads her over to where Auntie Diane had been sitting. She knocks Auntie Diane's knitting down onto the floor, quickly and furtively checks to see Auntie Diane isn't coming back yet, and then picks it up and drops it back on the table.

'Quick, before she comes back. Your turn,' Alice says.

Lisa hesitates, then quickly knocks the knitting onto the ground. It doesn't feel like fun. But she doesn't know what else to do.

'OK, we're even so far,' Alice says. She sounds disappointed. 'Your turn to think of something.'

Lisa points hopefully at Alice's book of drawings. She says, 'Let's draw.'

'That's not a dare,' Alice says impatiently. 'That would be a competition. A dare has to be scary.' She takes Lisa by the hand and leads her across the lawn to the big willow at the end of the garden. 'Like climbing that.'

They both look up at it. It is enormously tall, almost as high as the sky. But there are a couple of branches not all that far off that could be within reach for Alice.

Lisa pulls at Alice's dress to make her stay. 'No,' she says. 'Don't.'

'Don't be silly,' Alice says, and shakes her off. 'Don't be a coward, Lisa. You have to learn to be brave.'

'Too high,' Lisa says.

'Watch me,' Alice tells her.

The first step is easy. Up she goes. The next one is harder. Alice's feet slip as she reaches up, and she hesitates. Then she pulls herself up.

'Look at me! I'm so high! You look tiny down there.'

She already looks far away, like someone who is leaving. She is half disappearing into the green of the willow tree. Then she looks down and Lisa sees how happy she is. Her face is dappled with the shadows of the leaves and bright with sunlight. She gives Lisa a little wave and boldly reaches up again.

But the branch cracks and breaks off in her hand.

A great swathe of leaves bend and thresh as if in a sudden hurricane, and Alice's feet scrabble and slip.

'Help me!'

She screams as she falls, and lands with a splintery wet thump, the sound of something heavy and special breaking. And then she groans and lies there and doesn't get up.

Lisa backs away. She knows what she has to do. She must get help, the help Alice had called out for. She turns and runs back across the lawn towards the kitchen.

But Auntie Diane is already on her way out, moving faster than Lisa has seen her move since she had the baby in her tummy, and the look on her face tells Lisa for sure that what just happened to Alice is very bad indeed.

Which means she has not helped. She wants to help so much, and Alice is still just lying there. There must be a way to get her back. To fix it. Does she need to run faster? Be braver? Pull Alice right back down to earth? Or be the one to climb the tree?

THIRTY-FIVE

AMY

August 2009

Three days have passed since the fire and she has had time to rehearse what she wants to say before Joe gets back from New Zealand, but she doesn't want to launch into it straight away. He's come off a twenty-four-hour flight from Auckland followed by an hour-long taxi ride from Heathrow. What he needs is something to eat and a chance to see the children and a bath and a good long sleep. The truth has waited long enough already; it won't hurt for it to wait a little longer.

They've just had such a narrow escape. Surely the least she can do is let the big reunion go ahead before she blows the whole thing up.

She and the children are staying, for now, in a bed-and-breakfast place in Kettlebridge, which is in a medieval house on an old street tucked away behind the town hall. They have a family room on the top floor, with space for a double bed for her, a little bed for Tilly and a travel cot for Rowan. The room is bright and charming with a brick fireplace and exposed beams and bright rugs on the wooden floor, and windows looking out onto the rooftops of other old houses. There's a little kitchen along the corridor where she can prepare their food, and a bathroom which is theoretically shared but which they have to themselves for now, as there is no one else staying on their floor.

Mrs Paley had suggested the place to her and had said it was one of the town's best-kept secrets – they certainly don't seem to advertise because she had never heard of it before. The garden, which stretches down to the river, is open to the public most days but very few people wander in, and every now and then meditation groups or yoga classes come in to make use of the rooms that are open for daily hire on the ground floor.

It is calm, which is just as well because she has been all over the place and has barely slept since the fire. Although not sleeping has given her more thinking time. She wants to be honest with Joe, no matter how much it costs her. And with Tyler. And there is Lisa in hospital to think about, and the insurers to deal with, and the police, and a to-do list that she can hardly bear to look at, let alone get started on. Plus the children to worry about. But at least the three of them had escaped unharmed, and Lisa is recovering. In the scheme of things, the gratitude she feels outweighs everything else.

There's no TV in their room at the bed-and-breakfast, which is a minor disadvantage but liveable with since Tilly has already acquired several books from the various charity shops dotted around the town centre, and is working her way through them when not drawing in the new sketchpads Amy has got her from the nearby stationer's. Rowan has some new toys, too, acquired from the same charity shops. She would have thought that living with the children at such close quarters, in just one room, would be unbearable. But to her surprise it has actually been all right, in spite of the dire circumstances. Better than all right. It's such a relief to be with the two of them, she wouldn't care if they were living in a tent.

It is a joy to be sitting here in the sunshine on her double bed with a magazine on her lap, as usual unread, while Rowan distracts her with the tower of blocks he is gleefully trying to build, and Tilly, in the corner with a furious frown of concentration, attempts to knit.

Sometimes, though, especially at night, the fire comes back to her. The darkness. The choking air and the sound of flames and Lisa screaming. Rowan in her arms, and Tilly not there. Just not there. Vanished. Russell's instructions to Tilly echoing in her head, too late for her to counter them: *Find a really good place to hide.* Knowing the whole place might be about to go up in flames, and having to save Rowan, to get out and leave Lisa behind and probably Tilly too. Hoping against hope that Tilly would have gone outside.

She meant to go back. But they had stopped her. Someone took Rowan from her and she screamed and screamed. And in the despair of that moment she had known that everything that was difficult between her and Tilly meant nothing at all.

Then she had seen the light of a small torch circling and quivering at hip height in the darkness, and she had stopped screaming and run her fastest across the lawn and dropped to her knees to pull her sobbing child into her arms.

She could never repay Lisa for that moment. Never, never, never... She has been given something huge and beautiful, something that she has promised herself she will try to live up to for the rest of her life – a second chance. But what nobody ever told you about second chances is that sometimes they involve hurting people who don't deserve it. There is no way she can conduct herself the way she needs to now without smashing Joe's idea of who she is to pieces.

Somehow, she misses the doorbell ringing downstairs, and the first she knows that Joe has arrived is his tentative knock on the bedroom door. He comes in, lugging his suitcase, and he's the same old Joe, just looking more tired and a little thinner and more unsure than when he left. Tilly gets up and launches herself at him and he sweeps her up and hugs her, and Rowan gurgles in appreciation. Then Joe turns to Amy and embraces her before pulling back and eyeing her warily, as if he's not quite sure what she has in store for him. That's when she realises that however relieved he is that she is safe, he knows as well as she does that there is still more trouble ahead for them both.

They spend a quiet night together: they go out for dinner at the pizza place in town, he shows her and Tilly pictures from New Zealand, and then, back at the bed-and-breakfast place, he goes into one of the communal rooms downstairs to use his laptop while she puts the children to bed and borrows Tilly's torch to read. He comes in soon after and sleeps heavily, and she sleeps badly at his side and wonders if it will be the last time.

The next morning, they all eat breakfast together and it's sunny and everything seems hopeful. OK, so things hadn't been brilliant between them before he left. And yes, she owes him the truth. But what if there is still some way of making the future work that means she won't have to lose him? He's so pleased to see the children. She can't hurt him the way she had been planning to. It's cruel and unnecessary, because what will it achieve other than easing her guilty conscience?

Then Hannah, who is the mum of Tilly's friend Flora, swings by to pick up Tilly and Rowan in his pushchair and take them off with her children to the park, and she and Joe go down to the bench at the end of the garden behind the house they are staying in, by the edge of the river, and Joe says, 'OK then. You said you wanted to talk. Now talk.'

And she does. It is hard at first and then it becomes easier, but only in the way that anything is once you have forced yourself to start it.

'I have to tell you something about me and about your children,' she says. 'And when I've told you, you are going to be upset and angry and you will have every right to be.'

Joe turns very pale. 'Go on.'

'First, I have to tell you about Russell,' she says. 'The man who broke into the house and attacked me and Lisa, and started the fire. You know I used to work for him. What you don't know is that before you and I got together, I had a relationship with him. He was married at the time. It wasn't a good relationship. He was...' She shudders. 'It wasn't healthy. It stopped when I started seeing you. But then, after Mum's funeral, he took me out for dinner and he was so nice to me, and I guess I was vulnerable and I slipped up and I slept with him again. Joe... I think he might be Tilly's father.'

There is silence. Joe says, 'You *think*. How long have you been *thinking* this?'

'I didn't think. I knew,' she says, and begins to cry. 'I just didn't want it to be him. I wanted it to be you. That's why I didn't tell you.'

He makes no move to comfort her, and she wants to stop and take it all back but she can't. She knows she is breaking the dream of what their marriage could have been and she despises herself for having used him and made herself despicable. But at the same time it's a huge relief to have finally told him, and the relief is a complete surprise to her.

She had always thought that this – confessing how dishonest she has been, breaking his heart by telling him how she has deceived him – would be the worst thing she could experience. But it is nothing like as terrible as the time when she thought she had left Lisa and Tilly to burn.

'Russell knew that Tilly was his, and he threatened to tell you,' she says. 'He wanted to try to blackmail me into seeing him again. And he had figured out something else about me. He guessed I'd been unfaithful to you with someone else. Joe, last summer I slept with Tyler. It only happened once. But I can't be sure Rowan is your baby. Tyler asked me about it and I lied and said Rowan was yours. But it's possible he is not.'

He sits and listens. Because he is Joe, he doesn't rage at her or lose his temper or threaten her. The river slides by and people walk past on the other side, wearing shorts and eating ice cream and walking their dogs, enjoying the happy and peaceful small town existence that she has always belittled and pretended not to think much of, but has secretly wished she could properly share.

Finally he says, 'You made a fool out of me. I don't know if I'm ever going to forgive you.'

And then he says, 'You stole my children from me. I had two children, a little girl and a little boy. And now I have none.'

And then he puts his head in his hands and weeps. She says nothing because she does not know how to console him. What he has said is true. She has done that to him.

After a while he can't cry any more and he finds a handkerchief and blows his nose and she says, 'You are a brilliant, brilliant dad. I know Rowan would miss you and Tilly would be absolutely devastated if she couldn't still see you. You're her lifeline. You're the person who gave her all the love she needed when I wasn't there for her. I can see that she's soaked it all up and it's helped her turn into the sweet, sensitive, thoughtful person she's growing into. I want you to still see them. I hope you will want to.'

He turns to face her. 'You think it's that easy to make this OK? Just stop and think about it for a minute, Amy. Come out of the world where you get everything the way you want it, and try to see it from someone else's point of view for a change. How would Tyler feel about that? Where Rowan is concerned, I mean. I guess he won't be bothered about Tilly. And that man, that dreadful man who attacked you, who burned the house, who could have killed all of you. How did he get to have Tilly? Why should she be his daughter and not mine?' Then he turns away to look at the river. 'We have to be sure, Amy. I want to whatever tests we need to do. There's no way I can deal with this or process it while it's still a maybe.' He faces her again. 'Because there is still some chance, isn't there? That they're mine? There has to be.'

'Joe, for what it's worth...'

'Don't tell me you're sorry. That word cannot do the work you need it to do.'

'They're very, very lucky to have you,' she says.

'I'm not sure I can say the same about you.'

She doesn't reply. How can she defend herself? After what she's done? She can't. All she can do is try to do better from now on. They carry on sitting there together a while longer, looking at the water, until Tilly comes racing in with her friend Flora, with Flora's mum and Rowan in the pushchair following a little way behind.

Tilly demands to know if they have finished now and if so, whether Joe can come upstairs so she can show him some more of her drawings.

Joe turns to Amy. 'What do you think?'

'It's fine by me.'

'I'm not going to be able to look at your pictures for very long,' Joe says. He looks at Amy and she understands that he means he is going to find somewhere else to stay. 'I have some other things I have to do. But I can come up for a little while.'

'But Daddy, you've been away for ages and ages,' Tilly says, pouting. 'You can't go away again.'

'I'll be back to see you very soon, don't you worry,' Joe says, and manages a smile. Then he lets Tilly lead him back into the house.

Amy takes Rowan out of the pushchair and holds him close and takes comfort from knowing that at least someone loves her, for now, uncritically. Maybe, in the end, the thing she has struggled with so much, and sometimes felt she was barely capable of – being a mum – is what is going to see her through.

The following day Joe comes back, as he had promised, and they all catch the bus to the hospital to see Lisa.

She is on a general ward, still on bed rest. Her head is partly bandaged, and she's hooked up to a drip with an oximeter clipped to her finger. The first time Amy had come to see her she had been asleep, and Amy had sat with a while and left flowers by her bedside but couldn't be sure Lisa knew she had been there. This time, her eyes flicker open when they come into her cubicle and she smiles. She looks very pale, and the bruising on her face is all the more lurid in contrast. But it's hugely reassuring just to see her awake.

'It is so good to see you all,' she says, and her voice sounds thick and slow, as if she's got out of the habit of speaking. 'They told me you were coming, and I was going to try and get out of bed, but I don't seem to have managed it.'

'You shouldn't rush it,' Amy says. She has Rowan in a baby carrier on her front, facing outwards. He recognises Lisa in spite of the bandages and bruising and the unfamiliar environment, and beams and gurgles at her.

'We brought these for you,' Tilly says, holding out the flowers she had picked out at the florist's in Kettlebridge. 'We brought a vase, too, in case the hospital doesn't have any.' Amy had left the tulips she'd brought on her last visit in a cut-off water bottle.

Lisa takes Tilly's flowers and sniffs them. It's a big bouquet of white roses, baby's breath and love-in-a-mist, which was why Tilly had chosen it. She sets it down carefully on the cabinet beside the bed. 'Thank you so much, Tilly. They are beautiful. They are really going to cheer me up and make me feel much better.'

'I had to be checked by the doctor too, and so did Rowan,' Tilly says importantly. 'But we both did very well and they said we didn't need to be in hospital. Are you going to be in hospital long, Lisa?'

'I hope not, Tilly. They think they will be able to discharge me soon.'

'I want you to be able to come and see the place we are staying,' Tilly says. 'It's really quite nice, although it's only temporary. But Daddy has decided to go somewhere else.'

Lisa looks from Tilly to Amy to Joe as if not sure whether to ask for an explanation. Joe says wearily, 'It's been complicated.'

'I made you a card, Lisa,' Tilly says. 'Mummy, give Lisa my card. Rowan couldn't make you one, because he is still only a baby. He can't even sign his name yet, or write a kiss, so I did that for him in my card.'

Amy rummages in her bag for the card, a slightly awkward manoeuvre because of Rowan in the baby carrier on her front, and hands it over. It has a picture of Tilly and Lisa together on the front, surrounded by flowers. Lisa admires it and thanks Tilly and puts it next to the bouquet. Amy asks Joe to pass her the vase from the bag he is carrying and goes off to find a sink so she can put water in it. When she comes back, Joe is saying something she just catches the end of about how grateful he is to Lisa for everything she has done.

'We're all going to be all right. That's what matters,' Lisa says as Amy sets about putting the flowers into the vase.

'Yes. I suppose that's the way to think of it,' Joe says, and Amy feels the familiar burn of shame and remorse.

They chat for a little longer about how Lisa is doing and the place where Amy, Tilly and Rowan are staying, and then Lisa begins to look tired and Tilly becomes restless. Joe suggests that he could take Tilly out to the hospital café for a cake or an ice cream, and Tilly seems happy enough to go along with this. Amy is thankful all over again for Joe's kindness, and for his willingness to try and maintain his bond with Tilly in spite of what she has told him.

She is sitting on a chair next to Lisa's bed, and has taken Rowan out of the baby carrier to give him a little more freedom. He is on her lap, fiddling with his favourite rattle, content for now but perhaps not for much longer. When Joe and Tilly are safely out of earshot Lisa says to her, 'Is everything all right between you and Joe?'

'Not really. No, things are not good. But you don't have to worry about that. You just concentrate on getting better. And anything you need us to do for you, you just ask.'

Lisa's eyelids begin to drift downwards. 'Thanks,' she says. 'I just feel so sleepy all the time. But they say that will pass.' Then she opens her eyes wide. 'Can I ask you something? I've been going over and over what happened. Not much else to think about, in here. And I wondered if you knew why Tilly had gone down to the basement.'

'She came to the bedroom when I was in there with Russell. He told her to go and hide as a way of getting rid of her.'

'Is she really doing all right?'

'I think she's going to be OK. But we'll have to see. Physically she's fine. And because you came and found her so quickly, I think that's helped her cope with the shock of it. I'm sure it will have shaken her trust in other people. But it won't have completely destroyed it.' She hesitates. 'Can I ask *you* something? What made you go down there? Because if you hadn't, and if you hadn't pushed her out the window, the smoke might have got to her when the staircase went up. And it's worse for children than it is for adults. You said the door was open and you closed it – that helped slow down the smoke and the flames. If you hadn't gone down there, if you hadn't found her, she might have been seriously injured. Or worse. She could have died. And if she hadn't been able to tell them where you were, *you* could have died.'

Lisa turns to her and smiles, and her eyes are suddenly bright and clear.

'It was just a hunch. I guess I thought she might have gone down there if she felt threatened. She must have seen it as a safe place, even if it wasn't.'

Amy reaches forward and squeezes her hand. 'Well, thank goodness for lucky guesses. Though, of course, it wasn't just luck. You know her so well, after all the time you've spent together this summer. She loves you. We all do. I dread to think what would have happened if you hadn't been there. You're so brave. You didn't even hesitate. What you did was really heroic.'

'I'm definitely not heroic,' Lisa says, and turns her head to admire the flowers. 'I've always been a follower, not a leader. We were all just very lucky it worked out the way it did.'

Amy has the distinct impression that she's holding something back. Not lying, because lying isn't Lisa's style. But keeping something to herself. She doesn't get the chance to try to find out what it might be, though, because the next minute Lisa's eyes are closed again, and she has drifted off to sleep.

THIRTY-SIX

JULIE

December 2008

She doesn't know what she's done. The only thing she knows for sure is that it isn't good.

Broken neck? Is this what it feels like to break your neck? She can't move, and the pain is overwhelming. But if she has broken her neck, why is she still here? Why isn't she dead?

Is this how it hurt for Alice, after she fell?

Alice. A bold little girl, always disappearing ahead of you down the lane, always asking questions. *Why do I have to wait for my presents? Where do babies come from? If this is an old house, hundreds of years old, does it have ghosts? Are there really such things as ghosts?*

Julie knows the answer to that now, all these years later. Yes, there are ghosts. But they come and go as they please, and never in the form you might expect. You can't summon them. No matter how much you might long to see the people you have lost, you can't conjure them up. You can dream that you are together again and it is as real as life, but when you wake it will all fade away like mist burned away by the summer sun and you will be left holding nothing.

She has always believed she was protecting Lisa and that it was a sacrifice not to tell her the truth about Mike and Alice. They were Julie's burdens, to carry on her own. She didn't want Lisa to know what Mike had done, or how he had died – the heroin overdose in a squat somewhere, the shame and squalor of it. She had got as far as informing her mother, and the note she'd got back had been as short as it was brutal. *I'm glad he's dead*, it had said. *Elliott was like the son we'd always wanted. Mike was the son-in-law from hell, and if hell is real that's where he deserves to be. Your news brought back painful memories and I don't want you to write to me again. Your father doesn't know we've ever been in touch, but if he did, I know he would agree that I'm doing the right thing now. I'll destroy anything you send unopened, so save us both some trouble and leave me be.*

She'd burned that letter with shaking hands, but she can still remember every word. She'd burned the other letters her mum had sent her down the years, too. Why had she been so stupid as to stay in touch at all, however intermittently? Much better not to look back. She still had Lisa, and that was all that really mattered.

Lisa is innocent and surely Julie had been right to keep her that way. Innocence only lasts for as long as the people who are in the know protect it. And she's Lisa's mum. It's her job to protect her and to keep her away from *them*. From what was left of them. Her ruthless, broken family, and that old house on the hill with the bad memories and the old hatreds and the mistakes that had not been forgiven.

But maybe she should have tried to tell Lisa more. What if it's too late?

How often has she told Lisa to go carefully on the stairs? So many times. And yet she is the one who has slipped and fallen, and now here she is, and no one knows, and all she can do is wait for Lisa to come and save her.

She can almost see it now, the line of ghosts waiting in the shadows to be acknowledged and introduced, and Lisa living her life without ever knowing they are there. Having no idea how a family can behave when it needs somebody to blame.

But there's Diane's child somewhere. Amy, who'd had a baby – Mum had written to tell her. It had seemed like an olive branch, that letter, after the terrible one that had said Diane was dead.

Mum had clearly been thrilled to bits about Amy's baby, every inch the proud grandmother. She'd even told her which road in Kettlebridge Amy was living on with her boyfriend, and had sent a photo of Amy standing in front of the house, putting on a rather sulky smile for the camera, with the baby in her arms. A dear little thing. Julie had just been able to make out the house number in the background, and that had been all the information she'd needed to figure out Amy's address. She'd even made a note of it somewhere. She hadn't got in touch – that would have been going too far – but she'd thought it might be possible, one day.

And then she'd heard about Mike, and had written to Hillview House to let Mum know. And that had been that.

Her vision begins to flicker, on-off, on-off, as if someone is playing with a switch. If this is it, if it really is the end, Lisa would think she was all alone in the world. But she would not be.

Julie closes her eyes and summons up every bit of willpower she has left to wish her daughter strength and safety and companionship in the time ahead, and to send her all her love. And then the pain begins to fade, and she sinks gratefully into the darkness.

THIRTY-SEVEN

LISA

October 2009

The leaves on the cherry tree outside her flat are on the verge of dropping by the time she gets round to going through the final box of personal odds and ends from her mother's house.

All these months, and all through the summer while she was living with Amy, it has been sitting in a corner of her bedroom, tucked in a nook between her TV and her chest of drawers. If she'd been here maybe she would have tackled it sooner, because it's not as if she has space to spare, even for a box. But before she left for Hillview House she had not felt ready, and in the weeks since she has been back, she hasn't felt up to it. She has almost got used to the box being there, as if it has become part of the fixtures and fittings. It's on the way to becoming invisible. And she has put off opening it because she is nervous. She knows it'll bring back memories that she isn't sure she is ready to revisit – of going through her mum's house, of the lonely funeral, of the feeling of being all alone in the world.

Also, in her heart of hearts, she knows that opening that

box, and going through the last few things she had picked up for sentimental reasons, will feel like letting her mother go.

It takes her longer to do anything now than it would have done before the accident – another reason for having put it off. She needs to be in the right frame of mind, to have slept well and to feel relatively clear. The accident is how she thinks of what happened to her on the night of the fire. She prefers it to calling it an attack, which makes her feel more vulnerable, and makes her think about the man behind it. And the less she thinks about him, the better. He has hurt her; she is determined not to let him keep invading her mind as well.

Her victim liaison officer has told her that they still haven't found him, and they thought he had managed to leave the country. Not knowing where he is, and imagining that he might come back to try to finish the job, could obsess her if she let it. So she tries not to think of him at all, and every time he comes to mind she makes herself remember the little hand in hers that had led her down to the basement where Tilly was. That could not have been real, and yet she had felt it when she needed it most and it had taken her where she needed to go.

They had survived. The old house would survive too. It would be a while before it was habitable again. But that was just a question of time. Time and work. She hopes that's true for her, too – that in six months or a year or two years, she will be stronger and better able to cope.

She has healed well, apart from the headaches that sometimes lay her out for a full day, during which all she can do is lie on her back in the dark and wait for the pain to pass. Even the marks on her shoulder where he bit her are beginning to fade. Now they're a double set of pink crescents, shaped like the rows of his teeth. But her concentration is shot. Every now and then, it glitches if she's jumping from scene to scene, so she can be in the middle of doing something and realise she has no idea how long she's been doing it or why, or that she's done it already and is pointlessly doing it all over again.

Two things seem to help: swimming and work. In the pool she is weightless and disconnected, buoyed up by the water and free of any need to worry about either the future or the past, beyond reaching the end of the pool and turning for another length. And she has started working at the bakery round the corner, just a couple of days a week. There's something about the smell of bread that seems to focus her. The owner has suggested that she could train to work with the master baker one day, a possibility she has put on hold for now because she's not ready to be decisive and make commitments yet.

Even on good days, she often feels as if she's driving through fog. She recognises familiar things and places but nothing looks quite as it should, and the world around her seems eerie and uncanny, as if something unforeseen could come around the corner at any moment. Actual driving, for now, is still beyond her. She still hasn't replaced her car, and wonders if she ever will.

When she finally pulls the box out of its resting place she disturbs a skein of dust that has formed behind it and a spider that scuttles away out of sight. Well – high time she sorted it out. She carries it through to set down on her little kitchen table and finds a pair of scissors to cut through the brown tape she'd used to seal it. She'd done a pretty thorough job. It seems like half a lifetime ago.

The first thing to emerge is an old blue cardigan with one button missing, instantly familiar. She lifts it up and sniffs it, but all it smells of is cardboard box. She remembers so clearly seeing it in Mum's house, slung over the back of the chair she must have been sitting in before the fall that put her in hospital. And now it's just a cardigan that isn't in good enough condition to go to a charity shop.

She sets it aside and goes deeper.

Next are the framed photographs of her that her mum
had kept out on display. All those little signs of how proud
Mum had been of her. She opens up the frames and takes the
photos out and sets them aside, and puts the frames in
another box so she can give them away. Mum's watch also
goes into the box for donation – it wasn't as if Mum had ever
been particularly attached to it. She keeps on delving, setting
aside a few things to keep: Mum's wedding ring, a battered
copy of *The Tale of Peter Rabbit* that she remembers from
childhood.

Then she comes to the bottom of the box and a pile of
pictures on old computer paper that Mum must have been
given by someone, the type with punched holes at the side, all
covered in drawings Lisa had done as a child.

She takes out the first sheaf of pictures. A house, a garden, a
tree. Fairly typical, what you'd expect from a child coming up
for school age. She doesn't remember doing them – she doesn't
remember being into drawing as a child, particularly. Still, she's
written her name on some of them. They're definitely hers.

There's something familiar about the drawings. That
roofline, the arrangement of the windows, the tree...

Then it hits her. She knows exactly where that house is, and
that garden.

She gets down on her knees and spreads out the pictures on
the floor and studies them, but this time she doesn't look at the
house and the garden. She looks at the figures.

There are two of them. Two little stick people, drawn over
and over again. A small one with brown hair and a slightly
bigger one with yellow hair.

Alice. It had to be. Had they made friends while they were
together at Hillview House, that summer that had turned out to
be Alice's last, in the run-up to her seventh birthday? The
pictures are clumsy, as you'd expect, but somehow they're
evocative. There's a particular energy to the figure of the bigger

girl, who is always dancing into centre stage or standing her ground.

Lisa goes back to the box. More drawings on loose sheets of torn-off computer paper, more of the same. Under the next batch is an old newspaper with another, unbroken ream of computer paper underneath it. The second ream is a disappointment. There's just one picture on the top sheet of paper, of the two little stick-figures sleeping in their beds, and the rest of it is unused, as if Lisa as a child had got that far and then lost interest, or had been discouraged, or gave up for some other reason that is now lost to time.

She wonders why she'd stopped. Was it just one of the evolutions that you went through as a child, moving on from one pastime to the next for no particular reason, other than that you'd grown and were curious about something else? Had Mum, or someone else, said something that had put her off – criticised her, or found fault with her pictures in some way? Or had Mum seen one of her drawings and been upset, and that had prompted her to stop?

Had Mum meant to keep the newspaper that had ended up sandwiched between the piles of paper? It seems more likely that it had got mixed up with the drawings by mistake. She takes it over to the table and opens it out. It's all in black and white, apart from a bit of blue on the masthead. The ink is still dark and clear and the paper remains white and crisp, presumably because it's been kept between stacks of other bits of paper, out of the light. The smell of it hasn't faded, either – the faint, bitter reek of newsprint.

It's from 1978, the year after Alice died. The photo on the front page is of a beaming schoolgirl who'd won a raffle at a model railway exhibition. That girl would be in her forties by now. Lisa flicks through the pages, taking in the news items about strikes, a UFO sighting, an appeal for information about a fatal stabbing, a new school building opening. Then she goes through it again more slowly, and Mum's reason for keeping it jumps out at her. It's in the headline of the top story of the first right-hand page:

DOUBLE TRAGEDY AS DAD GUILTY OF KILLING AT FAMILY HOME

Father of two Michael Brierley, 27, of Holinshead Road, Tapley, Berks, pleaded guilty to the manslaughter of his ex-wife's sister's fiancé, Elliott Charles, 29, at Oxford Crown Court yesterday. Sentencing will take place at a later date, as yet unconfirmed.

Mr Charles passed away in September last year after Brierley assaulted him at Hillview House near Springhill, the seventeenth-century farmhouse owned by Brierley's former parents-in-law, John and Elsie Power, the owners of Power's Bakery in Kettlebridge.

Was that the standard reporting etiquette? The victim was a Mr, and the guilty party was just referred to by his surname. It seemed her dad had forfeited the right to a title.

At the time of his death Mr Charles was expecting a baby with Diane Power, 30, and the couple lived together in the flat above Power's Bakery where both of them worked. Mr Charles had a heart attack following the assault and regained consciousness in hospital but died of a second heart attack ten days later. Miss Power has since been delivered of a healthy baby girl.

The court heard that on the day of the assault, Brierley had been drinking in the Flowing Spring pub in Springhill for several hours before walking to his former in-laws' home at around nine in the evening, where he argued with Mr Charles and attacked him on the doorstep.

Earlier that day Brierley had met his ex-wife Julie Power, 27, of Nesbit Close, Brickley, at Portman and Sons undertakers in Kettlebridge to view the body of their daughter, Alice Power. Alice passed away in August last year on her seventh birthday, after falling from a weeping willow in the garden of Hillview House.

Lisa breaks off from reading, goes back and reads the last paragraph over again.

Their daughter, Alice Power, who died in August last year.

Either her eyes are playing tricks on her, or her mind is. This has got to be some kind of hallucination, the after-effects of the shock she has been through. There's no way this old newspaper can possibly say what she thinks it does.

And yet the words are the same on the second reading and on the third. The words say what the words say.

It could be a mistake. It's possible. Newspapers did get things wrong. And yet it would be such a big mistake to give the dead seven year old to the wrong parents. It's not like getting an address wrong, or an age, or even just the spelling of a surname.

Alice could not be the daughter of two sets of parents. She was either the daughter of Diane and Elliott, and Amy's older sister, as Amy had said. Or she was Mike and Julie's child, in which case she was Lisa's sister, and not Amy's at all. She couldn't be both. The version of events that Amy had relayed to her and the account given by the newspaper could not both be true.

Apart from the detail about who Alice's parents were, the newspaper and Amy's account fit together. That's the only point of difference.

But why on earth would Amy have lied about that? And Grandma Elsie too?

Grandma Elsie had been so hostile. It had seemed as if she'd made her mind up that Lisa was part of the bad side of the family, and Alice belonged to the good.

If the newspaper was telling the truth, and Amy had – for some unknown reason – misrepresented it, did Grandma Elsie even know what the truth was any more? Had she lied to herself for so long that she believed in her own lies? Was she still capable of deliberately maintaining a deception on that scale? Or was she just too confused to remember?

Lisa can't believe that Amy would have deliberately lied to her. Not about something like this.

What if Amy herself had been lied to? Why, though? Why would Lisa and Amy's grandparents have lied about such a thing? And Amy's mum too?

Had it been a way of justifying the decision to take sides? Amy had said that Lisa's mum had been looking after Alice at the time of the accident, and had implied that perhaps she'd been careless, or was in some way culpable. But what if it hadn't been her? What if it had been someone else?

Is it possible that Amy had never had a sister, but that Lisa always had? A sister called Alice, who had died when Lisa was still too young to remember?

The newsprint shimmers and shifts on the page in front of her. Lisa thinks she might be sick. It's like hearing the bell toll for one way of seeing herself and her place in the world, and not knowing where she will find herself when it stops.

She forces herself to concentrate, and the dancing letters fall become recognisable words again.

At the time of the killing both John and Elsie Power were at home, having hosted a small family gathering. They had invited Mr Charles and their older daughter, Diane, along with their younger daughter, Julie. Brierley and Julie Power

have a younger daughter, a sister to Alice, who was three at the
time and was also in the house that evening.

Mr Philip Hornbeam QC, speaking for the defence,
described Brierley as an affectionate father who had stayed in
regular contact with his two children following his divorce and
sent his ex-wife as much as he could afford from his irregular
income as a painter and decorator and handyman. However,
Mr Angus Penniman QC, prosecuting, described Brierley as a
volatile, unreliable and aggressive man with a drink problem,
prone to violent mood swings, who had inflicted fresh anguish
on his ex-wife's family while they were all still reeling from the
loss of little Alice, who had been much loved by them all.

Was it possible to be both an affectionate father and volatile,
unreliable and prone to violent mood swings? Perhaps it was.

Lisa thinks back to the photographs she had found in the
basement at Hillview House. Alice. Cheeky, bold, daring little
Alice, who had climbed the weeping willow and died. She
closes her eyes and the sense of being up high comes back to
her, and the sound of the wind in the leaves. But had it been her
who had been climbing? Or had it been Alice, and had she been
watching from below?

The ghost of a possibility of a memory, an image like something recalled from a dream, presents itself: the tall tree, the leg
and skirt of a climbing girl disappearing into its branches. The
same girl waving and smiling. *Look at me.* And then...

And then—

It's as if she is looking up at something too big and dark and
complicated for her to understand, that could destroy her if she
doesn't back off and keep away. And then it's as if she is falling
and falling, and there is nowhere for her to land.

Had she seen it? The little girl broken on the ground. Or is it a
false memory? She has seen the garden, the tree, and a picture of

Alice. And here, in front of her in print, is the suggestion. That's all it takes. Imagination is powerful, and the imagination of someone who feels wronged is especially so. How could she ever know what she might have witnessed, anyway? The only people who might be able to tell her are either dead or disinclined to tell her anything.

Her vision begins to redden as if she is hurt and bleeding again, and her head aches as if she is back in Hillview House, in Amy's bedroom with the fire blazing and Russell cracking her skull against the floor.

The hand that had reached for hers in the darkness, the little hand that had pulled her down the stairs to where Tilly was hiding in the basement...

She has never told anybody else about that. They would only think it was a delusion, created by the intense stress of the moment and the injuries she'd sustained. One of those tricks that the mind plays when it is approaching the danger of death. A way of rationalising the instinct to look for Tilly in the least accessible room in the house, and the one that was hardest to escape from, barring the attic. Is it necessary to tell the whole truth about something that other people would think was only in your head, and that would make no difference anyway?

Secretly, though, she has allowed herself to believe it was Alice. And now she knows who Alice really was. Her sister. Her older sister, still looking out for her after all these years.

Her headache lifts and she opens her eyes. The newspaper is still there in front of her on the table, and the words on it are still the same. And in a way, it's showing her something she already knew. Her family tells the stories it can bear. For her grandparents and her aunt, that had meant twisting the truth, and in her mum's case, that had meant saying almost nothing at all.

There is a framed picture of Mum in front of the kitchen window: Mum as Lisa chooses to remember her, sitting in her little back garden on a summer's day. Probably she had just been smoking, and maybe drinking, too, but in the photo her arms are folded and she is looking up at the sky, inscrutable and lost in the moment.

It's from about a decade ago, and her hair is darker and her skin less lined than when Lisa had seen her for the last time, a little over a year earlier. But there's something timeless about that picture, and what's timeless about it is that her mum seems completely unaware that her picture is being taken. There's no trace of self-consciousness. That's why she looks so free.

On the other side of the windowsill is a picture of the landscape where Mum had been buried – the gentle rolling hills and fields, all the colours bleached out by winter. Lisa's hoping to go there with Amy one day soon, when she's feeling a little stronger, maybe with Tilly and Rowan and Joe, too, if he would like to come.

She separates out the page with the court report from the rest of the newspaper and takes it to the newsagent's round the corner to photocopy it, then posts it off to Amy with a note saying she had found it in a box of her mum's stuff and what did Amy make of it? She hopes, after all they've been through together, Amy will take that in the spirit in which it's intended – as a question asked in good faith, not a reproach or an accusation.

A few days go by, and then a week, and she still hasn't heard anything. She begins to wonder if she's posted it to the wrong address. But she'd sent it to the place where Amy and the children have been staying, the bed-and-breakfast in the centre of Kettlebridge with the garden going down to the river.

It would be easy enough to check if Amy's received it. All she needs to do is to send a text message. But she holds off. She doesn't want to push it. She has a feeling Amy will get in touch with her in her own good time.

And then, one bright and gusty day in November when the pavements are cluttered with fallen leaves, she comes back from the bakery in the early afternoon and finds an envelope on the entrance hall carpet addressed to her, in Amy's loose, only-just-legible handwriting.

Upstairs in her kitchen, she sits at the little table in front of the window overlooking the street and reads the letter through before she's even taken her coat off.

THIRTY-EIGHT
LISA AND AMY

Dear Lisa,

Well, I am not much of a letter writer but I guess it is fair to say that I owe you one so now I am giving it a go. I am sorry it has taken me a while to reply to you. I don't really have any good excuses but here are the reasons. I had told you that Joe and I had been having a bit of a stormy time and were living apart. Well, that has been going on and we are not together any more. We are trying to work things out between us so Joe can see the children but it is not easy. Tilly misses him, as I know you will be able to imagine, but she is busy at school and has made some new friends, and has started dancing lessons so that is helping. We are getting by, but it is all a kind of chaos and Rowan is not far off starting to crawl, so I am not expecting the chaos to improve any time soon.

I've been looking for somewhere to rent for me and the children. Later on today, I'm going to look at the flat above the sports shop that used to be Power's Bakery. From what I can tell, it's on the poky side and has only a very small shared garden. But it's cheap (relatively) and there's not that much else available at the moment. I'm not sure whether the connection to times gone by is a reason to go for it or avoid it at all costs.

The old house is still a long way from being habitable, and I am not sure whether we'll ever live there again. It might be better to sell it and start somewhere new. But all that is some way ahead and can keep for another day.

I needed to think about what you had sent me and get my head round it and then I had a few questions to ask a few people. As you can imagine. At first, I thought it must be a huge mistake, but then I began to wonder, because when I really thought about it I had a sick feeling that it might be true.

I think I always did feel like there was something very wrong in the house I grew up in, but it was something I knew without knowing that I knew it. I told myself that what was wrong was my dad being dead and Alice being dead, and also, I told myself that it was me that was wrong, for behaving the way I did. But now I think that it was not just those things, and it was also because of the lie that we were all living with.

I grew up believing that my sister had died before I was born and I know now that I never had a sister. I don't know how to feel about this, really, except it is a kind of loss to find out that the idea you had of who you were is not true, and the people who you should have been able to trust have misled you.

What my mum and Grandad John and Grandma Elsie did is wrong, and I am ashamed of it. I have been trying to figure out why and I don't have any answers. Maybe you do. I can only suppose they did it for one of the reasons lies usually happen – to save face. No wonder they didn't want me to talk about it to other people in the village. They must have been at least a little bit scared that I would find out.

I am sorry that my mum decided to take your loss and add it to hers. It seems like a kind of stealing. I can only think that she must have felt guilty, and the way she told it was an easier version to live with. And I am sorry that your mum could never bring herself to tell you. I would have arranged to bring you Alice's things that we kept in the basement, but they were ruined by the smoke from the fire and I did not keep them. I am sorry about that, as well, because it seems like I should have at least asked you first.

Here is what I did after I had thought about your letter for a while. I left the children with Joe and went to see Grandma Elsie. I took the copy of the newspaper article with me, and I held it out to her and said, 'Look, this is what Lisa found in her mum's things.' She turned her head away from me and didn't answer. I said, 'Do you want to read it?' She shook her head. I held it out to her and she sat on her hands. She still wouldn't look at me.

So then I said, 'I can read it to you if you like. It is about Lisa's dad being convicted of manslaughter. But at the end there is a part where it talks about Alice and it says she was Lisa's sister, not mine. I was very, very puzzled by that and I think Lisa was too. I was wondering if you could explain it to me.'

What she did next shocked me. She turned to face me, and she gave me such a look, I knew I was not going to get anywhere with her at all. And then she turned away again.

I reminded her that you had rescued us. I asked if she would at least like to see you sometime, if you came over to visit. But she just said no and then she started yawning and said she was very tired, and I should leave. So then I had to go. I felt angry with her and sad, too, and I didn't know what else to say.

It seemed clear to me from the way she reacted that what the newspaper said was true, and the story I had grown up with was a lie. I'm sure there's someone in the village or in Kettlebridge who would remember – if I could bring myself to ask, or if you did, or if we did it together, which we could do if you wanted to. There must be official records somewhere, too, but I haven't gone digging for those. Anyway, I have accepted now that Alice was your sister and not mine. And I am sorry that what I told you after you made your way down to the basement has turned out to be such a twisted version of events. I hope you will believe me that I had absolutely no idea what had really happened. I misled you only because I had been misled too.

While we are in truth-telling mode there is something else I want to say. There is a chance that Joe is not the biological father of either of my children and we are going to do some tests soon that will probably confirm this is the case. I am sorry if this makes you think less of me but there it is. This is something he did not know until very recently and he was – and is – very angry with me which I guess you can't really blame him for. He still wants to be part of the children's lives, and I am holding onto that because that seems like the thing that will get us through.

I hope you won't think too badly of me and that you won't be put off seeing me. I suppose I couldn't blame you if you were, but you are one of the biggest-hearted, most forgiving people I know, so even if I don't deserve it, I am trusting that we will be OK.

Everybody wants to see you and Joe has a work meeting in Brickley soon so he can drive us over. I will call you very soon after I send this and see if that's something you would like. I am going to start having some driving lessons soon and then one day I will be able to drive us all over myself.

I hope you are feeling better and that your headaches are getting less bad. I'll bring you some lavender oil when I come. I don't know if I ever mentioned Hannah to you? The mum of Tilly's friend Flora? Well, she swears by it.

I think I would feel a lot more freaked out about the lie

that I grew up with if I hadn't had the chance to get to know you. I might have lost the idea of a sister but in my cousin I have gained a friend.

This is the longest letter I have ever written, and now I am all written out.

Lots of love, Amy

Lisa reads the letter through again and then sets it down on the table. Her heart aches for Tilly, who, if Amy is right, will surely have to be told that she has another father besides the man she thinks of as her dad. But Tilly has been so close to Joe, and him to her. As Amy says, it would be devastating for either of them to lose that...

But perhaps that means it won't happen.

And as for Rowan, he had such a placid, charming, easy-going nature, he will probably take whatever configuration of parents he is going to grow up with in his stride.

If Amy and Joe can figure things out between them, if they can be amicable – and it's hard to imagine Joe being vindictive, however bitterly upset he might be – maybe it need not be a disaster.

She presses her fingers to her forehead to massage it and is surprised to find that she has no headache at all. Not even the faintest shadow of one, after all that reading. She feels quite normal. Not sick. A little hungry, maybe. And she has a leftover loaf of bread in her bag, just right for toast.

But she doesn't stir because the low autumn sun is pitching in through the window in front of her, brightening everything as if it's summer again, and the light is too perfect to move away from. She closes her eyes and basks in it and offers up a word-less thank you. For Alice, her sister. For her mum, who had done her best in spite of all the losses that had broken her. For Amy and her children, the family she had lost and who have brought so much love back into her life when she least expected it.

And perhaps it's her imagination, or just one of the tricks that her concentration plays on her sometimes these days, but she feels a glancing touch on her hand where she is holding the letter, and then hears the quiet sound of footsteps heading away from her and fading, merging into the hum of distant traffic.

A LETTER FROM ALI

Thank you for choosing to read *The Family I Lost*. If you would like to keep up to date with all my newest releases just sign up at the following link. Your email address will never be shared and you can unsubscribe at any time.

www.bookouture.com/ali-mercer

When I was a little girl, we moved abroad to a house with a basement that had a bedroom in it. I was drawn to that basement room – I can still picture the shiny metal decorations on the chimney breast, which looked like curly bronze feathers. Perhaps it was the novelty. Our old house had neither basement nor fireplaces. I pleaded to be allowed to sleep in the basement, and my mum, though unconvinced, decided to humour me. I lasted one night. Nothing happened, but it was fantastically creepy, and the next day I begged to change to one of the upstairs bedrooms instead.

The basement at Hillview House in *The Family I Lost* owes something to that night, which made enough of an impression for me to remember it more than forty years later. Springhill, the village below Hillview House, is loosely based on the beautiful village of Sunningwell, which is near where I live in Oxfordshire. I walked there with my son one fine day in spring 2021, one of many countryside walks we've been on since the beginning of the pandemic. There are willow trees near Sunningwell's village pond, and they brought back memories of another willow tree, which was in the garden of the house in England that we moved back to after leaving the place with the creepy basement. I once attempted to climb that tree, and a version of it went into the garden at Hillview House.

This is the second novel that I've written since the pandemic hit. For me, and maybe for you too, 2021 was the year of cancellations. Parties and get-togethers were called off, or I found myself unable to get to them. I can count the face-to-face meetings I had with friends on two hands, but every one of those conversations was a treat. It was like putting your head above the parapet and seeing that there's a big, beautiful world out there just waiting to be explored.

I think that's part of what Lisa is looking for when she goes to Hillview House – that sense of connection that puts you back in touch with who you are and opens up the future. And it's what Amy needs too, even if it takes her a while to realise it. In telling Lisa and Amy's story, I wanted to explore the relationship between a pair of cousins who don't know each other, and yet come to need each other and end up changing each other's lives.

I want to say a huge and heartfelt thank you to all my readers, whether you're new to my books or have followed along every step of the way. I hope you loved *The Family I Lost* and if you did, I'd be very grateful if you could let people know! I really appreciate all the support I've had from readers who have reviewed and recommended my books.

Do drop me a line! I'm often on Twitter and Instagram and you can also contact me through my Facebook author page. I'd love to hear from you. Here's to happy and healthy times ahead, and maybe even a few parties.

With very best wishes to you and yours,

Ali Mercer

KEEP IN TOUCH WITH ALI

www.alimercerwriter.com

facebook.com/AliMercerwriter

twitter.com/AlisonLMercer

instagram.com/alimercerwriter

ACKNOWLEDGEMENTS

Thank you so much to Kelsie Marsden, my editor at Bookouture, for all your work on this novel and for your cheer-leading and insights. Thanks to the whole Bookouture team – it's been great to see how you've forged ahead through the last couple of years. Thanks to Natasha Harding (sorry my Zoom didn't work) and Ruth Tross. Thanks to Noelle Holten and the rest of the publicity team: Kim Nash, Sarah Hardy and Jess Readett. And thanks to Jon Appleton for the impeccable copy-editing.

Thank you to Judith Murdoch, my agent for more than a decade now, and Rebecca Winfield, who handles my foreign rights.

Thanks to friends and ex-colleagues here in Oxfordshire and further afield – it's been too long since I've seen too many of you! I have white hair now! Thanks Nanu and Luli Segal, Helen Rumbelow, and Neel Mukherjee, and here's a shout-out to North Cornwall Book Festival. And thanks to Jennifer.

Thanks to my family, including my cousins, of course. Thanks to Lyn and Ray, to whom this book is dedicated. And thank you to my husband and children, who have kept me entertained throughout the months we've spent closeted in the house together. Nothing is permanent but change and we're heading into different times now, but already, looking back, I can see how rich and precious our closeness has been.

Made in the USA
Monee, IL
09 September 2022